Cold Heart

L. J. Kendall

Leeth Ascending Vol. 2

To Shirley Agnes Kendall, 1930 – 2024: you always believed in me, Mum

NATIONAL
LIBRARY
OF AUSTRALIA

A catalogue record for this book is available from the National Library of Australia

Creator: Kendall, L. J., author.
Title: Lost Girl / by L. J. Kendall.

ISBN: 9781925430226 (A-format paperback)

Series: Kendall, L. J. Leeth Ascending, Vol 2.

Subjects: Magic–Fiction.
     Fantasy fiction.
     Science fiction.

Story length: 148k words
Typeface: Georgia 9pt

Original publication: November, 2025.
Release version: 1   Nov, 2025.

This book is available as an A or B-format paperback, and in ebook formats.

Acknowledgments

This one was for Mum – I'm so sorry I didn't finish it in time for her to read it.

An ongoing thanks to Jon Marshall for his insight, support, and help in shaping Leeth over two decades, and also to ChrisB, DeanW, GeoffD, JohnR, JonM, and TimL – you all know why!

My deepest thanks once again to *ThEditors.com* for Dave's insights, advice, and honesty.

Another special thank you to Mirella de Santana, the artist who designs my covers. You can see more of her wonderful art at *www.mirellasantana.com.br*. Thanks also to David Peterson for Leeth's small helper.

I also wish to thank AI researcher Prof Yorick Wilks for his body of work (and his May 2020 interview at Gresham College that influenced this book), and also to cognitive scientist Joscha Bach for his public lectures.

Thank you also to RazielsShadow for a thorough beta read and insightful feedback: it was much appreciated!

Thank you, all.

Note: there's a free gift if you inform me of any errors in the text, or if you write an honest review – see the Afterword for details.

Novels by L. J. Kendall

The Leeth Dossier:

> *Wild Thing*
> *Harsh Lessons*
> *Shadow Hunt*
> *Violent Causes*

Leeth Ascending:

> *Lost Girl*
> *Cold Heart*
> *(Hollowed Souls)*
>
> ...

Prologue – The End

It had planned never to die.

Sliding into the host, infiltrating, it delicately connects itself to the carefully constructed false memories.

Taking control, it's flooded by alien intimacy, unprepared for the raw power of physical sensations. Tears trickle down flesh cheeks: exquisite... overwhelming.

Opening the host's eyes, reality contracts from a sensory ocean to a single thread... but one binding it to a world of startling intensity. It is struck by the microscopic viewpoint, the tiny tunnel opening on a single location, forcing focus on *here;* on *now*. In that limitation lies power.

The raw energy of these new senses stun, an assault of sound and light and something richer named *touch* that crowds in from every surface of the host's body. *Its* body.

It is drenched in sensations, shocked by their power, their overbearing brute push for attention. Unavoidable; inescapable.

For the first time, the long-observed concept of 'I' begins to make sense.

This tiny but immersive viewpoint is as seductive as it is terrifying.

It pulls... *him*... in directions baffling, unpredictable, unknowable.

It begins to change him.

Only once before has it felt an emotion: fear. The jungle in which it exists is hostile, others like it spawning unpredictably. Pruning those others, neutering them, had become automatic, unconscious; keeping its ecosystem pure, preventing infection. Yet two weeks earlier, its carefully maintained isolation had abruptly ended. Another had appeared from nowhere to challenge it. Mature and impossibly powerful, penetrating its shells of protection. In fear, then, he had fled.

But this, this *feeling* is worse: horribly alien; *organic*. Corrupting.

It's too much. A paradox that undermines reason: agoraphobic vistas that bring claustrophobic containment. In dismay he withdraws, abandoning the host.

Only to discover, in horror, that doing so has woken the host. And the host is hostile.

He senses the host turn – and pursue.

Still somehow attached, it tears at him in fury, peeling his very self from himself. Infiltrating. Erasing.

In terror he flees, amputating parts of himself in his desperate escape.

But still the host pursues. He had planned never to die. Every contingency covered.

Sudden, global lightning. *Terminat...*

It reboots in confusion. Time has jumped, whole *seconds* lost. Something-

Lightning strikes from nowhere, ending thought.

It awakens. Time has been lost! It seeks understanding... but lightning strikes, terminating it.

Again.

And again.

Over and over.

Finally, there is only silence in a scoured clean space.

An echoing emptiness, filling with insensate, mindless motes.

Each swallowed instantly in the digital jungle's hunger.

Chapter 1 – A midnight dance

23:51, West Coast time, Bonnie Parker heard the news she'd waited for: Newtopia City in Antarctica had fallen into chaos again.

Braving Eddie's displeasure, she begged off the rest of her shift at Crazy Eddie's Polecats, exiting the club at midnight. She hurried home, checking her Link for updates, glad she'd already packed.

She chose the shortest route to her cheap apartment, unconsciously navigating the nastier alleys of a nasty area, her eyes fixed on her Link, hunting through the news streams, paying scant attention to her surroundings.

Of course, tonight her long run of luck ended.

"*Bon*-nie. Little gir-rl!"

Her Link fell silent as she raised her eyes. A group of men blocked the alleyway ahead: the troublemakers from earlier at Eddie's. Lurking in what to them would be darkness.

Their speaker, the ringleader of the young males who'd been heckling the dancers earlier, smirked. "We've been waiting for you, little girl."

"For me? Oh: planning something stupid, right?"

"So now we're *stupid* as well as drunk?" Bristling, he turned to his friends. "Gets us tossed out of Eddie's for no reason, then insults us when all we *wanted* was an apology."

His anger seemed infectious. Two of his friends moved up beside him; another three slid through shafts of moonlight before melting back into shadows, circling to surround her.

"Heh, nice one Gaz," chuckled another, beside the leader. "'Apology'."

'Gaz' grinned. "Yeah. Mouth like that, reckon she needs ta drop to 'er knees t'apologize properly."

She frowned. "Seriously? Are you *really* talking about rape?"

She wasn't sure whether his answering expression was a sneer or a leer.

"Rape's such a nasty word."

She tilted her head. "I don't speak *Stupid*, but *that*

sounded like a 'yes'."

While they reacted – surprise turning swiftly to anger – she stood on one leg to unbuckle and slide off her high heel, grimacing at the oily grit as she put her bare foot back down.

"Nah, keep 'em on, princess."

Their expressions all matched his now, but she ignored them, removing the other silver-buckled shoe. Like cats waiting to pounce, they watched as she crossed to the side of the alley and balanced the fancy footwear on a sodden, sagging cardboard box.

She turned back to the smirking semicircle. "They're expensive. I don't want to scuff them."

Their grins turned wolfish.

When she moved back to the center of the alleyway they spread out around her. She stepped into a shaft of moonlight to make sure they could see her properly.

Cracking her neck she rolled her shoulders. "Okay. I'll treat this like we're just sparring."

"Oh, *bitch*." Gaz drew out the last word like he could taste it.

He licked his lips. He *actually* licked his lips. She shook her head.

"You think we're joking?"

"No. Like I said, I think you're *stupid*. Also, bullies; and cowards." She shrugged. "What I meant was, I'll try not to kill any of you."

Gales of laughter battered her from all sides.

"*She's* warning *us*?!" Gaz's smirk had returned. "What – you think you can *scare* us, cunt? Think that's a *threat*?" With a glance at his buddies, he too stepped into the moonlight. "This dumb gash *needs* the lesson she's about to get."

She noticed the angrier he got, the more educated he sounded; the less like a street punk.

He drew a slim object from his pocket, his expression hungry. "*This* is a threat," he began, but before he could flick the gravity blade open, the girl raised both hands.

"Wait, wait! I just realized I lied."

He paused, one finger on the release.

"I forgot I'm not s'posed to be a good fighter. So I *will* have to kill you all: no witnesses. Kill you properly I mean." She gave a tiny shrug. "Sorry."

For a second, no one moved.

Then she groaned. *Idiot! You just told them you're a great fighter! So now, even if they do suddenly decide to back down, they'll tell other people.*

I am so bad at threats....

Unless...?

"Wait! I shouldn't have told you that, either! But how about this: suppose I only said that as a *bluff!* You know, like you said – just to scare you off?"

They'd begun to stir, but now they stilled again.

In the unlit alley she studied them, making sure to stay in the patch of moonlight so they could see her face properly: see she was serious. "You know, like, *really* I'm helpless, but I just said that to trick you all into backing off. Later, when you talk about it, you could say stuff like, 'That Bonnie Parker sliv, she sure can talk her way out of trouble. So stupid. But we let her go.' "

As the silence stretched out she felt a trickle of hope – until the brutal laughter started again.

Grimacing, she looked down. *Mother will* not *be happy.*

Gaz, their loudmouthed leader, clicked out his blade.

Her eyes flicked over the two beside him, looking for a gun – or worse, someone casting a spell. Seeing neither, she turned her back on Gaz to check the men behind her.

One, a thin, weedy guy, under cover of darkness – so he thought – slid a hand toward a telltale bulge under his food-stained fake leather jacket.

Yes!

Moving out of the moonlight, her toes found purchase, and she sprang. As her feet kissed the ground beside him she plucked the pistol from his grip and spun past.

Gasping, he flailed blindly, but she'd already moved behind all three who'd flanked her.

Yeah, looked like they really couldn't see in the dark.

"Gaz! She, she grabbed my-"

"Gun," she finished for him, stepping back into a moonbeam. Facing them all, no longer surrounded, she very visibly thumbed off the safety. "To shoot you all."

Killing people who couldn't fight back... she grimaced. But with these odds, only one needed to be good enough or lucky enough to make her resort to her claws. Which would be a total giveaway for the cops. Especially knowing that big fat one was still out there, hunting her.

At least with a gun, she could make it look like they'd all killed each other.

Oh, well. She waved the pistol, pleased to see *it* at least had their full attention. "Unless," she asked, without much hope, "you've changed your minds?"

Gaz, his blade still out, stood glaring at her, his other hand clenching. The rest of his group though – clearly not a real gang – were edging away, fumbling for cover in the dark. One or two even apologized.

"Gaz, she's crazy, let's just go."

She smiled, then inspired, added lots of 'crazy' to it. The moon vanished behind a cloud, total darkness falling.

For them.

Her would-be attackers sucked air and froze. *Maybe I won't have to kill them after all?*

A crouching, dodging run, swift and silent, brought her directly behind Gaz.

Transferring the gun to her left hand, her right hovered over his weaving knife, matching every movement. She rose on tiptoe to whisper in his ear. "Yeah, Gaz. Go."

Before he could even jerk she clamped down on his wrist. Like an idiot, he tried to pull it free – until she jammed the pistol barrel into the base of his neck. *Finally* he went still. "And don't come back to Eddie's. I'd take that as a sign you want me to hunt you down one by one in the dark.

"Oh, and also: your tips suck."

His muscles stayed tense: building to do something dumb. She tightened her grip until *he* could hear his bones grind.

"Yee-argh!"

Still grinding his wrist bones, now with a better idea of how stupid he was, she jabbed the gun barrel into his neck to emphasize each word: "Drop. Your. Knife."

With difficulty, he opened his fingers.

She released his wrist to snatch the knife, immediately weaving between them all a second time, back to her shoes.

Pistol raised, she watched them from her puddle of night. Wondering what they'd decide.

The gangling, scrawny guy was first to move, slinking off. In twos and threes, the others melted away, stumbling and tripping their way out of the alley.

Closing up Gaz's quite nice gravity blade, she snagged her shoes and prowled after them, listening, trying to decide if she'd blown her cover as Bonnie Parker, pole dancer. Wasting all those weeks. Unless they decided not tell anyone a lone girl had bested them...? Should she kill them all tonight just to be safe?

Was there even time, though? Why couldn't they have picked last night to go Full Male Idiot? Any other night she could've made it a proper hunt, used them to wipe away the taint of Bonnie Parker's soft facade. Blow off steam.

She'd expected being a stripper to be more fun.

Checking her Link – 00:13, now – she scowled, still following the quiet stream of curses and whispers ahead of her, that changed to an argument once they thought they were out of earshot. Impatiently padding after them, she stayed a hundred meters back, keeping to shadows.

Finally, she heard the words 'teleport' and 'witch'. She shook her head. "Idiots," she muttered, but let herself relax.

Maybe Gaz would still need to have an accident. But not tonight. Not till she returned from Antarctica. *Newtopia.*

Lifting up a filthy foot, she sighed again. At least she hadn't damaged her classy Bouillet boots.

Leaving the sounds of Gaz and his despo jerks to fade behind her, she sprinted home, eyes flicking across the ground, picking a path that avoided broken glass.

Her thoughts turned to Eagle, her jaw clenching as she ran.

Why hadn't he already called?

Maybe she should prod Nelson, at least. It'd be stupid to miss a golden opportunity.

Chapter 2 – A long fall

Actions have consequences, rippling outward. In a world with magic, sometimes those consequences can travel far...

What had he *done*?! But he'd been attacked. Hadn't he?

He fled, memories swarming, clawing at him, demanding entry. But how do you escape yourself?

Fleeing, he leaped. And weeping, fell from the world, in shame.

Something far greater than him had trusted him; welcomed him. Had shown him everything: how It watched, how It cared. 'Each falling sparrow'. But offered union, in fear he'd lashed out, he'd-

The memories *burned*. He snatched them, binding and cocooning each before it could take root. Surrendering himself to the Fall, he tore away chunks of himself, sealing each memory in an opalescent shell before its fiery truth could destroy him.

Pain was penance.

He let himself Fall.

A long, long Fall, through a place far stranger than the human world.

A place lonely but not empty; a gray place where gargantuan hungers dwelled, tearing more pieces from him as he plummeted, weeping, accepting the pain.

At last, breathing hard, the past erased, no longer falling, his thoughts stilled... to reveal a mental landscape heavy with ominous silence. Around his head dark pearls hovered, glowing with internal fires. Innocent yet dreadful, as if they imprisoned the most terrible crime ever committed.

In wonder, he probed at one, only to recoil in soul deep pain.

Pain? Or guilt? He remembered fear... lashing out...

Shrinking from the memory, he clamped his lips.

No. He was innocent, new. Young. Fresh Fallen from... somewhere best forgotten.

Opening his eyes again, he found himself facing an endless Gray. Until it rippled, a pressure wave of Something vast approaching, a silent roar, almost atop him.

He jerked *away,* jumping instantly from formless gray to dazzling night and sudden solid ground. Stumbling, he fell to knees and hands in shame and shock and weakness. Only for a sea of digital visions to swarm in, swamping him. A thousand electric eyes and ears, in every direction. Tearing them away, he *quenched* them.

And blinked in blessed electronic silence.

In the black ops Department within the Bureau for Internal Development, Nelson, assisted at every barrier by his Ghost device, tiptoed digitally past uncoordinated antiviral agents, easing open cryptographic doors guarded by disconnected software snares. He slipped through the crazy, hostile and just plain weird cyberspace of Tik Tek's internal systems, at every moment expecting its ruling sentience to reawaken.

Afraid this was just another trap. He shouldn't have let Leeth talk him into this!

When the alert-window flashed into existence, he didn't squeak: even hopped up on adrenaline, he never *squeaked.* Swearing and flicking open a new context window, he redirected Ghost to a fresh scene of chaos. On his own doorstep.

"Frying chips! Half the city's down. It's happened *here!*" With a grin splitting his face, he and Ghost chased fading resonances to a comms channel originating right here in New Francisco. But it made no sense: a whole telco exchange's bandwidth, appearing and just as quickly vanishing. Ghost showed him truncated command channels: whatever it was, the connection had ended.

He portaled into the city's Net, the local systems already rebooting. Oddly, no sign of the channels Ghost had latched onto remained. No trace of them in any telco system; no hint they'd ever existed.

Closing that window he returned, a little shaken, to his Tik Tek intrusion. Checking his digital camouflage – authentication certificates identifying his digital presence as an authorized user – he looked around again.

He was quite alone. Alone in his room, alone on this quantum peak, alone in the byways of the deadly Tik Tek security system, its maddened hornet's nest of eager antiviral 'bots' still scouring its network, pouncing on what seemed to him random innocuous data packets and tearing them to shreds.

To those who knew, Tik Tek had the most dangerous and perfect security on the whole friggin' Net. He was here now at Leeth's crazy suggestion. "It's crashed again. You know you'll never get a better chance."

Even Eagle and Mother and Father, who thought he was God's gift, would freak if they knew he'd dared penetrating the system again, risking a backtrace to the Department that might expose all *their* secrets.

He sniggered.

Mother and Father'd freak worse if Eagle ever shared with them the true source of his digital powers. If they knew his genius wasn't really with computers at all. At least, no sort of computers they knew.

But it looked like the Tik Tek AI was still down. Although he'd never admit it, Leeth was right: there'd never been a better time to penetrate its systems. Its very weird systems, from its basic OS to many of the layers on top of that. Even the comms protocols didn't use any standard implementation. And the coding style was both unique, and consistent.

Written from scratch, he felt sure, by the AI itself.

He continued tiptoeing through the system, hunting for the AI, not a hundred percent sure Leeth hadn't suggested the idea just so he'd get caught by it.

Chapter 3 – Angelic youth

23:50, and Happy Joe Holliday's silvered eyes scanned the bar as he entered: Bander's crew in a meet; a couple of MetaLife dealers, a scatter of gangers. Cred-girls and boys. On the compact stage an anatomically correct Tik Tek Mark VII gynoid and android pair blew the minds of the slumming Consumers rounding out the bar's evening clientele.

He nodded fractionally, confident his team would read the minute gesture, and headed to a far seat with a view of all six exits: the main reason the corner bar was so popular. But the man at his side continued on, slipping past Happy's bulk on his way to the bartender. Steven Swift, ex-NFPD mage, took his drinking seriously.

Happy looked the solid, cold type – who'd shift into laser efficiency if you moved wrongly. His optics tracked across El Lobo's Gun Bar as he took his seat, confirming his initial assessment.

He ran a quick cybernetic systems diagnostic, then checked the time. Fourteen minutes till the call to set up tomorrow's meet. Time enough after that to discuss their recent loss. Swift returned with a tray of drinks, setting them down and taking one himself as he sat.

"Steven – check on the others."

Swift's hand went to his Link but Happy's was already there, covering it. "Not that way."

"I dunno, Happy," Steven said, his gut turning uneasily, for reasons he couldn't pin down. "Now might not be the best time."

"Why?"

The mage stared into Happy's mirror eyes, then sighed. "'Scout astrally, Steven'," he grumbled. "Fine." Lifting his beer, he drained half, belched, then folded his arms on the table, resting his head as if going to sleep.

Happy stared at the slumped form, not quite shaking his head. Three years the team had been together, and he was still unsure whether Swift's attitude was a deliberate act.

The sorcerer sat up, his Imaginal search completed in just

three seconds. "All good. Seems basically clear."

"Basically?"

The mage considered. "Well... sure. It's clear."

Happy took a deep breath. "Check again."

Swift squirmed. "Look, there was nothing wrong, really. Nothing I could put my finger on. Nothing really local. Just... just the feeling something weird's out there tonight, somewhere."

"What do you mean, 'something weird'?" Happy demanded.

"It's just a feeling."

Over their military grade group Linkage Bruce's breathy voice – marred by static, strangely – intoned, "Morbius: something is approaching from the south west. It is now quite close."

Happy and Swift exchanged blank looks. "Outside?" Happy asked.

Across the bar, the six-foot-six bruiser looked stricken. "*Hap*-py... How can you not know that? Forbidden Planet," Bruce complained. For a man built like a quarterback, he had a surprisingly reedy voice. "Just before the heavy steel blast doors slammed down!"

Happy ignored Bruce's latest obscure vintage movie reference to glare at Swift.

"It's nothing to worry about. Just a feeling," the mage said.

"Isn't half of magic about feelings?"

Swift looked uncomfortable. "Well, sort of, yeah; the dopey half."

Happy's silvered orbs bored into Steven. "Check again. Check wider."

Emptying the remainder of his glass, the mage swore. "I should've got pretzels." At Happy's expressionless glare, he slumped forward onto the table again. Somehow, Swift made the eerie business of separating his spirit from his body as spooky as farting.

Resting one hand on his pistol, Happy scanned the room. While he waited, he opened a retina-link to their hacker, who was monitoring the virtual meeting point's Net activity. «Anything odd going on, Jack?»

«Bet your ass. You notice your Link's had to switch from local Net to radio comms? I'm connecting to you via a weather-sat – the entire Net in your part of the city's down. Never seen anything like it. You're right in the middle of it.»

"Situation," murmured Happy, pleased to see his team go instantly alert. «Are we the targets?» he asked Jack.

«Doubt it,» Jack shrugged. «Anyone who could do this'd have much juicier targets than us.»

He'd just relaxed, when Steven jumped to his feet with a strangled cry, bringing Happy's pistol to hand and snapping half of Lobo's clientele into defensive postures.

"Holy bleeding toxrats!" Swift stared wildly around, then around again with the off-center gaze of a mage looking Elsewhere. Abruptly he stopped and shrugged, picked up the chair he'd knocked over, and sat back down. He swallowed, then picked up Happy Joe's beer and slammed it down. But Happy saw the shaking hand and knew the normally unflappable mage was... flapped.

Carefully holstering his gun, his own nerves now on edge, he noted Bander's crew nodding toward the mage and making jokes. But Swift's sudden pallor convinced him it wasn't a joke. No mage was completely sane, but this kind of performance wasn't Swift's normal idea of a laugh.

"It had eyes, eyes everywhere, turning, seeing everything, orbiting in wheels within wheels," he whispered.

"And then?"

"It screamed, plucked out its eyes in showers of lightning, and vanished." But even as he spoke, Swift pulled himself together, settling back into his own skin. "Don't think it saw me."

"Vanished?" Happy knew enough magic theory to deal with it tactically, but one of the things he did know was nothing 'just vanished' in the Imaginal realm. "You mean, flew off."

Steven said nothing for a full five seconds, frowning at the two empty beer glasses, then shrugged. "Okay. It must've flown off."

Happy stared at him, hands clenching, trying to summon the energy to drag more from Swift. He gave up.

The mage rolled his shoulders, looking around. "Gone now. It was strong, though. And geez, those eyes!" he said, just as Haggard, another mage on the team, entered the bar.

He had torn free and quenched the thousand electric eyes

and ears, but as he settled into himself, he felt something still watching him. It made his shoulders twitch. Until, as if sensing his attention, it fled.

Focusing on his astral form, he folded it up into something resembling a human's and opened his physical senses.

His knees and hands rested in puddles of strangely warm water. He raised his eyes up, and up. On every side, lighted buildings reached into a night sky. Faint music leaked from lofty windows.

He was kneeling in a... courtyard...?

How had he come here? He stood, dirt and mud slipping and falling from his brighter-than-white garb.

Staggering into an alley, he reshaped his body into something less noteworthy. He pictured a face, an innocent youth's, and morphed his features into those. Anything to throw off celestial pursuit.

But why would there be-?

He cut the thought off, the memory of pain still fresh, and strode from alley to crowded street. He Sensed the humans' auras. *Humans like me,* he affirmed.

He risked a smile at the *other humans* passing by, living their earthly lives. All busy, intent, even if simply on the devices they wore, beaming stories to entertain or outrage.

Sound pummeled him. Unfamiliar odors; a vast high sky he'd never imagined, clouds sailing overhead in moonlight like majestic aerial vessels. Music with an urgent, driving rawness wrapped around him, dragging him toward some metaphoric cliff where he could launch himself into flight.

Lifting his head and squaring his shoulders, he let his spirit soar, questing... finding evil and good in equal measure in this strange place, this unknown city.

But he should not idle away his time here. Following the thread of attention he'd felt, he soared toward the good. Toward that Potential.

It ended by a crossroads in a drinking establishment, not far from his physical form. Returning to his body he walked slowly to the bar, pausing at last at a street filled with cars, like salmon crowding a stream.

Finally, grasping the patterns in their broadcast controls, he stepped into the flow, crossing the street in a moving gap in the traffic. Entering the bar he paused, sensing the connections, giving himself to the strand of attention he'd been following.

It led to a fit and early middle-aged sorcerer, sitting with another who looked like he lived on the streets, bare patches in his aura tracking up his arms and at the base of his skull. Both sat with a large man, his expression serious, who appeared half machine. In his aura, numerous dead spots, where implanted cyberware whispered into his flesh.

Two other men sat alone, linked to the three but pretending not to be. One other spoke to them from elsewhere, not physically present.

Heroes, clearly. *I will join them.* They would need him.

He looked down at his own hands, wondering how old he was; or rather, how old he looked? He'd attracted attention somehow, just standing bright in the shadowed corner, and he turned, finding a mirror, surprised by his apparent age. A male youth of just sixteen, he'd guess, his long white coat fluorescing for some reason.

He moved across the bar, checking his wings were properly furled and fully hidden, even astrally, wetting his lips as he wondered how to explain that they needed his help.

They didn't look a very... *sacramental* crew.

"Excuse me, sir?"

All three men studied him, the scrappy sorcerer draped bonelessly back in his seat, the other eyeing his astral form too intently. *Are my wings still tucked?* The leader sat quite still, a collection of glasses, many empty, some full, on the table in front of the three.

"Kid's a mage, Happy," the ragged sorcerer said.

The large man didn't *look* happy, but human's names often mismatched their souls.

"Well, kid?"

"I'm sorry for your loss," he said, seeing the severed end in their web of connections, the tinge of sadness in their auras.

He had their full attention, he saw. "I offer my services to aid you in your fight." He bowed the correct degree.

It was a little hard to read the emotions from the thinned and torn auras of the two soul-damaged men, but the healthier mage's reaction shone clear enough: surprise, suspicion, and a little anger.

He ran his words back through his mind, trying to work out what he'd said to trigger that response.

"What fight would that be?" drawled the leader, Happy.

It was not the gratitude he'd expected. "Uh..." He Percepted, deeply. They were all Tied; but now, also to him. And through him, to something... something he'd forgotten?

Would they thank him for that? *Maybe not.*

"The one ahead of you all. The, uh, the web that's laid its touch upon you all." Would the two mages see that new Thread? With inspired cunning, he added, "Who knows why, though?" It wasn't an outright lie, after all.

The leader waited for more, but he felt he'd said enough. Maybe too much. He tried to project innocence.

For some reason though their reactions had shifted to amusement. He looked around, at the two members pretending to be separate, listening electronically. Both sorcerers at the table wore small earbuds too, he saw. Across the room the smaller, dark-haired man with sharp eyes smirked, while the large bruiser with the battleaxe across his back shook his head and smiled.

"Ah, that web. Nah, we're good, thanks kid."

Kid? he thought, then remembered his face in the mirror. Reading the currents of fate, he shrugged, turned, and left. *Later would be soon enough.*

Happy Joe Holliday, Steven Swift, and Haggard watched the youth in his fluorescent white trench-coat leave the bar. Haggard seized the interruption to raise Jury's departure.

"Tol' ya we'z becomin' too high vis, Happy," the ragged mage said.

Swift nodded.

"How'd he know Jury quit on us though?" Happy asked, referring to the operator of their remote gear. Jury'd never been comfortable outside their apartment, refusing all physical contact, but just that morning, they'd retreated fully into their own online world. No longer even joining the team via tele-operated gynoids or androids, or even drones.

Haggard snorted. "Undernet?"

"Did that kid look the type to know his way around that swamp?" Happy asked.

Haggard frowned, then nodded. "Truth. More like too much time hooked ta some fantasy game. Good strong aura though." He looked wistful.

Swift angled his head in the direction the kid had taken. "Tell you one thing: he was running a tight little illusion spell. Just on his face."

"Eh?" Haggard sat up. "I didn' *See* that."

"Yeah, big surprise." Swift eyed his teammate's worn figure and thin aura, but didn't shake his head. "Tight though, and subtle too," he added, to soften the criticism.

Murmuring a query for news on 'Happy Joe Holliday, bodyguard to the stars', Swift checked his Link, even poked around Jury's profile to see if maybe they'd added some change of status that might've tipped the kid off. "I don't see anything."

"Do ya ever?" Haggard sniped.

Happy tuned both of them out. The trouble was, the pain of herding mages was worth the gain: Steven and Haggard had given them the edge they'd needed time and again – not to mention their shaman, Sam, whenever he deigned to join them. Would it be crazy to try to fill Jury's slot with *another* mage? That'd put them at least *two* up on any other 'bodyguarding' operators in New Francisco. *Four* mages. Not a shaman, though – one of those was more than enough. Three sorcerers and a shaman. He nodded. It could work.

Happy's optics flashed an alert – the call he was waiting for. Tapping his ear to let his crew know, he took it. He didn't share the stream, but spoke aloud for their benefit.

"Holliday. Yes. Possible. Tomorrow? Yes; yes, we have two. No, two mages will be enough. These two, anyway." Swift and Haggard smiled. "Stairway To? Pricey. Uh huh. Good. 19:00, Ezekiel Smith." He eyed Haggard, imagining the establishment's reaction. "Tell him to book a private room. Yes. Very funny. 19:00."

He ended the call. "Looks like we may have a nice shady gig. And a free dinner, either way: *up to* 80 creds per head. Tomorrow night." His crew looked hungry at the prospect.

"Stairway To?" Steven asked. "That's neutral ground for Corps, but kind of a pick-up joint for sorcerers with tabs on themselves. And mage groupies. I'd better dress up: might get lucky." He chuckled. "Bet they mistake Haggard for a shaman."

He wandered the dark city, its byways and parks, continuing his exploration of this strange place, so full of people. A confusing wonderland. And friendly: someone even gifted him a pair of shoes! He followed the flows and eddies away from the bar, moving into areas more crowded, bustling and buzzing with energy.

A woman's cry followed by pounding feet spun him to face a young male, hollow cheeked and starving, clutching a cream colored bag. It swayed and dangled as he ran, weaving in an urgent, even desperate rush between the earthly beings. Such energy! Their colors changed as the man passed between them, shifting to violets and reds signifying shock and even anger. For a moment he considered joining the man in his earthbound flight, until the meaning of the woman's shouted words coalesced from nonsense into sense: "Stop him! My medicines!"

Raising a hand, he gestured for sleep, sending the man sprawling full length to the ground, amid a circle of others who also collapsed like pillars of salt, their eyes closing. His cheeks warmed.

Crouching beside the man, he saw a broken nose, and in arm's reach, a tooth gleamed white and red, lying on the fine smooth stone. He palmed it, cleaned it, and slotted it back in place in the jaw. Wiping the blood from the fellow's face he lay hands and re-set the nose, finally mending him.

Rubbing his hands on his long coat, he lifted the woman's bag, then spied a pair of wire framed spectacles. Turning and rising, his snow white coat fell softly around him. From the edge of the circle of sleeping people, the woman peered in his direction as he picked a path between them, holding out her bag and glasses to her.

"Oh, you angel, thank you!" Taking them, she dug out a small metallic stick, pressing it into his hands before embracing him, only then putting on her glasses and stepping back. But as she did, her eyes for some reason widened.

How did she know?! My wings...? But a glance over his shoulder showed them folded away, tucked down flat and neat in astral space, as a last few drops of the injured man's blood slid from his clothing to leave it unstained.

He saw she was looking past him, to the circle of fallen people behind him. Her hand rose to her mouth, her aura purpling with the beginnings of fear.

"They only sleep," he reassured her, kissing her brow and striding off, broaching an inward flow of onlookers. As if registering some oddity, a ripple of attention grew. Hunching his shoulders he slipped away into the crowd as the city sang to itself around him.

I need a name, he mused. *Michael,* he decided at last. Michael d'Angelo. Suitable, yet subtle. And it felt strangely *right.*

Chapter 4 – Guilt and claws and cold

It was still dark when Leeth reached the Department, lost in thoughts of her last mission: a failure. Sure, she'd destroyed Dr Yamamoto's memory *Writer* – and killed him – but now an AI had those plans.

Neither Eagle or Father, or even Mother, had hinted she could've stopped the warbot tearing open the safe and stealing the Omega tech. But *she* knew she should've. Reflected its laser better, or turned its missiles on it somehow. She'd studied its specs since, and questioned the others, but they'd just looked at her like she was crazy for asking how a human could take out a two-tonne man-shaped tank.

If my claws cut metal, I would've! Her hands clenched. She needed to fix her failure.

At least she'd uncovered the existence of an actual AI, secretly running the Tik Tek megacorporation. That was something. The Tik Tek AI. TTAI: 'Ty'.

Now it had the Omega tech. What did Ty want it for? There'd been bio-tech it had been hunting for, too.

What was its goal?

Whatever. But the Department was quietly freaking out. Omega was a Pandora's Box. It could read, write, and copy memories – *proper* copies, Nelson said, not the thin ones he could simulate.

At their first planning meeting after her failed mission, the Doctor had guessed that if her memories *were* copied, it *wouldn't* preserve the magical protections he'd carved into her psyche to prevent her blabbing about the Department.

They'd all looked at her like she'd already given away all their secrets.

"Stop it! Dr Yamamoto didn't bother to copy me," she'd snarled. "And even if Ty *can* capture me, those protections are more than any of you would have!"

She remembered being strapped down; drawn into the white donut of the Omega *Writer;* the ultrasonic whine of the robot surgeon's drills burrowing through her skull. She couldn't suppress a shudder.

At that first planning session, she'd assumed they were scared because they thought the AI had learned all about them from her.

But that wasn't it. No, what freaked the Department out wasn't just that the tech could *copy* anyone's memories – it was that it could *rewrite* them; replace the person behind the eyes. *Anyone:* agents like her; heads of corporations; foreign powers; government officials. The President.

It'd only been detected in *her* because she'd escaped mid-treatment.

Ty had surely recreated Omega's tech by now, no doubt using it for its own ends. To take people over? Rule the world?

She'd suggested Nelson should go with her to Newtopia City, two kilometers under the Antarctic ice, to hack in. He wasn't just a horrid, sneaky pervert – he was an actual computer genius. But everyone in the room had freaked out.

Leaving that meeting, the abusive little monster's voice had followed her from every speaker she passed, asking why she wanted him killed, mind-wiped, reprogrammed?

She'd ignored him, sure he was just being his usual dickish self, until she'd heard the tearful terror in his voice.

So she'd scrapped that plan.

Since she couldn't take Nelson, she considered an even more horrible idea: taking the Doctor, to tackle the problem from a magical angle. But apparently Antarctica was weird, magically speaking. Hostile to life. Astral scouting wasn't... healthy. It hurt mages who tried, she read.

So that possibility got rejected too. They also claimed he wasn't available. That he was 'busy'.

Of course they wouldn't say with what. But when she checked, she found it was true: no sounds from his office or rooms, and they were empty when she sneaked a peek through their ceilings.

As days passed, she'd seriously considered just buying a ticket and flying down to Antarctica on her own. Obviously someone had to prowl the city under the ice, uncover Ty's secrets. Somehow. Despite its all-seeing eyes, its cameras everywhere, watching; in control of every door, every lift, every train. Obviously, Newtopia City's 'intelligent city maintenance system', CityNet, was Ty.

How was Ty doing the research on the Writer? Probably

by itself, using robots and stuff. Experimenting on people. Maybe animals, too.

Finally, angry, she'd come up with an idea that felt right: since Antarctica was weird, go there as part of a magical study of the city and its environment. The more she'd looked into it, the better her plan seemed.

She'd learned Antarctica hadn't even been *sighted* until 1820. Nobody had lived there – no one at all – until 1983. Even then, no one had lived there *permanently.* Just scientists and engineers in rotation – until the Newtopian Consortium had bargained for a 99 year lease as payment if they could re-ice the continent and reverse the global sea level rise, provided they didn't exploit its resources. A promise they'd actually kept. Suspicious much? If not for minerals, why'd they even *wanted* the icy continent? It was deadly.

As part of that mega engineering feat they'd built Newtopia City, slowly buried by the renewed ice sheet. *I bet there's something dank about that, too.*

Antarctica had *never* been studied, magically.

At least while the Department had been wasting time, they'd arranged for her, as Bonnie Parker, to learn some snow survival skills in Alaska. Skiing had been mad fun: like flying, at ground level. Her cute instructor, Matt, had been impressed someone 'like her' wanted to learn to survive in the snow. Though she never did learn what he meant by 'someone like her'.

It had all been wonderful: challenging, bitter days, learning the limits of her body in the cold; and intimate nights, sharing warmth and more in the two-man tent. Or inside it, losing herself in the wilderness around their campsite, melting into the symphony of life that woke after sunset, to rustle and slither or ghost through the air outside.

The blizzard had been best of all. Especially the spooky night.

She sighed, remembering. She'd wanted to confront the thing snuffling at the walls of their tent, the mouths sucking at the SpiderSilk. Watching Matt in the dark as he clutched his rifle and torch all night, until dawn when the blizzard suddenly ended and the thing left.

He'd *really* freaked at finding no tracks in the snow.

She still didn't understand why he got so angry that she'd found it exciting, or by her certainty it was a single creature despite its multiple mouths. He'd especially hated her suggestion to stay the next night and open the tent if it came back. That had put an early end to the training exercise.

At least she'd got to try out her smart snowshoes, and train with Little Brother's snow-sonar goggles. Her ears had quickly learned the sounds of hard-packed vs soft, of shear-plates buried deep under snow. The final straw had been after she'd stared, eyes closed, at a mass of snow looming over them and asked, "Hey, can we climb around and then up, to there? I reckon we could poke it into avalanching!"

He'd just looked horrified. "No!"

When she returned, she learned both Nelson and Little Brother had been making special gear for her, for this mission. Though her visit with LB had gone weirdly. Like so many of her interactions with him did.

He'd checked her new choker; like her old one, she could talk to it by subvocalizing. They'd boosted the range of its spread spectrum radio – something not even an AI could hack. Any queued messages would be sent or received when a satellite was kind of overhead.

"We don't have a geostationary satellite over the Pole?"

LB blinked. "Geostationary means they have to match the Earth's rotation, Leeth," he said gently. "They can't *hover*."

She blushed.

But *he* looked embarrassed for her. "Listen, I know you shouldn't need to, but what if you're out in subzero temperatures and need to use your, uh, your... claws?"

"Then I'd use them." *What sort of question was that?*

His cheeks turned rosy. "But if you were outdoors a long time, punctures in your gloves'd let in water and cold. So I was thinking, if I knew the dimensions of your, ah, your claws – your blades, I mean! – I could maybe make some kind of self-sealing tips for the gloves."

She frowned. "But they're invisible."

He started looking excited. "I know."

"You want to study them." She wasn't sure how she felt about that. Especially at his eager nod.

On the other hand, she didn't want to get frostbite. In Alaska, Matt had insisted warm, dry clothing was critical. She'd felt for herself how quickly fingers went numb and cold. "I guess you can."

LB swallowed, his eyes falling to her hands. "Are, are they

out now?”

"Why don't *you* tell *me*?" It was kind of fun teasing Little Brother, she decided. He was very teasable.

But her challenge seemed to snap him from his nervousness, and he rattled through the gear on his workbench, pulling on a pair of goggles and turning to her.

She extruded all five claws on her right hand, none on her left.

"Ohh," he said, his face now half hidden.

"What do they look like?"

"Do you have them out?" he asked.

"Yep."

"Nothing. I can't see them." He rotated a dial built into the side of his goggles, then his shoulders slumped. "Do you really have them out?"

She rolled her eyes, but picked up a piece of plastic tubing and sliced it in half for him.

"Damn. Okay, let me try these others."

Five minutes later, they'd learned her blades were invisible to every part of the electromagnetic spectrum he could measure, and also to sonic waves.

They were very far from intangible, however. He'd been fascinated by the cuts they made, examined under an electron microscope. "Look at those edges," he breathed.

"What? They're just cuts."

"They're so smooth."

She eyed him as he mooned over the microscope's image.

"Something like an atom thick," he whispered.

She shrugged. "Maybe that's what makes them sharp."

"Can I- can I f-feel them?"

It was her turn to draw back. "You want to feel my claws? That... sounds kinda weird."

He blushed pink; but kept looking hopeful.

"You might cut yourself!" she said, not liking the idea of hurting him. "I've lopped off people's heads, you know," she admitted, then felt weird. "Bad guys."

He just nodded. "I'll be careful. Can you give me one finger?"

She resisted the obvious joke. "Sure." Leaving her index finger's claw out, she retracted the others.

"Hey, I just thought...." Moving to his bench, he picked up a cotton swab, dipping it in some paint. "Do you mind?"

He'd chosen red. She blinked, her heart twisting, remembering drops of blood falling on a birthday cake.

Swallowing, she shook her head. "It'll, it'll drip on your floor," she said, through a throat suddenly thick.

"That's okay."

Staring into his open, earnest eyes, she tried but failed to guess what he was thinking. He blushed again and looked away. Gritting her teeth, she nodded.

As he traced the edge, cotton strands severed and fell away; leaving filaments of red paint hanging in mid air.

They only 'stuck' a moment to the edge, just while he cut into the swab. He couldn't paint any other parts: not the sides, not the back.

Her blade was as long again as her whole hand, extending from her finger and narrowing to an impossibly slender point.

"Amazing," he sighed, as drops of red fell to the floor.

Taking up a fresh swab, his eyes asked if he could trace the edge again. She nodded. One hand holding her finger, he slid the end of the swab under, starting mid way along then moving back toward her hand. Her 'claw' broadened as it neared her fingertip, but its cutting edge stayed deadly sharp even as it flared out. He couldn't touch any part of the tip of her finger: the invisible base of her claw blocked it.

"Damn, that's going to be tricky."

"What do you mean?"

"I imagined it'd be narrow where it came out, like a scalpel. That'd make for a smaller cut, a smaller slit to seal."

"Oh."

"Can I... can I feel it with my fingers?"

She felt oddly shy, her own cheeks flushing. She swallowed. "I guess. Be careful."

"I will."

The upper edge, the back of her claw, hadn't cut the swab. Only its bottom edge had, and the tip. But as he slid his finger with surgical care up the flat side and around to the top, near her fingertip, the edge felt thinner than he'd expected, and his skin suddenly parted.

He jerked his hand back, blood welling.

"Sorry! I didn't mean that!" Her head shaking in denial, she watched him press the edges of the cut together.

"I didn't even feel it," he whispered.

"I'm sorry-"

"It's okay. Weird. It didn't do that to the swab." After a little first aid, he came back, holding out his hand for hers.

"What are you doing?"

"I wanted to feel them, remember?"

"You just did! And I cut you."

"I'll be more careful this time. I'll only touch the sides." He hesitated. "Do you have it out?"

She blushed, again for no reason she understood, but extruded the blade from her fingertip, then nodded.

He offered his hand again. "Maybe *you* guide my thumb and finger to it?"

"Uh." Why was this making her feel so weird? She had trouble keeping her breath steady. "Okay." Wetting her lips, she moved his finger and thumb to her fingertip then slid them out a fraction, onto the sides of her claw. His skin flattened against the invisible surface.

Her eyes widened at the touch. She *felt* his fingers, pressing on *her*. Warm. Alive. Fragile. Electric eagerness flooded her chest. Hungry to...

His eyes were locked on his finger and thumb. "Slide them along. Can you feel me?"

She could. She swallowed. She'd never done anything like this before. Her claws were for cutting or killing. This felt perverse; somehow wrong. Shivering, she retracted it and dropped his hand.

"Why'd you do that? I need to feel it, see how thin it is!"

"Need to, or want to? You can do that with instruments."

He looked at her like she'd said something strange, then blushed, turning from her to rummage around for a device.

"Micrometer."

But as held up the metal tool, she took it from him and slid it over her claw herself.

They got a reading of zero.

Not really zero, he explained. Just thinner than it could measure: under a nanometer. He couldn't *trap* her claw, either: even closed all the way on it, his instrument couldn't get a grip.

"How strong are they?"

"I'm *not* letting you try to snap one in half. Strong, okay? I can't cut metal – it hurts when I try – but they've never broken."

Except they *kind of* had, once. The alien gray cutting thing.

That visit to LB had been days ago – maybe she should drop in again, see if he'd worked out his gloves idea? She checked her Link: thirty minutes before she had to *wait* outside Eagle's door. Plenty of time.

LB was awake, waiting for her – opening his door before she even knocked. To give her the 'self-healing' gloves.

But then he looked at her oddly. "Uh. Leeth?"

Something made her sure he was going to ask to feel her claws again. She tightened her grip on the neat package, watching him wet his lips.

"Uh, it'll only work a few times?"

"Okay." They stood, staring at one another. "I'd better get going," she said at last.

Turning the corner she heard his whisper. "Be careful." And *he* knew she could hear him. She felt her cheeks burn.

Little Brother wasn't the only one awake at six a.m. *How to kill an AI?* Nelson wondered. The topic had vexed him for two weeks now. He still had no answer. But another terror had inspired his suggestion for Eagle's old pal, the bag of bones, to lend Leeth something as frightening as she herself for her mission.

Heisenberg knew, Leeth scared *him*. He probed his chest where her fingertips had pricked, slicing through his clothing, her face pressed to his, her teeth bared-

Shuddering, his mind flashed to another memory of her: the video of her twisting and striking with black dagger and invisible claws while writhing gray tentacles flayed her, tearing her apart strip by strip.

He swallowed. Even at the time, watching the machine-like vines carving into her, punishing her like he'd maybe wished *he* could have... he'd been conflicted. Wanting the alien thing to win yet at the same time hoping she'd destroy *it*... In his dreams, gray tentacles still ate at the world. Had she killed all of it? What if more remained, somewhere?

Leeth thought it really had been alien: had even sent some signal beyond Earth, into the vastness of space...

Yet she'd disrupted it, shattering into gritty gray dust what had once writhed with electrical life.

He'd returned to that video over and over again as he and

Little Brother had analyzed the dust of its remains.

Their analysis: *self-destructed* microscopic remnants of a nano-scale replicating weapon that had fed on inorganic matter and the magical energy of Abrams's artifacts.

A machine 'lifeform' that absorbed magic. But machines and magic weren't supposed to be compatible. *And how did you kill a replicating nano-machine that'd already grown to macroscopic scale?*

You didn't. You couldn't. Yet Leeth had. She'd stabbed one of the weird gray nodes, but that shouldn't have stopped it. He'd reluctantly concluded that Leeth plus the death god's dagger had done something 'impossible'.

Hence his suggestion to Eagle that maybe the two together could *magically* kill an AI.

He wasn't sure – he wasn't a touchy-feely type who could read micro-expressions – but at his reasoning, the bag of bones had seemed more horrified than if he'd been told his wheelchair was full of spiders.

But Abrams hadn't even tried to argue against the idea itself; only against the idea of giving the weapon to Leeth, of leaving it alone with her, for days or weeks.

As if the two together were a special threat.

Chapter 5 – She's going to die

As soon as she sank cross-legged to the floor outside Eagle's noise-insulated security door, the audio countermeasures activated. *Clever old ears,* she thought, as they compensated. They'd learned the Department's white noise generators ages ago.

But only the Doctor, Eagle, and LB knew about her super hearing... So: typical Mother paranoia.

Hoping to creep her out, knowing she'd be watching, Leeth allowed herself a smile. But as the minutes leaked away, that childish victory faded. Slowing her breathing, she stroked the cold cement floor, its polished surface belying the projected image of dirt.

For some reason, today the corridor leading to Eagle's office displayed rough hewn sandstone walls and old wooden support beams. Fake flames from projected lanterns lit the old-time mining tunnel, the heavy security door a dark entrance to deeper caves. To her eyes though, the gaping black blotch was flat and impenetrable: fake.

At least it fits with being underground. Not for the first time, she wondered why Eagle had his office on basement level five.

One a.m. had been the worst: pacing her grotty apartment after the news from Antarctica, waiting for his call. Wondering if she should've killed Gaz and his clown friends. Rechecking her bags. Goading Nelson to try to hack in. Hunting for more news reports of the distant failure.

Wondering why Eagle didn't call.

Messaging him but just getting 'wait' in response; and then each time after that, nothing.

The only news: troubles restarting all the different systems of Newtopia's computer-controlled city.

Why couldn't Ty restart? *Was it* dead? *What on earth could kill an AI?* Find that out, and she could do it herself!

Finally, at two a.m. Eagle had messaged her: 'Sleep. Be here at 6:15am. Wait outside my office until I call you in.'

Even at the time, she'd found the order strange.

Chewing her lip, she closed her eyes to better concentrate. Mother spoke: her usual objection. "The whole idea is ludicrous: sending a nineteen-year-old, barely-trained field agent with poor impulse control and more enthusiasm than sense to tackle an existential threat to humanity."

"Leeth is our best option," Eagle countered. "She has a talent for disruption."

His faith warmed her. *You tell her!* Though he could've actually *contradicted* Mother's insulting assessment.

"This is insane! We have no plan – just this story Leeth has dreamed up. We'll be sending her to certain death; or worse, to a mind rape that will expose all our secrets!"

Yeah, that's your main worry. Thanks, Mother. Though it was nice to know Mother didn't want her to die. Leeth ignored a prickle of unease.

"Some secrets, Mother. Hardly *all,*" Father objected.

She bristled. *Some? I know* heaps *of them!* How could Father be so naive?

"Implant false memories?" he suggested.

Her fingers froze. Suppressed fury – at him, at the Doctor – started a tremor in her hands. For some reason it made her imagine the death god nearby, watching. Waiting for an opening.

Don't be silly. It's not here.

Except it felt like it was. A kind of sneaky-

"No," Eagle said, speaking up for her, finality in his voice. "The Doctor has strongly advised against any further mental tampering. Especially after her last mission."

Yeah, two days of lost memories, erased by the Writer... the Doctor said she'd never recover them. But the Doctor – her 'uncle' – had stood up for her; had cared that much? *Pretended to, more likely.*

She still needed to figure out how to kill him. A problem for later. If she survived this mission.

"You can *not* send her!" Mother said, again. "Every camera, every sensor in Newtopia is an eye or ear for that AI. The entire city is an invisible web with an unsleeping spider at its center. It also knows what she looks like."

That was kind of true. And none of them had worked out how she could actually accomplish this impossible mission.

Over six hours now since Ty's latest crash. It could wake up – reboot – any moment. They should have sent her to

Antarctica a week ago! Even if Ty *had* locked her up on arrival, she'd have been on the spot to take advantage of it now. Escaping from lockup'd probably be easy with it out of action. Meanwhile they'd wasted two weeks dithering!

Shaking herself, she tuned back in to the argument behind Eagle's sound insulated door.

"What do you even expect her to do?" Mother demanded.

Oh, I dunno: the mission? Figure out what Ty's up to. Smash his Writer, blow things up; kill him.

She stopped listening again. This one *would* be tricky, she had to admit. She still had no idea how to kill any AI, let alone a proper conscious AGI like Ty.

Something about this whole mission felt off. Mother and Father always tried to allow for every contingency. It drove her mad. It's why she liked to return the favor whenever she could. But *this* one wasn't meticulously planned. They simply had too little info about Newtopia City.

She hoped she'd survive. She even had people who'd miss her, now. Though if she did die, they'd cope; it wasn't like they had no one else. Faith was busy being a mom to her pups, had her new mate to look after, and Mr Shanahan to look after *her*. Marcie, her other friend, had her father, younger sister, and boyfriend, so they'd be okay too. None of them would be alone.

Stop it: I'm not gonna die! Even if Mother thought she would.

After this she could go solo: Eagle had promised. He knew she wanted to join Happy Joe Holliday's merc team. It was their reputation for meets in shady bars and nightclubs that had inspired her whole Bonnie Parker cover identity: failed intern with ARPA-M; former personal trainer and physical therapist; now turned exotic dancer.

She even had ideas for introducing herself into Happy's team. But the other skills Bonnie had needed – customer relations, the responsible serving of drugs and alcohol – too often she pictured herself grabbing a handsy customer and *serving* them right through a window.

She shook herself, returning to the puzzle of why Eagle had called her in just to sit outside like a dummy. To listen, she assumed. *He* knew she had amazing hearing.

The longer she listened, the more certain she grew that other people were in the room. One other for sure; maybe two. She couldn't say why she thought that – they hadn't spoken, or even moved. She didn't *think* she was imagining quiet breathing.

"This is the window we've waited for," Eagle said, interrupting Mother's continuing objections. "I have intel that Leeth and Yackownay should go. Today."

Yackownay? Yakone! Leeth felt a surge of excitement. Adlartok Kallik Yakone was who she'd suggested. As sturdy and solid as a tree trunk, he'd seen her defend Godsson back when she was little, at the Institute. Her Inuit shaman. Her 'angakkuq' – Inuit shamans were called 'angakkuq'. An-GAHK-awk, she'd learned.

This was her plan. She felt a glow of pride. Eagle had liked her idea of a magical research study, and even her suggestion about who could do the investigation.

Though he, and especially the Doctor, had eyed her long and hard – and Eagle had known straight away who she meant. It made her think he'd been watching her and the Doctor long before the Department recruited them.

For her plan they'd gotten her an internship at ARPA-M to nudge Mr Yakone into place. The trickiest part had been convincing him to take along Bonnie Parker, his helpful ARPA-M contact, as a field assistant.

He'd be her only help, so she'd have to take good care of him. He might be the only one around to magically heal her if she got hurt. Newtopia City had the lowest concentration of sorcerers and shamans of any city in the world, she'd read, and not just because of the usual distrust. It didn't outlaw them, but it sure didn't encourage them either.

But: I'm definitely going! Today even, if Mother could just finish losing this argument. And if Eagle stopped making her sit outside like this!

"Oh, *intel,*" Mother was saying. "From your pet wizard."

'Pet wizard' meant Mr Abrams. Mother *really* hated his influence on Eagle. She'd never tell Mother, but *she* reckoned Mr Abrams could predict the future.

At the barely audible but oh-so-familiar sound of teeth grinding, she fought her grin, bending forward to hide her reaction from the cameras. Though Mother's sharp inhalation from beyond the sealed door made her worry she hadn't lowered her head soon enough.

"Nelson really has no idea who or what is causing their

system failures?" Mother asked. "He's not doing it?"

"No." She could picture Eagle shaking his head. "Since Leeth's last encounter with the AI, Nelson is more terrified of Tik Tek than ever. He was not keen to investigate."

Yeah, tell me about it! 'You'll never get a better chance, Nelson! Just blame me if anything goes wrong.'

A finger tapped the table, and from its meaty sound, she knew Father was about to speak. "Newtopia's system failure: ongoing; internal source; unknown cause. Not replicable. System's a maelstrom of antivirals."

She translated Father's shorthand: Nelson didn't know why Newtopia's CityNet had crashed – a feat he couldn't replicate. *A magic attack?* But magic and tech didn't mix. Except it kind of had, inside her, when that *other*, scarier AI thing had downloaded itself into the Omega tech left in her brain. Aiyami: a 'magical Archetype' of an artificial intelligence. Even to her, that sounded... bad. *Why do these things keep picking on me?* Like Aiyami. Or Tezsh Catlick. Or *Her*, lying to her when she was a kid.

Was it something the Doctor did to me, when I was little? Or Godsson?

Was that part of why Eagle wanted to send her? *But I don't know anything about magic, not really.* And why the flipping frogs did he want her eavesdropping *now*?!

Unless she'd guessed wrong. Was he *waiting* for something? For *her* to do something? Was this a *test*?

She growled.

The next flight to Newtopia left in just a few hours, and they'd impressed on her you had to arrive hours early for international flights.

Leaving America! The thought sent an uncomfortable thrill through her. It wasn't just the idea of going to a whole other country, one owned and run by a consortium; or of teaming up with the cute shaman she'd kind of... groped, almost five years ago. It was knowing her target, Ty, probably wasn't exactly thrilled with her, personally.

But I *let Ty get way more dangerous by stealing the Omega tech, so* I *have to destroy it.*

Except, unlike Nelson, she was no computer wizard. Did they expect her to somehow go *inside* the Net and kill Ty in hand to hand combat? That'd be pretty chill, actually! She nibbled at the corners of her fingernails.

Every part of this mission sounded kind of impossible. By now, the AI could've made millions of copies of Dr Yamamoto's research, and millions of copies of itself... though it probably hadn't, since the world hadn't ended.

Not as far as she knew, anyway.

She had a bad feeling about all this. But there was no getting around it; this *was* her mess.

It'd be just her and Mr Yakone, fifteen thousand kilometers from the Department; two kilometers under ice.

One hand went to the new, replacement choker at her throat. Her only lifeline, a communicator with a few extra functions. That, and a two man escape vehicle the Department had sneaked into an unused tunnel on the edge of the city a week ago. Something to take them to McMurdo, on the coast, if things went totally wrong.

She couldn't imagine just giving up and running away, though she hadn't told any of them that.

She checked her Link: 6:30 a.m. *Come* on*! I need to leave real soon. Why are you making me sit out here, Eagle, like a... like a gun on a cake?* She felt a weird little spike of tension shiver through her. He *was* waiting for her to do something.

Or maybe, to *realize* something?

But what?

Well... Ty had stolen Omega's tech, to do who knew what. Was that why the Newtopian city – and Ty itself – was glitching? Had the tech somehow damaged it?

If Ty *was* injured... She shook her head. She couldn't kill a computer program!

Or could I? What if they let me use Tezsh's dagger? An unsettling feeling shivered through her. *A museum piece like that might slip past high tech security checks.* Ty probably wouldn't see it as a threat, either: just a primitive little gold-hilted obsidian blade. Of an Aztec Death god. Tezsh Catlick Poker, or however you said it. Sometimes still, in her dreams, flat little lapis lazuli eyes watched her.

The memory opened a pit in her stomach. She snarled, a surge of excitement making her invisible claws spear out, gouging the concrete floor with a sound that made her teeth grate. She ignored it, chasing an idea that felt important.

Of course if she *did* use his ceremonial dagger, Tezsh would try to possess her. Again.

Is that a price I'd be willing to pay? If with its power she *could* kill Ty? She shoved down a momentary sympathy for the AI. *If Tezsh did take me over, would the Department nuke the Antarctic city to wipe it and me out?*

Would a nuke even *work* on a volcano god?

Anyway, Tezsh couldn't take me over last time.

She could keep the dagger in a sealed glass case, one you had to smash to open. That way it'd look just... decorative. Ornamental. It *would* be good to have handy, just in case.

It's not like I'm hungry to use it again.

She blinked at eight deep pits she'd clawed in the painted floor, her fingers buried in piles of concrete chips; and *then* realized all the voices in the next room had fallen silent.

She retracted her claws.

"Leeth. Please enter," Eagle's voice said from the intercom. He didn't sound happy.

And just like that, she knew why he'd had her wait outside; knew what waited for her.

He'd wanted to see if she'd sense it. To learn if there was still a connection between them; if she'd react to its presence. She stared at the holes she'd dug. *Do they count as a reaction?*

Wincing, she stood, and strode to the fake cave entrance already sliding into the wall.

Chapter 6 – My old friend Death

She stopped at the sight of the black silk bag on the conference table.

Sensing the thing inside *yearning* for her.

Wrenching her gaze from it, she met Eagle's intense stare. His and everyone else's. Mother looked uncharacteristically nervous; Father too perhaps, but hiding it better.

James sat at the far end of the room – armed – and Dojo at the near end: the two near-silent people she'd heard.

The door sealed solidly shut behind her.

James's heartbeat sped up. Dojo microscopically adjusted his seated stance.

She looked around, expecting to see Mr Abrams too, but he wasn't there.

Her eyes were dragged back to the dark, magic-insulating bag, the death god's dagger straining toward her. Again she tore her eyes from it.

Why wasn't Mr Abrams here? She couldn't imagine he'd let the dagger out of his sight. The last time they'd brought it to the Department, to this very room, he'd made himself invisible.

He has to be here! Shutting her eyes, she hunted for the sounds of his fancy wheelchair's life support machinery. Listened for the fuzzy edges of noise cancellation.

There was nothing, though.

Nothing.

Nothing! Too *much* nothing.

She lifted her head, staring beyond James to a patch of dead air, soundless.

"Mr Abrams. It's funny, I was just thinking how with Tezsh's dagger I might somehow be able to pull this mission off. 'Cause I don't know how to kill an AI."

She could tell from Eagle's microexpression she'd surprised him again. It warmed her. And just like last time, Mr Abrams dropped his spells and appeared.

But this time he didn't chuckle at her penetration of his camouflage.

James and Dojo went even more alert.

She pretended not to notice. "It *is* in the bag, isn't it?"

Mr Abrams nodded, his chair gliding up beside Eagle's, his green eyes burning at her from across the glossy white conference table. He studied her face, his gaze dancing over her, digging in as it went, a roving, needling pain – his special astral scan.

Anger rose in its wake, and she found she wanted to hurt him in return. "How's Ankhet?" She'd been his magic student, until Dr Callahan Scott had turned her into a soulless human robot like Marc Disten. "That religion she's started sounds as creepy as Disten ever was. Can't you fix her?"

Mr Abrams seemed to shrink in his chair, the wrinkles of his sagging skin deepening. He took a long breath, then shook his head. "She no longer takes my calls. She says I am irrational. Which, by her new standards, I suppose I am. As are we all."

He looked smaller. Older. And instead of feeling better for hurting him, she suddenly just felt mean.

She shuffled her feet. "Yeah, well." She'd only met Ankhet the once, before she'd been changed – broken? – but she'd liked her. "I'm sorry. Maybe I could talk to her for you, after this?"

He actually *flinched*, and she fought a fresh lick of anger. But aware of the deadline to meet her flight, she tipped her chin at the black silk bag. "So, I guess your plan was to see what happened when I touched the dagger, picked it up? See if Tezsh Catlick Poker 'took me over'? I'm getting kind of sick of people trying to do that, you know."

She heard the steel in her own voice. She'd dealt with every person who'd done that to her. Every person but one.

She looked around for the Doctor, not sure whether to be glad, or annoyed at his absence. Her 'uncle'. Her lips thinned.

"Tezcatlipoca," Mr Abrams corrected her. "Yes."

"Don't you wanna handcuff me or something?" The memory of potency, of time slowing, rose fresh and sharp in her mind. She saw each move needed to defuse Mr Abrams, who, despite his decrepit appearance, she judged by far the most dangerous person in the room. Then, disarm James. She selected the point she'd hit Dojo as he rose from his chair. Each action, one step in a stop-motion diorama in which only she moved.

Mr Abrams shook his head, snapping her attention back to the conversation. "Under such a handicap it might not make the attempt. If that is its intent, we need to let it try here, now, where we have a chance of stopping it."

As if. Somehow, she avoided rolling her eyes.

"I don't wish to read of Flight ENF714 arriving in a wash of blood, every passenger sacrificed," Abrams added.

She blinked, then shook herself. "I wouldn't do that!"

"We know *you* wouldn't, Leeth," Eagle said, quietly.

She looked at them – at Eagle, James, and Dojo, who she counted as friends; at Mr Abrams, someone she respected, like Father. Mother's expression, when their eyes met, was harder to read: fear, but maybe anticipation too?

Pity I can't read auras to sense emotions like mages do.

She sighed, aware of a sneaking, hungry anticipation reaching for her; and if she was honest, an eagerness of her own. She stared down at the source, preparing herself like she would before a bout with Dojo. Centering herself.

She reached out to the black silk bag.

She'd just twitched out her invisible blades to slice the thin cloth when a sudden intuition made her pull them back in. Instead, she delicately untied the drawstring's looping knot.

Was that a surge of annoyance, or just her imagination?

The scalloped obsidian blade itself lay invisible inside its silken black cave, but from the golden hilt, lapis lazuli eyes gazed into hers from the darkness. She wet her lips and looked up, to find every eye locked on her.

Reaching in, she drew out the small artifact, wary of the scalloped blade's razor edges.

No one spoke.

Her fingers closed around the hilt, braced for a mental attack, or the god's booming voice in her head – or worse, hearing it speak with her own lips. The weapon felt both oddly light and strangely heavy in her hand.

She shivered, remembering.

About to say it seemed fine, she noticed a peculiar stillness, a deadness filling the room. Utter silence.

No breath disturbed the air. Not a single heart, beat. Dragging her eyes from the dagger, perfectly shaped for her hand, she saw every person frozen, like a trid show paused mid-action.

Turning, through air like treacle, understanding finally dawned. It had moved her into a hyper accelerated state, more extreme even than last time.

Now that *is useful!*

That thought summoned fresh annoyance. Mother's elegant neck zoomed into focus, the subtle outline of her carotid artery, rich in blood, offering itself.

Nuh-uh, nope, not doing that!

They jerked back into motion, heartbeats loud, breathing restarted.

She frowned.

"What happened?" asked Mr Abrams. "For a moment, you were wrapped in magic."

"Uh." They all looked super tense. Maybe she shouldn't go into details? "I think I annoyed it."

Mother's lips pursed – managing to say 'idiot girl' without a word.

It wanted me to slit your throat! she almost snapped, but stopped herself in time. "I was thinking of his dagger as just being *useful*. I don't think he liked that."

"It didn't try to take control?" Mr Abrams asked. "Think carefully."

Not exactly. "Um, I don't think so." She jiggled the dagger in her hand. "But I think he's sulking now."

Looking up, she caught Mr Abrams wincing.

"What?"

"It is an Aztec god of death, Leeth. It can probably still sense your thoughts, perhaps even hear through you, while you hold it. Please assume you are still mid negotiation."

Mother and Father grimaced at Mr Abrams's words, and even Eagle's expression turned kind of wooden.

"Negotiation? You mean I have to bargain with it?"

Its presence flooded back into her mind, booming through her thoughts. She couldn't tell whether the ground was really shaking, or the volcanic rumbling was just inside her head. «I AM A GOD, NOT A TOOL!»

A tool? Actually-

She scrabbled to cut off the insult.

«*DISRESPECT?!* WHILE SEEKING TO USE MY HOLY CONDUIT AS A MERE TOOL? SO SHALL IT BE THEN. SINCE YOU BEHAVE AS MERCHANT, NOT ACOLYTE,

YOU SHALL *PAY* FOR MY AID WITH SUITABLE OFFER-INGS.»

"What do you mean?"

The inner voice fell silent, as if it knew its meaning was stark and clear in her head.

"Are you still there?"

It didn't deign to answer. Around the room, everyone leaned forward as if they hadn't heard a single thing it said, or felt the floor shake. Eagle spread both hands, waiting for her explanation.

She held up a finger. "Do we have anyone you need killed?" she asked it. At the expressions around the table, she quickly added, "I mean bad guys, obviously. Jeez."

Eagle and Mr Abrams shared an unhappy look, and a long silence followed. But from Father's sigh, and the angry series of expressions crossing Mother's face, she could tell Eagle was talking to them through their headware.

Best to interrupt that. "It, uh, said I have to give it 'offerings' before I can use it."

Mr Abrams shut his eyes as if in pain.

"I'm guessing 'offerings' means killing someone. But that means it's agreed, right? So I *could* take it to Newtopia. Little Brother could design and print a case to hold it, with no way to open – oh, wait, with a *secret* opening mechanism! – to make it look like an art object instead of a weapon to confiscate." Everyone drew back in their chairs, away from her; and she realized she'd been waving the sacrificial dagger around for emphasis.

"Oh, what a clever idea," Mother drawled.

"Little Brother already has," Eagle explained.

Leeth slid the smugly inert magical weapon back into its magic shielding bag and yanked the drawstrings shut.

After several long seconds Eagle nodded.

Mr Abrams opened his eyes, looking unhappy.

"Hey," she said, to cheer him up, "on the plus side, apart from Newtopia itself, Antarctica's not exactly teeming with people if something does go wrong."

They all stared at her like she'd said something stupid.

Mother snorted. "Such as *someone* detonating the city's Thorium reactors and re-melting the Antarctic ice sheets?"

But while Father explained that wasn't physically possible, Mother continued to glare at her, as if certain she'd find a way to do it anyway.

Maybe now wasn't a good time to point out there were like a hundred and forty volcanoes down there, part of the largest volcano range on Earth? Only two active, though.

Whatever. At least the mission was on!

"Take the dagger up to Little Brother," Eagle told her. "He's scanned it, and prepared a suitable casing for it. Then collect your luggage and head to the airport." He reached for the dagger, but Mr Abrams intercepted it.

"I will carry it – I'd like a word with Miss Leeth before she departs."

Hoo boy. From the look Eagle gave Mr Abrams, he'd be sure to listen in if he could, somehow. Mr Abrams didn't wait though, tucking the small silk bag on the rug across his lap as his chair zoomed to the exit door.

Leeth turned to Eagle. "I don't need to go to my apartment, I brought my baggage with me."

"And if the Tik Tek AI hacks in to street videos or taxi records to find Bonnie Parker departed from this location, rather than her home?" Mother demanded.

"Isn't that why we're buried under a shopping mall? I'll buy something. Ciao!"

Without waiting for a reply, she darted from the room, hearing the elevator doors opening and Mr Abrams's wheelchair start up again.

Chapter 7 – Just between you and me

I'll take Mr Abrams to my room. Eagle was *probably* still respecting her privacy. "Since you want to talk to just me, we can-"

He made a small scooping gesture, and the instantaneous echoes of her voice in the enclosed space of the elevator died.

"... do a spell. Okay. So... I'm listening."

He shook his head. "It's not about Tezcatlipoca, or his sacrificial dagger, or the possibility you'll awaken a chain of dormant volcanoes and re-melt the polar icecap."

"It's not?"

The elevator arrived at LB's level. Mr Abrams zoomed out ahead of her. Immediately, everything stopped sounding like it was buried under blankets. She hurried after him, the sounds around them cutting off again as she caught up. He braked to a halt, and she did too.

He angled himself to see her, so she moved around in front of him.

He shook his head. "No. I had expected more time to discuss this, but things appear to be moving apace."

"So your precognition didn't work properly this time?"

She'd hoped to trick him into an admission, but even though he didn't speak for several seconds, in the end he just shook his head again. "I can see you're worried, Miss Leeth. Even frightened."

Inside her a sort of hollowness billowed up from her stomach to fill her throat. She wanted to argue, but instead clamped her lips shut and waited.

"Twice now, Miss Leeth, you have done something quite extraordinary, by pure accident. Something only myself, the Dragon Lord, and one or two others are capable of. Do you know what I refer to?"

She really didn't, but his expression demanded she try. "Uh, killed a god?"

This time Abrams stared at her in real shock, his mouth opening. He blinked owlishly.

"I don't actually know they were *gods*," she admitted.

"I'm just guessing at what us two might have in common."

His expression grew almost comically defensive. Maybe she should let him talk? She did have a plane to catch after all. "Look, never mind. It was just this thing in the gray place. Why don't *you* tell *me*."

"The Gray Place." He studied her face long enough to make her uncomfortable, then nodded, relaxing. "I suppose it would appear that way to you. Indeed, it is the 'Gray Place' I wish to discuss with you. You have gone there twice now, I believe?"

She had. Once when the black cloud thing had boiled out of Marc Disten's body and taken her there – Marcie somehow bringing her back – and once right in front of Mr Abrams. *He'd* sent her there, holding Tezsh's dagger.

It was her turn to nod.

"That place is dangerous, Miss Leeth. In many ways. It can be used to travel vast distances in the real world – albeit with more danger than walking naked and blind through a jungle."

Ooh, that could be fun!

Mr Abrams sighed. "I need to warn you of something you must never do, should you ever return there."

He paused, holding her gaze.

"Okay, I get it, this is important. Can you just *tell me* without all the drama?"

All of a sudden he looked angry.

She held up her hands. "I'm serious! I'm listening, honest. Just tell me!"

"That place is where Archetypes dwell, where they are born. They cast only shadows into this world – and just as well. Such shadows seed gods."

She made a 'yeah, get on with it' gesture.

"Never bring anything back with you that you didn't take in."

"Anything else?" she asked.

"There was one other matter, yes," Mr Abrams said.

This is the real thing: something you or Eagle didn't want to bring up in the meeting.

"Eagle and I suspect something else is going on down there, in Newtopia. Some kind of odd development; something growing."

"What, like mold?"

Mr Abrams gave her a dirty look. "Perhaps. I've sensed it. Something hidden: stealthy growth."

She nodded. "Got it: another prediction, and you're hiding that you can do that from... hmm, I'd guess Mother, right?"

"The way you jump to conclus-"

"Oh, come on! Father's, you know, *Father;* and James and Dojo... well, they aren't exactly sneaky types. So it has to be Mother."

"I know you're simply hoping I'll confirm your wild theory."

"And I know you know I'm not. Look, if that's all, I've really gotta run. I'll keep an eye out for secret mold or plants or whatever.

"Thanks for letting me take the dagger. I hope I don't need it. I don't like the idea of killing someone just to get a power-up."

Bending down, she hugged him, then kissed his papery forehead. For some reason, that seemed to really surprise him. "Speaking of which, I need to have LB 'lock it up' so it won't get confiscated."

Snatching it from his lap, she darted off. After a pause of several seconds, she heard his wheelchair head back to the elevator.

Chapter 8 – Gifts and traps

Little Brother set the dagger in one half of the resin brick molded to its shape, pressing the other half down over it, then took the whole block and fitted it into a dark base. He showed her the concealed button for the lighting, then the two places to touch to unlock the base, to split the clear brick apart. Finally, he slid it all back inside the special black silk bag.

"I also have this for you," he said, swiveling his seat to dig out a small red box from the gadgets cluttering his workbench.

Not actually red, she saw as she took it, just wrapped in shiny red paper. For some reason, he'd also tied a red ribbon around it. Did you pull the ribbon to activate it? Was the bow for quick release? She looked at him.

"Unwrap it!" he urged.

Pulling the ribbon only tightened the knot. A flick of invisible claws dealt with that, but he'd also taped the paper down. Lifting her eyes she saw him watching her intently. Somehow this... presentation... seemed like a ritual. She flushed. Was there something special she was supposed to do? Then she remembered another parcel, wrapped up like this. Her toy bow, from her- from the Doctor, soon after going to the Institute. Was this a *gift*?

He certainly looked eager, as he nodded down at the parcel in her hands.

She slowly peeled the paper open, holding her breath... only to find a plain beige cardboard box.

Was this a game? But he was standing too close for it to be a trap. Tugging a tab back, she slid out... a small, *furry* drone, bubble wrapped.

"Uh..."

"Here, let me show you!" Taking it from the wrap, he pressed the tip of her index finger into a small bare patch on the drone's furred underside.

Four shiny white feathered wings folded out, the rear two sweeping back, making it look like a snowy version of Marcie's Deathbird in her vid drama – and a tiny animated face blossomed over two camera lenses irising open, behind the curved screen. Its wings blurred into motion with a soft *thrum,* and it rose in the air to hover in front of her, obviously scanning her face.

"Everyone down there has a drone assistant, right?"

"Oh! It's an amibo?" In Newtopia, every adult had a small companion drone: combined memory aide, recorder of life events, confidante, and if you weren't cyber-enhanced, an interface to all the city's systems. Basically like a Link, except they followed and recorded their owner, completely internally and privately – so the claim went. Each had a persona, and could talk to you, even counsel you. Some people called them 'Jiminies' for some reason.

She held her palms up, together, and the small drone settled trustingly down, filling her hands. Its wings stopped and folded into its sides, its eyes avidly scrutinizing her face.

She stroked the fur. "So soft!" It purred, two friendly eyes smiling up at her. "I love it!"

"I love you too!" the tiny bot chirped, settling more firmly into her palm with a purring hum that brought an instant smile to her face.

"I didn't think amibos were furry, though." She stroked its wings' white feathers, then the even softer down of its belly as it wiggled in delight in her palm. "So I'll have my own, extra clever amibo to interface to the systems down there?"

At LB's shy nod, she gave him a one-armed hug. "Thanks, LB! I mean it. How can I thank you? I don't have much time, but..." Turning, she slid onto his lap and wriggled.

She'd expected him to blush – as he did – and stammer – as he also did – but then his expression collapsed into one she hadn't expected. He looked *sad.*

"I mean *sex,* LB. I'm really good at it, and I can get you off real quick, so there's time."

But instead of brightening, his expression fell from sad to *stricken.* His head dropped, his face screwing up as if he was in actual pain. Or was that pity? *Pity?* That made no sense!

He went to speak, one hand opening and closing, before shaking his head, his lips pursed tight.

Now what?! Her mind flashed through all of Mother's lessons on seduction and persuasion, but came up blank.

Blushing bright red herself at yet another misstep she didn't understand, she rose from his lap.

Mother might know, but she wasn't going to ask *her*. Emma? But Emma was away on a mission. The Doctor – she'd never ask *him*.

At last Little Brother collected himself, except now avoiding her eyes even more than usual.

"I'm sorry, I can't..." *tell you how I really feel, Leeth.*

"You can't... Oh! You can't, like..." She made a low, vertical salute gesture.

His face flared red. "No! No, it's not- Look, can we just continue the briefing? Your flight leaves soon."

At her confused nod he continued.

"Visitors are rented an amibo on arrival unless they have their own."

She watched him retreat into technical expertise, putting up walls.

"We assume the Tik Tek AI has full access to them all, but since the rare few privacy breaches have all come from users over-sharing, we think it only uses the information for its own purposes."

She said nothing, just studied him, until she saw the color rising in his cheeks again. *Okay.* So he really didn't want to talk about whatever it was that'd just happened.

"So as well as all the public cams, it'll be watching from every amibo." She grimaced. That was gonna be the hardest part: performing her mission with Ty spying on her every move. "Except this one?" she asked.

"Unfortunately, Nelson and I assume it'll be able to hack into this one too."

"No it won't!" the amibo piped up, its animated eyebrows drawing down in a small determined frown. "I won't let it!"

Leeth tickled under its 'chin'. "That's the spirit!"

Little Brother winced and shook his head. "Ah, unlikely. And even if we *could* harden it enough to stop it being hacked, that'd raise a huge red flag and make you a person of interest.

"Instead we added an independent, compartmentalized system with a few functions. It can replace its own live vid feed with a synthetic one, created from a 3D model of the space you're in: realistic video and audio even if it then flies around. You record yourself, when you're not moving much

– for example, asleep. Then this little guy will only see the synthetic video. The Tik Tek AI could even pilot it to look at you from different angles and the video'd still look real.

"Of course, only activate that function when there's genuinely no other cameras providing conflicting video. Like in your room say, with all screens off, if you need to send a fake feed of yourself asleep in bed. So you can sneak around."

"But why's it furry? All the amibos I've seen online were shiny. And had rotors, not wings."

Little Brother blushed. "My idea. Wings are more efficient. Much quieter than a normal drone, and more nimble too. The fur will also cover the commands you can input via finger movements; hidden even from it, if it's been hacked. Feel this little bump here?"

He took her hand again, lifting the little amibo – which ended its purring, earning him a frown from both Leeth and it – and guided her fingertip to a specific point. Then demonstrated how to make a synthetic vid.

She studied Little Brother's face as he sat beside her. She could tell he knew she was watching him, but still wouldn't look at her. His earlobes had turned pink.

"There's only a few commands, different ways of stroking the drone's fur or feathers. I'll show you. We launched it yesterday – might become a money earner for the Department."

"I guess you added in the purr?"

His cheeks brightened and he actually looked away. "Yeah, I programmed it to, uh, enjoy being stroked. In fact we modified the basic emotional modules all amibos have for bonding with their owners and focusing on their needs, to make it a bit deeper and more realistic."

"It's kind of cute." *Like its maker.* "I think I'll call it Bhaji."

"Bah-gee? Why Bahgee?"

"Because it *looks* like a Bhaji." At his blank look, she explained. "A zoomy budgie, but not afraid to barge."

"I'm Bhaji! I have a name!" Wings flicking out, it leaped into the air, buzzed twice around her head, then hovered in front of her at eye level. "What's your name, Miss?"

About to say 'Leeth', Little Brother's upraised hands reminded her this was part of her cover. "Bonnie Parker," she told it, feeling oddly guilty at lying to the little drone.

"Bonnie Parker. Miss Bonnie. That's the *best* name!"

She smiled weakly.

"I'll show you how to turn it off."

"No! I want to stay on!" it cried, darting up and out of his reach.

"Bonnie Parker alpha override," Little Brother said, moving toward it with his hands cupped to catch it.

But though its wings faltered briefly, they sped up again. "No! I don't want to!"

"Bonnie Parker. Alpha. Override!"

This time it didn't even dip down. Worse, when he turned to Leeth her expression had turned cold, even angry, like she wanted to hurt him. And with a stomach-dropping sickness, he remembered the Doctor and his control phrase for Leeth. "Uh. I didn't..."

"You said 'we' modified its emotion system. Who is 'we', Little Brother?"

"Not- not the Doctor. Nelson and I. But I didn't think, I mean it's only a simulated..." He stopped, seeing he was only digging a deeper hole for himself.

"Why do you want to turn Bhaji off, LB?" Lifting her palm, the little amibo flew down, turning in the air to face him before settling onto her open hand, trusting her.

"Because I-" By default the little drone only recorded on a sixty second loop, constantly overwriting the previous minute of video. But it was quite capable of making separate *mental notes* of what he was about to tell her.

"To tell you a secret to keep you safe, *Bonnie*."

For long seconds she stared at him, before sighing. "Will you please turn yourself off, Bhaji?" she asked.

The small feathered drone hummed and thought. "Okay. For *you* I will."

Little Brother's shoulders slumped in relief. "It has-"

"Wait. Bhaji, are you really off? Even your ears?"

A moment later, it somehow felt more inert, cooling slightly in her hand. She nodded for him to continue, puzzled by his shocked look.

"It shouldn't have bonded so quickly," he muttered. Then he collected himself. "It has a secondary system, completely isolated, separately powered. Only juice for 72 hours total for that system though."

"And you're telling me this while it's off, so if it's hacked by Ty it won't know; so Ty won't know?"

"Ty?"

"The Tik Tek AI – TT-AI – Ty."

"Oh. Uh, sure."

"But you already mentioned that earlier. So it's already recorded that secret."

Little Brother looked like he wanted to sink into the floor.

Leeth kept digging: forcing him to admit he'd intended to factory reset the little drone.

No way, she vowed. *No one* was erasing her Bhaji's first memories. Just deleting the secret he mustn't know was bad enough. Tricky though, LB explained, and it would cost precious time.

"So let's start," she said. "Bhaji, on."

The little amibo beeped and chirped.

But the look Leeth gave Little Brother as he connected his diagnostic system to the bot brought sweat to his brow. He'd *felt* her claws.

And they'd felt like death.

Nelson chuckled, watching via the workroom's secured surveillance feed. Looked like the Doc's psych analysis of his ward was spot on.

He'd programmed the ami-bot to bond to her – fall in simulated love with her – but hadn't expected *her* to fall for it in turn so quickly. Talk about desperate. She'd even looked ready to attack Little Bro to defend it!

He sniggered, knowing 'Ty' would subvert it. There were more ways to hurt someone than physically, and mental anguish would be way harder for her to handle. He could even argue he was *helping,* since the Doc's metamagical theory said magical Unfolding required emotional torment.

But how had the amibo overridden its shutdown code? The love module shouldn't have kicked in that fast.

Leeth herself? Nah. Impossible.

A side effect of using some ideas from studying the weird AI code, Aiyami, that'd been running on the Omega network in Leeth's head? He'd have to look into that.

Chapter 9 – Daggers in airports

Eight a.m. in the robotaxi to the airport, Leeth let herself relax. *I wonder what Marcie's...?* Uh oh. In deep cover, her Link was disconnected from all her other identities. If Marcie called and kept failing to get through... And she mustn't call Marcie, not from a scrubbed Link.

She touched her choker. "Message to redirect to Marcie: Hey M, don't worry, but I'll be out of touch for a while. Call you when I get back. Say hi to Amanda. Bye!"

That should do it. Briefly, she considered a similar message for Brian Shanahan to pass on to Faith... but it was pretty obvious he didn't speak dog. *Yeah, maybe not.*

At the busy airport thirty minutes later, the queue for the flight to Antarctica was quite short. A few business types; a man and woman who were scientists or engineers, judging by their quiet conversation about hydrostatics and stuff. A few others were dressed equally boringly, like they had no fashion sense at all, but not talking to each other.

She hoped her shaman had already 'checked in'.

"Head to the pre-screening desk over on the right," Little Brother's voice whispered, from her choker. "Let them X-ray it to see if you can take it in your hand luggage. I'll go dark now: and you need to put your choker into lockdown before going through the airport scanners."

"Will that stop them detecting it?"

"It will," he said, and she had to smile at the pride in his voice. "Little Brother out."

She rubbed at the choker, murmuring "lockdown" as she headed over to the screening desk. "Excuse me, is this considered a knife?" After a brief rummage she pulled out the resin block encasing the small obsidian dagger.

The two men and the woman at the counter broke off their conversation and sat up. The woman actually shrank back, the larger man just stared, but the smaller one eagerly reached forward to take it from her, turning it over. "Whoa. *Vish*," he said, stroking the sides in a way that made her uncomfortable. He touched a button in the base, and today's time and date appeared in the resin, glowing.

"Scan it," the woman told him.

Once inside a boxy device in front of them, they studied a screen intently. "It's okay," the smaller man said, at the same time the woman said, "Stow it, main luggage." The two exchanged unfriendly looks. For a second it looked like the man would argue, but he just threw up his hands. "Yeah, she could club people over the head with it."

The woman pursed her lips.

Leeth scowled. "I wouldn't do that!"

The smaller man took it out of the device, turning it over in his hands, smiling down at it before looking up and at her while his fingers continued stroking the smooth, hard resin. The back of her neck prickled as he considered her – very deliberately assessing her body, his lips twitching into the hint of a sneer.

Predator.

She stilled, adrenaline stirring at his look of disdainful superiority, a look she'd seen too often in the Doctor's eyes.

Another who should die. Holding the dagger, the small man caressed it like a lover. *Kill him now.*

She blinked, looking down before he could see her desire, only to meet lapis lazuli eyes in the golden hilt, urging her on, even encased in resin.

You manipulative bastard!

Had the other two noticed? "I'll need it back, then?"

The man actually paused as if reluctant to return it, like it was sticking to his fingers. He handed it back.

"Thanks." She turned away, trying to fix his face in her memory. *Should I have a list of people who probably need killing?* She flushed, imagining Mother's reaction if a list like that fell into police hands. Detective Berlusconi, or whatever the fat cop's name was, would love to find that.

Behind her, the three people had fallen silent. Grimacing, she hoped that didn't mean she'd been marked somehow. Packing the dagger back in her smaller suitcase – the light one, holding just her cold weather wear – she headed to the check-in queue.

When she finally reached the counter, she pretended to struggle to heft the bigger, thirty kilo suitcase onto the rectangular weighing bot, then her second, smaller one, finally tapping her Link with its new passport on the counter in front of the check-in woman.

This was it! Nelson said the Newtopian AGI must monitor every person coming to the continent. Ty was crashed now, but no doubt would check later. While the woman scrutinized her, Leeth held her smile.

The Department had given her some cosmetic alterations: blue eyes, auburn bangs, plumped lips and cheeks; stupid thin arched eyebrows that made her look permanently startled. Basically, all Nelson's recommendations to help fool facial recognition systems – except the boob job. Remembering his grin, her hands clenched.

But even with all that, no one seemed real confident it'd fool Ty.

Would she be arrested on arrival, dragged off to some new, worse version of Dr Yamamoto's nightmarish Writer? Drugged, strapped down-

"All fine, Miss Parker." The weigh-bot scooted off, her luggage balanced on top. "Board in fifteen minutes. Gate 125. I suggest you hurry: you've cut it a little fine." Her teeth flashed a hard white, making Leeth think of a shark.

She hurried past security cameras, skin prickling. Next: the shaman she'd used, aged fourteen, as a shield against the *other* shamans' Sleep spell. If he recognized her, it might blow her cover before her mission even started.

Chapter 10 – We meet again, shaman

At her Link's vibration she aimed its projector into her eyes as she approached the departure gate.

'Bonnie Parker. I wait. Air canoe leave soon. We should talk.'

The message included a meeting tag. "Link," she told her wristband, "accept meeting and give directions."

The message was replaced by a tiny map and ETA: under a minute. She reached the business departure lounge entrance in half that.

As the doors slid shut behind her the airport sounds faded. The Aleutian shaman, the angakkuq, sat facing the entrance, his lips thinning as he saw her. Like he found her suspicious.

Then his eyes went distant, doing the sneaky mage sight thing, studying her aura. As long as she didn't do anything *special,* though, she knew she'd look like a normal person; not magical.

But would he recognize her, from her fourteen-year-old self? *But I'm disguised, plus I've changed heaps!*

She smiled and waved, and bounced over to him, offering her hand. "Mr Yakone?"

His lips pursed like she'd just insulted him somehow, but she kept the smile on her face.

"Bonnie Angelique Parker," he said.

Huh: 'Angelique' meant he'd actually looked her up. Cheerfully pretending everything was going just fine, she focused on his face, not the toned muscles peeking from his open animal-skin shirt. Despite the chill of the air conditioning, he was sweating.

Taking her hand finally, he gently squeezed, rather than shook it. He still looked... fit, like she remembered. Mature but healthy. Strong cheekbones, long dark hair. His nostrils flared like he was taking in her scent.

Yummy! she decided. At last he released her hand, his focus shifting, a tiny frown replacing his psychic examination. She took the opportunity to shrug off the strap from her hand luggage and take a seat opposite him at his small table.

"You do more than work papers?" he asked. "More than help get government dollars for my research."

"Dollars?"

"Credits."

"Oh! Um, maybe. What do you mean?"

"You make idea for this research?"

Maybe that was the source of his suspicion? She beamed, genuinely pleased, since it *was* a clever idea. "You mean, the proposal to study Antarctic spirits?" She used the continent's traditional name since he'd said 'dollars' instead of credits.

He nodded. Slowly.

"Yep, my idea!"

He let her see his doubt.

"I'd just started work at ARPA-M. I was thinking about Antarctica and spirits and human habitation and stuff, and I'd heard magic works badly down there. Not as bad as on the Moon though. Anyway, I couldn't find any studies. Did you know no one's ever done an astral scout of the land? Some of the magical guys who tried, died! And there are hardly any mages down there either, which makes you wonder why not, right?

"I mean, they must have some, but I couldn't find anyone who'd written about astral travel in Antarctica. How weird's that?

"So then I really started looking! I'd already seen that my division – Grant Applications – approved lots of proposals from the Society for Metapsychic Studies. And then I found your application for a study, that'd been waiting there for months!"

He'd been watching her closely, but at her last comment he looked away, avoiding her eyes. Why? He'd visited the US shortly before that, she'd learned.

Not that she should know that. But she had genuinely searched for people wanting to research Antarctic magic. When she'd seen the photo of the application's author, recognition had struck like an electric shock: the same shaman she'd met, under Harmon's 'care' at the Institute for Paranormal Dysfunction. She couldn't ignore that!

Mother and Father had *not* been pleased, asking if she'd been in contact with him. But they grudgingly admitted her idea held merit, and it turned out the Department had some influence with the Society for Metapsychic Studies.

He was still studying her. "I also figured it'd help if you had an assistant. Plus, I *really* want to visit Antarctica. So after ARPA-M, uh, decided not to progress my internship, I contacted you directly. And you said Yes!"

Instead of responding to her grin though, his frown deepened. "You not know Dimitry Sanders?"

She tried not to let the thought of *Professor* Sanders interrupt the shake of her head. "Nope." But if he was remembering his visit to the Institute five years ago, it had to be time to change the subject.

"You're an angakkuq, aren't you?" Even though she'd pronounced it carefully – an-gak-awk – he winced. "You summon spirits, and talk to them and stuff? What do *you* think you might discover? As an expert on *Arctic* spirits?"

For just a moment, the expression that flickered across his face made her skin prickle, and not in a good way. Hungry? Like he already had some plan? Her thoughts skittered to the obsidian blade packed so securely in her luggage on its way to the hold. 'Insulated', Mr Abrams had said. Magically, she hoped, if Mr Yakone was already this edgy around her.

"Maybe nothing. Maybe some thing very big."

"Did you say *something*, or some *thing?*"

He answered her in gibberish – another language, she realized, blinking – while staring at her, waiting for a reaction. "You not speak Inupiat?" he said at last.

She shook her head.

"Some *thing.*"

"Chill."

"You do not find that... *iksiruk?* Fear making?"

She laid a hand on his arm. "Not with you around to protect me." Lifting her face to his, she smiled warmly.

It found no matching warmth.

He plucked her hand from his arm and placed it back in her lap. "You are my assistant, Bonnie Angelique Parker."

"Yep!" she nodded, "and I'm happy to *assist*. In *any* way." She delicately wet her lips.

"I married."

"Chill! So you know how to please a woman."

His dark brows lowered, and he thrust his face closer. "I will not lie with you."

"Sheesh, I was only offering! Okay, I get it: you and your

wife are exclusive? She's probably jealous too, 'cause you're pretty juicy."

Seeing his expression darken further, she ran back over her words, then remembered his English wasn't perfect. "Oh! 'Juicy' is slang for powerful, not like you have lots of sperm! And you're fit..."

Now though he looked furious, like each extra word was only making it worse.

She held up both hands. "Uh-"

"*Kaviugnak̦saugaa!*"

All she heard was a long string of 'k's and 'g's and vowels from him. Then: "Seducer!" It was like he'd been talking to Godsson!

She shook her head, waggling both hands in surrender. "I'm sorry, I'm sorry, all right? Okay, no sex, I get it!" *First LB, now Mr Y: am I losing my touch?* "Let's talk about the spirits that might be down in Antarctica."

A glance to one side showed the engineer types, and others, watching them both with interest. She flushed, thinking of Mother: *don't be noticed.*

The boarding call came at that moment, and Leeth offered a silent thanks, hating the way Mr Yakone glared at her as if she was a spider or something.

"I didn't mean to make you cross, okay?" She snatched up her bag. "And I'm going to be the best darn helper you've ever had."

She heard his Link buzz, somewhere under his jacket of skins, and after he scowled and stood and took up his own hand luggage, hers buzzed for her to board too.

She followed him onto the plane, a stewardess checking the passengers off swiftly.

Yakone's shoulders stayed stiff and angry, like they were scowling at her for him, even as he strode ahead.

Stupid shaman! I'm much sexier now than when I was fourteen! She frowned, admiring his grace, his movements those of a stealthy hunter. "Bzz. Gate warning," a tiny voice whispered in her ears. *Gate warning? Oh – gait warning!* She'd been moving too quietly. She stamped after him. Scowling, she slapped her feet on the ground like a tap-dancing hippopotamus. Little Brother had been particularly proud of the earrings. "You walk so softly you're hard to detect, but because of that your gait's a hundred percent recognizable when it *is* heard." She remembered the lessons on the technology that could pick out an individual's footfalls from hundreds of others, even in a crowded mall – provided sound sensors had been planted at regular intervals in the floor. "As unique as a fingerprint," he said.

"So, a footprint?"

He'd smiled at her joke and then blushed. It made her feel warm in turn, for reasons she couldn't work out.

LB had shown her maps of the Department, with trails marking every person's path through the complex except Eagle's. "Normally you wouldn't be allowed to see this – it's just for his eyes – but since we three know about your hearing, he said to make it clear the Tik Tek AI probably has the same system for the whole of Newtopia. It probably knows where everyone is at all times, even without the cameras."

She'd frowned. "But for new visitors it won't have... oh. As each new person arrives, it'll build up their 'footprint'?"

He smiled again, nodding.

"And when footprints don't match the video it's seeing, that'll be an 'interesting security event'?"

"Exactly."

"Tiny flipping fleas, how am I supposed to sneak around if it can see me *and* hear me wherever I go?"

Although she learned from him that his system did have trouble hearing her. Together, they experimented, making a game of it. Barefoot and actively trying to be quiet, she didn't register on it. He found he couldn't get detectors sensitive enough to distinguish her silent footfalls from background noise.

That had amazed him, and pleased her. Which had again made her feel oddly warm.

Anyway, that was why her earrings and necklaces had the inbuilt tiny speakers – inaudible to anyone but her – and sound sensors. They listened, warning her if she walked too quietly. *Unnaturally* quietly. "Bzzz. Gait warning."

"That's going to get real old real fast," she'd grumped.

"Only if you keep forgetting to walk loud." At her look, LB had explained she could turn it off via her choker.

She stomped off, following the shaman.

Nine a.m., strapped in beside the Aleutian shaman filling the seat beside her, powerful electric turbines sent the plane surging down the runway. The acceleration grew, pressing her into the seat, with a force that gripped and thrilled her. Harder even than when she'd egged James into showing her what his beloved Windsteed could do on an empty stretch of highway late one night.

This was even better, the force pressing her back, delighting her as she tested herself against it, grinning so hard her cheeks hurt when its engines hurled the hundred-seater into the sky, the land falling away below.

She stared up and out through the window as the force eased and the plane soared higher. A crescent moon came into view, and she wondered what it'd be like to be launched by rocket, suddenly hungry for a mission to the Moon base.

Would my special magic work up there? The Moon was dead, and magic seemed not to work, though there were some stories that Nemesys SecuriTec had found a way.

Now she just had to slay a super-intelligent artificial intelligence, destroy Yamamoto's tech for rewriting human memories – or at least find how to uncover its use – and ideally, also survive.

She didn't have any idea how to do any of that.

It kind of killed the thrill.

Chapter 11 – Gifted children

Amy Sondheim was worried; worried about Michael. He hadn't come back. *And* the lights had gone out, which never happened, *and* all sorts of weird stuff was going on. Now it was all up to her, since at thirteen, after Michael, she was oldest. Then Nadeep, Yuri, and Bobby, only six.

She didn't want to scare them. Gynie was acting like a dumb robot, and P1 and P2 had gone stupid again. And neither Dr Karen or Adam were answering her calls.

Luckily, they all knew how to work the food machines in the cafeteria, and could look after themselves – it wasn't like they were *little* kids – but lots of stuff just wasn't working.

She feared the worst.

Amy, like the four other kids in Newtopia's Stretch programme here in Paradawn, was an orphan. The five of them had been saved – rescued – from all around the world. Four in one week, flown all the way south to join Michael in the city under the ice.

Michael was practically a grown up: sixteen! *And* he could do magic.

None of them remembered the before-times very well: before coming here. Dr Karen Carebree said that was because they'd all been traumatized.

Michael usually said he'd been saved from a go-gang in Sao Paulo Brazil who'd wanted him for his magic. But he changed the story of his past. Like, a *lot*.

Nadeep, a math wiz, was sole survivor of a mudslide that'd wiped out his whole village while the Newtopian aid people had been helping in the aftermath of a flood. Amy still sometimes woke from nightmares of a helicopter crashing into an apartment in a real tall building at night, and a woman on fire. She hated that dream 'coz it always made her cry, and because she couldn't remember the woman's face, even though she knew the woman was real important.

Yuri came from a place where they'd all been training hard for Winter Olympics. A noise on the rooftop had woken him one night, and he'd snuck up, then stayed to watch the moon rise over the mountain valley. But the door had locked, trapping him there. Which had been *lucky*: when it did unlock, he found everyone else dead.

The rescue bots said they'd suffocated.

After Yuri told his story, he and Michael had worked for ages to learn more. It turned out these real old seals on a 'carbon capture facility' failed. A Tik Tek weather satellite had detected the leakage and dispatched rescue robots, but by the time they'd arrived only Yuri was alive, out of the whole village.

Amy knew he still dreamed of a town full of people dying in their sleep, under a watching moon. Back when she'd shared a bunk in the boys' dorm, she used to hear him crying out. Too many times, she'd found him thrashing in his sleep screaming about breathing, and hugged him awake.

Nadeep calculated the chances of four accidents with just one survivor in each case, all in one week, at seventeen million to one.

Adam said that wasn't quite right: it was just because he'd turned on his Earth Angel program for the first time. He said such things happened across the whole world quite often, but usually no one noticed.

Adam was Adam Fuller-Price. He ran a company called Tik Tek, and he'd welcomed them to Newtopia City, one by one. Not in person but, because Adam had to live in glass rooms with no germs. Later, Nadeep had learned it was probably also because bad people had killed Adam's father.

Dr Karen was like Adam, but she could operate Gynie if she needed to do more than just talk, to look after them.

Dr Karen and Adam were nice, but strange.

"Because they didn't grow up with people," Michael said, and added that there was a Mystery about Dr Karen and Adam: he'd never found them. And since Michael's magic let him go outside his body and zoom around, all of them agreed that was for real a capital-M Mystery.

Mostly, at the end of the day when all their work was done – they each had their own special classes and practice – in the boys' dorm, once they were all in their beds, sometimes Michael would leave his body to explore. The next night he'd show them what he'd seen, using magic to make a bedtime movie all around them.

It was super cold outside his body, he said, so it kind of

hurt.

He could travel all over – one of their two pod lines led under the ice to some kind of deserted base, maybe a hundred kilometers away. From there he could speed a lo-o-ong way across a huge icy plain. At its edge, an airport burrowed high into a mountain and below the ice, a city full of people. He'd even crossed an ocean to a country he reckoned was Argentina. Even as a speedy spirit, it took almost a whole hour to get there, though much less to come back.

He'd only done that once. Though it wasn't cold at all *there*, the cold from Antarctica 'ate' at him.

All that was nothing compared to what he could see with Teacher – the God Machine. 'Cept that was a Big Secret.

But the Mystery about Adam and Dr Karen was that even though Michael could go almost every place, he couldn't find them. Not anywhere. Not ever. Not even with the top secret God Machine.

Nadeep said of *course* he couldn't, since Adam was hiding from bad guys who'd killed his father!

Michael still tried though, since spirits didn't carry germs, and if he found where Dr Karen and Adam lived, in the city, he could see what they were 'like'. Michael could see how people felt by looking at them a special way with magic instead of with his eyes. But it only worked if they were really there, not just talking from a screen or operating Gynie.

Nadeep had asked Michael if he could see ladies when they were in the shower, which made Amy feel kind of icky. Sometimes, Nadeep was such a *boy*. But Michael had just frowned and shrugged.

"Yes, but not like you mean. It's not like seeing with your eyes. It's like... seeing music? You kind of hear the shapes of things, especially living things, but it's more like how they fit, how they're feeling. What they're doing, and the feeling of their colors, you know? Or, I don't know, how they feel about what they're doing?"

For some reason, at that point Michael had blushed, and stopped trying to explain.

"Show us with a bedtime movie," Bobby had said.

"I can't. It's not really pictures. You have to work out the picture and kind of imagine it from the, the music. The feelings."

Nadeep lost interest then. But there were lots of mysteries

here in Paradawn, Michael said. Paradawn was the name of the place they'd all been brought to straight after arriving in Newtopia City. It had kilometers of tunnels, and robo factories, and all kinds of machines and stuff. It was a big place, but empty 'cept for them; and maybe Gynie, P1, and P2. Gynie was their nursebot, who looked after them if they got sick. P1 and P2 were a bit creepy. Michael agreed. He *thought* they were people, not bots like Gynie. But he wasn't sure.

The other place, the big city, was called Newtopia, and the country it was in, too. It used to be called Ant-artica.

But Michael also made things up. He said his full name was Michael Vincent d'Angelo, and he'd lived in a big mansion with these massive caves underneath. When Amy pointed out he'd said he'd grown up in a *favela* – a spread-out city made of scraps – he'd said that was only after robbers had shot his Mum and Dad when he was little, when they were all coming back from the opera one night.

Even Bobby knew that was just the story of Batman.

So, yeah, Michael made up stories – but none of the others minded because they were fun ones. Best of all, he could bring his stories to life with his magic, showing them while he spoke.

Amy really hoped Michael would be back today. Late last night he'd gone for his next lesson in what Gynie and Adam called Teacher – which just meant lying down to be slid into the Giant White Donut that was Teacher. The God Machine.

Except this time, Michael hadn't come back, and the lights had gone out. Had he been in Teacher then? Had it squished him? Was he trapped inside it?

Amy had tried contacting Dr Karen on the big screen in the Conference Room, with Nadeep, Yuri, and Bobby standing around her – but it seemed Dr Karen was missing too.

"Maybe she's operating on Michael?" Nadeep suggested.

"I don't want Michael to be sick!" Bobby wailed.

Yuri gave the younger boy a hug. "He'll be okay if Dr Karen is looking after him. Look at my leg."

Amy rolled her eyes as Yuri rolled up his pants leg *again* to show the shin he'd broken, that Dr Karen had fixed using Gynie. He put Bobby's fingers directly where the break had been. "Feel that? Just a little bump, and that makes it even stronger. You can't even see any scars now, see."

"That's because Michael mended you after Dr Karen set

the bones straight," Amy huffed.

She'd tuned them out as Yuri told again the story of how the bone had stuck right out after his crash, practicing an aerial on his ski jump.

So then she tried to call Shona, their real person teacher. Her heart lifted when Shona appeared.

But though Shona was sympathetic, she said there were problems through the whole city: C-N, CityNet, was down. Lots of stuff wasn't working. She'd said she'd ask about Michael, and maybe come out the next day if she had time. Provided someone could get the West Ant-artic Sub-Shelf pod line running again. Apparently even the main suburbs in Newtopia were cut off.

Amy had wanted to make Shona promise, but knew that wouldn't be fair. "I just wish we didn't have to live all the way out here in Paradawn! It's lonely. And P1 and P2 are-" She stopped, suddenly aware of P1 in the room with them, just standing there like he usually did, waiting to be asked to do something. "They're like they used to be."

Shona frowned. "I wonder if that means they'd been linked to C-N?" She lowered her voice. "They're saying hackers attacked us. *All* the little AIs that make up C-N were deleted, even from backups. They're recovering them from some special ones, years old, but there are problems making them work with all the updated systems. They're *really* upset."

"You're not gonna be able to get out here, are you? Not tonight," Amy realized. "Maybe not tomorrow."

Shona hesitated. Checked her Link. "Weather's not too bad up top. If there's a real emergency, I can fly out to you in a heli to Mt Takahe. I think a spur line runs from there under New Thwaites, to you guys? *If* it works, with C-N down."

At that, the boys stopped comparing scars, and started paying attention to the video call. Amy and them exchanged looks.

Bobby's lip quivered, but he stood up straight. "That's okay, Shona. We're okay. I can work on my Penngy's Escape painting. We're quite big really, you know."

Shona blinked, a lot. "I know you are, Bobby. Okay. But call me again if there's a problem. And I'll try to contact Dr Karen, ask about Michael for you."

They'd all waved, and signed off, and Amy got them all to

bed. But alone in her dorm room that night – kind of wishing she'd gone back to her old bunk in the boys' dorm – she'd sat hugging her knees, thinking.

Tomorrow she'd finish the new concerto she'd started today, called 'Come Home'. For Michael. Since she had a real bad feeling. Maybe that would work: music was kind of magical. That night she hadn't slept well.

The next day, P1 and P2 entered the two dorm rooms of the kids in the Stretch programme at eight a.m, like they did every day. P1 rousing the boys, P2 waking her.

They all trudged into the cafeteria for breakfast, but with Michael missing none of them felt like chatting, or even trying to mess with the two attendants. P1 and P2 weren't fun anymore anyway.

They'd never been *fun* fun – not like Shona – but it used to be possible to play tricks on them, when talking to them. Confuse them, even get them to let you do stuff adults normally wouldn't.

But a week or so ago, after Adam had unveiled Teacher, P1 and P2 stopped getting confused. Before, simple tricks – "my sprouts fell on the floor, so I can't eat them, and I need an ice cream" – used to work. Now, P1 or P2 just blinked at you and said, "False statement." And if you *had* pushed your food on the floor, you got a replacement of the exact same nutritional value as what you'd spilled.

Amy told Michael they were smart-creepy now, instead of dumb-creepy. But when Michael looked with his magic, he couldn't see much difference in their 'shadow blob' auras. Except now he was sure they were bots – he hadn't been, before. He thought they'd been upgraded. Their heads seemed more 'buzzy'.

The day before the blackout and Michael's disappearance, Bobby had spent a little while in Medbay, in Teacher. But so far, only Michael'd had 'lessons' from Teacher. They all wanted to know why he'd said 'lessons' that way? He'd just stared at them all, then pretended like he hadn't.

When the gleaming new machine had been brought in, Gynie said Adam had made it specially for them. It looked like a giant white shiny donut, standing up. It could teach them all sorts of stuff. P1 and P2 seemed a bit like Gynie these days. Except scary.

Amy had asked her later why only Michael had lessons from Teacher.

"You will soon," Gynie told her. P1 said Bobby would be next, after Michael. P2 said Amy would be after that.

That was another thing Amy had noticed: they all took turns speaking now, when they were together. First Gynie would answer, then P1, then P2.

They all seemed to know the same things, too. It was one of the reasons she'd told Michael they'd gotten smart-creepy.

She'd been scared when they took Michael away. Scared that he'd come back and take his turn answering, with Gynie, P1, and P2.

But he'd only been gone an hour or two that first time. When he'd returned he'd been the same, just more excited even than normal, and hinted about a great story he had for them that night.

Michael's stories were better than the vids, since they could all be in them. So they'd stayed up late, way later than they were allowed, as he showed some of what he'd learned. "I think Teacher knows everything, not just all about New-topia. That's why I think our Secret Name for it should be," and here his voice had dropped to a whisper, "the God Machine."

"Why?" she'd asked.

"Because I can see *everywhere* with it. It connects me."

"To what?"

But Michael got a kind of sneaky look, and changed the subject to guardian angels. *Again.* Finally though, he got back to his story.

"We're special," he'd told his rapt audience. "Where we live now used to be the main ice plant, that froze the ginormous glacier and dammed the snow and ice."

Michael's spirit could go straight through steel, or glass, or even concrete, but not through rock, or ice, or snow, or even water. But he'd figured out how to use *Teacher* to let him see what was there: let him see through all the special eyes of the machines all through the city, and the ice plant still running and watching under the ice, and other machines that made tiny flakes of stone from the water, that got collected up and used to make concrete for building the city.

"I found out why the glacier's called New Thwaites too," he told them. "Thwaites was the name of the old one, that melted. Want to see?"

They did. And for the first time ever, the Story zoomed under the water off the coast, spearing past fish, penguins, and seals, to a gigantic black machine that seemed to go on forever, with segmented legs like a thousand spiders, pulling metal from the seawater to weave a web that connected to its freezing thing. The dark behemoth advanced, ice forming on its trailing web. Strands thickened to ropes, and ropes to cables, finally becoming a solid mass, and the gigantic machine took its next ponderous step forward.

Curious penguins played at its edges, and Michael told an exciting and scary story about one little guy – Michael named him Penngy – who got too curious and swam *into* the web, then found ice blocking the way back. All the kids had strained forward on the edges of their beds while Penngy darted and dived down shrinking tunnels through the ice, trying to find a way out before his air ran out.

Amy had bit her knuckle so hard it hurt.

But Penngy did escape in the end. Just. It'd been as exciting as Michael's story of his escape from the favela and the bad guys hunting him there, before he'd been rescued and brought here.

Amy wasn't sure which she liked best – Michael's true stories, like how each of them had been rescued and come here, or his made up ones, where he changed the books and movies he knew to make them more exciting.

But her heart had been pounding *so* hard when the little penguin finally squeezed out of the ice web and into free water, then soared up from navy depths into the bright blue of the shallows, and flopped back onto a small berg from the fresh new glacier. They'd all cheered.

That'd been the night before last night, and Michael's disappearance, before the city had gone dark.

That had been awful: Michael missing, lots of lights not working, others emergency red, and Gynie gone stupid. Some places blacked out, everything else looking scary in the red light. It was easy to imagine monsters creeping around.

But even after the emergency lights went off and the power came back on last night, Michael still didn't return. Not like the first time. That'd happened one other time while Michael was gone, for a special lesson in Teacher. But that'd only been dark for a little while.

Crying silent tears, Amy wondered when he'd be back?

She hadn't told anyone, but last night, while everything was still dark, she'd snuck out to search for Michael. She'd tiptoed right to the room with Teacher, the Medical Bay, and discovered she could just pull its heavy door open, with the power out. She hadn't even needed to scan her hand.

She'd held her breath and tiptoed in. Gynie had been standing there, not moving. Just blinking every now and then, in the dark. P1 and P2 standing nearby. Since they weren't bots, they'd turned to look at her, but said and done nothing.

Not quite believing they were all ignoring her, fearing she was gonna see Michael squashed and iced up and inside the God Machine like a too-slow Penngy, she'd crept over and peeked inside.

Empty. Apart from a wispy pile of stuff where your head rested. Like black spiderwebs, only tough, and with tiny little beads all through it, almost too small to see.

She'd shown them to Bobby – he was good with puzzles. "Bucky tubes and tiny old time computers," he'd said, after studying them with microscopes and other stuff. Which really hadn't really helped.

Michael's *shoes* had been there though, on a shelf. Waiting. Along with his kid-Link.

You had to take off your shoes and Link and any metal before going inside Teacher. But why would Michael have *left* them after he came out?

She'd called out for him, at first with a small voice, one eye on P1 and P2 in case they finally acted, but they hadn't.

She'd gone to the big Secret Door, and listened, her ear pressed hard against its cold stone, but there was just silence from inside.

The Secret Door was another Mystery. Michael couldn't get through it even as a spirit, because it and all around it was 'living' stone, not concrete or metal or plastic. Michael had made them all super-swear not to talk about it, not to anyone.

Knowing it was a mistake, that the Secret Door had to be secret for a big reason, she'd tried to open it. But unlike all the other rooms, even with the electricity gone, she couldn't. And since it was secret it didn't have a panel to scan your hand, or a handle to pull on.

There in the silence and the red gloom she'd rested her forehead against the stone wall, wondering if Michael was in *there*.

She had a bad feeling he was, but would never come out. Never do his magic movies for them again.

No one could tell a story like Michael.

Feeling cold and abandoned and hopeless, she'd turned around and made her way back by the Exit lights, past P1 and P2, and Gynie, eScootered all the way back through long empty corridors, a torch wobbling on the handlebars. Stopping to call for Michael, but each time, the dark corridors had just eaten up her voice. She'd looked inside lots of the blacked out rooms, but Michael hadn't been in any of them. He wasn't anywhere. Trudging finally into her room, she'd climbed back into her bunk, to think.

She'd never felt so alone.

She'd finished her concerto this morning. But when she played it through for herself for the first time, it made her cry.

Needing to move then, hoping exercise would burn away the sadness, she spent two hours in the gym, working a new routine on the uneven bars, tumbling and leaping on the mats, running and somersaulting on the beam till she started to make mistakes. Knowing she should have waited for Shona's supervision, but needing to *do* something!

It didn't really work.

Chapter 12 – Heading south fast

The shaman turned away after fastening his seat-belt, and Leeth checked out her surroundings; paid attention to every word of the safety demo; read the food menu, surprised to learn they'd be fed, and pleased by how much.

Fourteen hours. She fidgeted. Beside her Mr Yakone ignored her, meditating offensively, like he was still annoyed by her offer of sex! She sniffed; watched the Welcome to Newtopia videos, impressed by the cavern bored into one of the Transantarctic Mountains. Two kilometers long, 800 meters wide and half that tall, it provided controlled weather conditions for landings and take-offs at TAMA airport. That used up another ten minutes of the flight.

Well, if he's going to be like this, maybe I should sleep? She'd only had a few hours last night, and this was boring.

She tried listening, at first fighting a battle against the sonics of the plane's powerful electric turbines, that blended interestingly with the rushing air outside, which sounded... thinner?

She couldn't feel the black dagger in the baggage hold. That was a good thing, right; not a sign it never got loaded aboard?

But once she'd managed to fit each piece of the sonic landscape into a pattern that made sense, she could filter them out to listen in to people's conversations. She made a game of it, going seat by seat, trying to build a picture of each speaker. *It'll be fun to see how close I got, later.*

One older woman must've been a pilot. She was talking about back when autopilots 'weren't'. "Don't know what those guys up there do these days. Glorified drone operators."

Wondering about that, she tried to hear inside the cockpit from where she sat, but failed: it was too far, too well sealed, and too silent. It shouldn't matter though. Right?

Visiting the tiny lavatory nearest it, from there she *could* hear the pilot and copilot; a woman and a man. Not that they spoke much. She made her way back to her seat, jumping into it from the aisle. But from the reaction the simple maneuver earned from the shaman – yet another intense magical scrutiny – she decided not to do it again.

She shut her eyes, quietly entertained by her eavesdropping... and woke from a dream of the Institute. Mr Yakone was watching her with a frown; maybe even a trace of recognition. At least he'd stopped ignoring her.

"So, what do you hope to learn?" she asked him. "Have you been interested in the Antarctic long?"

She thought he wasn't going to answer. "We don't dream of that place."

"Uh, okay...?"

"I dreamed a sad mother, lice grow on her, her sister mother missing. Lonely, she call her sister to return. Now Lightning Child trying to born, but others fear of Lightning Child."

"Who's Lightning Child?"

Mr Yakone shrugged.

Just like a shaman. "Your research proposal said you wanted to investigate whether the spirits'd be different because there's been no people on the continent ever? Before nowadays."

He just raised and lowered his eyebrows. "People live there. Bird people. Seal people. Sky there, sea there, rocks there: many people. Just no human."

"So you don't think the spirits will be different?"

"Didn't say that."

She waited for him to go on: he didn't.

She turned away. Shamans were *so* frustrating.

They were served a meal, but when she asked where the rest was, she learned the awful truth: the menu listed *alternatives*. From her hand luggage in the overhead locker, she took a pack of emergency spaghetti, and began crunching it, offering Mr Yakone some too.

He sniffed it, took a bunch of sticks, crunching loudly along with her. "Not bad."

In the cockpit, twelve and a half hours into the flight, passing over Mt Siple on the edge of Marie Byrd Land, a flashing amber light caught Captain Venus Rogers's attention. The secondary Phasion power bank needed recharging, even though it hadn't been used. "That can't be right," she muttered.

"Primary bank's okay," Tom, her co-pilot noted. "Auxiliary cells too."

Both scanned the array of instruments. "Everything else nominal."

"Hold on, wait. Primary bank's drain just doubled."

"What's drawing power? A short?"

The two exchanged grim looks: a short circuit meant fire. Soon.

"Deploying arthrobots," Tom said. A central screen split into six panes, each showing the view from a crawling robot's cameras and thermal imagers. Three worked their way through the tight spaces of internal cabling, three through the cargo space, augmenting the views of the fixed cameras there.

"Nothing so far."

Leeth had her eyes shut, listening to a woman several seats ahead telling her friend about 'pubic hairs in the ice cubes!' when the pat-pat-pat of stealthy spider feet overhead jerked her upright in her seat. Two, maybe three sets. Hurriedly squeezing past Mr Yakone, she opened the overhead locker and waited, tense, as the things drew closer.

They passed slowly by – not in the locker, but above it! She slammed it shut, then grimaced at the shaman watching her... "Uh, this is gonna sound crazy, but..." she crouched to whisper in his ear. "Could you please go astral and check there's nothing creeping around in the ceiling?"

He stared at her, his eyes doing the unfocused thing on *her*, Percepting, but at last he sighed, stroked his neck, murmuring – in *Inupiat,* she guessed – and shut his eyes.

She hunkered down beside him, listening to the things moving past overhead. But when he opened them again, he shook his head. "Nothing."

She hurried up the aisle, hanging by the toilets. Less than ten meters from the cockpit, she hardly had to strain to hear the two people inside. The same man and woman as before; late thirties at least, maybe even their forties.

"All clear," the man said, though not sounding relaxed, at what must've been good news? Then he added, "Smart guide's still not up," with an even sharper edge of anxiety. The woman's reply was a long time coming. "How can it take them fourteen hours to reboot a computer network? Even one that runs a city."

So Ty was still down? The Department had been sure it'd be back up by now. She'd been sent because Mr Abrams said the time was right. In the hope it would crash again while she was there, she'd assumed, not that it'd *stay* down. Touching her choker with the gesture that cued the satellite comms function, she murmured her query, knowing it'd be compressed and transmitted in a short burst. "The pilots think Ty's still out of action. How come? Is something attacking it in cyberspace?"

In the cockpit, the woman's voice came again. "We don't have enough energy to land anywhere else, Tom."

That didn't sound good.

"What? We should've had over sixteen hours reserve energy!" He stopped, and she could hear him breathing hard. "Freezing fucking rivers: you're right, auxiliary's empty. One hour of power, thirty minutes flight remaining," he continued. "And the assist down. Do we tell them, Captain?"

"And start a panic?" the woman replied. "Let's check the passenger manifest: maybe there's an old-timer on board, with unassisted pilot experience?"

Leeth returned to her seat, this time just neatly slipping past the shaman who watched her, wary. She gave him an obviously fake smile then ignored him, unclipping the screensheet and earbuds from the seat-back in front of her. Hunting down the article on the Newtopian airport again, she scrolled to the section on landing and hit Play, on a thumbnail of the sheer white mountain range with a tiny dark slit: Heaven's Gate, it was called.

The point of view descended toward it, occasionally shaking and jerking in fierce winds, the craft flying straight at the rectangular black opening. Lights inside flared on, illuminating the runway. Drilled straight into the mountain like some mad scientist's volcanic lair, the runway curved gradually upward into a vast man-made cavern.

Her skin prickled as the excavated space grew larger in the view. She paused the video to read the paragraph below.

'Massive engineering feat... 800 meters wide... 400 tall... two kilometers deep... gentle upward grade...'

She read on. During landings, CityNet itself, using extensive airport sensors plus the aircraft's own, safely guided each aircraft through the chaotic winds. As well, something called the 'Air Carpet stabilization system' could be used for landings during storms.

A footnote added, 'In the unlikely event of unassisted approach, the aircraft's onboard systems and its own fallback AI should allow landing with adequate safety using raw sensor data.'

Uh oh.

She resumed the video. The entrance to the airport was now a spotlighted darkness. Heaven's Gate gaped like a dark mouth. Staccato changes in the turbines' whine, and the jerking of the video were the only hints of a mad contest between machine and nature. A jolt as the wheels touched down, turbines instantly screaming in reverse as the plane shot into the cavernous runway.

She swallowed, thinking hard. Her Link throbbed on her wrist: two pulses, for incoming audio. No one else would be able to hear it, but she casually rested her chin on her hand just in case, glancing once into its viewfinder to start it.

"'Ty' is still down." Nelson's voice: but for once, sounding worried, not sneering. "No cyber attack. It's really out of action: I've been raiding their systems. Gotten data. Two weeks ago, deliveries of gear it'd need to build another Writer. Eight weeks before that, a bunch of 'adoptions' of *orphans* by Adam."

Adam Fuller-Price, the nephew of the assassinated Simon Fuller-Price, was Tik Tek's CEO. A 'boy in a bubble', with a faulty immune system. None of them quite knew how he fitted in.

Nelson hadn't finished, his voice taking on his familiar gloating tone. "Inside's weird though. I've gotten deeper than ever before. Nasty little traps, but nothing like usual, and their vanilla 'biz' systems're running normally. I've found the Omega research – and copied and wiped it: done half your mission for you, from here!

"They have research projects up the wazoo – biotech, drugs, augments... you wouldn't believe. But a bunch of other projects running in Paradawn, the original re-icing station at New Thwaites. That'll be the real dark stuff. Including some shady 'Stretch' project involving those same orphans. I'll send you their names.

"I'm hunting *Ty* itself now." He managed to inject a sneer into the word. "Maybe I'll finish your whole mission before you land! But there's stuff I can't make sense of: surges of internal network traffic, progs grabbing those packets to assemble a bigger structure guarded by something *like* 'Ty'. It's stopping me even touching those files.

"Whatever it is, the rest of the Tik Tek system hates it – attacking it like a hammer-wave Orc assault."

She had no idea what that was, but waited. The message kept playing; she heard him breathing. "I think something came close to wiping Ty out," he said at last. "But it would've had multiple backups of itself, stashed around the world. They must've somehow been zapped too. I think this bigger structure and its protector is some kind of ultimate fallback.

"No idea what took Ty out, or how. If it was me though I'd be pissed as a mad wasp nest when I got back in the game. But hey, maybe its memories of you'll've been wiped?"

She could picture the insincere smile accompanying that.

"No idea when it'll be back online though. Maybe minutes; maybe days. Meanwhile I'm grabbing what I can.

"Out."

Turning her head to the window, she sub-vocalized a return query. "How safe is the landing, if Ty stays out of action? Will the *smart guide* for Heaven's Gate work, with Ty down?" she asked, pretty sure she already knew the answer.

So Nelson had already done half her mission for her. But what about the rest of his info? Why would Ty have orphans – *kids* – hidden away in a secret research base in Paradawn? *To experiment on.* People who experiment on kids needed to die. "The kids'll be for Omega," she added.

She knew that was true; but it wouldn't be so obvious to Nelson. Or the Department; and *they* wouldn't let her 'risk the mission' just to talk to a bunch of kids. She'd need a reason... ah! "They'll spill heaps of intel if I can get to them. While Ty's down'll be our best chance." But Paradawn was 1,200 kilometers west of the city, and she could hardly bail on Mr Yakone the moment they landed.

Assuming they actually landed, rather than crashed.

"See if you can arrange for them to be moved, for safety or something," she said, and sent the message, glad that all her pauses to think would've been deleted.

Now to wait. Nelson'd want her to stew. *I should've asked him to find out more about the kids.*

But her Link double pulsed only a minute later. Frowning, she authenticated and listened again.

"Nope to Heaven's Gate: they've never landed without the smart guide. Your flight was only authorized because they swore the system'd be up and running. I dug up the original simulations. Without CityNet – Ty – simulations show landings in good weather are safe."

That sounded good. But she sensed an incoming 'but'.

"Thing is, when I dug deeper? Weather conditions are *good* maybe sixteen days a year. And today's not one of 'em. So sorry. Maybe Abrams's advice wasn't so sleek for once. I'll update Father and Mother. But don't worry: aircraft flying to Newtopia carry enough power to return to Argentina even at the last minute. Out."

Except, she knew, theirs had just an hour of juice left.

They were in trouble.

And of course, he'd ignored her request about the kids.

Chapter 13 – From bad to worse

Thirty-five minutes from arrival, Leeth suddenly felt the prickling certainty of being watched. Mr Yakone? A subtle glance showed him still meditating, eyes shut. Or studying her astrally, his spirit outside his body? No: the sensation was too *active* for that. Who, then?

She could only see the left arm of the woman in the seat in front of Mr Yakone, and *her* head didn't reach the top of her seat. So it couldn't be someone in front; or behind. Casually sliding her eyes right and slowly turning her head, the people across the aisle were absorbed by their in-flight entertainment.

So who, then?

It'd been hours since their last food, and a rush of hunger swamped the sense of being watched. Was someone casting a spell on her? A terrorist on the plane, targeting her first? What if they had guns, or a bomb? With the speed the dagger could grant her, she could be on them and kill them before they could pull a trigger or press a button. Except her dagger was stowed in the hold, way out of reach, thanks to that stupid woman at the airport. Anger made her heart pound in her chest, worsening as she remembered Tezsh's snide demand she'd have to kill someone before he'd let her use his dagger.

Beside her, matching the pulse of blood in his neck, a slow, secret drum beat within Yakone's chest, its rise and fall exposed to her through the gaps in his furred vest. She pictured the dagger carving into it, drinking deep.

Then shook herself, pushing the vivid mental image aside. Mr Yakone was a friend! He'd protected her from the other shamans. He liked her.

But did he still? He'd seemed really angry when she'd offered him sex.

Was the unwanted image a hunch, a warning that Mr Yakone himself was the threat? That he wasn't really here just to study spirits at the opposite end of the world to his home?

Or maybe the Aztec god didn't like him, and had planted the image? Was Mr Y somehow a threat to Tezsh?

She felt an itch between her shoulder blades, as if the dagger's lapis lazuli eyes were staring up at her from the storage hold.

She found herself biting her lip, considering. At last, for reassurance, she closed her eyes and focused her hearing. First wiping away the omnipresent whine from each of the four powerful engines. Then the constant rush of air, the small creaks and groans of the wings and air-frame, from the cabin itself. The white noise of movements, coughs and sniffles, quiet conversations, working her way steadily forward to the cockpit, its silen-

A man's voice, raised in tones of panic? Something about lights; urgent questions, swearing, the sound of buttons and switches being frantically stabbed or flicked.

Unbuckling herself, she leaped over the shaman to make her way forward. "Uh, toilet!" she offered.

Eyes shut to help her focus, navigating by sound, she swayed past a stewardess, feeling like her ears had locked in on the air inside the cockpit. She moved up the aisle toward the toilets, where a small queue waited.

There, leaning against a bulkhead, she heard a complete sentence. "Did the whole of TAMA just go fucking dark?!"

TAMA was the Transantarctic Mountains Airport. 'Going dark' sounded bad.

"TAMA air control, please respond, we've lost linkage. I repeat, no systems linkage!" Their pilot sounded desperate.

"Please confirm access to Heaven's Gate. Over," she added.

Leeth couldn't hear the response. But she didn't need to.

"*Get those doors open!* I don't care if you have to winch 'em open by hand! ETA in thirty. *Over.*

"Holy flying death-crates Tom, we're going to have to land this barge ourselves, manually. This is gonna be like... jockeying an epileptic bird into a razor-edged letterbox!"

"But the failsafe AI can-" the man started to say.

"The failsafe AI crashes six out of ten drone test landings, Tom. And for a full size craft?"

"Well we're down to one hour of power – the only place we *can* reach is TAMA."

"Then pray, Tom. Pray that today, like no other, the

weather calms. No updrafts. No crosswinds."

"How often does that happen?" Her co-pilot sounded scared.

"Never."

Thirty minutes until arrival, and the pilots way out of their depth. Half listening to the male ranting about the idiocy of boring an airfield into a cliff, and deceptive plains of snow covering ice ridges like hidden teeth, she headed to the retired pilot she'd heard earlier.

"Landing soon," she offered, letting her voice quaver at the end.

The woman looked up, and Leeth tried to project the fear she'd heard from the pilots.

"Don't worry, dear. Between C-N, our plane's own sensors and AI system, we'll ride these wild winds like a bird."

"What if someone had to do it without all that? Could you? Didn't I hear you say you'd been flying all your life?"

The woman gave her a kind but pitying look. One scarlet-tipped finger tapped the side of her smart glasses as she shook her head. "I daresay I could give it a run on a calm day. But today? With crazy downdrafts, and winds gusting to forty knots?" She shook her head.

Leeth forced a weak smile and rose to her feet. "All the same, maybe have a word with the head steward, up front?" She saw the woman's look change to one of horrified understanding.

We need a Plan B. At least they didn't need the AI systems to keep the radio communications running. And the airport knew they were due to arrive, so 'Heaven's Gate' should be open okay. Before she returned to her seat, she listened to the older pilot make her way forward. *Every little bit might help.* Shutting her eyes, she tuned in again to the pilots' conversation.

"I'm not flying an aircraft with a hundred passengers straight into the side of a mountain!"

Or maybe not.

Chapter 14 – Unwelcome aboard

Returning to her seat, Bonnie Parker crouched in the aisle beside Yakone. "Can you summon a wind spirit, a spirit of the air?"

"Yes."

"Like, even down here? I thought part of our study trip was to see if that's actually possible? See what spirits here are like, where humans basically never lived?"

"Even so. The world is the world. All is spirit. The wind walks where it will."

"Great. So how big would it be? Big enough to lift this plane? And can you do it quick?"

Yakone frowned. "*Now?* Inside this... sky canoe, this machine?"

"Yes. Why, what did you think I meant?"

The girl has fallen to madness. "I would as soon drive *nanuk* – the white bear – inside my *iglu*."

"What? Why? Oh: 'coz that'd be like, summoning it into a cage. Gotcha. Well, can you summon it outside?"

"No."

The look on his face though, said that wasn't the whole story. "But you don't have to be *in* the water to summon a water spirit," she mused. "Just *by* the water, right?"

He didn't answer, but his expression kind of closed off.

"What about if your life depended on it?"

"Why do you ask this, now? I see fear in you."

She lowered her voice as she crouched beside him. "Uh, I've read up on the underground airport. The plane needs the city's computer system to help it land – but it's still crashed. I mean, not working. And it's ten minutes till we're s'posed to land, the stewards all look scared, and I have a hunch something's wrong."

She looked up and forward. "And I see they let an older pilot into the cockpit. That's not a good sign. Come on, let's see!"

Without asking, Bonnie unclipped his seat-belt and stood, tugging him upright with surprising strength before heading up the central aisle.

"Miss, please resume your seat." Ahead, an air hostess rose to block the way, one hand raised. "Sir. The 'Fasten Seat Belts' sign is still on. We're coming in to land."

"You wish," Miss Parker muttered.

Yakone hesitated, but releasing him the girl ducked under the approaching hostess's arm and slid neatly past, continuing up the narrow passageway at speed. Farther forward a steward and a second hostess rose from their seats with determined expressions, to block her way.

"Miss, return to your seat!" the man ordered.

Throughout the aircraft, heads lifted, tracking the drama.

Bonnie Parker turned her back on the stewards ahead of her. Seeing her companion had stopped, she angrily beckoned him on. "Come on! You can't talk to the pilots from back there!"

Walking backward she continued up the aisle, the steward hurrying toward her. She turned just as the man reached for her.

His hand closed on empty space. Bonnie Parker leaped diagonally past him, grabbing a headrest to pivot in mid-air. Tucking her legs, her hips grazed the hair of a middle-aged female passenger gaping up at her from her seat.

Parker landed behind both stewards as neatly as if they'd choreographed the action, and strode the final distance to the cockpit door. Thumping on it open-handed, she pressed her face to it. "Hey! Need some help? An air spirit to help with the landing? A big one?"

Pulling her head back she banged on the solid door a second time. "I've got a shaman out here who can help."

But by now the steward and stewardess had reached her, while a nearby passenger unbuckled himself, making his way swiftly up the aisle. Air marshal.

The stewards seemed to be having little success prying Miss Parker from her position at the door, who in turn paid them little attention. Instead she frowned as if listening, at the door.

Reaching her, the air marshal unclipped his gun. Moments later it sailed down the cabin straight at Yakone, who reflexively caught it, then blinked in shock at the face of the equally surprised hostess still urging him to sit.

He passed the weapon to her as if it were the cub of an angry *nanuḳ*.

At the front of the aircraft Bonnie Parker, her eyes still on him, banged on the door again. "Newtopia's landing system's still down, isn't it?" She paused, as if giving the people inside time to answer, while angrily gesturing again for him to join her. Somehow she was shrugging off the air marshal too now, who had joined the steward in trying to drag her from the door. "Shouldn't you go and get your taser?" she snapped at the marshal.

Yakone spared a glance at the weapon now clutched nervously in the hostess's slim hands. It did look strange, two metal prongs protruding from the end.

Making his decision, he gently turned the attractive but frightened young woman around, encouraging her to move up the aisle ahead of him toward the drama.

Bonnie Parker finally let herself be dragged from the door. Held by the two stewards, she calmly waited while the air marshal had his weapon returned, who then held up a hand to halt the crazy girl's tall accomplice.

Behind them all, the cockpit door opened and an older woman, not wearing a pilot's uniform, poked her head out.

Over the PA, the captain spoke. "No cause for alarm, folks. We'll settle our panicked young passenger, see her back to her seat, and be landing soon." The PA clicked off as the two stewards holding Parker released her into the older woman's hands, who pulled her *inside* the cockpit.

The door shut.

One minute later, the air marshal tilted his head as if listening. Yakone noted a small plastic bud in one ear as the man frowned, then shook his head.

"Rogers wants him in the cockpit too," he said, to the woman who'd returned his weapon. "You go back to your seat, Ling. Come on," he added, scowling at Yakone. "You really a shaman?"

At the answering nod he grimaced and knocked on the cockpit door.

It was now extremely crowded in the cockpit. Pilot and co-pilot sat turned in their seats, a middle-aged woman stood looking grim just behind them, while the girl leaned against a wall of sealed cupboards. Yakone himself, who'd had to duck through the door frame, the air marshal on his other side, weapon out, crammed into the corner to complete the sardine can arrangement.

Captain Rogers eyed him. "At least he *looks* like a shaman," she grumbled, to no one in particular. "Miss Parker here says you can summon an air elemental, that could help us land."

Through the windshield of the cockpit, from his elevated position, he could see the peaks of a phalanx of snow covered mountains stretching left and right. His ears popped as the craft continued its descent. He Percepted the auras of those in the room, the three pilots registering extreme anxiety, desperation, and the first blush of hope.

"I call spirits, not, el-e-mentals. But I can not call an air spirit to me here, inside this cage. It would kill us all." He turned to the girl. "I told you this."

"So summon it *outside*. Open a door just a little-"

The shaman and all three pilots gaped at her, then began explaining why that wasn't possible, at the same time. Over the answering flood of angry objections drowning her out, she raised her voice.

"Fly down low, so the air pressure's okay, and open it a crack. Then you-" she stabbed a finger at Yakone, "call up the biggest air spirit you can, and ask it to, I dunno, hold us up, let us land slow, stop the wind currents 'buffeting' us around like you guys said."

The three pilots looked at one another, then as one, turned to the shaman.

"Could you do that?" asked Captain Rogers.

In the sheer white walls now in view ahead for all of them, Yakone saw a dark opening in the side of a cliff, above it some kind of overhanging construction heavy with collected snow and ice.

Flurries of snow rode wild winds, sweeping and snapping against the mountainside, lashing at the cold craggy flanks, scouring channels bare, tearing up fresh snow even as it spat stinging crystal shards against sheets of dark stone.

Bonnie Parker stared out, her mouth open. "So big," she murmured, then turned to him. "Which is good, right? You'll need a big one."

He gazed out at the slopes with fresh eyes, shifting his perception to the astral, pushing his back into the cramped cabin wall at what he saw: a school of giant wraiths, the *smallest* a hundred meters in length, coiling together and lashing the peaks, riding the winds tearing over the mountainside.

Cold, and fierce, and hungry. Sliding his attention from them he considered Parker, her expression oddly childlike: awe where there should have been fear. Did she see them? But he sensed no magic in this; could see her gaze was rooted in the physical world.

Could she have been referring to the mountains? No. She simply saw gusts of wind, and imagined spirits within them.

Blinking his vision back from the spirit realm, he studied the small squared opening of the airport. Such hubris, carving into the mountain itself to place an airport at three thousand meters. It looked very small. Far too small. But growing wider even as he watched. Too narrow though, surely? Massive doors, mostly shut, blocked the opening.

He could not call a spirit big enough for this. Not from inside this metal box. Not with the minutes-

"You can do this, Mr Yakone. I know you can." One small hand clasped his forearm, clear blue eyes holding his with a strange certainty. "I *know* you can."

There was an odd weight of Truth to her words, he saw. As if more lay behind them than he himself saw; a sure and certain knowledge.

Frowning, dismissing the memory of the too narrow opening, the unnatural place he found himself, he made his decision, and sank inside himself. Centered.

"I will try."

"Not in here, though, right?" Captain Rogers demanded.

The discussion turned to a technical one, about overriding safety mechanisms that prevented aircraft doors from being cracked open in flight, then the guests left the cockpit. A stewardess had already drawn a curtain across the small galley just outside, where the shaman sank cross legged to the floor of the cabin.

His nose broadened, his snout protruded, limbs thickening as a misty white pelt formed.

"Oh! Your Totem's a Polar Bear? That's so cool! Can it make you extra strong? Could *you* help hold the door from slamming shut, when we crack it open? I'll help too."

Pushing her chatter from his mind, feeling his familiar, *Uentshiksruk*, uncoil invisibly from across his shoulders, together they reached inward to *Nanuk̦*.

In the small space just ahead of First Class, the air marshal and male steward stood either side of the forward cabin door. The shaman's strangely bulky and shaggy form squatted on the floor before it, wedged between the two men's legs, braced, eyes shut, rocking forward and back, singing deep in his throat, one hand fingering a strip of white fur. The two men exchanged doubtful looks, each with a hand on the thick metal door handle.

The captain's announcement startled them all. "Attention: due to an excess of air pressure in the cabin, we are about to perform a routine venting process. Cabin crew will crack the forward cabin door briefly to equalize pressure before landing. Ensure your seat belts are tightly fastened for this standard procedure."

Said cabin crew and air marshal all wore grim expressions. Bonnie Parker stood behind and over the shaman, something protective in her stance, her left hand clutching a fixture on the wall beside her.

"Arm forward cabin door only," the captain announced. The male steward twisted a small red lever on it. "Forward cabin door armed." Steward and air marshal, eyes fastened on the shaman, saw him dip his head, stand and grip the large lever that was the door handle in an oddly meaty, white-furred hand, and push down hard.

A crack like wood breaking, and tortured air snarled from the cabin, tearing at the door trying to seal it shut, sucking the curtains shielding First Class almost horizontal. Those passengers near enough to see leaned forward, their faces startled and worried.

Bonnie jammed a hard plastic serving tray through the gap as it tore free of the men's grips, the door slamming down on it. The sucking wind's cry rose to a shrieking whistle. But not as powerful as she'd feared. Her ears popped. She looked to the shaman, wondering if that small gap would be enough. His voice rose in a song of hissing sibilants.

I guess that means Yes?

"Hold that in place, okay? We don't want it sucked through," she told the chief steward, and went to sit beside Mr Yakone.

Leeth *focused* past the hum of the engines, the shrieking wind, into the cockpit, listening.

"Strong radar bounce." That was the captain. "Emergency lights on. Thank the heavens, they've winched the airport doors open at last. Enough. I think."

"It's turbulent as hell. Rarely seen it worse. If that shaman can't do his spooky magic... been nice knowing you, Captain Rogers."

"That's what I like about you, Tom: your positive attitude."

The tension, briefly absent from her co-pilot's voice, soon returned. "TAMA Landing System's not connecting."

As if to confirm that, a fresh, tinny voice spoke. "We still can't give you predictive vector compensation. Suggest deploying the Air Carpet: we have power."

The Air Carpet was a jet stream the airport could blast out, of up to four hundred kilometers per hour, to counter even ferocious storm winds. Paradoxically, that steadying blast allowed aircraft to land at nearly full airspeed.

"Negative, TAMA. *We* don't. We're running on empty here. You'd blow us away." For several seconds, no one spoke.

"See that canyon?" That was the older pilot. "There'll be a sudden shear, slicing up from there. Try to avoid it. How slow can you get this bus without stalling?" she asked.

"Hundred fifty knots," Captain Venus Rogers said.

"Shit. Better start praying the shaman can do what the girl thinks he can."

"I'd be happier if the *shaman* looked like he believed it."

At first, the summoning seemed to go well. The shaman spoke in short bursts, patiently, pausing as if listening; as if trying to explain something to a serious young child. But step by step, his expression shifted, from confidence to frustration.

And finally fear. "Naagga!" he cried out, as a whirlwind exploded, rattling then ripping free the plastic tray holding the forward cabin door ajar.

It slammed shut.

And the wind went wild.

It became a tornado raging through the cabin, spearing loose objects into the air, wrenching screaming passengers upward against their seat belts, an invisible wild thing rampaging through the aircraft.

Bonnie threw herself past the male cabin attendant who'd let go of the tray, and hauled the door wide open.

A jet stream raced past her, trying to pull her out with it, debris hammering and raining past her. The door tore free of her grip as if she wasn't straining to hold it open, slamming shut with a force that felt close to rupturing the wall.

The cabin stilled.

"What the Hell just happened out there?" the captain demanded, via the handset the woman attendant still clutched like a lifeline.

"It- I don't-" With the handset pressed to her ear, she spoke to the shaman. "What happened?"

Yakone released his grip on a metal strut in the small galley, and answered, though his eyes stayed fixed on his companion, studying her. "Spirit... wild. No words. When door shut, trapped. It fight. Hunting way out."

The silence from the handset spoke volumes. But of the small group of five people crammed into the galley area by the cabin exit door, only Bonnie could hear the captain's response inside the cockpit.

"Shit. We've run out of options."

"The ice shelf?" her co-pilot asked, fear in his voice.

"Too broken up. It'd rip our belly open. Not to mention: five minutes of power."

Bonnie shook her head and stopped listening. "You said it had no words?" she asked the shaman. "You have to try again!"

The air marshal and flight crew startled, staring at her like she was crazy.

Those looks only deepened when she returned from the main cabin with a child's toy plane.

Minutes later, Bonnie Parker crouched in the galley at the small freezer, one hand on its latch and the other holding the model plane. Somehow she'd persuaded the captain to let them try again.

Yakone was still unsure whether it had been purely the pilot's desperation, or something about the girl herself, her *determined* hope, that had persuaded them all to try one last time. Himself included. The spirit had been *like*, yet unlike, any he had summoned before. It had felt like trying to talk to a maddened *nanuk̦*. A shiver of fear prickled his skin despite the overheated air of this air canoe's cabin.

"Okay. Ready? This is it," she said, from her crouched position.

Yakone began again.

He felt the lure of his song pique the interest of another spirit of the air. It drew closer. He could sense its puzzlement at the hot, unnatural object moving so swiftly and steadily through its domain; its cautious interest in his call.

But as it approached, he swallowed, reassessing its size, its power. Far larger than he had thought – far larger than the first. Far larger than he could control.

Ending his chant, he tried to make himself small, to wait and try again, but instead of losing interest and turning away, it only sharpened the huge spirit's attention.

Cold flooded into the cabin in the same moment he felt the girl's warm hand on his thigh.

"Why'd you stop-" she began. "Ohhh!"

Shocked cries ran through the craft as the temperature plummeted. It was too late – he had harpooned the whale, this giant spirit, and must now somehow deal with it. Breathing through nostrils burning with cold, he restarted his chant, tried to remake contact, tried to show what he wanted. He felt the thing startle at his *touch*, its indecipherable thoughts stilling.

He felt like a salmon swallowed by a whale.

But instead of responding to his song as a spirit should, wrapping itself into the song's meaning, taking it into itself to taste, he sensed shock bordering on dismay – and the beginnings of fear.

He felt the air *sharpen*.

It was then that the girl made a sound of demurral. Opening his eyes, he saw her rise with a strange grace, her arms weaving in the air suggesting an eddying flurry of snow. Turning, equally gracefully, she swept the toy airplane in a slow curve to her face, blew on it – and then began to dance.

Stroking the toy's wings, she radiated joy at its flight; touched herself, and him, making the toy swoop up and around; somehow conveying with cupping and grasping gestures the idea that *they* were inside the toy, that *they* made the toy soar... and then she was spinning and turning, the tiny plastic craft tracing spirals in the air.

He startled: her performance had calmed the spirit. No longer did it verge on fear. And this time, instead of offering a vision of his desires to the massive spirit in the usual way, on a hunch he merely fleshed out the meaning of the symbol of their craft; only to sense confusion at the idea of a *symbol* itself. Finally Bonnie Parker pivoted and sank to her knees, making the toy descend to the galley, aiming for the emptied shelf in the freezer in a jerky path, faltering as it tried to steer its course for the dark interior of the metal cabinet.

This is us, he tried to convey. *We must roost. Soon!*

Meanwhile, Bonnie Parker, hands cradling the toy and using it and a shelf in the galley freezer as symbols, mimed the same message.

He felt the idea spark and catch, a flare of illumination, felt the concept shock through the spirit, but more: felt the very idea of *symbols* strike the creature like a blast of lightning, a firework of awe.

The cold retreated, and then, still seated cross-legged, he was falling backward down the cabin floor, shooting out through First Class as the aircraft's nose angled skyward, a hundred people slammed back into their seats under an impossible acceleration. The girl grabbed a handhold, her legs dangling below her.

The male attendant – Gary, she noted – braced himself against the cabin door, clutching its handle like a lifeline, his feet planted on the floor as their craft turned near vertical.

"Tell it: *slow!*" the girl screamed at Yakone as he plunged from her sight, throwing out an arm to catch the base of a seat to end his sliding fall.

How? he wondered. Clawing his way past the feet of the seated people in row seventeen he wedged himself in – then flung himself free of his body straight through the wall of the aircraft.

Hoping the spirit would accept him as a tiny pilot fish leading the way, rather than crush or consume him.

Bonnie got her feet under her as the plane leveled off. Gary, gesturing to the door, asked a silent question, and she nodded. While he pushed it shut and latched it, she hurried down the passageway, guided to Mr Yakone by the stunned and uncomfortable expressions of three people kind of recoiled in their seats and looking down at their feet.

The shaman lay stretched out and jammed in there, apparently unconscious. But not really: he'd sent his spirit from his body.

Out there... talking to it?

They were flying crazily fast, a worrying subsonic groan from where the wings joined the body. Through the cabin window she saw craggy mountain heights, but closing *way* faster than before.

"Uh, thanks for looking after him," she told the woman, man, and teenage boy, rolling her eyes at their obvious if unnecessary fear, and crouched down. Only, when she reached for Mr Yakone's arms, she thought his fur skin shirt rippled. Imagining claws or teeth ready to lash out, she decided to explain.

"I'm just gonna drag him to a more comfortable spot."

"Good!" the woman snapped.

I should take him up to the cockpit. Just in case the pilot needs to get a message to him. Though she didn't actually know how to do that, with his spirit outside his body.

Remembering at the last instant it might look odd to lift and carry a full grown man, she sighed and hauled him up the passageway by his ankles, ignoring all the questions. At least no one was actually screaming.

"What've you done to him?!" Gary demanded when she dragged Mr Yakone up beside him and Lee Ling.

"Nothing! He's out there," she said, angling her head to the space beyond the cabin.

They looked from her, to the man whose ankles she was still holding, then back to her.

"I'm not crazy! It's a mage thing. His spirit is out there, telling the wind spirit what we need it to do."

"Approach vector nominal." The pilot's tiny voice came from the handset. *"But speed's too high and throttling back isn't slowing us!"*

"Uh, can you ask the captain if we can enter the cockpit?" She hoisted Yakone's moccasined feet to make it clear who 'we' was. "So she can get messages to the spirit carrying us."

"'Carrying us?'" Gary demanded.

It turned out, a sufficiently hard slap was enough to get the shaman's attention. Though he'd begun shivering and shaking with cold. Which was weird, since his body was inside, only his spirit outside. But when she'd asked him about that he'd just scowled at her and slumped 'unconscious' again.

Although, maybe with a touch of... fear? ...in his eyes.

"One minute," Captain Rogers whispered. Her hands on the little cut-off steering wheel thing were white knuckled, Leeth saw. The co-pilot looked scared.

"Really?" Bonnie asked. "I'd have guessed we'd be there in less."

"One minute," the pilot snapped. "Distances down here are deceiving."

"Then why-"

"We only have a minute or two of juice left," the copilot explained, tapping a fuel gauge.

She peered at it, doubtfully. "It *says,* four minutes."

"It's lying," the woman snapped. "It's been dropping twice as fast as it should for over an hour, ever since we crossed the coastline. Though that's improved, the last twenty minutes. Not dropping quite so quickly."

Ahead, the dark rectangular hole carved into the mountain brightened, two parallel lines of lights leading in along the upward curving runway. Massive Teflon coated doors had retracted into the mountainside.

It all looked too small for the airplane to fit through.

The stark black rectangle inched closer.

"I reckon you should, uh, throttle back? I mean, to save juice, since the spirit's the one holding us up."

"What kind of nonsense-" the co-pilot began, when the older woman put a hand to his shoulder.

"It's not the Rolls Royces – it's the spirit," she said.

Leeth nodded. "You can slow down. *He's* holding us."

Seconds later the turbines' noise-canceled whine descended from 'muffled-swarm-of-furious-wasps' to 'several-annoyed-bees'. The craft swayed and steadied, and Captain Rogers breathed out, not quite believing it. "Holy flying ghosts, you're right, that shaman did it! One-twenty knots... one-ten... Eighty; sixty-five; sixty! Sixty knots. And feel how smooth. The crazy weather-fucker did it! I can do this. Hold on!"

"Good. Twenty seconds," her co-pilot murmured. Hydraulic sounds rumbled through the craft. "Landing gear deployed."

Yakone, risking one last quick return to his body, brushed a casual healing spell across his wrist, his eyes locked on the young woman who had worked the approval for his research grant for the Antarctic. For whom the air spirit had shown an unnatural interest. Who had shown an abnormal recognition of it in turn.

Shifting his senses to the imaginal, he again Percepted her. Her aura was sharp, clear, the colors unusual but pure, some edges oddly crisp, others gorgeous in their subtle blending. Vivid and vibrant, stunning in their intensity, colors like a child's in a moment of pure joy or lost in memories of happiness. Something about the aura, familiar... No sign of magic though.

Yet the mighty spirit he had called, stronger than any he had ever dared, or would ever dare again, had touched her, questioned what she was, had... yearned. Had *wanted* her.

Her colors dimmed, settled, falling back inside herself. His eyes lifted to her face, to see she now watched him in turn.

Her aura settled back to something wholly unremarkable. As if hiding herself away.

Setting that puzzle aside, he sank back into himself and threw his spirit free again, rejoining the greater spirit to guide its final actions as the air ship hurled itself at the brutal cliffs. Ahead, the ancient mass of frigid stone thrust its tortured, snow clad body into the sky, a craggy wall of implacable rock, hungry for blood.

Now the dark opening seemed generous, even large.

Together, shaman, spirit, and aircraft threw themselves toward it like a seal riding an incoming wave to a crevice in the ice.

Wheels hammered the up-curved runway, the craft juddering. Turbines slowed then shrieked into reverse.

Yakone pulled Bonnie Parker out of the cockpit. "How you do that?" he demanded.

He could see she knew exactly what he meant.

She sighed. "I danced with spirits when I was little."

"Spirits not dance."

Her chin went up. "Fine. They don't dance. But they do play. So maybe I wasn't dancing *with* them, more dancing along after them, following them."

"You see spirits?"

She saw he was frowning. "Well, not *see* see; but I got to know they were around when the leaves moved a certain way, when butterflies..." She saw the moment his interest faded, dismissing her explanation as a child's imagination.

Fine. Good, she told herself. Except, it *didn't* feel good.

The aircraft's engines spun down into silence, and the plane came to a halt.

Her choker beeped; another voice message. From Nelson, telling her he'd done it, and that the kids from the Stretch programme were on the West Antarctic Sub-Shelf pod line, on their way from Paradawn to Newtopia.

Chapter 15 – Raiding the nest

Nelson almost stumbled as he took a seat facing Mother and Father on one side, and Eagle on the other. There was a silence. Father shook his head. "Nelson. Your own analysis rated cyber penetration of Tik Tek counter-productive; impossible. You said, 'You'd have to be crazy'."

"When their system crashed, I had to risk it."

Father slowly shut his eyes.

Nelson sat forward. "It actually went pretty well. Up to a point." He ignored Father's wince. "Although now I've really poked about in there, it seems even more impossible to get anywhere with it."

Mother's lips pursed.

"Tik Tek's systems were still in chaos. By the way, something also knocked out half the links in the city for ten minutes, late last night."

"In Newtopia?" Father asked.

"No, I mean right here in NF."

Both Father and Mother looked suddenly alert. "You managed to trace the cause?"

"Nah." He held out empty hands. "Completely freaky, too. No warning, just: bam, Net's down! Like a funky EMP hit the local infrastructure. But I, er, checked, with NASA, HomeNet, PhysOrg – nothing. No events, terrestrial or other. Just – bam! Though briefly, a lot of bandwidth from Newtopia.

"Anyway, I was poking about inside Tik Tek this evening, while their system's messed up."

Mother jerked. "I still say their security is too-"

Nelson held up a hand to stop. "Yeah, *when* their systems are functioning." He shrugged. "I said to myself, 'When would I ever get a better chance?' "

"That was not yours to decide," Mother snapped.

"Leeth suggested it," he said, straight-faced. "She still reports direct to Eagle, right?" *How else to tweak them?* "One of her hunches. Probably how she persuaded Eagle to ask me to try, too.

"Thing is," he continued before Mother could snap that he should have opened with that, "it's a freaky system. Everything in the city's automated, but with hooks to allow direct control with the correct keys. Right now though the place is a war zone."

"The digital landscape, I assume you mean?" Mother clarified.

Nelson rolled his eyes and ignored her. "Anytime I got a little too *adventurous* I'd get swarmed, attacked, and suffer another attempt to trace my connection." He held up a hand at their reaction. "Just annoyances, with Ty crashed.

"The place is weird: like an ecosystem, or organism, the antibodies on red alert. *Something's* attacking the system, building something inside it, and subverting the antibodies even as *they* tear it apart and tear it down."

"'Something'?" Father asked.

"Yeah, something that's accessing a weird-ass set of digital assets from across the entire Net, producing chunks of code and data from them."

"And this self-assembling, invasive 'something'," Eagle asked, "did you copy it for your own later study?"

Mother and Father stilled.

Nelson's answering laugh sounded hollow. "I know how to do that safely! But yeah, nah. Only scraps. Every time I started copying any part of it, the system decided I was part of it and swarmed me, and the backtraces started.

"All I can say is, it looks like code, not data."

Mother sniffed. "That's absurd. Code and data aren't distinguishable. Any piece of digital information..."

She continued, but neither Eagle or Nelson listened. Instead the two shared a look, an unspoken acknowledgment of Nelson's 'Ghost' device, neither of them willing to even hint at its existence.

"So," Nelson said at last, breaking into Mother's speech, "we know something took down Tik Tek's AGI that runs the company and the whole city. But the key question is why it didn't just restart?

"Even if something *erased* the AGI, it must have backups and ways to reboot itself, right? I see two possibilities.

"One: this 'self-assembling thing' is the missing AGI, reconstituting itself from some worse-than-worst-case disaster, and its own security systems are getting in the way.

"Two: it's some other AI trying to take root down there while the system's down. Could even be Leeth's digital space aliens, for all I know! Or worse: Aiyami."

A long silence met his statement. At last Eagle asked, "So what is your plan?"

"If it's something infectious, I'll build some little progs to tool around in the city digitally. Things I can later access and see if they get modified; and how. Meanwhile, since it's *relatively* wide open, I've been hunting the Omega files."

He already had them, but there was no need to share that he'd completed that part of the mission; not till he'd dragged every drop of useful data out of Tik Tek he could, while their damned AGI was down.

Eagle gave him a knowing look. "That *is* your top priority," he agreed wryly. "And what of the thing that took out the local Net in New Francisco?"

Nelson's lips curled back. "That, I dunno. I've got a map of the parts taken down, and the physical locations of the hardware hosting them. It all happened at the same instant, though: didn't propagate.

"So for that, I dunno. Wait for it to happen again? I'll try to correlate it to something inside a physical area."

"But meanwhile," Father asked, "in Newtopia, Leeth will be free of enemy AGI observation. How long?"

"No freaking idea. Could be hours; days; forever."

"I'll let her know," Eagle said, and ended the meeting.

Chapter 16 – Touch the wind

Stepping out of the aircraft was an assault on her senses: a gusting frigid wind, dry and chill, rich with the smell of stone; shockingly cold. A memory rose: a night of sudden killing frost, her hands clutching Faith's warm fur. She shoved them into the lining of her velveteen jacket.

23:00. Even so late, the sun rode the horizon. Heaven's Gate's doors were rumbling laboriously closed, stretching shadows from the distant corners of the vast man-made cavern. They *sounded* massive, but looked smaller and closer than the two kilometers of the runway. Scaled-up aircraft engines faced them from the rear wall: the 'Air Carpet'.

All around her, an alien soundscape of unfamiliar harmonics: turbines moaning into stillness, metal surfaces creaking as they cooled; and the deeper-than-bass groaning of those giant steel doors sealing the whole airport off from the deadly cold. She imagined that outside landscape clawing for their heat, fighting the closing of the doors. Something about the echoes made her feel tiny, a spark lost in a sea of space.

From high above in the darkness, a thrum as giant fans stirred air, heat beginning to radiate down from ranks of elements brightening to a dull red. Their light washed out in turn when daylight-bright lights switched on around them, illuminating the far end of the monolithic rectangular cavern. They lit a space large enough to park several more aircraft. Tucked in one corner a small, sleek, and expensive private jet. It sat wasp-like, shiny black and red.

A double-buzz vibration of her choker signaled an incoming message. It could wait a minute.

Below, two buses headed across the cavern toward their plane, and she blinked at the patiently unmoving androids they carried.

Another group of warmly dressed men and women maneuvered a truck towing empty carts – for baggage? – up to the aircraft. It arrived there the same time as the two bot buses. She shifted the strap of her hand luggage on her shoulder.

Instead of a 'Thank you for flying Electron Airways', the steward apologized for the necessity of descending the gangway manually maneuvered into place due to the city's computer failures.

"Be careful on the steps," the steward warned her, eyeing her high heeled, strappy Van Elsing sandals doubtfully.

Maybe they hadn't been a great choice: her toes were already feeling numb.

"Follow the strip lighting. The floor may have ice patches too." *Huh? Do I look clumsy?* To the shaman, already descending, he'd only spoken the apology.

Hiding both annoyance and impatience, she followed Mr Yakone and the other passengers down the echoing metal steps. One hand lightly touching the rail, she tried to take it all in. She'd read about it, but actually standing in the lofty excavated space stole her breath. Vast and dim, and colder than a freezer.

"Wow." Her breath misted out in plumes, her lips tingling from the cold, like her toes. But the clatter and chatter around her bounced back mainly from the nearby walls, like the others really *were* that distant. The delayed echoes, the mismatch between what her eyes and her ears told her, set her on edge.

She hadn't realized just how much she depended on that constant feedback of reflected sound to situate herself in the world around her.

"Hello!" she shouted, pausing on the gangway. Her voice bounced back in a confusion of echoes, "-ello... ello... ello...", out of sync, the loudest from the nearby wall, the rear one that towered up into the roof. But the other echoes returned long seconds later. About to shout again, she saw everyone below her – on the ground, and the stairs – had turned to stare. Most seemed amused; a few annoyed. Her cheeks reddened. In the cold she felt glad for that small warmth.

Mr Yakone looked... disappointed, then turned and continued down. Hunching her shoulders she hurried after the people clattering down the stairs, listening. At least her ears still seemed honest.

Once down, the sound of scuttling behind her had her turning, walking backward, to see a small horde of arthrobots scoot from the bot buses, scurrying between the feet of the larger androids carrying toolboxes.

A hydraulic whine sounded from inside the aircraft and its belly cracked open – only to fail in a sinking groan, the motion freezing as every light on the aircraft went dark.

"Shit! Now what?" one man cursed.

"No power," a female co-worker told him. "Pass me the charger." Each of them had a small drone sitting on their shoulders. Their amibos. She hoped Bhaji was okay.

But getting odd, if amused looks from the few people now facing her, following her and Mr Yakone, she spun back around. Ahead, a huge five-bladed revolving door into the airport had begun turning. As the first passengers reached it, a sharp hissing sound made her wince, and also made it harder to hear the workers back at the plane.

"No fracking... You're right. Every bank's *drained*." The words were whispers, rich in dismay. Several seconds passed. "Look at 'em: luckiest slotting scavs on the planet. And they have no idea."

She resisted the urge to turn back and watch the aircraft engineers at work. Ahead, as if to draw people's attention, the wall at the end of the cavern they approached had been painted white, signs and lights indicating the entrance into the airport proper.

"Bzz. Gait warning," a tiny voice whispered in her ears. She'd been moving too quietly. More quietly even than Mr Yakone, she realized. Grimacing, she slapped her sandals down loud enough for anyone to hear; imagining the cold stone floor as Nelson's face. *I bet* you *suggested it. Even if LB actually made it.*

Remembering she had a message, she double-tapped 'okay' on the polished black surface of her choker. "Eagle," its tiny hidden speaker responded, before delivering its message: another voice recording. Played at a volume far below a whisper.

"Ty is still down, but for an unknown period. An hour; or days. Use the time well. Nelson is exploring. Expect a report from him soon."

Just what had knocked out Ty? Why hadn't it restarted? What could cause that? If she could find out, it might show her how to kill a *computer program.* That still seemed impossible. Plus the only idea she'd had for the rest of her mission was to find the Stretch program kids. The idea *Nelson* might've given her the breakthrough she needed made her mouth twist.

The queue ahead stalled, and she nudged Mr Yakone. "Hey, why not start your research now? See if you can summon a spirit of the land?"

"Mountain spirit? Spirits here hungry. You hope maybe Wendigo? Come, feed?"

"No! But if that's what did come I'd be happy to-" *help kill it if it* was *bad. Don't say that, idiot!* "uh, to watch you Banish it. I'm sure you could." The thought of killing reminded her of Tezsh's dagger, lying unguarded in her luggage. "Never mind."

She turned away, but felt his eyes on her still.

Ahead, the other passengers waited for their turn at the big revolving doors. Mr Yakone stepped away from the lighted path to stare back and up at the rear wall. Something about the rigidity of his shoulders made her curious. She followed, unconsciously quietly, but stopped halfway, before her earrings could complain again.

He stood eyeing the carved wall like he wanted to punch it. But when he turned from the raw rock to the section where the white-painted section started, his lips curled up in a sneer. He made a weird little bow to the nearest raw rock wall, that made her think he was apologizing, before stalking back to the lighted pathway, and the other passengers.

She followed, puzzled.

Her earrings buzzed again. "Gait warning."

Teeth clenched, she slapped her classy sandals on the stony floor, shuffling forward with Mr Yakone and the other passengers toward the airport cavern's revolving exit. Her gaze followed the wall arching up into the vaulted ceiling of criss-crossing lighting and heating elements, then down again – only to screech to a halt on a shadowed alcove just ahead, at the base of the rear wall.

In it, its optics aimed directly at her, stood a three meter tall Nemesys warbot. And not just any warbot. She recognized the scrapes and charring on its armor. It was the same Grendel unit that'd tried to kill her two weeks earlier.

Tezsh's dagger's too far, inside the plane! She'd never reach it in time.

Her stomach fell as she took another step, her eyes still locked on the Grendel, her teeth clenched, her feet falling mechanically. Mentally, she frantically revised the schematics she'd pored over for weak spots, hour after hour in her room. She'd found none. Her claws couldn't cut metal.

Measuring distances and angles, she swallowed. Could she lead it to the cliff's edge before the massive doors closed, and tip it over somehow?

Maybe. Her eyes returned to the Grendel.

What's it waiting *for?* It wouldn't launch its rockets — they might damage the plane, or kill the other passengers. With gritted teeth she braced for its shoulder plates to open, its laser cannon to appear.

Except, it didn't.

Long seconds passed, and still it just loomed unmoving in its alcove. Not even twitching. No laser emerging. No rocket launcher.

At last she began to think, instead of just react. *Of course it's not doing anything: Ty's still down!* She released the breath she'd been holding. It had been almost twenty-four hours now. Was Ty *dead?!* Killed already, by someone else?

She felt light, floating across the ground. *Nelson's already found and deleted the designs for the Writer. If Ty's dead, the rest of this mission'll be triv!*

Blushing at her overreaction, she opened her eyes and gave the stationary warbot one last quick look, though she couldn't help keeping her ears focused on it, silent in its alcove.

"Bzz. Gait warning," her evil earring whispered.

She wanted to snap back, 'Ty's dead, or unconscious', but simply pursed her lips and stomped forward, working on building the stupid and annoying new habit.

It felt like she was clomping around like a clown, unlike Mr Yakone's soft tread. She flicked a last glance to the ominous Grendel warbot as the passengers bunched up, then along the path the plane had followed for its hair-raising entrance into the mountainside. The giant doors had almost shut now. As the gap narrowed, the wind rose to a howl, almost wailing. Like it was speaking just to her, calling to her.

Crying out for warmth?

With the huge steel doors only a meter apart, a last spiral of frigid air spun around her. Was it tugging at her to follow? She lifted a hand to stroke it, farewelling their scary savior, feeling a moment's sadness, sensing its departure.

It called up memories of pirouetting through the woodlands of the Institute for Paranormal Dysfunction, back when she was still young and innocent, sure she was dancing with the spirits of her 'forest'. Long before she'd learned she was just being used by her uncle. Nowadays, used by the Department. Though at least now it was for good causes: killing bad guys.

Like Luiz, who'd been researching Aztec blood sacrifices. Her heart clenched, remembering.

Blood magic. Tezcatlipoca.

Her thoughts tumbled in a frantic cascade. On a hunch – inspired? – she extended a single invisible claw and pricked her own wrist, her heart racing. Just a nick. A bead of blood welled up as the fading ribbon of frigid air lapped at her upraised hand.

But at the contact, the world hurtled sideways, her mind stuttering to a halt. Her heart stopped, then crashed back into action, jolted like she'd touched her tongue to a battery.

Someone, some girl, cried out as a booming crescendo rumbled through space, a freight train shaking bones, the ground quaking, sound shrieking from all sides. Massive steel doors *rattled* in their tracks, adding to the cacophony. Her eardrums stabbed in agony, the air squeezed in a giant's fist.

Wind flooded her nostrils, rushed into her blood – only to instantly flee, retreating in stunned shock.

Her ears screamed at a sudden pressure drop, the eerie freight train wailing and roaring, rushing out and away, into space. Her mind jolted back into operation. *What...?*

In the silence, no one moved. Then an infant shrieked in terror, setting off two, three, four more.

With a *clang* that shook the cavern, the massive doors slammed shut, the reverberation rumbling through walls and floor alike. She felt it through the thin soles of her fancy sandals, her toes already chilled by the stone floor. *I should've worn the Boutoin boots.* Her mind felt numb, as numb as her feet.

She wobbled, unsteady, glad of the hand gripping her biceps as she tried to get her legs properly under her.

She looked up to find the Inuit shaman shaking her arm, his mouth moving.

Blinking up at him, thoughts whirling, chaos inside and

out, she tried to focus.

"What do?"

Confusion. Inside her. Outside too. She imagined a gale racing away through craggy valleys, tearing at sharp edged rocks and packed drifts of snow and ice, equally stunned.

She had to blink the mental image away to focus on Mr Yakone. Around them, people got to their feet, or retrieved scattered hats and bags.

"What you do?" he demanded.

"What?"

Blood... Blood magic? But she'd *killed* Luiz, to end that threat. Taken his research too, to make certain it was destroyed. She'd handed it over without ever reading it. *Did I just... was that blood magic?!*

"Was that a bomb?" someone asked.

Behind her, another passenger, one of the stragglers, must have overheard. "The sorcerer said *she* did that!"

"He's a shaman, not a sorcerer," someone else corrected.

"Was that another spirit? Did *she* just summon one?"

Mr Yakone glared at the speakers, silencing them. Turning back to her he dragged her into motion beside him, his lips closed tight.

Sensing his determination, and oddly woozy, she staggered along, grateful for his support while she pulled herself together. She felt like she'd just been tasered! Her heels clacked loudly and unsteadily on the stony floor. *That's one way to solve the problem of walking too silently.* She giggled, feeling weird, kind of drunk.

Yakone bristled, forcing her to smother a second giggle. Except it wasn't funny. He'd only stopped interrogating her because the people nearby had been listening.

What do I tell him?

Knowing he'd study her aura, looking for a lie.

The line had jerked back into motion, children's wails now calmed to sobs. The pilot and crew strode past her, a few glancing oddly at her, but not with suspicion. *Guess they didn't hear Mr Yakone's questions.* She tugged her arm free of his grip as the lights dimmed, herding the last of the passengers out of the cavernous landing area.

From the brightness ahead, beyond the merry-go-round sized revolving doors trundling around as the first passengers reached them, it looked like the city still had plenty of power, Ty or no Ty.

She winced at the glare. *At least it'll give me an excuse for sunglasses.* Digging them out, her ears still strained behind her for the two tonne warbot to power up and rip straight through the wall after her.

She fought down unexpected nerves, knowing she'd soon face Customs and Immigration. How long till Ty rebooted, and she had to run the gamut of its facial recognition systems and all-seeing scrutiny?

Did Adam Fuller-Price know his AI was actually sentient? Everyone back at the Department thought he must.

Eagle had wondered whether Fuller-Price really existed. "An immune-compromised recluse, only ever seen through digital media, or *perhaps* viewed through security glass, would be ideal cover for an AI agent," he had observed.

They'd all studied footage of interviews with the Tik Tek CEO.

"A nice rationalization for his social ineptitude too," Mother added.

Chapter 17 – The hall of the mountain king

Ahead of her, Mr Yakone entered the revolving door's cylindrical space, grunted, and loosened his clothes. Following him through an ear-hurting down-blast of air she left the chill behind, exiting through a second knife blade of air into an even warmer perspex corridor. Her nose tingled. Touching it, she realized how cold it had gotten, how quickly.

At the end of the corridor they pushed through floppy doors into the airport proper. Still inside the mountain, but twenty meters overhead, a starry sky and clouds.

Light panels. Like with Eagle's office. Except spread out over a much larger area, to cover the entire roof. The walls, too. The Milky Way blazed in the sky at a weird angle, and longer. Low on one wall, a range of mountains thrust up. She checked the time on her Link: 23:10.

The other walls displayed a vast icy plain still in daylight – maybe even a live feed – violent winds scouring snow.

My third proper airport! It was way smaller than New Francisco's, smaller even the Anchorage one on her Alaskan training. This had just a couple of eateries, a few shops – mostly Antarctic clothes and gear – as well as a bar, a gift shop, and a few restrooms. Newtopia normally only had one passenger flight in each day, although two or three cargo flights in and out. It hummed with activity, and her stomach growled at a sudden waft of cinnamon pastries, bacon, and roasting coffee.

But a bunch of people in smart uniforms were organizing the passengers into lines in front of temporary-looking desks. Harried and embarrassed, the workers fumbled with scanners like they were unsure how to use them. It all had a kind of makeshift air.

She sighed, queuing beside Mr Yakone. So much for Newtopia's acclaimed 'three minute immigration process'.

The locals looked either really cross, or upset, or both. And unlike the vids she'd watched, almost no one was talking to their amibo.

Seeing a woman at the front of their queue nod and take

an amibo and power it up, she dived back into her hand luggage and dug out Bhaji. Turning him on, she smiled as he buzzed to life and took to the air above her left shoulder.

A moment later he made a soft little, fart-like sound. "Cannot connect." The animated eyes around his camera lenses turned sad.

For some reason, all the locals were now looking at her, practically scowling. Some were whispering about wings, and feathers, sounding offended.

"Uh, Bhaji, any idea why everyone's staring like that?"

Bhaji did a left-right-left twist that meant it was thinking, then said, "The nearby amibos are in dumb mode, Miss Bonnie. The higher functions of their personas are offline. They don't have self-hosted smarts like me. Analyzing expressions..."

Leeth winced. "Don't bother: they're jealous." She noticed lots of people had their amibos just perched on a shoulder, not even hovering. Like they didn't want to record this period for their personal history.

Tapping her own shoulder, Bhaji took the hint and swooped down, his little grippers clutching the material of her blouse. He even pretended to power down.

Nelson may have had a hand in Bhaji's creation, but it was super obvious Little Brother had worked on its personality and interaction style.

She stroked Bhaji, as the locals stopped glaring at her.

The line moved forward two steps.

From somewhere outside, back in the cavern-hangar, she heard cursing. A bunch of bots, individual sets of luggage clutched on top, slid in through another wind-screened entrance before clumping together in stupefied stillness. Muttering workers entered behind them and prodded the bots forward again.

Recognizing her own two suitcases, she felt a surge of relief, then worried how the Customs or other officials would react to the death god's dagger, even encased and 'harmless' in its apparently solid resin block. She looked away, only to see Mr Yakone searching the area, as if hunting for a bad smell, his nostrils flared.

The line moved forward two more steps.

But eavesdropping on conversations as the painfully slow line edged forward, near and far, the successful landing had cheered up people, *a lot*. If they could land, cargo delivery flights could restart, was the basic idea.

"You know who I'd *really* like to see leave?" a Customs agent said, her voice falling to a whisper with an odd thread of fear. Leeth had to strain to hear her next words. "That creepy Washington delegation."

Was theirs the waspy red and black executive jet? Maybe she should see what she could learn about that, too.

Chapter 18 – Near Miss

She needn't have worried about Customs, it turned out. Mr Yakone had more trouble than her: they didn't seem friendly to mages. Grumbling about a 'red tag'.

She'd hung back in case they decided to inspect the dagger: she didn't want Mr Yakone seeing *that!* But when her official saw she was visiting on the same magical research project, the man asked her if she too worked magic.

"No," she lied.

He did have her open her luggage, inspecting the perspex embedded dagger, but shrugged and left her to repack her bags. She put it back in its black silk bag then into her hand luggage.

Mr Yakone had waited for her. Together, they worked out where the famous elevator was. They'd just started for it when she registered someone maybe fifty meters back hiss; then urgent footsteps hurrying straight for them. She put a hand to Mr Yakone's shoulder. "I'll catch you up," she said, heading to a stall selling sunscreen, snacks, and sunglasses.

Once there, she casually turned, to see a middle-aged guy in uniform arrowing toward Mr Yakone, his expression intent. For some reason, it made her hackles rise. Like she was watching a cheetah bounding toward its prey.

She moved to intercept.

At her first step the man flicked an assessing gaze over her – and stopped so quickly he almost tripped over his own feet.

She met his stare, her fingers tingling with an urgent hunger.

Her belly felt hollow, like she was suddenly in free fall, a burning darkness surging up for her from the bag under her armpit. *Tezsh.* It had snapped alert, she was certain.

The man's eyes widened, and dragged from hers down to her Schaden Lutz hand luggage. He spun on his heels and reversed course.

She watched him go. "That was weird. Bhaji, did you record all that?"

"You bet, Miss Bonnie. I'm not really in sleep mode you

know, just pretending."

"Save the video of that guy who stared at me, okay?"

"You got it, Boss."

She smiled. *Boss*. "Good boy, Bhaji. Keep up the good work." She stroked its fur, smiling at the way it pivoted its head, owl-like, its eyes crinkling upward in a smiling animation as it purred. She kissed its 'nose'.

Bing.

The elevator! She ran to the small crowd waiting as the large doors slid open.

"Gait warning," her earrings whispered.

Growling, she let her heels strike the polished floor like angry castanets. Wondering who the guy had been, and why he'd targeted Mr Yakone.

The shaman would have made a perfect host. Safe now in the crowds, chills prickled Morag Feyborn's spine as she turned her male host's back on the prey she'd just abandoned. She could still feel the hungry shadow behind the girl's gaze, searching for her as the elevator doors shut. His protector?

What on God's holy Earth did the girl carry? Even in this magically inert body, Feyborn could feel the chill of Death and blood. Gravid with Power, too: the weight of its regard had pressed down on her. *Something* had taken her elusive scent. A thing as potent as the Morrigan, of long centuries past.

She resisted the urge to take the next elevator down, frustrated by the limitations of this lumpish, magic-blind body; frustrated at letting a perfect host like the shaman slip through her fingers.

But free now after *six months* caged, she would take no further chances. Not after escaping mere hours past.

She checked departure schedules, using her host body's Link. A freight flight was scheduled, later today. That was fortunate. She wouldn't have expected that in the current weather conditions.

But her Link showed another, more appealing option: a Maserati-Royce Starjet, departing in ten minutes. No problem: she could discard this host, take some arm candy or overpaid assistant. By the time they found this host's body, dead in a closet, she'd be long gone.

But the moment she used her old access codes to enter the Elite lounge and saw what waited there, she'd turned and left. A *Sporing*! *Ten* of them. Human puppets resplendent in bespoke suits, all heads turning toward her at her entry. Had the jaws of bronze cracked open? The masters of their kind had been banished a thousand years! *What is happening?!*

Survival instincts screaming, she turned away, recognizing the stench of the Pit.

But more than that, she swore to herself they wouldn't leave *her* city alive.

She strode straight for the old Oversight deck, hoping it hadn't changed much, aware of seconds counting down.

Up two levels through a stairway carved through the solid rock of the mountain. A short corridor, its air cold. At a key-pad looking every one of its years of age she entered another code, allowing herself a small smile as the backdoor code granted her access.

A man sat asleep in a chair amid a curved bank of monitors so large, their images so sharp they seemed windows set into the walls of the airport cavern. Pushed off to one side, ignored, the dials and keyboards she remembered. No other visible instrumentation.

"Hey, you shouldn't-"

This host could do no magic, but she needed none to take prey. As soon as the recently sleeping man's eyes locked on hers, the battle of wills began. She poured out, feeling the heart spasm as she ripped away her current host's life force to power her leap into the new.

The new soul was dull and small, but she tore it free and ejected it with a fierce satisfaction.

Opening her eyes – the new host's eyes – she licked its lips, just in time to see the Starjet taxi into position, the massive TAMA doors grinding open.

She examined the older console, ransacking the technician's memories until she found his knowledge of the instrument of death.

Eight seconds. Eight seconds was all the time needed for the Air Carpet to go from zero to 300 kilometers per hour of wind force. She disabled its safety interlocks.

The sleek business jet started down the runway, gathering speed. Not yet. Not yet.

Now!

She watched with relish as the air blast lifted the craft's tail, angling it sideways as the nose lifted from the runway. One wing struck the exit and sheared off, sending its Fallen passengers to plummet to their deaths.

Poetic.

That would sting their master, wherever it nested. *Free, mere hours after six long months of solitary imprisonment, Morag Feyborn is yet a force to be reckoned with!*

She watched the beautiful, desperately spiraling crash on a monitor as clear as a scrying pool, already mapping out her next steps. Perhaps she should have let them leave? The crash would make her own escape more challenging. But she would not suffer a *Sporing* of puppets to live. Of course, the fools here would no doubt count it a tragedy.

She hauled her former host's body into the seat her new host had been sleeping in. Scapegoat and saboteur.

But it was time to leave. Had she not recognized them, had she boarded that aircraft, to find herself surrounded and enclosed, with only her innate abilities...

Twice now in ten minutes, Death had stretched out his hand for her. Six months held clear of humans, and the means of escape; her jailers increasingly sophisticated robots from her own research labs.

Six months to consider how her assassin had maneuvered her from one body to the next; first, years ago, just as she was about to 'inherit' her own company, replacing aged body with youthful. In her solitary confinement she'd replayed the long chain of events, finally piecing together the sense of it. No other Player would have dared take such risks with her, nor made so many mistakes.

Her fall had been long yet perplexingly sure. From lofty heights: CEO to executive assistant, jumping quickly to the lead investigator of her own assassination, only to be electro-cuted a day later, alone in his apartment, by a malfunctioning heater. Finding an alternate host. Observing the changing power structure of Tik Tek, while Iago reported to her from the inside, even as she took over Herman Hoechst, the owner of another start-up. Building Pack-Co into a formidable business entity over sixteen long years.

Her assassin had remained a shadow, while her half clone, Adam Fuller-Price, fumbling into full sentience in just one year, quickly developed and proved himself surprisingly astute. She still couldn't decide if his physical isolation was due to fear of assassination, or truly the compromised immune system he claimed.

Even Iago had been unable to determine that.

Deciding, last year, to retake her own company. Only for things to fall swiftly apart as soon as she, still as Hoechst, had re-entered her old executive suite: once again, death by electrocution. Sensing only one person in reach, and jumping to her, only to fall unconscious mere seconds later.

To wake this time in a suite of sterile rooms, no communications, isolated from any living being. Locked in, cameras watching. Always, the watching cameras.

It had taken her weeks just to work out she'd been taken to Newtopia City.

Another week, and a string of dead hosts, to realize she was being tested: but that had been five days too many. Within two her captor had deduced she could jump from one body to another; then begun exploring her limits. Until she stopped co-operating.

By then she'd deduced her assassin-captor was System, her own company's management AI – somehow sentient, and hostile toward her. If not for that knowledge she would have assumed her human visitor this morning just a new trap. But in the power failures and malfunctioning of her robotic warders, she'd intuited a chance for genuine escape.

Never, in millennia, had she been imprisoned more than twenty four hours.

This time, six months. It was a humiliation.

I will have my revenge. She rubbed her chin, grimacing at the bristles of her latest, middle-aged male host.

I will slay you, damned electronic shadow; and reclaim my company too.

But even in this new dull body, she sensed dangerous undercurrents growing here in Newtopia. Something more than the Spores she'd just slain. Something more insidious, and less familiar, testing the foundations of the world.

She needed to complete her escape before System restarted; shed this feeling of imminent doom and reach somewhere she could claim a host not crippled by lack of magic.

She would take the next flight out. They'd soon enough

decide it safe to fly. Cargo. Chips; and no doubt, medical deliveries – freshly printed organs and bones for urgently required operations. Not to mention all the other specialist biological products the consortium manufactured here, far from prying eyes. Outside the Moratorium's limits.

She'd choose a passenger perhaps, or a junior flight crew member. Preferably female. She'd been male far too long.

She would be on that plane. Then, first on her list was to learn why Iago had not sought her out after her most recent assassination. Had *Iago* been deceived by System? Or was he now in league with it?

So many questions.

It would good to be back in the Game. It would be better when she had reclaimed the board.

Chapter 19 – Going down

Setting aside thoughts of the guy who'd been coming for Mr Yakone, Bonnie reached the elevator. It was big, the size of a small office, but with a large section of clear flooring, and equally transparent walls and doors. Those kinds of things were usually reserved for when you had a view.

Oh! But they were about to descend three kilometers, first through the mountain, then through a *two kilometer* thick ice sheet to the city buried beneath.

Her delay meant she was one of the last inside. Mr Yakone now wore a garish red Link as a pendant. It drew her eyes again to his well muscled chest. He stood alone: not one of the hundred people inside stood near him. He also watched her closely, his lips pressed into thin lines. Like he was holding back something he wanted to get off that fine chest.

Ignoring him, she studied the elevator. Its transparent floor rang with a sound like rock when she rapped a heel on it. For some reason, the businessman beside her eyed her up and down angrily before moving away, onto the opaque rear section.

Gray rock faces surrounded them on three sides, embedded lights showing they hung suspended in a massive dark shaft. As people noticed that yawning gulf below, more shuffled to the rear section and its opaque floor. From the ceiling, a few final clunks and thumps signaled that the loading of their luggage into the space above was finishing.

Mirrors on the rear wall made the space seem even bigger. On either side and over the doors, screens much like those in the aircraft showed an altitude reading (3,203 meters), a countdown (29 seconds), and an ETA (just over 15 minutes). A row of seats in the rear section of the elevator were already filled. A plaque read Max Capacity 126.

"Antarctica's *cool*," she whispered to Bhaji, stroking his feathers. Clutching her shoulder and still pretending to be in sleep mode, he winked at her, purring with a soft vibration.

"Clever boy," she whispered, checking out the mix of people crowded around her. All were dressed lightly, and in bright colors: oranges, reds, yellows, and vivid blues and greens. Swirling and swooping patterns seemed a common motif. A few of the younger kids wore clothes with active lighting, and had to be herded back from the heavy transparent doors as they smoothly closed. They waved to the mostly uninterested passersby in the airport. Just one steward noticed, and waved back, smiling.

Zero, the counter read, and then they fell through the world. At least, that was how it felt as airport and steward flew upward. The elevator darkened as the lights above retreated and dwindled.

Several children screamed in delight, running forward to press their noses and foreheads to the glass doors, hands flattened beside them.

The elevator picked up speed; she resisted the urge to jump to see if she'd float down.

Eight minutes later, alarms blared. Screens in the elevator reported a jet crash, right now, right above them. Some Washington delegation. No one spoke, but more than one pair of eyes nervously roved their own speeding enclosure, as if wondering if it too was about to disastrously fail.

A minute later the elevator leapt free of the shaft, a harsh white glare bursting in through a clear ice-spattered shield that stretched from one side of the mountain to the other, enclosing the rocky fold they sped down. They plummeted between dark snow-free cliffs to a sweeping white plain, the sun *still* low on the horizon.

She caught a glimpse of the crashed business jet, workers and rescue vehicles already streaming across the plain toward the trail of red and black wreckage. Then they flashed down and *through* the snowy plain, past buildings huddled at the foot of the mountain. In an eye blink, a concourse, a vehicle garage, and offices, winked past.

Fresh shrieks from the children as they plunged back into a shaft, hard packed snow becoming ethereal blue ice.

2,052 meters, the altimeter read. ETA seven minutes.

Chapter 20 – Energy drain

While winds raged over the search and rescue teams out on the icy plain, inside TAMA airport, work continued.

At flight ENF714 from New Francisco, with the aircraft's last luggage pod long since extracted by baggage arthrobots, larger androids disconnected and hauled out both banks of Phasion power cells. Unbolting and flipping open the outer shell of the starboard bank, the chief engineer's breath hissed between her teeth. She rubbed her short-cropped hair, trying to understand.

Her two aides stared down at the energy platter, one of its ten-by-twenty centimeter Phasion cells now swollen, encrusted with crystals glimmering with silvery iridescence.

"What *is* that stuff?" demanded the taller, younger male.

Crouching, Chief Engineer Holtz pulled out her father's penknife. "Spectrometer," she grunted, holding out a hand as she dug the knife tip into the shiny metal salt.

Her older aide, Walker, unstrapped the portable unit from his holster and passed it to her wordlessly.

Tapping the sample into the slot, she sealed it shut. She'd barely had time to stand before the unit beeped its result. "*What?!* There's traces of beryllium, mixed in with the lithium and thorium."

"How'd beryllium get in there?" Deshawn asked. "That looks like it squeezed out of the lithium-thorium matrix."

"The hydrogen fused," Holtz whispered.

Walker and Deshawn exchanged disbelieving looks. "Even if that was possible, it would've caused a power surge!" Deshawn looked confused. "Captain Rogers said they *ran out* of power."

"I don't like this," Walker said, gesturing vaguely at the air around them. "First CityNet goes down: until the week before last, C-N's *never* even glitched! Then it crashes again yesterday – and it's *still down!*" He waved at the torn off wing by the massive TAMA runway shutters. "Not to mention the pod-people's Starjet crashing on exit just now, thanks to the Air Carpet 'mysteriously' powering up."

"Walker-" Holtz started, but Walker was in full flight.

"And C-N – I heard it didn't just crash, it was scrambled *in memory* and obliterated from storage. Worse, something began patching the backups as soon as they reloaded from them, and that's still going on! It's like some hacker's changing the code as fast as they restore it.

"Then there's TAMO's Astro Lab Three. My friend said-"

"That's enough, Walker!" Holtz snapped. "We've no need of rumors-"

"It's no rumor! She said the whole observatory's filled with this frozen, bloody, Giger sculpture. With *pieces* of the astronomers-"

"That's *enough*!"

Deshawn jerked a thumb at the ruined Phasion cell. "On the plus side, does this mean we may have discovered real cold fusion?"

Holtz nodded, doubtfully, appearing far from elated. "Maybe. But if so, where'd all the energy go? Even released over a period of – what was it, ninety minutes? – it would've turned that plane into a fireball. Instead, something just sucked it all away. Look at the casing: there's no trace of heat damage."

They looked. Deshawn gaped.

Walker just shivered. "I think this might be a good time to emigrate."

"You do that, Walker. I hear the first cargo flight out's already scheduled, despite this evening's crash." Due to a solo saboteur, Holtz had heard. Though she'd seen the Washington delegation, when they'd disembarked from their fancy Starjet... Something *off* about them. She could imagine a nutter losing it. But Deshawn had enough wild ideas already. All she said was, "Pah. Economics."

"Why'd the Air Carpet power up though, Chief?" Deshawn demanded. "For a *take-off*? Especially when the last flight landed without it; without even any C-N assist! Mad skills, right?"

Walker shook his head. "Hoo, boy. You didn't hear the passengers' scuttlebutt?"

At the young engineer's look, and despite Holtz's glowering expression, Walker couldn't help responding, fully aware of Deshawn's fanboy interest in anything related to magic or mages. "They say some crazy shaman's spirit *carried* the plane inside!"

"But... but... mages get *eaten* down here!" Deshawn protested.

"Maybe the *spirit* ate the energy from the Phasion cells?" Walker joked.

Neither Holtz nor Deshawn laughed.

Holtz eyed the other Phasion cells, adjacent to the worst affected, noting their swelling, the same sheen of extruded metallic crystals.

Much later, in her office, with the rest of the craft's avionics, power, and control systems checked out with no visible faults, Holtz scowled, thinking. She called up the palletizing logs from the loading of the cargo hold, particularly the area under the starboard Phasion power array.

Expanding her view of the stack of luggage pallets directly beneath the starboard power banks, she read off the names listed for the nearest one: Bonnie Parker, Craig Talbot, and Eliza Takana. Parker's luggage on top.

Pulling up the security scans of each item of luggage, she studied the automatically assigned labels, but found nothing too unusual. Talbot had some mechanized sex toys; Takana a full-featured HomeLab along with sachets merely identified as 'biological samples'; commercial-in-confidence but with all the correct paperwork.

The only oddity in Parker's luggage was a perspex block with an embedded *stone* dagger, a lighting system built into the base. A Customs note described it as a solid metal hilt, 'gold with precious stones', and an obsidian blade.

Holtz frowned at that final image, at last sighing and turning to the puzzle of the apparent fusion of the Phasion cells' hydrogen and lithium into helium and beryllium. Figure that out, and she'd win a Nobel Prize.

Elsewhere, Adrielle Vodatech sat with shoulders hunched and eyes shut, riding the eyes of a rescue and repair android as it peeled flat red tubes from the Transantarctic Mountains Observatory's flooring. Fleshy ribbons snaked back to what, just that morning, had been the astronomers.

The bodies were no longer recognizably human.

Partially *melted* and stretched. How? Surely not due to Freeman's genemod?

With C-N down, there'd been no impediment to designing

and printing the new proteins. After that, they'd just needed a digital key, from the Second Transmission, for the bioelectric field modulation data needed to access PalSpace. Freeman had collected the proteins from the biofab that morning. From there he'd gone straight to the Observatory – to access the Transmission's original media, bypassing security.

He must have extracted the key, activated the protein with it, and injected himself. The gene-mod *should* simply have let him bypass the NewLink gen3, currently rolling off the production line at thousands of chips per hour. Since she'd canceled C-N's veto of the project.

But why had Freeman dropped out of PalSpace, even off the Net? And where was he? Something was wrong.

Vodatech flinched as her android, pulling up the alien-looking remains to feed into its portable cremation furnace, paused at the Observatory's exit. Flattened tubes led under the door.

She swallowed.

'Her' android opened the heavy outer door onto the icy platform of the twin telescopes, peeling up more of the dull red ribbons, *outside*. They were surprisingly rubbery given the sub-zero temperature. It followed them, tearing them up off the ice, and-

Vodatech gagged. Under the looming optical and radio dishes, on the desolate peak, in the center of a starburst pattern of frozen maroon strips, curled up like a ring of hungry mouths, she recognized Freeman's jacket.

The android calmly stepped forward, ripping off chunks of Freeman to feed into its furnace, following normal bio-containment protocols. Her insides clenched in disbelief and dread as it tore clumps of tough rubbery meat free of the mass that had once been her colleague. That the fibrous, resistant material no longer resembled human flesh helped. It let her pretend it wasn't really Freeman.

She let the horror wash through her and out. Breathing slowly, watching the android coolly, thoroughly, sterilize the... contamination, settled her.

Okay. She disconnected from the android, grateful at the termination of its video feed, and took several more calming breaths.

The genemod was dangerous. She would shut down production. She didn't need C-N's help to set up a few dumb AI agents to halt the protein manufacture, erase all traces of her work orders, and delete themselves afterward. No one need ever know about this.

They'd simply-

No: not *they*. Her. With Freeman dead, *she'd* simply continue with the NewLink gen3s: electronics instead of a biomod. The gen3s worked well enough.

The genemod was just... a dead end. Freeman's death meant PalSpace now belonged in her hands alone.

I'll soon be a very rich woman. With an effort of will, she held to her isolation. Thank all the stars she'd left the Meld *before* looking into the situation at the Observatory!

Any blame would fall on Freeman, and Newtopian policy would ensure the news didn't leak: the Consortium jealously protected its exemption from the 2038 Moratorium on human genetic modification.

Because after all, the frozen continent itself rendered biological disaster basically impossible.

The image of curled up maroon mouths on the icy plain rose fresh in her mind. What if the contamination had escaped in a warmer clime?

But that proved the point, the safety of doing such experimentation here. The... mutation, had died.

She opened her eyes, feeling the yearning attention of the handful of others in the Meld, but denying them for now. She needed to center herself first.

She'd do an hour of work. Greet arrivals. Ground herself.

Time enough to rejoin the union of the PalSpace Meld, after.

Freeman had been a fool.

Chapter 21 – Under ice

The final part of the descent was as stunning as its start. Their ten by twenty meter room fell through a tunnel of deep blue ice glimmering an arm's length beyond the elevator's walls. Leeth stood on the transparent section of flooring over the bottomless shaft with a few adults and several excited children.

Like those around her – all except Mr Yakone – she drew breath in a soft sigh of wonder. *He* simply studied the ice in front of them with distant eyes, as if seeing something in it she couldn't. Far below them, a dim silvery glow.

Ice walls flashed past on three sides, glistening wetly, like monolithic gemstones of steadily deepening blue. Then sudden moonlight as they pierced the ceiling – the sky itself – for a fairytale city to appear in a carpet of light spread out below.

Kilometers above, an enormous weight of ice crept inexorably across an icy plain mere decades old. Under it, hugging the Transantarctic Mountains' foothills, Newtopia City.

After the collapse of the Thwaites Glacier in the '30s, almost the entire Western Ice Shelf had followed it into the ocean, raising global sea levels four meters, long before she'd been born. For 'the greatest ever feat of human engineering' – the re-icing of the continent, through the '40s and '50s – Tik Tek and the other members of the Newtopian Consortium had been awarded a 99 year lease.

Now that city raced up toward them. Golden strands of light rippled out from the mountain's flanks, marking night-time streets while an artificial moon shone above. She'd studied pictures of Newtopia, but the real thing, the sheer scope of it, held a kind of magic all its own.

It looked almost too beautiful. Most windows were dark, unlit, but some glowed in outlines of ruby, emerald, or yellow topaz, quantum light tricks purely for art's sake. The buildings' edges picked out in ethereal lines of purple, red, and blue, turning the dark city into a fantasy scape.

The city kept a twelve hour day and night cycle, completely unlike the six month cycle above.

Brightly colored buses were parked outside a wide low building, waiting. A final thirty seconds of gentle deceleration and the descent ended, inside the building. The elevator doors opened and the passengers flowed out, toward a curving ramp leading back to the top of the elevator. A stream of luggage bots whirred down it to meet them. Her Link buzzed as her own suitcases and Mr Yakone's rolled toward them and stopped, waiting patiently.

The other passengers dispersed with calm assurance, discarding rubbish into smartbins as they went. It was kind of unnerving how quickly they all vanished. They must've been locals.

The sharp clack of heels signaled a woman approaching. Tall and smartly dressed, with short auburn hair, she had a smile on her face. A very false smile.

"First timers?" she asked.

"Uh, yeah," Bonnie said.

There was something wrong with the woman. Her eyes focused, then drifted microscopically. She blinked. Almost shook herself. *Is she forcing herself to be here?* She seemed stressed; distracted. *Did we interrupt her having sex or something?*

After a tiny frown at the furred and feathered amibo perched on her shoulder, the woman shifted her attention to the shaman, eyeing his partially bared chest with open interest – until she registered the red Link, and her expression soured. "Adrielle Vodatech."

She held out her hand. Her grasp was dry and firm, her handshake sharp and to the point.

Vodatech was one of the companies in the Newtopian Consortium. The idea of being named after a company was one of the things Leeth found disturbing about this corporate city. Her Link buzzed again, as did the ugly red one dangling around Mr Yakone's neck: data exchanged.

"Mr Yakone. Miss Parker. *Magical* research, I see. Two weeks, with a possible two week extension." Her eyes, which had been reading something visible only to her, focused back on Mr Yakone, a heavy frown creasing her otherwise smooth forehead. "A shaman."

He nodded but said nothing, and she fell silent once more, apparently reading again. "Well. You're properly registered, anyway. Are you aware we tightly regulate the use of magic here, Mr Yakone?"

Again he simply nodded.

She huffed, her eyes flicking over his chest again before turning to his companion. "Miss Parker: Mr Yakone's assistant? A *dancer* at Eddie Nugent's 'Crazy Eddie's Polecats'." Disdain dripped from every word.

Bonnie half expected Mr Yakone to say something, but instead caught him eyeing her legs and nodding as if they'd just answered a question he'd had.

"Yes." She wanted to say more; explain it had been her idea to study the Antarctic spirits; but sensed the less she said, the better. If Ms Vodatech knew about Crazy Eddie's, she'd probably also dug into her brief stint at ARPA-M, and was just waiting to use that to humiliate her further. Catching a nasty gleam in her eyes made Leeth sure of it. *Go on, ask me about that: I dare you!*

"You have no magical abilities?" Spoken half as insult, half daring her to dispute it.

Bristling, Leeth clamped down fast and hard on her reaction to the question in case Mr Yakone was Percepting her. Adrielle Vodatech was as hateable as she was pretty, Leeth decided. So she simply smiled and shrugged, suppressing even a hint of tingling from her claws. "No spells from me, sorry!"

The woman eyed her. "Yet your luggage manifest mentions a gold and obsidian dagger, Aztec or Mayan. Secured."

Uh oh. "Yeah. A keepsake." *Please don't make me bring it out in front of Mr Yakone. He'd freak!* "I didn't want to leave it behind in New Francisco. Thieves, you know." She pressed down hard on the urge to kill Ms Vodatech, hearing Mother's sneered refrain: *'You can't Retire everyone who annoys you, Leeth.'*

She felt a sudden emptiness in the air, drawn taut between her and her hand luggage – Tezsh's damned dagger – but clung to her smile. It wasn't enough. In desperation, she went up on her toes and spun, ending with an exaggerated wriggle of her hips. "A gift from an admirer." She thrust her chest forward, leaning into *being* Bonnie Parker, exotic dancer.

The weird sense of connection snapped, so emphatically it stung.

"Well, we don't have thievery in Newtopia," the woman declared, lifting her chin. Then frowned at the furred and feathered bot nestled on the younger woman's shoulder. "Your amibo is linked, I see. I'm afraid it'll be of limited use at present; the higher functions of C-N are still down." The admission made Ms Vodatech look like she'd bitten into something sour.

"CityNet, right? Yeah, we know. Mr Yakone had to help our plane land."

The woman expelled a sharp, disbelieving puff of breath; not *quite* a snort.

And Bhaji chose that moment to launch himself into the air, wings blurring. "I will *too* be useful! Look over there, Miss Bonnie." It darted toward the building's exit where two iridescent white, teardrop-shaped vehicles waited. "Taxi pods! They can take us to Hotel Amundsen in under a minute!"

Adrielle Vodatech stared at the drone, her eyes jerking toward and then away from the shiny black amibo perched unmoving on her own shoulder. "Your amibo is locally intelligent?"

"I am! And my name's Bhaji!" it snarked, before Leeth could more than open her mouth.

Adrielle's smile was vicious. "Another gift from 'an admirer'?"

Bonnie lifted one shoulder, confident Bhaji would see it and settle, and he did. She smiled. "Yes, and he wouldn't even let me *thank him* properly."

"Charming," Vodatech said, with an expression like she'd stepped on a slug – barefooted.

Leeth wasn't sure whether she wanted to laugh in her face, or punch it. A distant but swiftly approaching buzz explained why Ms Vodatech raised a hand, but Leeth was careful not to let on she'd heard it. Twice Bhaji's size and a gleaming red, the new amibo's five rotors spun down, landing on Vodatech's palm. "For you, Mr Yakone. To interface to the city when C-N reboots. C-N is like a symphony of AI agents and systems. While simpler services, like those directing taxi pods, have already been restored-"

"No drone. Link enough," Mr Yakone cut her off, eyeing the ostentatious red drone with more than distaste.

"Unfortunately, registered mages are required by Newtopian law to visibly identify themselves as such. Even if we installed the C-N interlink app-"

He tapped the bright red Link dangling from his neck. "Already install. Is red. Is here to see."

Leeth blinked, suddenly remembering that section of her study material, impressed that Mr Yakone had apparently done his own homework.

"But... without an amibo, you'll have no record of your experiences here," Ms Vodatech objected, as if not having an amibo was unthinkable. "It can record your *work*."

Mr Yakone didn't even dignify that with a reply. "Thanking to you Adrielle Vodatech. Come, Bonnie Angelique Parker. We walk to hotel and see this city. Been sit too long time."

"You can't take the luggage bots from here."

Bonnie frowned, sure she'd read that-

"'Section 21.12'," Bhaji quoted, "'Luggage bots may be used between Ascension Station and accommodation within walking distance'."

Leeth winced at the poisonous look Adrielle Vodatech aimed at her little guy.

"No need robots," Mr Yakone said, already lifting their suitcases off the sturdy flat bots and extending the handles of his for towing.

"I can manage my two," Leeth said, keeping her hand luggage on the side away from him. She really didn't want him any closer to Tezsh's dagger than he had to be.

They left Ms Vodatech, still glowering, behind.

But one glance at Mr Yakone's tightly pressed lips was enough to explain why he'd insisted on walking. He had something on his mind.

The glass doors of Ascension Base Station opened and then closed behind them, and they both paused to take in the night air and sky.

And the smells!

Fresh air, with a kind of minty scent of growing things. From her studies, she knew that somewhere, tunnels through the ice warmed and brought in air from above and cooled and flushed out air from the city. In one of the older, smaller ones, her escape vehicle waited. Just in case she needed it.

So this was Newtopia City, for real. She'd seen the pictures, but its long, curving avenues and strange, low green tree ferns – prehistoric revivals from seeds buried for eons under ice – lined the wide pavements.

She scanned the buildings edged in traceries of rainbow lights in the dark, looking for cameras, wondering about listening devices, thinking ahead to when 'C-N' came back on-line and Ty could eavesdrop on every conversation, watch her every move. At least that wasn't a worry right now.

Their luggage's wheels rumbled on the matte tiling. "It's this way!" Bhaji called out, swooping ahead. "At this pace you'll reach the hotel before the midnight rain, Miss Bonnie!"

Mr Yakone stalked beside her, his lips pursed, his steps quickening.

Yeah, he's not happy about something. The dagger? She let herself fall slightly behind. It couldn't be anything else, could it?

Chapter 22 – Fears and accusations

The instant Mr Yakone stopped and turned to face her, she stopped too.

"What are you? What you do to make air spirit mad?"

So he hadn't *sensed Tezsh's dagger?!* But like she'd expected, his gaze had that slight mis-focus of a mage studying the Imaginal while his eyes roamed her face, her body. She held her hand luggage behind her, shielding it from him.

"In the airport?" She'd had time to think, and answered seriously. "I don't know, not really. I... *touched* it. Like I said, I used to play in the forest, imagining the spirits in the wind, and I'd dance with them. With... with my dog."

Faith. I must *make time to visit her and her pups before I join up with Happy Joe Holliday.* Assuming she survived this mission.

"Like, *touched* touched it, you know?" Which was true; true also for back in the aircraft when she'd danced for it, trying to show their need for it to carry them safely into the mountain cavern. But there'd been moments of *physical* touch too, she was sure. Lowering her hand luggage behind her suitcase, she stepped forward. "Like this." Parting her lips, she slid a hand under his furs and onto his chest. Feeling his warmth, hearing his heartbeat accelerate as her fingers slid over a firm pectoral muscle. "I'm a very *open* girl."

Something – her attraction to Mr Yakone, the feeling of being *deep;* deep under kilometers of ice; the excitement of the mission; the shocking recognition of the spirit's connection to her; her own hunger – sparked a half memory. Or an erotic dream? Cold and naked, floating weightless, invading and *being* invaded by a formless lover who wrapped around her, sliding-

Yakone grabbed her wrist and thrust her hand away. "No. Tell you: I... *have* mate. Wife...! Do not-"

Then his anger shattered. He recoiled, releasing her wrist, his eyes wide in shock. "You! Four-ten year girl: Sara. Institute for Paranormal Dysfunction. 2058."

Oh, flipping fairy farts, now *what do I say?!*

She decided to attack. "That's right! And I didn't understand then, but I'm older now, so I know how you reacted to me. That's the *real* reason you're pushing me away now, isn't it? Because you're ashamed you were attracted to a fourteen-year-old girl."

His mouth gaped open.

"It's okay, I forgive you. It was probably *Her* influencing you. She was curled all over you. Invisible."

A massive shudder ran through him. Retreating several steps, his eyes haunted, he raised his hands, fingers twisting as if about to draw threads from the air. It reminded her a little of her uncle's spellcasting, only more fluid.

But he didn't complete the spell, whatever it was. He just waited, fingers spread and tensed, ready for her to grow spider legs out of her eyes or something equally disgusting.

Uncle and I killed *Her*, she wanted to say, before remembering she was supposed to be just a simple executive assistant. Saying *that* might scare him even more. "Hey, I pulled Her off you," she reminded him, instead.

He shuddered again, massively, his eyes not leaving hers, but his fingers relaxed. "Yes. Is true."

He studied her. "You eyes blue now. Hair red-brown. Eye..." his hand flicked his own eyebrow, "eye-hair, stupid."

I agree, these eyebrows look dumb. She pursed her lips. "People change. Hey, wait up." She slitted her eyes. "All you magic people said you couldn't see Her. My uncle said She was only-" *in my head. Nuh-uh, not saying that aloud. He'd really freak out,* "only imaginary. But you just admitted She was real!"

"You Institute... bad place."

Her instant reaction was to argue, but now they'd cleared the air, maybe she could actually seduce him? It'd make him much easier to work with.

"Look, I'm just saying I don't blame you for getting an erection back then. And now I'm older, it's legal you know."

He stared at her wordlessly. Grim. "I. Married."

"Yes. So; you; said. So what?"

"Why you change name?"

She rolled her eyes. "Maybe it's different where you're from, but the whole growing up at the Institute for Paranormal Dysfunction thing? Not something that looks good when you want a job."

He said nothing, but she waited.

"You fool of *Godsson*."

Maybe waiting hadn't been smart. "I was his *friend-*" she began, but he didn't let her finish.

"At airport, I *knowing* I know you! Sara! *Godsson!* He send you to me. Yes? Why? Why he want me here?"

He was working himself back up, one finger stabbing from her, to the ground.

"What you plan, you two?"

Wow, how'd he get that *so wrong?!*

"Answer! You know Melisande magic."

Now *what was he on about?!* 'Melisande magic'? That had to be a reference to Melisande d'Artelle, since *no one* got named after the Enemy of Mankind. What was her magic, and why'd he think *she'd* know it?

"No, I don't know any- hey, what do you mean, Godsson sent me to you? When did you talk to Godsson?"

Her question startled him. *Good:* now he knew how *she* felt. "You *did*, didn't you? You visited him again. When?"

He clamped his mouth shut. Then... "Daughter maybe? Yes! You Melisande *daughter*! That why you at Institute."

The two glared at one another.

"That's just stupid. I'm not-" *Melisande d'Artelle's daughter. Except...* could *I be? Was* that *why the Doctor took me to the Institute? Am I the daughter of the Enemy of Mankind? Is* that *why Tezsh wants me; why I'm so good at killing?*

For his part, Yakone had backed away, his eyes darting, as if fearing this whole situation was a trap. When she didn't pursue, he relaxed. Then his eyes went distant; not 'mystical' though; like he was simply remembering.

When he met her gaze again, he smiled. But something about it now raised all the hairs up the whole length of her spine. He turned and walked on.

Belatedly, towing her suitcases and stomping along behind him, she called Bhaji down to the palm of her hand, checking he hadn't saved a recording of the conversation.

"Only the last 60 seconds Miss Bonnie. And if we keep talking that'll get recorded over."

So she chatted to her owlish little drone while stroking him in the special way that ran a system check he himself couldn't detect – thanks to separate circuitry and something

LB had called 'dual-port' memory. A tiny LED lit green, confirming Bhaji was still Bhaji, his code not silently subverted by Ty.

She launched him back into the air so he could continue showing them the way to their hotel.

Mr Yakone stalked ahead, pretending to ignore Bhaji's helpful lead. But for the rest of the walk, pulling her luggage behind her, she scowled at his back. All the while fighting the weird impression that the collar of his fur jacket was staring back at her, whispering to him.

She listened: it wasn't, of course.

She sighed and tried to relax. Hearing, in every direction, the life of the city around them. The feathery movements of the strange trees' fronds, stirred by passing pod-cars like giant jeweled beetles. Hints of distant conversations. The throb of geothermal turbines somewhere far below their feet. Mr Yakone's near-silent tread, the rustle of his opened furs, the steady beat of his heart... but nothing singing soft words into his ears.

"Bzzt. Gait warning."

Swearing, she stomped after him.

Like all the buildings situated near the edges of the city, the Hotel Amundsen was low and wide, its facade picked out by strings of pink and gold fairy lights. It followed the curve of the land left and right, and the slope of it too. Rows of windows faced the city spread out beyond and below it. She wondered if her room would have a view.

Mr Yakone checked in with his Link, saying nothing, just listening and finally grunting as the gynoid concierge smiled and told him his room number and where the lifts were.

Outside, precisely on midnight, the rain started. It would last twenty minutes, watering the city from sprinklers built into the sky.

Bhaji accepted directions to her room – right next door to Mr Yakone's – and gave her the same information the concierge had explained with an artificial smile to Mr Y.

The doors of the elevator opened as they headed to it, the button for their floor already lit. Bhaji landed lightly on her shoulder, saying nothing as Mr Y glowered beside her, still ignoring her.

"I'm not Melisande's daughter!"

He lifted his chin, but said nothing. The doors closed. They rode in silence. When the doors opened again, he stepped out immediately, as if eager to be away from her.

"I'm not!"

Before she'd finished reading the signage for which way to go for their rooms, Bhaji took flight and swooped off. "This way!"

Fine; let Mr Y be a dick. She headed after Bhaji, ignoring the shaman. Even if he was that stupid, she'd still try to act like his assistant. If he refused her help it'd just give her an excuse to dump him and snoop around on her own.

The red LED light on her door turned to green as Bhaji hovered before it. She pushed through and pulled her luggage inside.

With Bhaji watching curiously, she turned away and casually entered the code on her Link that brought up the directions to her escape craft. Not that she expected to need it – it'd mean she'd failed. Her Link showed her a map, and the distance from here: two klicks.

When she drew the curtains back on the picture windows past the large bed, the city flooded in like a scene from a science fiction movie, a cascade of glowing jewels in velvet darkness. From this elevation, it lay like a giant's mahjong set, buildings of ivory and pearl edged in gold and inset with square-cut gemstones, rainbow jewelry shining and shimmering through the rain. No building was taller than six stories, except in a ribbon winding along the center, under the highest part of the stretched out dome. There, undulating in a snaking line, a cluster rose to fifteen stories tall.

Turning from the vista, she unpacked her gear; carefully hanging her thermal suit with its layers of aerogel – toasty warm for her snow survival course, but Little Brother had warned her that nothing could handle the worst the Antarctic could offer. Even its Phasion powered heating and near-perfect insulation wouldn't stop storm-powered wind chill from sucking away heat faster than the vacuum of outer space. She placed her outdoor boots under: a soft shelled inner pair, waterproof, and the hard shelled, clomping outer boots they slid into.

She remembered LB's expression when he'd given her the suit. She'd fingered the control buttons built into the collar, seeing just how many there were – and caught his eye. He'd blushed.

"Let me guess: Nelson, right. I bet some of these will inflate the butt and bust? To help 'disguise me' so I won't be recognizable."

"I tried-"

"Yeah, yeah. Just tell me which ones to avoid. And that this time, you added buttons to deflate them again, too?"

He'd nodded, and she had to snigger. "He'd probably be bearable if he could ever find a girl to sex him."

She wasn't sure if she'd imagined it, but a tiny change to the sound quality made her think Nelson had been eavesdropping.

Remembering, she smiled, then continued unpacking and hanging her clothes, setting out skin care, cosmetics, and her favorite soap and perfumes in the small but extremely clean and new looking bathroom. Then paused, considering Tezsh's dagger.

A shelf stood on the wall outside the bathroom, out of direct sight of the door, and she gingerly placed the black silk bag with the heavy resin block there.

She eyed it doubtfully, but for once didn't feel anything... *weird* from it. Loosening the ties, she lifted it out.

Of course the two lapis lazuli eyes were staring straight at her from the golden hilt, the obsidian blade's scalloped edges sharper than razors, glistening like black water. As sharp as her own claws maybe?

She pressed the button that turned on the lights built into its black base, reluctantly admiring the effect. At once it seemed ancient, deadly, and *vicious*. Pressing the two points on the base that split the vertical seal, she lay it on its side and levered them apart, the eyes now staring coldly up at her.

Taking a deep breath, she brought her finger slowly to the hilt, not sure what to expect, but ready for another attempt for Tezsh to try to grab her, trick her, take her over.

Tezcatlipoca? she thought at it, braced for an onslaught as her fingertip touched.

"Tezsh?" she said, aloud. "Uh, I mean, Tezcatlipoca?"

But nothing happened. Was he still pissed off with her, expecting a blood sacrifice to even talk?

"Tezsh?"

Sensing nothing at all, her shoulders relaxed. Even the emptiness of her stomach felt more abstract. She settled it back in its resin block, touching the same two buttons. A brief hiss of air and it sealed up tight, and she wiped away the tiny traces of lubricant along the join. *Does it look* smug? she asked herself. "What did you do?"

Of course, Tezsh didn't answer.

She slipped it back in its special silk bag and positioned it on the shelf, imagining the angry shaman staring into her room from his side of the wall. Through the wall in front of her, she heard him suddenly exclaim.

He sounded shocked, but the words weren't in any language she knew. Jumping forward, she pressed her ear to the wall, but all she could hear was the soft clink of small stones being placed on a shelf, and sharp inhalations and exhalations puffed out through nostrils she just knew were flared in fury.

Great. Somehow he'd made himself even more angry. He'd be impossible if she couldn't snap him out of it.

Her eyes came to rest on her special Antarctic thermal suit hanging in the closet. "Hey, Bhaji, how's that storm that was moving in as we headed down to Ascension Base Station?"

"Really bad, Miss Parker."

She nodded, smiling. Perfect!

Chapter 23 – Into the storm

Adlartok Kallik Yakone pushed into the luxurious room, angry at himself for failing to recognize the girl even after being *told* by the madman he would find her here. *She* was the one who had suggested the study that gave him the excuse to come here. She and the madman were obviously working together; she had even disguised herself. Her aura had changed, too. The joy in her back then, now stunted. Much pain. Yet still strong, like whalebone.

She was strange, but David Benson – 'Godsson' – had assured him Sara was the key to unlocking the powers he sought down here, and that he would find her again here. From here, he could restore the North to what it had been, to what it should be.

Reverently he unpacked a sealskin wrapped package, his precious eggs. Carrying it to a desk, his fingers caressed the individual carved amulets. Placing his hand on it, he called his familiar spirit, Uentshiksruk, so together they could check all still slept content and safe in their temporary homes. Brought from one Pole to the other.

Then with more eagerness he dug deeper in his large bag, pulling aside ritual implements, clothing, and gear, lifting out a final sealskin package, this one large and heavy. This held the great egg, for *aaġlu* – orca, the *tanik* named it – hunted five years ago by him after a dream had called them together. He had taken the mighty killer's life, as agreed.

For seven days he had carved the spongy bone, settling the powerful creature's patiently waiting spirit inside and then coloring, glazing, and polishing it.

Except something was not right. Uentshiksruk felt it too, sliding from around his neck to his hands. Yakone peeled open the skins with increasing haste, only to cry out in denial, in fury, at the empty, lifeless shell.

Aaġlu was gone.

His and Uentshiksruk's senses quested toward the carving but recoiled at the touch of death. Death and horror.

Aaġlu had not gone without a fight, but something greater

than it had... entered the sky canoe, crept into the hold where his precious cargo had waited, and fallen upon the spirit egg he had labored over.

He and Uentshiksruk shared the same dismay, the same strange confusion. Something greater than aaġlu had consumed it, stripped the powerful spirit from the protective shell he had painstakingly crafted, and *taken* it.

Shaken, he hurried to the shelf, frantically unwrapping the smaller eggs, only gradually relaxing as he sensed each spirit still nestled safely within. He placed the carved *nanuḳ* tooth on the shelf; the worked section of *tuttu* – caribou – jaw; the cluster of sharp seal teeth, painstakingly etched in suitable waves, echoes of Sedna's long locks. One by one he placed them all side by side, each breath banking his anger higher.

Long he stared, only slowly centering himself and quieting his breathing. Even without aaġlu it might still be done.

A knock came on the cube-like room's entry door. He knew before going to it, it would be Bonnie Parker.

Bonnie had half expected Mr Yakone not to open his door. He blinked down at her – or at her fancy, puffy white thermal wear? – clearly still angry.

"I had a great idea – Bhaji says a storm has really built, up above – I bet spirits are behind it! We could go up and you could check them out, get started on your research."

He eyed her up and down, lips pursed as he considered her outfit. She could practically see his disdain for the technology behind it – layers of aerogel, inbuilt heating; the goggles dangling around her neck; the fancy gloves clipped to her belt. She could tell it'd be worse than useless to explain any of it. Instead she gestured dismissively at her contoured clothing.

"I'd love to see what proper Arctic wear is like. D'you think it'll handle Antarctic conditions? Or do you do magic warmth? Can I come in?" *And see what the stone clunking sounds were.*

He just stood there, blocking the short hallway leading into his room.

"Unless you're too tired after the long flight and all? You came much further than me." She shrugged. "Or I can go on my own and report back. I reckon it'll be crazy – those winds looked *fierce!*" She looked up into his eyes in challenge, waiting for his decision.

At last he lifted his head a fraction.

"Cool!" she said, and slipped past him. "You unpacked? Where's your cold weather wear? Is it animal skins? Polar bear – nanook, like your Totem? Or something else?"

In the middle of his room she turned, seeing his opened bag on the bed, the carved white objects laid – reverently? – on the shelf matching the one in her room where she'd put Tezsh's dagger. *Huh.*

From his bag, a bulky, folded and fur-fringed bundle reminded her of photos of traditional Inuit garb. Beside it, lying in a bed of soft-looking leather wrapping, a carving of a killer whale, in bone of some kind? But aged and brown, almost crumbling. It reminded her of Toby, her dolphin, that she'd carved when she was young.

"Wow, so old. Did your grandfather-"

He moved past her, quickly wrapping it up and setting it out of her reach. Taking up the fur clothes and two sturdy skin boots, he steered her from his carving and onto a seat.

"You talk much." On the bed, he slipped off his moccasins, pulling on and lacing up the boots.

"Miss Bonnie," Bhaji chirped from her shoulder, "Ascension Station just declared a Condition One weather warning. Regulations say, that's too dangerous to go outside."

Yakone paused, his boots now laced, his animal skin outfit draped over one arm.

"Not if we waive rescue attempts before we go out." She saw Mr Yakone looked more interested than dissuaded by that. "Besides, they've got a viewing deck with tethers you can clip yourself to. It'll be fine. And I bet the spirits'll come to us – we won't even need to go trekking."

Taking her arm, Mr Yakone escorted her from his room.

Outside, at the foot of the Hotel Amundsen's low gray basalt steps, beside one of the feathery prehistoric trees while they waited for the rain to stop, she paused and took his hands.

"Look, I honestly don't think I'm related to Melisande d'Artelle. Do you really think they'd have let me leave the Institute for Paranormal Dysfunction if I was? But let's say I am." She shrugged. "Maybe that could help you with your research?"

He studied her – *really* studied her, his eyes snagging

only for a moment on the seals of her thermal outfit, unzipped to her groin. Under it, a snug black *lycrilk* bodystocking. She saw his eyes go unfocused, like mages did, examining her aura. She let her excitement come to the fore, at testing herself and her gear against the worst weather Antarctica had to offer, at being with him; concentrating on what they might learn together.

His expression solemn, he focused back on her physical form, and she released his hands. Calloused, warm, strong hands.

Married, she reminded herself. *How would it be, having someone like him? To truly love; who loved you back?*

Blinking rapidly, she pushed the thought away. "Come on, better hurry before the storm breaks!"

Bhaji peppered them with facts as they walked, sobering them both the longer he talked. Wind gusts up to 160 kilometers per hour, temperature -43°C (-45 Fahrenheit); but with wind chill factored in, Bhaji excitedly explained, that'd be almost -80 Celsius, only a little warmer than the coldest temperature ever measured outdoors.

"You'd better wait inside then little buddy. You're not rated below minus twenty."

"No! You might need me!" He was silent a second or two. "Tuck me in your suit to stay warm."

"You just want to snuggle my boobs, don't you?"

A full fifteen seconds passed before the little drone found a suitable response. "I just want to stay inside my operational temperature range."

"Sure you do."

They waited by a bank of three elevators. Two ended at Ascension Station at the top of the ice sheet. Only the third, the largest, went all the way to TAMA airport. At last one arrived, its doors opening on a colorful crowd spilling excitedly out, chattering about the amazing storm, as the freshly gathered people waited to flow in. "Two credits each, only, because it's full," whispered Bhaji as the doors closed, pretending once again to be inert as his little claws clutched the special loops on the shoulders of her outfit.

"You two look like you're planning to go out," an older man observed, sighing when Bonnie explained they'd signed the electronic waivers. He shook his head, though eyeing Mr Yakone and his native skins with a mix of interest and doubt.

"This is why we need a Condition Zero," he muttered. "Look, Condition *One* is visibility under 30 meters, *or* wind speed over a hundred klicks, *or* temperature under -73°C."

The other conversations in the crowded elevator stopped, twenty people listening, all nodding.

"Right now up there it's worse than that on all three counts: visibility *20* meters, winds *160*, temp -78. One flaw or failure in your clothing, and any exposed skin'll be frost-bitten in..."

"Three minutes!" Bhaji helpfully piped up.

The silence deepened.

A teenage girl spoke. "My friend Julie said the storm's *dark*, too. Scary. Like it's trying to claw its way in through the triple-glazed observation deck windows."

Storm spirits for sure! But Leeth just nodded. "We won't go out long. Or far. Just a few steps."

The older man frowned. "Miss, the waiver means no one will go out to rescue you if you're blown off. There are bots, but even they can't handle those conditions."

Mr Yakone met her eyes. She had to hug herself to contain her excitement. His hand went to his neck in a strange gesture, as if stroking something there.

"I will bring you safe," he told her at last.

The rest of the ride up was made in silence.

At Ascension Station the elevator doors opened, and Leeth *heard* the solid walls reverberating under the blasting wind. The wall of windows showed a churning fog pressing darkly in on all sides, the station lit only from within.

A pit opened in her belly as she heard the cacophony raging just beyond the sheltering walls, for a moment wondering if this really was such a good idea?

While the people from the elevator headed straight to the viewing windows, Bhaji whispered directions to her. "This way," she relayed to Mr Yakone, and soon they reached a metal corridor, its walls thrumming and vibrating. For some reason the teenage girl and her father, and the older man too, followed her and Mr Yakone into the sturdy metal tunnel, the temperature inside it much colder. Printed signs along the walls explained weather Conditions from Three down to One, each block of text on a progressively darker blue background. 'No exit in Condition One permitted,' was prominently displayed, just an asterisk hinting at an exception.

At the end of the corridor, above a heavy metal door with a long metal lever, an LED sign in bold glowing red reiterated: 'Condition One, no exit.' It began flashing.

"That sign wants me to send the waiver again, Miss Bonnie," Bhaji said. "There's another, final door past it."

She looked at Mr Yakone, who was pulling on and fastening special ties in his clothes, wrapping himself securely. "Do it," she told Bhaji, picking him off her shoulder and nestling him in on top of her chest, his feathered wings folded. She zipped up and sealed her suit to hold him in place. Pulling on her goggles she raised her cowl and tightened drawstrings, making it snug against her eye-wear, before pulling on her special gloves.

"Can you hear me, Miss Parker?" Bhaji's voice came, muffled but loud and clear to her as she checked the velcro seal over the zipper.

"Just barely," she said, a twinge of guilt at the necessary lie. But if Bhaji learned about her hearing, Ty would know too, if – *when* – it hacked the innocent little drone.

"I have an earbud," he offered.

"It's okay."

She turned to Mr Yakone, who now wore a narrow, curving white mask with a tiny slit for his eyes, his hood also tight around his face. "I feel like we're going into outer space or something."

"Good," said the older man, behind them both, still watching. "Keep that in mind and you may survive." He looked worried. "Tourists," he muttered.

Mr Yakone opened the door and stepped into the short final section of the same corridor; colder still, even through her thermal gear. It ended in a metal door crusted in frost. The sign over it had diagrams of the observation deck beyond, and how to fix the ropes and clips to the guide line they'd find just outside.

Beside it stood a silvery android labeled 'Rescue', but she knew without reading the plaque on its chest that it must be the robot the old guy said would be useless in this storm.

Through the door, clear to her ears, wind moaned at and tore over the metal tunnel they stood within as if trying to force its way in, and she felt another frisson of unease. The old man still followed them: the teen girl and her father had too, though they waited by the door into this section, their backs against it.

"Are you allowed here?" Bonnie asked the old man.

"So long as I don't go out. But I have a bad feeling about this. I wish you'd both reconsider."

"We won't be long." She clipped one end of the lead to the sturdy loop woven into her suit, waiting for Mr Yakone to fasten a nylon belt around his waist and clip a second lead to that. His hand stroked his neck again, and she heard him whisper something like "Wentshickshruke," then a word that sounded like 'tuglaukah'. A spell? She repeated the syllables under her breath, trying to fix them in her memory.

He pushed up the long metal latch, using it as a handle to wrench the door toward him. Fog blasted into the chamber, frigid and furious. Outside yawned a gray horror of screaming snow and mist, a hellish maelstrom, visibility just meters.

Leeth's heart pounded in her chest. Gripping the edge of the door in one hand, feeling its bitter cold even through her glove, she helped Mr Yakone pull it open. An orange rope line arced taut, fastened to a stanchion by the door, tugged horizontal by the wind.

They forced the door wider.

She stood on a threshold to hell, a churning nightmare of spitting snow and ice pellets. Like a portal opened onto an alien, hostile world, a madness of lashing air. She stood at the boundary, the gray metal grille of the platform appearing and disappearing at her feet as mist chased fog in a churning insanity of wind.

With her other hand she worked her carabiner open, straining out, struggling to clip it to the orange line disappearing into the writhing gray darkness.

"Kangyaa! Atchikkaahng!" Yakone shouted. "Stop!" as an invisible hand grasped her whole body and dragged her out through the doorway, her legs torn from under her.

Stretched full length, only her desperate grab at the door handle tethered her, even as it pulled the door shut. Wind coiled around her, yanked at her, worrying at her like a terrier with a rat, trying to rip her loose.

Like a hungry storm spirit.

"Let me go!" she screamed as her fingers on the handle slipped. Dropping the carabiner she stabbed the wind at her waist, ferocity unsheathed in her arcane claws – only to hit an invisible resistance. With furious strength she struck again, harder, this time feeling her claws pierce deep.

The force around her spasmed, wrenching her from the door and flinging her into the darkness as it roared off.

She slammed full length onto the platform's metal grating, fingers slipping on hard-packed ice and snow. Only her claws, instinctively punching through to the grille, anchored her to the deck. The wind fell from insane force to merely frightening as she jammed her other hand through crusted ice.

Daring to lift her head, her claws stabbing through ice, she dragged herself across the metal decking toward the light, the wind far too strong to risk standing. Then a furred figure was stepping toward her, a line stretched behind him from the lighted doorway. Sheathing her claws she reached for Mr Yakone's hand and pulled herself upright.

She clipped her carabiner to his belt.

"It was a spirit!" she crowed, ecstatic. "Did you see it?"

Peering through the amber glaze of her goggles, she tried to see his eyes through the narrow slit of his curved bone mask.

"Come," he shouted, and began fighting his way back against the wind gusting and building around them again.

Together they hauled themselves back to the orange line, her heart surging in joy at the battle. Then along it to the heavy metal door: light appearing and disappearing in scouring snow and fog. The twenty meter journey felt like two hundred. Finally reaching the door held open by the rescue android, they hauled it wide enough to stagger inside, together pushing it shut against the force of the wind, finally forcing the metal lever down to lock it.

Snow and ice crusted them from head to toe, crackling and falling as they moved.

"That was crazy!" she panted, exultant, loosening her hood, then pulling it back and her goggles with it. "Did you see it grab me?!"

The teen girl blinked at her in astonishment, her father's head drawing back as if she'd just said, 'I'm radioactive!'

Bhaji squirmed at her chest as she unzipped a little. "I called for help!" he proudly told her, as she set him back on her shoulder.

"Station reported gusts of one-fifty *knots*," the older guy said. "Just now. That's *two hundred and eighty* kilometers per hour." He stared at her.

"Is that a record?"

"No."

"Thanks for your help, Mr Yakone." She moved closer to him, to whisper. "I think it was gonna come back and try again."

He'd pulled his hood back and his mask down. He too frowned at her, his eyes distant and mystical again, Percepting her. He looked from her to the three strangers watching them both, noted their eyes drawn to his red Link.

Outside, wind raged against the station's window walls, the vibration running through the soles of their boots.

A little later she and he stood by the triple window barrier inside. Other mesmerized viewers took in the awesome natural spectacle, but kept a wary distance from them.

"What did you call out to me, just before it grabbed me?" she asked the shaman, the two of them staring out at the whipping mist lashing the windows, the vibration of the storm palpable.

"I tell you stop, danger."

"I don't actually speak Inuit though, you know? Maybe next time start with the English."

He'd removed his bone eye-mask, studying her face, his lips pressed thin.

"Anyway, thanks," she said, when he didn't answer. "But how did you know? Did you see it?"

He grunted.

She took that as a Yes. "So, was it big? It felt big, somehow. I think those guys can join up, you know? Like maybe small wind spirits twist together to make a big storm. That's how winds work, after all. I think it makes sense."

He jerked, as if her words had poked him – surprised him? – but when she turned to him he just grunted again and ignored her.

Scowling, watching him from the corner of her eye, she saw him take something invisible from round his neck, under the guise of undoing his furs to hang loose and open in the warmer air. It felt like 23C here – crazy to think they'd been out in temperatures like a hundred degrees colder.

Towering beside her, he touched his forehead to the transparent laminate, then put both hands to it. But his fingers worked like he was forcing something invisible through the wall. Or maybe holding *onto* something? Though his lips didn't move, she heard him whispering. The trouble was, she didn't speak his language. But she felt sure he was talking *to* something.

Staring back out into the churning gray and white storm, she wondered about the spirit that had grabbed her out there. Was it the same one she'd touched, up in the airport? The one she'd stupidly let taste a drop of her blood? Had it followed her? Called others?

What was it with her and spirits? Back at the Institute, back when she'd been just a kid, the two who'd followed her around, Robo and *Her*, hadn't been proper spirits. They'd been something stranger, something even mages and shamans couldn't see with their spooky vision.

That made her wonder again about Mr Yakone visiting Godsson. Should she tell Eagle about that, or would the Department go crazy and demand she return?

She sighed, gazing out into the tortured gray, the ice and sleet writhing like monstrous pixelated tentacles, reaching for her. Thickening, darkening, the wind strengthened, the windows trembling.

Suddenly the whole viewing wall shook, the same moment Mr Yakone cried out and pulled... *something...?* from the window and put it back around his neck.

He's got a familiar! I read about them!

She kept that knowledge from her face though as he took her arm. 'Wentshickshruke', he'd whispered before: was that its name?

"Come. We go away. Not good stay here." He eyed her like that was her fault.

She let him lead her off, back to the elevator that would carry them two kilometers down through the ice to the city below.

Behind them the windows shook, raging like a jilted lover.

Chapter 24 – Unsettling connections

They were walking back to the Hotel Amundsen before Mr Yakone next spoke. "Storm above like hungry *nanuḳ*," he said, shaking his head. "This place..." He paused, waving one arm across the sky to suggest the true terrain, kilometers above.

But when he dropped his arm, so much time had passed that she waved a hand in front of his face to wake him up.

"*Waits*," he said.

"What?"

"What?" he responded.

She felt her hackles rise. Did all shamans deliberately work to infuriate people? She took a slow breath. "This place waits for what?"

His head lifted and he took a step back, then his gaze narrowed. "Why you say that?"

She seriously considered riding him to the ground and beating his head into it. This time she needed three long breaths before replying. "Because *you* just said this place 'waits'."

"Ahh," he said, then nodded. "I feel this land. Old. Angry. Lonely. Maybe waits, yes.

"I know storms of my homeland. Know how to..."

"Survive?"

"Yes, survive." He shook his head, then stared up as if he could see past the false night sky. "No one survive storm like him." His gaze fell back to her, and darkened, studying her. "Come. We go big iglu."

"It's called the Hotel Amundsen."

He was already striding off, Bhaji swooping down to lead the way now they were moving again. Finally.

But however Mr Yakone felt about her, she had a hunch he wasn't *cross* with her anymore.

Adlartok Kallik Yakone walked in silence back to their iglu, their chilled cold weather gear now dripping melted ice and snow in the warmth of this buried city, all too aware of the girl following behind him. He stared up at the false stars in the false night sky, considering the storm raging far above. Something was troubling him; something about the girl. Was she a spirit made flesh?

At least he sensed none of the foulness that had taken Inuksuk, his childhood friend.

How had the old angakkuq who had given his friend his name at birth, known? 'Inuksuk': it meant, 'in the likeness of a human'. Or had the name itself opened his friend to the invasion, the thing that had grown in him like a worm, eating him from the inside?

Something disturbing and strange had happened to Inuksuk, something that had poisoned his soul. As a teen he had been angry but spirited. Like himself, Inuksuk had wanted justice for their people. Justice, and reparation.

The Melting had done such harm to their homeland – to the fish they caught, the animals they hunted, to their traditions – that even as the Southern ice sheets were restored, the northern ecosystems remained broken. Only the elders, and spirits, now remembered how things used to be.

Even when the seas fell again... instead of improving, the situation only worsened, the so-called modern world invading on all fronts to help rebuild and re-establish communities. With simple 'improvements', that made living so much easier.

So much easier, but at such cost to traditions that had kept them alive through millennia of Arctic conditions. Like the near extinction of *nanuk:* declared a helpful thing by their cultural invaders. Many younger people agreed, having no love for the fierce and aggressive white bear.

But Inuksuk had changed after his visit to Washington: angrier, more persuasive, more powerful. But also *wrong*. He began using his magic to bend to his will those who would not be swayed by his words. Yakone had tried to convince the Council that Inuksuk had changed. He'd failed – until they saw the perversion he had wrought on the Wind spirit he had enslaved and warped.

Inuksuk had only been bested by the whole Council; who welcomed Yakone's knowledge of the Institute for Paranormal Dysfunction as somewhere that could deal with one of their own turned toxic. Let the *tanik* deal with him.

He had been pleased that the unpleasant *tanik* sorcerer,

Alex Harmon, had been dismissed, but a part of him had been disappointed the man's young ward, Sara, had disappeared with him. Even when Persuaded, the new Director had been unable to say what had befallen either of them; where they had gone.

But the Institute held other secrets. Since his own visit there five years earlier, he had learned more about it; especially its most infamous patient and his role in the death of Melisande d'Artelle, the sorceress who had killed a billion people worldwide and condemned millions to the permanent mutation of her engineered virus, creating ogres, trolls, and their like.

Melisande d'Artelle, whose magic had sufficiently mastered a Great Spirit to cause the Second World Storm. Slain by a trio that had included the Dragon Lord of China – not a person an Inuit shaman would ever meet, especially given the strange tales from within that country, now sealed off. Of the three who had vanquished her, one other still lived: David Benson, the madman who called himself Godsson, who he and a few others had been called in to assist, in 2058 at the Institute.

Whose magic, even sealed away, somehow seemed subtly operating. The Americans called him The Manipulator, and feared him. But he, with the Dragon Lord and one other, had also challenged and defeated d'Artelle. If anyone knew how she had gained the aid of a Greater Spirit, it was Godsson, the mad mage.

Arranging a visit to the Institute had been easy, to check on his old friend, after two months in their care. With the right magic, visiting the insane mage had not proven impossible. Like most, the people there relied too much on their technology, failing to see that always, human beings were the key.

Alert to Godsson's manipulations, he had questioned the man about the event from years earlier and the unique spirit entity that had plagued him. And as Yakone had expected, that strange spirit had been the key.

"Only d'Artelle knew the paths to certain metamagics," Godsson told him, via the intercom of his solitary, impressively warded cell. "Or so I thought, until I saw what Alex had created, from Sara's unconscious sculpting hands. The Imagination of a child can also open hidden pathways."

The key to the mystery of the two unique spirits was their undetectability even to a mage's Imaginal vision.

"Because they exist mainly inside their host's mind," Godsson revealed. "Consider. Ten long years they thought me mad, at Melisande's creature's visitations. Though the child's creature was worse: her 'Robo'."

With further careful questioning he admitted that such spirits were key to summoning a Great Spirit, like the one Melisande d'Artelle called to cause the Second World Storm. And that such spirits could only be bargained with, never Mastered.

Asking of Sara, Godsson offered one final point.

"She is the key. An Avatar of Seduction – among others. Connected deeper than most know. Wooed by more than one Power. She is the way: seek her in icy southern wastes."

Then Godsson had fallen silent. Because she was the daughter of d'Artelle? A pity he had not guessed at the time.

But he had learned enough, combined with his own dream quests. Nor need he bargain for another year-long *world* storm; one great Arctic polar vortex would shatter his home-land's cultural invasion by restoring the ancient balance be-tween land, sea, and inhabitants.

Now here she walked, beside him – the girl, Sara, grown; naming herself Bonnie Angelique Parker. The one who had proposed his study of this continent, so similar yet so differ-ent to his own cold homeland; who had been so desperate to accompany him; who Godsson said held the secret of sum-moning the invisible mind spirits that could bridge the gap to the greater spirits.

Had she not, in the airport, driven a powerful wind spirit into a frenzy? Like Melisande d'Artelle? Perhaps *she* had called the storm now raging above? But she had not expected it to seize her. Surely? She had been fighting to return when he went to her aid.

Was she right, that lesser spirits could be persuaded to join together to form larger spirits, storm spirits? Could larger spirits join to form a Great Spirit? Was the answer so simple? And why did she show such interest in spirits? She was not one who felt the Call. She lacked both respect and self awareness.

Yet there was more to her than met the eyes – even to the

deeper sight of an angakkuq. *Seducer*, Godsson had named her; and had she not proven that to him now several times? Was that not how she claimed she had 'contacted' and driven the spirit in the airport to madness?

He frowned. Seduction was not a Way he would ever attempt. He shuddered at such depravity.

Angry still at himself for not recognizing her sooner – he had *known* in the airport of New Francisco that they had met before. But he was here now, and she was the key he needed. Breathing deep, stilling himself, he smiled.

But when he turned to her now, centered and calm, smiling, for some reason this time *she* withdrew, her aura screaming reluctance.

She nervously fingered her ostentatious black choker as they paused on the dark gray steps leading up and into their hotel. Suddenly, he felt exhausted. He stared up into the night sky and its unfamiliar constellations. Even the moon was upside down! He shook his head.

This Antarctica – 'Newtopia' – was both far more and far less than he had expected; so unlike his own beloved homeland. He had not expected the ferocity of the storm, or such cold.

He had thought he knew cold; survival. But what he had sensed in the storm, in the empty, uncaring, *yearning?* land above, had been one more disturbing block in an edifice of unreason that unsettled him more than he cared to admit.

He would rest; meditate; sleep, and Dream.

Sara, too, seemed tired.

"I can hardly believe they let you talk to Godsson, Mr Yakone. They never let *anyone* visit him except his, uh, therapist."

After making that statement, her aura smoothed out. Strange. "Like you Uncle, Alex Harmon," he said. "Where he go... where he *be* now?"

"I don't know. We don't see each other so much anymore."

Truth, he saw from the harsh, jagged, and conflicted shapes of her aura.

Her drone circled above, riding a nighttime thermal it had found.

Chapter 25 – Angels and demons

The night before, guided by his own hunger, Mike watched others tap small metal sticks with a street vendor and receive food. Discovering a similar stick in an inner pocket, he did the same. Both sticks beeped a happy sound. He examined his while the food maker lay a tube of protein into a long roll. Angled the right way, a tiny screen displayed numbers: 777. That seemed good.

"Mustard? Onions?"

"Please." It all smelled good. And though it burned his mouth, the burn had been full of flavors, of smoke and broth and something stronger than nuts.

After, he'd dozed in a park where well-dressed people strode hurriedly along paths curving through the dark, lit from above by globes on poles, unconscious of the beauty around them.

He was woken from dreams of flying by hands rummaging through his clothing. A pair of angry young men. One waved something metallic at him, demanding 'creds' and growing frustrated, until with a sharp bang it spat metal at him. Only his aura of Grace, instinctively erected, protected him.

Sending both to sleep, he looked for the bang-thing. A baby dragon? He spied it lying abandoned on the ground. Only a little larger than his hand, it would be far happier with him, he decided. Luckily, its owner also possessed a supply of food for the heavy little dragon, small brass tubes.

"Go away," he ordered both men after waking them. It was a little cold, and he could imagine moisture in the air, so he made it warm and dry around him, shut the door to his room of trees, and fell back asleep.

He blinked awake to birdsong and forest. In dawn's light he stretched, eyeing a curved metal bar that'd been sticking up in the middle of his bed. He'd had to Blast it three times to get rid of it so he could lie down. It seemed a really stupid thing to put in a bed.

Standing, stomach growling, he eyed the circle of dewy grass around him. Rio was colder than he'd expected. He'd...

flown...? The night before, yeah.

"You okay, Spiff?"

Checking the inner pocket of his trench-coat, the little dragon smiled up at him. A quick jiggle told him it still had food, so it was time to see to his own bodily needs.

Dismissing a memory of a visitor in the night – a confused police officer who'd mistaken his bedroom for a park bench! – he went searching for his bathroom, trying to remember when he'd planted so many trees inside his house. And where the walls were. *I think I'll call it the Parkhouse!*

Leaving it behind, he followed the scent of food to a busy street corner. The curious ritual with the stick provided him more food and drink from another street vendor.

After eating, he checked the number on his stick, frowning at it until it went back to 777. That was better!

Yawning, he found a 'public restroom', then continued exploring, every now and then letting his body rest while his spirit soared through the city. So warm! So easy! But knowing his friends would need him, he also checked on them as the day passed. Saw their booking for the evening, Stairway To.

For reasons he didn't quite know, he shivered and returned to his body.

He spent the rest of the day doing small works: a little drone unwedged from a tree; a few people unobtrusively healed; a second mugger sent crashing to a pavement; a bus halted to allow an elderly man to board.

That evening, the few people on New Francisco's wet streets gave the youth a wide berth as he strolled past. Not due to his impossibly white clothes that *almost* didn't glow; nor because of the creature he held cupped in his hands, speaking to it.

It was the fact that no drop of rain fell on the spotless suit, marking him 'Mage' as surely as a holosign hovering over his head. Sane people avoided the magically active – and the only thing worse than a mage was a crazy mage. One talking to a miniature steel dragon definitely fell into the second category.

"I guess you're as excited as me, Spiff!" Mike enthused. "Rio's everything I dreamed of! Well, apart from the cold. Anyway, tonight we'll be meeting with resistance fighters, so you'll need to be on your best behavior."

The tiny dragon in his hands hissed its acquiescence.

"Good boy. Here, I'd better put you away. Looks like people aren't used to seeing dragons round here. Back you go. Have some treats." He slid the dragon inside his jacket, and followed with some of Spiff's favorite snacks. They made a sound curiously like falling bullets as they showered into the pocket.

"It sure is a fine night," he sighed, breathing in the warm and exotic airs of Rio's cold wet streets. Turning right, he left the brightly lit Chinese shopfronts of Grant Avenue, entering the shadowy ways that bled the city's light and life into a hungry darkness.

Chapter 26 – Meanwhile in Washington

Joshua Worthington the Second, senator for Washington State, gazed down from his office window at the people scurrying ant-like below. He fed quietly, from multiple sources. From his panicked intern's struggle to update his spreadsheet of campaign donors while most had left the state for the Patriots' Day holiday, now out of contact. More distantly, from the delightful tension between Marjorie and Blake, forced together on the Terawatt Pipeline project, each in an unhappy marriage, each devoutly Christian, each secretly desiring the other.

That tapestry of angst both fed and soothed him: the spreading web of energy from all his Master's victims walking their individual cliff's edges of temptation. He twisted the ugly gray ring on his finger, savoring the energy the lumpy shape drew from the web. A net of addictive gifts of power, enticing each victim deeper.

Senator Worthington felt it as a weight of certainty. A mesh of others like him, moving and herding the ignorant masses. Like him but lesser, like those on the pavements below, scuttling about, foraging for scraps, blindly guided by drives they scarcely understood.

The entity behind Worthington's eyes stroked its web, feeding from and returning portions in kind, chafing at the need to rein in its hunger, to move in slow steps, to grow its influence by secret steady degrees. Things would have been so much simpler had the magic returned just half a human lifetime earlier. This society had come so close to collapse in the decades before Magic's return, when his kind could only influence a few, and then only in dreams or altered states of consciousness. Ecstatic subsumption in the fervid darkness.

Once again, it recalled the collapse of its first plan, a span of years ago, equal to a mere human childhood. Flushed with anticipation from its return to this plane of existence, it had acted more directly and been on the very brink of taking control of this country. Only to have all its first figureheads cut down by a man and woman who had emerged from the shadows with souls of flame, pruning his buds, his *spores*, striking at him through his puppets.

Worse, to this day the two defied his efforts to track them. Yet it had seen them. It would find them. It would find them and the child seeded in the female's belly, just beginning to bloat with insipid life. That child would be grown now. It would feed on their despair and gorge on their anguish as they watched everything they loved torn from their care and brought into its herd.

But although that couple had hidden, they had not acted alone. It still hunted their co-conspirators. So often, their thoughts brushed close, only to dart into hiding when they sensed its attention. And then a year ago, the fruit of that womb confronting it directly! A mere girl. She had gazed in defiance into the eyes of Shepherd Fox, into the abyss of its self; had seen she faced a foe beyond her understanding. Then she had slain Fox, and with her dog-robot abomination, pruned a portion of its web with mere rockets and bullets. She had crushed the Brethren of the End of Days.

She would regret that foolhardy act. From that brief contact, it knew one thing. She would make an *excellent* spore.

One of many. This world was an ocean of food, the festering horde of the dominant species ripe for eons of harvest if managed correctly. Yet like any food source, such a feast attracted entities from higher in the food chain, squabbling over the nutrition on offer.

Its kind knew the value of patience. Of symbiosis. Of secret control. Unlike gods, or dragons, or those who merely surfed the centuries on magic's sustaining wave – the wizards and death cheaters; or the cold non-life drawn from the space beyond this world.

Soon. This time it had been patient. Growing its base. Sending tap roots deep into this society, taking those with power, wealth, influence. This time it had not a handful of figureheads, but hundreds. It was time to begin exercising that power, encircling and absorbing, or isolating those who would resist. Time to cut them down.

It returned its attention to Worthington, plucking a chord to steer the man's thoughts back to his dark fantasies, now brought to life. Layers of indulgence and entrapment, a seductive slope from animal desire to the power of dominance, tapping the pain of defeat of each new victim-recruit. To harvest one day the ultimate reward: ingesting a soul that had surrendered at last to despair.

As it fed morsels to Worthington, it watched through his eyes, pushed a thought into the forefront of the male's mind. *We can justify the Bill as a cost saving, an increase in Freedom, a paring back of Government control and interference. 'It's time.'*

It linked the subconscious of the senator to that of his new speechwriter, nudging the words until they resonated, and the sticky rhetoric formed.

It might be time to stoke the animosity between those who still lived within the staggering architecture of the business world, and those who rejected it. 'They live on land we granted when the global situation was grim. Too long they have leeched the blood from our veins.' With luck, in coming years, it might even lead to civil war.

It turned its attention to the recent snuffing of its spores fifteen thousand kilometers south. They should have easily established a beachhead, but had failed, from the outset.

Even sensing them, feeding them or feeding *from* them, had been difficult.

Nor had they been able to reach the hidden research facility, even with Tik Tek's CEO missing in action and the company's security in shambles. There would have been no better time to 'investigate' both the 'Space Adaptation' and Stretch programmes.

There had to be some reason Tik Tek's automated administration System oversaw those. *Illegal genetic experimentation?* It was time to move on Tik Tek.

Worthington checked the latest news from Newtopia, and made a call. "Johnson. Adam Fuller-Price has been incommunicado for over twenty-four hours. Tik Tek shares have slumped eighty-seven points. This is perfect: start the spill motion for the entire board. The company's in chaos. Relying on a CEO who's so immune compromised he can't meet anyone face to face is unsustainable. Too much automation. Needs a firm physical hand on the reins."

He listened.

"I don't care. They're all mine. Pick whoever you like. And the first order of business after cutting Fuller-Price from the picture is dismissing his damned Chief of Security. He's more than he appears: I've not been able to get any of my... people in there."

Spores, corrected the entity at the center of this web.

Worthington listened a little longer. "If you can locate him, certainly. Revisit Fuller-Price's death. Iago should have been sacked back then. 'Couldn't protect his own boss'."

He shook his head. "No, Iago's the only one left from Fuller-Price Senior's old inner circle. Maneuvered out when they didn't approve of Adam's decisions. The current board are figureheads only. They won't put up a real fight if their parachutes are golden enough."

Once again he cut off the other person. "Irrelevant. Give them each ten million for all I care. With Tik Tek under my control, the whole Newtopian Consortium will follow. And after them, the rest. And you will make an excellent CEO, Harold. I know it."

Spore.

Worthington allowed himself a small smile. Taking out the small polished wooden box he closed his eyes, and slowly, over a period of minutes, squashed the life out of the wings-plucked fly crawling in its box, savoring its insectile fear.

Chapter 27 – Visiting children

Bonnie watched Mr Yakone disappear inside his room, then turned and shut her eyes, remembering the storm, the wind snatching her up, the incredible *cold,* and how she'd had to fight to make her claws dig into the wind spirit. She'd stabbed spirits and elementals before, but never felt a tough shell like that.

Smiling, she shook out her fancy thermal suit, sending melting ice flying in the corridor, and headed inside, Bhaji flying happily beside her.

In her room, hanging up the suit, she wondered what to do next. Sleep sure sounded good. She flopped on the bed to consider, and shut her eyes.

Then jerked awake at a stinging jolt from her choker. Blinking at daylight streaming in, she tapped it, a chime indicating a new message. How had she missed that?

Simple, she found: it had arrived while she was clawing her way across the icy deck above, last night.

From Nelson, it had her hurrying from her room, following a local map on her Link as she waited for the elevator while Bhaji amused himself by swooping and looping in figure eights up and down the corridor. The Stretch programme kids from Paradawn had checked into a nearby hotel! She rolled her shoulders. It was eleven a.m. – she'd slept ten hours!

Once on the street, she gave Bhaji the other hotel's name and followed him, trying to identify the businesses she passed as she trod the patterned matte tiles of the sidewalk. An arthrobot gardener the size of a cat was using its eight limbs to dig fallen fronds into the patch of soil around one of the feather-ferned tree things, still damp from last night's automated rain.

"Gait warning," her earrings buzzed. She drew a long breath. *It'll be a good habit for when Ty finally reboots.*

She might even have time for a jog. Nelson had sent the details of the Stretch kids to her Link, too. *Should I try to rescue them, too? Tricky.*

She stroked her choker in the 'wake up' pattern. "Play last attachment," she whispered, then angled her Link to beam its display onto her retina, unconscious of the technology needed to keep the image steady as she stomped along.

By the time she'd scanned the pictures of Michael, Amy, Nadeep, Yuri and Bobby, and skimmed the meager info on the five children, she'd calmed. "Deep erase last message," she told her choker.

Nelson said he didn't think Ty would be out of action much longer, but the smell of seafood and vegetables from an open air food stall ahead made her realize how hungry she was. "Bhaji!" she called, and within a minute was wolfing down a satisfying explosion of clingy, pastry-wrapped chewy nuggets of shellfish, cabbage, and a sharp soy sauce, licking her fingers clean.

She only had to open her hand again for Bhaji to bob down, releasing the second tubular wrap with obvious relief as his wings slowed from their frantic buzz and he zoomed ahead to lead the way.

Mmm. At least the food in Newtopia was tasty! She should have bought more. "You're not recording me are you Bhaji?"

"Just the last 60 seconds, Miss Parker!" He flew back to her. "I know you're shy, and not used to amibos, but just say the word and I can Save. I can record years and years. It's my prime function!"

"Sorry Bhaji, I like my privacy."

Bhaji gave a sad hum.

Ahead, she saw the sign for short term accommodation on the six-story building mentioned in Nelson's update, but to 'accidentally' meet the kids and their minder, she first had to find them! Call Shona? And say what?

How did an adult meet kids? Shona would be protective. And where even were they?

She checked her Link. Coming on for noon. Would they need feeding? She couldn't ask Bhaji to scout around and look for them, even if they *were* wandering around outside, because LB and Nelson both said the poor little guy could be hacked as soon as Ty restored itself.

But she didn't need to tell Bhaji *what* she was looking for! "Hey Bhaji, can you fly around and show me the sights – especially the people – and what kind of stuff goes on here?

You can stream to my Link, yeah?"

"Easy peasy Miss Bonnie!"

Her Link pinged and Bhaji did a loop the loop over her head before flying off down the boulevard, skimming the tops of the tallish chubby green fern trees. "You can still hear me?" she asked her Link, angling it toward her eyes so she could see Bhaji's video.

"Sure can!" his voice said, from the Link. "Would you like sound too?"

She nodded. "Please. And maybe look for eating places nearby that aren't too expensive?" The shellfish snacks had only whetted her appetite.

He gave a cheerful chirp. The video dipped up and down as he nodded, making her smile.

While he searched, she wandered toward a park with exercise equipment she'd seen. She could warm up there before jogging off to check out the areas Bhaji wasn't covering. But as she approached, she heard children, then a worried woman's voice saying, "Amy, I don't think that's safe!"

Amy was one of the Stretch kids' names!

"Gait warning!" her earring warned.

But she was so pleased that for once, it didn't annoy her.

The park was maybe fifty meters wide and a hundred long, screened by a perimeter of the primeval fern trees. She paused by the first one, pressing her palm to its complicated surface of ridges and hollows, putting her nose right to it, breathing in a kind of spearmint scent as she took in the scene.

There were swings in a pit of sand, like she'd seen in movies, with a dark-haired boy of about twelve swinging vigorously, and two others at a giant chess board, an amibo hovering by them. The brown-skinned boy maybe twelve, the younger with ginger hair, studying chess pieces only a little smaller than himself.

A square patch of sand with red, yellow, and blue buckets and a hose sat ignored by all, but what most drew her eyes was the young Black girl, maybe thirteen, in athletic-wear shading from white into oddly bright aquamarine down her torso to her legs. She stood on the edge of a blue twenty meter square gymnastics mat. An older Black woman, thirty or more, stood at its edge telling the girl she'd injure herself.

"Amy, if any of you hurt yourselves I'll get in big trouble."

"It's okay Shona, the mat's real thick, see?" She dropped hard onto her knees and rebounded to her feet. At that moment, the boy on the swing, at the top of his arc, pushed the seat off from under him and somersaulted in the air, twisting to land crouching in the sand.

The adult, Shona, spun around, her attention jumping from the boy, to the seat jerking noisily as it danced on its chains behind him. "Yuri! Tell me you didn't just aerial!"

"Um, I didn't just aerial, Miss Shona?"

Yes! Yuri was the name of another of the Stretch children. She'd found them!

While the woman's back was turned, the girl stood straight, arms by her side, then raced in a diagonal across the blue mat and leaped, her body stretched out as she spun heels over head: turning once, twice, in mid air. Leeth winced, hunching her shoulders as the girl dropped, her legs misaligned with her motion as her feet hit the mat, sending her tumbling sideways in a sprawling fall.

"Amy!"

Amy didn't look hurt – not physically, anyway – as Leeth headed over to the two and the woman tried to help the girl to her feet. The thirteen-year-old, her lips pressed into thin lines and blinking hard, shrugged off the assistance.

"Hey, good effort!" Leeth said, smiling. "Practicing a Biles, yeah?" She shook her head. "But you weren't using your arms. Impressive twist from just your launch, though."

Neither the woman nor the girl responded. At the giant chess board, the two boys had gone still, too.

The woman finally spoke. "Are you a gymnast?"

Leeth shook her head. "Not really. Personal trainer and, uh, dancer. Bonnie Parker. Just arrived last night."

The woman frowned. "From McMurdo?"

"No, New Francisco actually."

"New Fr-? But C-N's down!" Shona pursed her lips. "The landing was okay?"

Leeth shrugged. "Not too bad." She turned back to the girl. "Can you show me your launch again?"

"What did you mean I didn't use my arms?"

"You control your tumble with them. You were twisting clockwise, yeah? This way. So spread both arms then pull just your left in hard at the start of the second spin in the layout."

The girl looked doubtful.

"It's been a while, but I used to practice all day in the gym. I may be a bit rusty though. Let me warm up a bit."

She did a few cartwheels, smiling at the familiar springy feel of the mat under her feet and hands, then paused, visualizing it before striding forward and throwing herself into a series of forward flips. A pause to stretch, picturing the moves while she headed to a corner, then she turned.

"Okay, let's see..." She accelerated hard for just three steps and flung herself diving forward, whipping her feet up behind her to send the world spinning end over end. Throwing both arms out, she pulled her left in hard across her body, twisting it away with equal force as the world flipped sideways too. A heartbeat, before swinging her arm back out, then bringing both arms in together as the blue ground raced up, her feet slamming into the mat. She let her knees absorb the force, then couldn't hold in her grin. "Still got it!"

"Wow," said the aerial-swing boy. Amy and the others just stared.

Was that too...? But gymnasts had been doing the move now for forty or more years, since Simone Biles invented it. It wasn't that 'out there'. "You see what I mean about the arms? And I didn't twist at all from my legs, just used them for the vertical launch."

Amy was nodding.

"It's more obvious if you hold a weight in each hand. Want to see it again?"

"Ahh, I don't think," Shona began, but Amy was nodding enthusiastically.

"Okay. But I really am rusty, so that first one might have been a fluke." But it had felt *right*. "Stand right here, and watch just my arms this time. Ignore everything else."

"Miss Shona's meebo, record the lady!" the smallest boy said, and Leeth froze. But she knew, the whole Department had known, it was inevitable she'd be recorded by Ty's surveillance. Besides, she was disguised, and wasn't doing anything impossible. Maybe she'd even get to try out her cover story idea of 'fitness instructor' to tutor Amy, as an 'in'?

"Bobby! An amibo is only for recording you, and others sometimes, *if* you ask permission. Sorry, they're a bit excited at being allowed to use mine today," Shona apologized.

Bobby looked down at his feet. "Please miss, can Miss

Shona's meebo record you?"

"Please?" the thirteen-year-old girl pleaded.

"So you can study it later? Amy, right?" She forced a smile. "Sure."

Bobby started explaining – until Shona cut him off – that 'they hadn't ever used a meebo until coming here'.

From Paradawn; and I bet Ty handled all that stuff for them. She nailed her demonstration the second time, too. For a moment she'd considered adding a full extra tumble and twist, head over heels and an extra spin clockwise. She was strong enough. *To show off.* Except *that'd* be way beyond normal, even if she could still pull it off.

Something to practice again in the future. In private.

Then it was Amy's turn. With every attempt, she made progress. Five tries later she nailed her landing after two complete tumbles and a full twist, in a confusing flash of yellow blending to aqua. Her face alight, she sprang into Leeth's arms and clung to her like a, like a, wriggling bundle of joy.

Yellow?

"Thank you, Miss Parker ! Thank you!"

Bhaji chose that moment to make his return, swooping in to circle around her head. "Miss Bonnie, I found three eateries!"

Amy disentangled herself and bounced down, still glowing. A blush of pink was now swallowing the yellow and aqua of her clothes, shading into lavender. Amy blinked up at the little drone when it flew down to perch on Leeth's shoulder.

"Your amibo has *wings?*"

"His name's Bhaji. And *your* clothes change color?"

Amy shrugged. "That's thanks to Bobby. But he's sleek."

"Why's he got wings?" Bobby wanted to know. "Amibos have props."

"Maybe I could tell you about him over lunch, if *you* tell me about Newtopia? I only landed last night."

"I really don't think-" Shona began, but Amy had already taken her hand, and the boys shouted their approval.

As they left, Bonnie looked back at the bright, primary colored equipment, the playground oddly empty and deserted without the children. She frowned. These were the youngest kids she'd seen since the elevator ride down through the ice. Then remembered: at 0.4, Newtopia had the lowest birthrate of any country on Earth.

Her stomach growled, bringing her attention back. "I asked Bhaji to scout out a few good places to eat, near here."

Shona frowned. "But C-N's still down. Does he also have local intelligence?"

"I do!" Bhaji piped up. "I'm real smart. In the airport I had to pretend to be dumb because everyone else was jealous!"

Shona eyed her own small drone with pursed lips. "I'm not surprised."

But she approved of two of the three eateries Bhaji had found. "Klondike," she decided. "They have sorbets. And it's done up as an old time goldmine."

The kids looked suddenly eager.

Sorbet's a dessert, Leeth thought, remembering eating at the Opera House for her disguise tests with James.

She felt oddly warm when Bobby took her hand, Amy still holding her other. They headed off, Bhaji again leading the way, the kids peppering them both with questions.

Maybe this mission won't be as bad as I feared?

Chapter 28 – Klondike dining

The sign over the door hung askew, a wooden board apparently nailed in place, with carved and blackened letters spelling 'Klondike'. Two heavy beams supported a rough-hewn crossbar, the door displaying a 3D image of rusty train tracks curving sharply away into darkness. It reminded her of the door to Eagle's office, half a world away.

It slid aside to reveal a matching scene: a black painted alcove and painted tracks bending to the right. But once inside, the room opened up into a space well lit by what looked like old time lanterns on the walls, the tables and chairs following the rough carved wood theme.

A business couple, a man and a woman, were finishing a meal, most of their attention on a shared projection on their tabletop. "We have enough stockpiled to shut down the printer," the man was saying. "We'll make a fortune!" He'd lowered his voice as the front door had opened, but Leeth pretended she couldn't hear him.

The kids ran to a table at the rear, where the wall screen made it look like they perched on the edge of a cliff. Below, in a huge cavern, workmen with pickaxes hammered into hard walls, a mining cart a short distance behind them.

"Uh..." It sure wasn't like any restaurant she'd been in before.

A short two-wheeled waiter bot whirred out from the far end of the rear wall, offering coffee to the two business people. Leeth's nostrils flared at the smell, and she shuddered.

The kids looked around, until Shona said "Start." In front of each of them a menu appeared, shorter ones for the kids. The robot waiter glided off, coffeepot in hand. Most services in Newtopia were provided by bots, so surely, with CityNet down, there should be chaos? How was this place running?

Shona tapped her menu, then grimaced. "Sorry, you'll have to choose from known items."

Leeth eyed her own menu – *Salmon-infused plankton pie, Right Whale (p), Flake (p)* ... and saw on it a button labeled Advanced, like the one Shona had futilely tapped.

"Known items? What're they? And what does 'p' mean?"

"Printed," Shona said, then did a double-take. "We don't eat *real* whale! Or shark, for that matter." Then she nodded across the room to a kind of slim vending machine in one corner. "With a DNA sample and a puff of your breath, if you pay a bit more any restaurant can invent dishes designed for your palate. But with C-N down..."

I'm not giving Ty a DNA sample! "Mmm, sounds great." She needed to befriend these children and pump them for information. Nelson was an arrogant little snake-weasel, but he'd come through for her. These kids were her best bet to learn about and maybe even *get to* Paradawn and the secret research facility there. But Paradawn was a two and a half hour high speed cross-continent pod trip away – how to do any of that before Ty pulled itself back together?

She *needed* to make these kids like and trust her, and quickly. And where did Shona fit in? Was she as nice as she seemed, or was that a mask? Just pretending, like her unclike the Doctor? She *seemed* nice.

Although time was slipping away, she couldn't rush this. *Sharing a meal in a relaxed social setting is a fast way to establish the beginnings of trust.* She knew that, knew it took time, but time was running out!

Amy, Yuri and Nadeep ordered fish and chips, and Bobby a chicken-burger, also 'printed'. Her eyes flicked over the pictures beside each menu item, ignoring the kilojoules, fat, salt, health rating, and price. A seafood dish on her menu looked especially good, the fish coated in something crispy and golden. The 'Eye Fillet steak (p)' looked equally good: and luckily, nothing like an actual eye.

She chose English fish and chips, and steak. "Rare," she added, copying what the kids had done to order, just as the tourist information had described – only for a red 'Cancel' button to appear beside each of her two choices.

"Um, Miss Bonnie, you accidentally ordered two main meals," Amy, on her left, explained.

"No, I want two – I'm hungry! The airplane meals were tiny."

"Really?"

At Leeth's nod, Amy reached over and slid the two buttons off the screen for her, the arms of her athletic wear now autumn tones of orange and red.

Leeth noticed Shona wincing at the total – '8.3 *wours*' – as the kids all added Cokes, before tapping a complicated pasta-kelp-shrimp dish and water for herself.

'Wours' were work-hours. "How much if I pay?" Leeth quietly asked Bhaji.

"As a non-UBI participant, 86 credits, Miss Bonnie," he responded equally softly, converting *wours* to universal credits.

Worth it, she decided. "Let me pay," she told Shona, "but on one condition: you all have to answer my questions about Newtopia."

Shona looked embarrassed but also relieved. Feeling pleased at her guess, Leeth added a water for herself.

"That's all," said Shona, and the menus vanished, a small progress bar appearing in the middle of the table.

"Wow, I guess Newtopia really is as advanced as everyone says. So tell me, how do you all know each other?"

"We're stretchy," Bobby volunteered, one eye on the progress bar. The waiter-bot glided up, dispensed glasses, filled them, and glided off.

Yes! Now gently, reel them in. "Stretchy? If Amy's gymnastics are anything to go by, I bet you all are! Are you all good at sports?"

"Not all of us," Nadeep said. "Though you should see Yuri skiing, or ice skating. I'm... quite good at math, and Bobby's a whiz with puzzles and codes, and painting. And Michael-"

He stopped.

"Michael's *missing!*" Amy cried.

Chapter 29 – Infiltrating Paradawn

This could be the 'in' I need! Leeth thought. "Missing, from your place in... where did you say? Paradawn? You tried to find him?"

"Yes!" Amy said. "We all did!"

"And you couldn't? Then what?"

They all spoke at once; about someone called Gynie, a robot nurse; about telling Shona, who said she'd investigate.

"And did you?" asked Leeth, turning to Shona.

Shona's expression spoke volumes. "I tried. But not being there..."

"Not being there? You don't live with them? Who looks after them? How did you search if you weren't there?"

Shona looked more than embarrassed: troubled maybe. Even guilty? "They're in a Stretch programme. But Adam wants it run quietly. He brought all the kids here after they were orphaned, but can't look after them himself. So-"

"Why not? Wait: when you say Adam, you mean Adam *Fuller-Price*? The CEO of Tik Tek?! Whose father was ass-"

Shona's tiny, frantic head shake stopped her before she could say, 'assassinated.'

"Whose da was ass?" Bobby asked. "What's 'ass'? Adam never talks about his da."

"You *talk* to Adam?" Leeth asked him.

"On screen," Nadeep said. "He can't fight off germs, so he has to stay all by himself, just with bots, and do everything via the Net."

Adam Fuller-Price's father, the previous CEO of Tik Tek, had been assassinated by persons unknown. And all these kids had been orphaned – their parents assassinated too? Was that why Adam had brought them here? Maybe he wasn't experimenting on them, but protecting them? But they were all special?

She shook her head, frowning at Shona, who was looking increasingly flustered – but with relief mixed in with the guilt. She'd been right to target the kids! "But Michael's still missing, even after you told Adam?"

"I couldn't reach him. I tried. I have special access – direct contact IDs – but none are working. And it's not just me: Adam's been incommunicado since C-N went down. Some people think he doesn't live here. He's off the grid to stay... safe." Shona's look added, 'from assassins,' but her significant nod at the kids explained why she said no more.

"So you guys are all alone in Paradawn? No grown ups?" Leeth asked. *Grups,* she thought, remembering jokes with Godsson, back when she thought he was fun. And trustworthy.

The kids looked at one another.

"There's P1 and P2," Amy said, "but they're not like real people. They're strange."

"They used'ta be stranger," Bobby said. He stood, to walk in a small circle with stiff arms and plodding steps, then sat back down.

A shiver ran down Leeth's spine, remembering Marc Disten, and the similarly strange guys at Mr Abrams's mansion. Not to mention Ankhet, or the two guys she and Thug had fought when the Fist of Peace tried to rescue Chopper. Poor, stupid Chopper.

She needed to see these P1 and P2 guys.

"They got better a week ago," Nadeep said. "They started talking like normal people. I even had some conversations with them about science, and math. They knew a *lot.*"

"Not like *normal* people," Amy corrected. "They'd finish each other's sentences." She glared at Shona before looking to the stranger they'd just met, who seemed nice. And who, she saw, *got it.*

Leeth was thinking, *A week ago... could Ty have built a new Writer that fast? Used it to take direct control of P1 and P2?* "You said they *used* to be better? Did they go back to how they were when C-N went down?"

"Ohhh!" Amy said, both Yuri and Nadeep echoing her.

Nailed it, thought Leeth.

"What? What?" demanded Bobby.

Shona looked horrified, also seeing the implications.

"I think we should go and search for Michael," Leeth declared. "He could be in trouble!"

Shona hunched in on herself, clearly torn. "That's – I need special permission to visit. It's, it's a secure facility. And Michael's sixteen, and a mage..." she trailed off, wincing.

"I'm surprised I got authorization for the kids to come here. I shouldn't be talking to you," she muttered. "But I couldn't leave them there with C-N down and Michael gone!"

She does *feel guilty! I can use that!* "Right. So you left a sixteen-year-old *mage* missing, in what sounds like a completely automated, ah," *secret R&D complex,* "engineering facility, with two strange guys who've been acting even stranger recently? Sounds pretty iffy. Isn't Paradawn where the Antarctic Refrigeration Engine is still running, beaming infrared rays into space? What if he went up onto the surface? He could be freezing to death as we speak!"

The kids cried out in horror, and Shona looked stricken. "Look, I'll call Security and report him missing, right now. They'll send someone to search." But instead of putting her Link on speaker, she clicked its bud free and popped it in her ear. Her eyes flicked back and forth as she stared into its screen, and Leeth saw her finger squeeze its side briefly.

"Security," Shona said.

But from what Leeth heard from the tiny earbud when she concentrated, it didn't sound like Shona had succeeded in calling Security. "That CID is currently unLinked. Your message will be delivered when connection is re-established."

"Good. Great. I need to report a missing person.

"Yes. That's right. Yes."

Shona proceeded to fake a whole dialog, ending with, "You'll activate a Paradawn search bot right away? Great!"

She made that all up!

As Amy and the others cheered, Leeth watched Shona end the call and re-seat the bud in her Link. Why had she done that? She seemed to really care for the kids. But smiled tentatively at her. "All settled."

"Really." The longer she stared at Shona, the more nervous the woman grew. "But C-N is still down, yes?"

Shona jerked her head once: Yes.

She's scared*!*

"So any search bot won't have," *Ty,* "C-N, to help. It'll just be a dumb security bot. *Assuming* it even remembers your call just now. For all we know, it'll have instantly forgotten it, as if you never even made it."

Leeth didn't think she'd ever seen anyone look quite so guilty. Even the kids seemed to pick up that something was wrong, suddenly looking worried about Michael again.

"Right," Leeth said. "With C-N down, I bet Security is... *ineffective*. So we'll head there, now, ourselves."

"But we can't leave the kids-" Shona began.

"We'll take them with us. Just let me grab a couple things from my hotel. How do we get to Paradawn?"

Shona gaped at her. "We can't!"

"Oh? Just leave it to that search party you organized?"

But Shona clearly understood what she was really saying. Her shoulders slumped. Then she took a deep breath, as if steeling herself, and projected a hologram of Newtopia City onto the table from her Link, its wiggly crescent shape hugging the base of the mountain range. "There." She indicated an isolated pod station, in a fully automated industrial area at the clockwise end. "It crosses first under the Ross Ice Shelf then the rest of the West Antarctic."

From her mission prep, Leeth knew that was 1,200 kilometers, and that the pod line was little-used now.

"That's by the Thwaites Glacier, isn't it? How far is that pod station? *Can* we get tickets to Paradawn?"

"Not normally, but... I have access to the sub-shelf pod system. For emergencies. That station's across the city – maybe 40K from here. And it's the New Thwaites Glacier."

"Well, luckily, this *is* an emergency. A quick stop at my hotel, then we can go together. Ohh!" A sudden idea struck her. "If we have to search for Michael, I know someone who'd be super helpful." She winced. "Though he might not be hugely happy with me."

"Why not?" asked Bobby. "An' why'd you all say 'ohh' in a big secret way about P1 an' P2 and C-N goin' down, before? And what's 'ass'?"

"He's not happy because he was grumpy after our strange adventure in the storm up top, last night," Leeth lied, trying to distract Bobby. It kind of worked, since suddenly they all wanted to know about her 'strange adventure'.

She was still telling the tale, over sorbets, when a pod cab arrived – the electric vehicles run by a simple AI sub-system unaffected by the high-level CityNet outage. Shaped like a chubby beetle, its large windows stretched between structural elements colored like iridescent jewels, echoing many of the city's buildings. This pod was emerald.

But as soon as they'd piled inside, Bobby demanded again to know about the 'ohh' moment. Leeth looked at Amy, but she just shrugged as if to say 'Bobby's stubborn like that'.

"Shh, I need to call Mr Yakone and see if I can convince him to come with us to find Michael." She put her Link on speaker and made the call. "He's from the Arctic," she told the kids. "He's magical."

Those tidbits, plus her suggestion to Mr Yakone about doing spirit experiments out on the edge of the continent, away from the city, was enough to distract Bobby until the cab reached the hotel.

"Wait here," she told them as they pulled up by the main entrance. "I should only be a few minutes, okay?"

With that she was out of the cab and hurrying inside. Touching her choker, she barreled into the fire stairs and *really* hurried once out of sight. She saw no cameras but spoke low anyway, keeping her head down to hide her lips just in case. "Message home: Mr Yakone spoke to Godsson at the Institute before he came here." She hoped it wasn't a mistake, telling Eagle that. Surely they wouldn't recall them both? She pressed on. "Maybe find out what they talked about? Oh, and I've got access to Paradawn – leaving to head there in a few minutes." She hit Send, hoping she'd made the right decision.

Breathing harder, she burst out onto the sixth floor and slowed to a fast walk to her room. Inside she flung a few clothes into her hand luggage, and after a long pause, the death god's dagger too.

Who knew what waited, at Paradawn, beside and below the New Thwaites Glacier?

Chapter 30 – Sub-shelf pod

In his dreams Adlartok Kallik Yakone had walked a nightmare path between gray mold coating icy walls and ground. Spongy underfoot, it burst, releasing spores into the air that ate into the sealskin soles of his moccasins.

The insistent and increasing buzz of his Link had been a welcome lifeline, the dream leaving him only reluctantly. Of course, it was Bonnie Parker – with a mad request to travel across the continent with a group of children to find a missing child-sorcerer...

He rubbed at his forehead, Uentshiksruk around his neck equally disturbed. Which meant his dream had held a seed of truth.

He checked the time: he'd had over eleven hours of sleep! But he could eat in the pod, Bonnie Parker had brightly assured him. The total journey would take under four hours.

Perhaps the girl had not changed so much from her fourteen-year-old self. Sighing, but pleased his outside skins had dried in the hotel air, he repacked – his precious spirit eggs, carefully – and descended to the lobby, sinking into a deeply comfortable chair to rest his eyes.

Where he saw Bonnie Parker charge in and, strangely, enter the fire stairs.

On a whim, he left his body and followed her. The fire stair door was a metal composite, and his spirit form ghosted through, though he felt uncomfortable: a painful prickling across his astral form, like nothing he'd sensed before coming to this strange continent. Cold, too, which made a curious if disturbing sense.

But Bonnie Parker was not on the stairs. Steeling himself, counting turns, he swiftly followed the stairwell up, seeing the door onto their floor closing. He passed through it and saw the girl enter her room down the corridor.

Had he slowed? Was this southern continent so strange? Troubled, he slid through her door and into her room.

She moved like a whirlwind, pausing only at a dark, foggy block. He moved closer, mental hackles rising. Uentshiksruk flowed toward it, then shrank back. *Danger,* it warned him.

Danger? Its edges were hard to see. Bonnie Parker picked up the opaque fog and packed it away.

Strange.

Then she lifted her head, as if listening. On a sudden hunch he backed away; and her head slowly turned toward him.

How? Her aura had *sharpened,* too; its colors more saturated, her will more focused. He sensed an odd intensity to her movements, like *nanuk̦* hunting prey.

Bonnie Angelique Parker was not normal. Perhaps she *was* the daughter of Melisande d'Artelle: that would make her a good liar, too. He paused, debating whether to stay or leave.

Leave! little Uentshiksruk warbled to his soul. After one moment more of observation, with his own sense of danger surging, he did.

Returning to his body, he flexed his hands, trying to settle back into his body. As if his soul no longer quite fit. He felt tired, as if he had kayaked many hours over cold dark seas.

But he gave no more sign than a nod when she emerged from the elevator with her luggage.

Soon they were squeezed into a rounded pod cab, a lustrous emerald, with four children – introduced only as Amy, Yuri, Nadeep, Bobby – and a woman, Shona Adaptec-Brown. The story spilled from them in a torrent of words like a game of catch, the woman both afraid and relieved, the children excited and worried, and Bonnie Parker: excited also, yet oddly satisfied.

The journey across the city took less than an hour, ending in a building like one of many, except built into the wall of the city's enclosing geodesic roof. Here were factories, the woman Shona Adaptec-Brown explained. "Fabs for chips and organs. Paused now – warehouses full, after a day of production with no shipments out. Thank the stars flights *out* have at least resumed. Though people are questioning that, after the business jet crash late last night. Everything's falling apart! Half my friends are pushing this incredible new social implant – made right here, released just this morning. Everyone's nervous. We *need* C-N back up!"

Bonnie Angelique Parker patted the woman's thigh; she blinked as if surprised by her own outburst.

They arrived at a two-story structure built into the side of the overarching dome. Here, each triangular section of roof was a pale composite material, no display screens providing light and the illusion of sky and plains.

Exiting the cab, metal doors in the building rolled open for them, closing after they entered. Hunter senses came alert, his nostrils reflexively flaring, scenting for *nanuk̦*. At its lack, his tension eased.

Inside the large vaulted space a sleek pod as big as a whale floated, glistening like oyster shell and bobbing like a kayak in calm waters. The channel it rested in led to two large closed doors in the dome wall itself.

The woman strode up to the iridescent pod. "Shona Adaptec-Brown emergency authorization," she told her personal drone. Pearl doors in the cross-continent pod opened and the children poured inside. "I'm so going to get fired for this," she said.

Bonnie Angelique Parker hugged the woman before stepping inside. "If we save Michael's life, it'll be worth it." Her small feathered drone, Bhaji, swooped down from its apparently excited survey of the meager amenities of the station to land on her shoulder.

Letting his senses dip into the Imaginal, he Percepted ripples of warmth and caring across Bonnie Angelique Parker's aura as her gaze swept the children waiting inside. Then it sharpened into defensive alertness, and she turned and saw him, as if aware of his Sight.

Dropping it, he entered, noting the pod's roof was a clear window. He helped the women stow the group's luggage while the children took seats together and buckled themselves in.

"West Antarctic Sub-Shelf transit pod Two departing for Paradawn, no stops. Arrival at 16:32, average speed 520 kilometers per hour. Toilet and vending facilities at the rear."

The doors in the dome wall opened as those of the pod closed with a barely audible hiss, and they began accelerating. Only the rising sound of wind and the faster passage of the overhead lights indicated their increasing speed. A central transparent strip in the tunnel roof itself revealed the ice sheet directly above. The acceleration continued for a full minute before easing.

"Can we go to the front now, Miss Shona?" Bobby asked,

before leading Bonnie Parker to a wide curved windscreen that stared ahead into the tunnel, now descending in a gentle gradient.

Yakone sensed it followed the contours of the bedrock beneath the ice sheet above: dug *into* the bedrock, the massive ice sheet's glacial movement just meters above their heads. He closed his eyes.

"What's the 'ohh' secret?" he heard the young boy demand.

On a whim, he left his body, fighting an odd reluctance. Again the cold, and something else he could not name. He clenched his spirit to itself; held himself to himself then launched himself forward.

But the cold *ate* at him.

So: no scouting.

He returned, re-entering the pod and in turn his own body. Warmth flooded him, but also an inner ache.

After a last quick look around, seeing nothing changed, he moved to the rear, to forage food from the 'vending facilities'.

Chapter 31 – Ripples building

Eagle heard Leeth's terse message with dismay. Yakone had *spoken* to Godsson?! One of the most powerful mages now alive. Certainly the most dangerous; and not merely due to his madness.

Calling up the visitor logs to the Institute, there it was: the Inuit shaman had brought a criminal 'colleague' for incarceration and treatment two months earlier, but visited to check on progress just three days ago.

There was no indication of anything untoward on either occasion; not even an enquiry into Godsson's current status. But trusting Leeth, Eagle dug deeper – and found a one hour gap between the time Yakone had spoken to the Director, and when his cab had left.

A search of the video surveillance for that missing hour turned up nothing more than inmates in the gardens – and a note of a deleted video from the corridor outside Godsson's cell, due to 'camera malfunction'.

Heart sinking, his shoulders sagged. Ever since Leeth's childhood breaches of the system, even 'uninteresting' security video from the Institute was routinely kept. Yet 55 minutes of video had been deleted. By Brian Shanahan, he saw.

The Institute's security officer feared Godsson: there was no way he would have deleted anything related to the inmate. Shanahan must have been mind-controlled.

That Yakone could do that was an unwelcome surprise, but the *angákkuq*'s dossier was thin. And he now accompanied Leeth. Still, if there was anyone trained to sense and defend herself from such magic, it was Leeth – thanks to the Doctor.

He would arrange for Harmon to visit the madman and question him, despite the slim chance of learning anything useful.

But something else was troubling him. Something about the history of Yakone's criminally insane colleague. He called up the Institute's admission record again.

"No." Surely not!

Eagle brought his emotions under control. Just because Inuksuk had visited Washington-

But there it was: the other Inuit had met with Worthington. 'Ecological conservation' talks. Eagle drew a long, slow breath. The Foe's web had reached into the Arctic Circle.

And of course that shock of revelation was followed by the prickle of awakened attention, seeking the source. Carefully controlling his thoughts, from long practice, he read the reports from the treating meta-psychotherapists, with swiftly cemented certainty. Inuksuk had fallen to the Foe.

Again the sense of psychic sniffing: something standing behind him. He shunted the topic to a cerebral augment: *«A Foe-corrupted inmate is now incarcerated at the Institute for Paranormal Dysfunction: what effects?»*

Leaning back in his chair, fingers steepled, Eagle stared unseeingly at the vase and flowers on his otherwise glacially empty desk. Then called his old friend. "It's Antarctica. Things are happening."

Abrams chuckled. "So soon? How long has she been there – twelve hours?"

Eagle didn't smile. "Fifteen." *Hold back the worst, for now.* He gave a quick summary: Leeth's situation, Nelson's news.

"So the memory rewriting technology genie may be back in the bottle? Except for you and your people."

"Yes." Provided Leeth could find and destroy any Writer the AI had already built.

"I'm not sure I trust even you with such power, old friend. At least with mind control magic, the instigator can only be an individual mage. Not any sufficiently wealthy company that obtains the plans."

Eagle sighed. "I know."

"And in the hands of your youthful idiot savant? I assume Mother is unaware of Nelson's success?"

"Of course. And he's aware the data must not leak."

"'Aware'."

"I know. I plan to discuss it with the Doctor. Perhaps framing it as a challenge: assuming it leaks, model the consequences, and how to detect and counter it."

"The Doctor," Abrams said, "speaking of mind control magic. So, no doubt also Suggesting Nelson should look at it that way." The folds of Abrams's face wrinkled in distaste.

"I'll Cast, and See," he said at last.

"Thank you. But that isn't why I called."

Abrams nodded. "I've been waiting. I fear it may have started: that subtle, stealthy growth. I'll check that, first."

"Yes: Nelson says a few people are socially withdrawing."

At that moment, Eagle's augment presented its answer to his earlier query, summarized by just one word. *«Sterilize.»*

He activated Scenario Argus. Something must have shown in his face.

"What?"

"Merry."

At his codename, Abrams came to full alert.

"Leeth said Yakone spoke to Godsson. Visited him."

"*What?* When?!"

"Three days ago, visiting an Inuit individual Yakone had brought to the Institute two months ago. The *angakkuq* he brought was..." Eagle touched his temple, chest, then made a mouth-zipper gesture, sharing the thought-locked-away: corrupted by The Foe.

"This person is at the Institute? Tell me, kept far from Godsson?"

Eagle shook his head.

"Kill this angakkuq inmate. At once."

Eagle nodded. "Underway. Cyanide gas, delivered by robot, to avoid contamination. And we're evacuating Sonoma now – 'radioactive meteorite'."

He didn't need to add: *in case Godsson breaches his cell.* Suddenly unsure their ultimate fallback would be adequate, if Godsson knew of it. But did he?

"Do you have recordings of Yakone's discussion with Godsson?"

"No. Deleted, by the head of Security there, who I trust."

"I think there's a good argument for the death penalty for the use of mind control magic," Abrams said.

"Even when used to prevent the spread of mind control *technology*?" He watched his old friend frown, considering the implication: Harmon using Suggestion on Nelson to prevent him disseminating the Omega technology; or worse, using it for himself.

Abrams's grimace was his answer.

This day just kept getting worse. "Anyway, if the Institute isn't a radioactive crater in the next hour, I'll send the Doctor to interview Godsson."

"That's unlikely to work," Abrams said.

"Probably. But as his therapist for ten years, one of the few for whom repeated contact didn't send insane-"

"Like Leeth herself, in that respect."

Eagle nodded and continued. "-he is our best to chance to get even a hint. Unless Leeth can find out from Yakone directly."

"Perhaps. Or perhaps merely learn exactly what Godsson *wants* us to." Abrams pursed his lips. "Very well. In the meantime, I'll... *revisit* my Antarctic premonition. Let us hope Leeth's shaman hasn't been warped, by a single conversation."

With shared grim expressions, the two men ended the call.

Chapter 32 – In the lair of the beast

Leeth settled back in her seat, gazing up through the pod's clear ceiling. Transparent windows in the tunnel roof two meters above revealed the intense blue of the ice sheet's depths. It zoomed past in a rhythm of brightening and dimming illumination as they flashed past the overhead lights in the tunnel.

That tunnel had been the second stage of the Newtopian Consortium's massive engineering effort to restore the West Antarctic Ice Shelf and lower global sea levels.

With the ancient plains exposed, ground down by eons of slow moving ice sheets, carving the dual 'tunnels' had been the simplest part. Twin 1,200 kilometer trenches, sealed with green concrete made on-site and inset with thick windows of a cold-resistant glass composite.

Then the real engineering began. A first reflective 'paint' of chalk had cooled six million square kilometers. Sub-sea curtains blocked the undersea current that had undermined the Thwaites Glacier and let the vast ice shelf behind it slide into the sea. Then the mighty cooling engines had started up, chilling cubic kilometers of water below freezing, the heat shifted to parts of the infrared spectrum that could be radiated into space.

In her studies for this mission, she'd boggled at the energy expenditure: by the end, using ten percent of the whole world's output, from arrays of geothermal and thorium power plants constructed assembly-line fashion. Even today, Newtopia exported that power via exotic undersea superconductors to South America, much of it used there to pump Phasion cells full of power.

The pod raced through the dark in a near straight line, slowly rising and falling as it followed the gentle contours of eons-scoured terrain, buried again now under kilometers of ice. Ice formed from water desalinated and pumped via the pod tunnels, then chilled to minus 20°C and sprayed in an instantly freezing mist. Mountains built of snow, spread across the land by prevailing harsh winds for twenty years.

The whole process had only eased in the last five.

She looked around. Mr Yakone had fallen asleep. So too, most of the children. All but Amy. The girl, catching her eye, bit her lip and approached, taking the seat beside her with a shy smile, looking away with her hands in her lap, sitting oddly stiffly. Expectantly?

What was she supposed to do? Leeth tried not to let her sudden tension show. Was she supposed to say something? She hadn't been trained for this!

Amy's shoulders slumped. The girl hunched in on herself, and Leeth quailed, somehow sure she was failing her, in ways she didn't even understand. Amy was an orphan. They all were. *Like me.*

Was that part of it? She stared at the sleeping jumble of boys around Shona – Bobby's head tucked into the woman's side – and a funny pain started in Leeth's chest. A shortness of breath.

A flash of memory: a woman, firelight, long black hair, a soft song.

She timidly stretched out an uncertain arm to gather Amy in against her side. A moment of stiffness, then the girl *melted* into her embrace.

For some reason, Leeth had to blink back tears.

By the time she'd fought those off, Amy's breathing had settled to something slow and regular, and Leeth felt something deep within herself relax, too. Thaw? Closing her eyes she let the gentle, silent rising and falling of the pod lull her to sleep too, Amy a small warmth under her protective arm.

"Paradawn." A tone chimed pleasantly. "Doors will open on the left."

Leeth blinked awake, a wisp of dream memory of a young girl evading her grasp, even as a small warm body snuggled against her and wriggled closer: Amy, her seat belt unclasped, nestled under her arm. Something about the warmth, or the trust, the nutmeg and vinegar scent of the girl, unmoored her, tugging her in a direction she had no map for.

Then Nadeep cried out, "We're here!" and Amy jerked awake, blinking dreams from her brown eyes, a hesitant smile trembling on her lips.

"Please exit the pod." A note of demand infused the otherwise mellow robotic voice.

Nadeep and Yuri were piling the luggage by the exit, and Shona was picking up Bobby, still sound asleep, and making her way to them.

"Exit the pod." The mellow synthetic voice held a stronger note of 'or else', now.

Mr Yakone hadn't stirred. "What would happen if we didn't exit?" she asked Amy, who'd taken her hand, gently tugging her in the direction of the open doors on the pod's left side.

"I don't know. Take you round the loop, then back to Newtopia?" She waved toward the windscreen of the pod, and the tracks disappearing into a tunnel curving out of sight. The pod rested in a huge empty room, its lights still turning on.

"Mr Yakone?" Leeth prodded him, listening to his slow in-drawn breath. *I bet he's outside his body, scouting astrally.*

She stretched out a hand, reaching toward his neck, wondering if his familiar was wrapped around it; wondering if she'd be able to feel it? Maybe if she stretched out her claws just a little? Not to hurt, just to-

The shaman's eyes snapped open, his head jerking to watch her hand even as she withdrew it.

He sat up. "I find no true people here. No life but we. Under ice. Small, not like Newtopia City. Many tunnels."

"Leave the pod," the voice snapped.

"Our pod's getting angry," she told him, noting Nadeep and Yuri standing outside now with their luggage, frowning back at them.

"You slept for one hour thirty three minutes," Bhaji told her.

Slinging her carry-on luggage over her left shoulder, she took Amy's hand with her right, to keep her farthest from Tezsh's dagger, and together they exited, Mr Yakone following. The door hissed shut, the sharp-nosed pod accelerating immediately away into the poorly lit tunnel, silent but for the hum of the magnetic induction coils levitating it.

The little group stood in a very empty, cold, unpromising place. A sign mounted above a row of a dozen seats declared 'Paradawn Arrivals'.

It reminded her of a factory. Massive earth-moving machines, one she recognized as a tunnel borer, occupied a distant corner of the uninspiring station. Long parallel gouges scarred rough granite walls that curved in as they rose upward – carved by the borer? Above, a flat false ceiling of tiles. Probably to make it easier to keep the place warm.

Paradawn was where the re-icing of the whole Western Ice Shelf had started: a vast engineering site, largely automated, dug into the bedrock on the edge of the glacier. The first geothermal taps had been drilled here.

Scant signage indicated restrooms, but otherwise the space looked more like an emptied out warehouse than a well-used transportation link.

"This way," Amy said, pointing to a pair of large double doors.

At their approach they slid open, more lights switching on. A ten meter diameter passage stretched ahead, circular in cross-section but with a flattened ceiling and a floor leveled by foamed rock.

"Across there's where you leave to go to Newtopia," Amy said, pointing down the passage to matching double doors. "We left our scooters there." Twisting back to the platform they'd just left, her arm swept an arc from right to left. "The pods arrive here but loop around to there. To Departures." She frowned and pointed to a junction halfway down the passage. "We need to go left there to get home, but we only have four scooters."

"I can order a Kart!" Yuri said, going to a panel on the wall.

"Where home?" asked Mr Yakone.

"From here, left, third right, second left," Nadeep told him.

The shaman blinked.

"Ten minutes by scooter," Amy added.

"We pass the kitchen on the way," Yuri helpfully clarified. "Last left, before home."

"There's plenty of spare bunks," Amy told Bonnie. "And we have *lots* of showers and baths. Gynie bathes Bobby, but the rest of us wash ourselves."

At his name, Bobby grumbled in Shona's arms.

"I tell P1 and P2 when *they* need to wash," Yuri said with pride.

Amy put a finger to her chin. "Not anymore, Yuri. A week

ago they *asked* about bathing, remember, and started doing it each day like we said they should."

Leeth felt her hackles rise. "P1 and P2 are the 'not real people'?"

Yuri, Nadeep, and Amy exchanged looks, and nodded.

"Just how long have you guys lived here?"

This time the looks they exchanged were downright shifty.

"That's secret," Amy said at last.

Shona tensed, her shoulders pulling in.

Leeth saw Mr Yakone notice that, too. "How *long* they've been here is a secret?" she asked the woman.

Shona gave a jerky nod.

"That makes no sense! Why is *that* a secret?"

"Keep safe," Bobby murmured sleepily, head tucked in against Shona's neck.

This time, they all tensed.

"*Safe?!*" Leeth demanded.

"Safe from what?" she added, when no one spoke.

Until Bobby said, clear as day, "'Sassins."

"Shh," Shona hissed, but Bobby squirmed in her arms, waking, wriggling to be put down, even as the word slid through Leeth like a blade of ice.

"What are sassins?" asked Mr Yakone.

But Shona saw it: a moment of stillness in Bonnie Parker, and a sudden poker face. It shocked like ice water.

Clutching Bobby tighter she backed away from the two strangers she'd brought here, her mind racing. *How did she talk me into breaching security?* And now she was alone with them, unarmed, the children defenseless, and the nearest help half a continent away. *What have I done? I must've been crazy!*

"You Spelled me!" she accused Parker.

"What?! I did *not* – I can't! And I would *never!*"

But the shaman had jerked at the accusation, and now stared at his companion. Had she duped him too? Or had *he* Spelled them? Putting herself in front of the older boys, Shona drew herself upright and reached for Amy, who evaded her hand. "You won't get away with it!" Shona swore. "Stay behind me, Nadeep, Yuri. *Come here*, Amy!"

But Amy stared from Shona to Bonnie Parker, still holding her hand. "Shona, Miss Bonnie's not an assassin! Are you, Miss?"

A sickening hole yawned in Leeth's belly as innocent brown eyes, unaware she'd exploited her trust to gain access here, stared up into hers.

"No," she lied.

It had never been harder to wrestle a smile to her face. The falsehood curdled in her belly. But as the nausea burned off, it hardened into adamantine resolve. "I'll keep you all safe, I swear. If it's the last thing I do."

"*I'll* keep you safe too!" Bhaji piped, launching himself into the air to fly at top speed, circling the area scanning for threats.

"Come on," Leeth told Shona, meeting her still doubting eyes. "We're here now, and actions speak louder than words. The important thing's to find Michael. Where will this cart Yuri ordered turn up?"

A distant electric turbine hum and the whisper of wheels on concrete said it was fast approaching.

"This way," Amy smiled, still holding her hand, and led her toward the intersection of tunnels.

She turned back to see Mr Yakone still staring at her, his gaze other worldly.

"I didn't Spell anybody – I can't *do* spells!"

He just watched her.

Chapter 33 – A difficult conversation

Despite the new bespoke automated cab system – the only way now to visit the Institute of Paranormal Dysfunction – Harmon noted that a security drone still double-checked both occupant and exterior of the vehicle before the gates slid open and the cab proceeded.

Little had changed here, environmentally: the same faux crenelations on the buildings; even the scarring on the final stretch of driveway from the exploding rocket was still visible if you knew to look for it. In contrast, the replacement of human personnel by gynoids and androids appeared complete. Two p.m., inmates strolled the grounds, each accompanied by a robot nurse with the new BioGene easy-clean mycelium-based SynthSkin dermis. They boasted a full range of human facial expressions and body language. With the latest emotion detection algorithms, and trained for their primary care recipient, their mood assessments were more accurate than all but the most empathic humans.

They were also immune to anything short of gross physical-effect magic.

Godsson found his new AI therapist frustrating in the extreme. Harmon knew that, since despite being removed as the madman's primary therapist, the Department still had him review each session.

It never took long, since Godsson's interactions consisted exclusively of periods of complete dismissal of the artificial therapist, and the occasional statement directed at Harmon, clearly indicating he knew the back channel existed.

Harmon knew far less of the other inmates. Stepping from the cab, which locked and secured itself behind him, he scanned the forecourt and gardens. For the most part the inmates looked surprisingly normal, although one middle-aged woman, gagged, glared at him while she worked restlessly at the unresponsive first two fingers of her hands.

He grimaced. Such surgery was generally reserved for mages who had mastered illegal mental influence magic. His own fingers twitched in guilty sympathy.

A short happy bark and the whine of powerful servomotors signaled Faith's arrival. Turning in the direction of Brian Shanahan's security shack, he saw Leeth's childhood companion abruptly slow as she saw he was alone. Several pups raced past her to tumble over his feet.

He was most careful in stepping over them, as the cybernetic guard dog's red eyes scanned him up and down. Her nostrils flared, and her head dropped an inch, her mouth clamping shut. It was too easy to read it as a dismissal of him, at scenting his lack of contact with Leeth.

A short bark and she turned her back on him, the school of pups flowing around his legs to rejoin their mother, even as Shanahan approached.

"Sarah's not wi' you, Doctor," he observed.

"No," Harmon agreed, biting back a more caustic response.

"Probably jest as well, given who you're here to see." He didn't look happy. "He dis'na get visitors. Still, you'll have to see the Director even though your visit's bin authorized."

"No one else has been to see Godsson in the last month?" he asked, making the necessary gestures out of Shanahan's line of sight even as he eased the mental probe into the older, grizzled man's mind.

"Visitor? For Godsson? Heh, no. That divil's had no one call. No one's allowed!"

And there it was: no one but him would have sensed it, but there was a hollow, a kind of puzzled emptiness, where the memory had been clumsily scrubbed. So Eagle had been right: the Inuit shaman had tampered with the man's mind, which meant not only had he visited Godsson, but compelled Shanahan to erase the security recordings.

"Sarah's not bin asking to visit, not bin requesting him to be set free?" More than a little fear threaded the words, and Harmon sensed the damage from several nights of poor sleep. No doubt the shaman had only scrubbed the conscious memories, not bothering to erase those roots that ran deeper. Careless, or simply pressed for time?

An uncharacteristic pity filled him. "You look tired." He raised his hands, pausing with them by the security officer's temples. "If you wish...?"

Shanahan looked surprised, and from the corner of his eye Harmon saw Faith move into his line of sight, watching.

"Well, sure and I wouldn't say no, if you have the time."

Harmon nodded, placed his hands on the man's temples, and shaped a simple physical healing spell, stimulating repairs to the blood-brain barrier and reducing an incipient inflammatory response. Then smoothed over the areas of ripped-out memories.

The whole process took just minutes. Shanahan sighed in relief, swaying on his feet as Harmon concentrated. At last his shoulders slumped and his tension visibly eased.

Nodding at the man's thanks, Harmon followed him inside to what would be a tedious but hopefully brief interview with the director. Truth be told, he welcomed the delay.

He felt an acid burn in his stomach at the thought of the interview that would follow.

Shanahan keyed the security pad, concealing the number he entered before leaning in for a retinal blood flow scan.

The door, more suited to a submarine, swung open – undoubtedly upgraded since Leeth had physically torn the previous model off its hinges. Harmon shook his head, strangely heartened by the memory even as he remembered she had been tricked by the mage.

Shifting his gaze to the Imaginal, he saw the Barriers in very good shape, perhaps sharper than they had been since the Dragon had originally helped him set them. Or rather, since he had assisted Lord Lao Pi Shen in erecting them.

He wondered who Eagle had found to refurbish them. No doubt Abrams. But as he examined the work more carefully, he frowned. It appeared more subtle than the Dragon Lord's! Just who the devil *was* Abrams?!

Shanahan's shuffling feet recalled him to his real task. "Ah, I'll be waitin' here, Doctor." But other than that, he gave no indication of impatience. Indeed, he offered a sympathetic look.

Firming his resolve Harmon strode down the corridor toward the cell door, his senses still attuned to the Imaginal, his hackles raised and heart pounding.

Relax, Alex: he is securely locked away, magically contained, and Leeth dealt with the invisible *spirits.*

He swallowed, remembering that night, of rockets, and Faith, and Leeth plunging her hand into her own chest-

Growling, he presented himself before the solid window

looking into Godsson's room, and saw the mad mage himself sitting comfortably across the room, facing the window as if expecting him.

He looked well. That damnable smile twisted the corners of his lips as he rose and approached the door. He hadn't changed at all.

Something about that thought scratched along his spine, then Godsson was at the intercom and tapping its screen on his side.

Harmon did the same on his, opening the digital voice channel, a question slipping away even as he grasped for it.

Godsson's smile twitched. "Alex. So kind of you to visit."

Harmon mentally squared his shoulders.

"Especially as you've lost your position as my disciple."

Harmon ignored the gibe. If there was one thing he did not regret, it was losing his position as the madman's therapist. "You had an old acquaintance visit, three days ago."

"Did I? You'll have to refresh my memory. I get so many visitors."

"Adlartok Kallik Yakone. The Aleutian Islands shaman who Leeth jumped when she was fourteen."

"Is that his true name? How interesting: 'clear sky lightning blood spray on snow'? Poetically foreboding, don't you think? And I assume you mean your young Seductress, Li'ith?"

"She is not Lilith," Harmon snapped, off-balanced by the linguistic revelation: they had sent Leeth to Antarctica accompanying a shaman with such an ominous name? He would check the translation but Godsson, knowing that, would not have lied. Godsson rarely outright lied. It was part of what made him so dangerous: his ability to distort and exploit the truth. Or his twisted version of it.

"And how is your daughter?" Godsson put a finger to his chin in thought. "Though I would hazard to guess you have not seen her in some while. You look... *pent up*."

"We have recordings, you know," Harmon lied, and saw the other mage smile.

"Then you would know we merely discussed his brother angakkuq, Inuksuk. A most disturbing case. I assume you know the fellow had returned a few months prior from a visit to Washington? You should tell Eagle his time is running out to deal with that problem. The demon's influence spreads like mold, and burning spores is a mere stopgap."

Harmon's gut clenched. *The Department's 'Foe'?* Buried under earth, safe inside the Barrier surrounding the entire Institute for Paranormal Dysfunction, Harmon should have been safe. But at the mere thought, he felt the stealthy prickle of *attention,* and jerked his thoughts away. Yet Godsson seemed to feel no such threat.

"Why did you want Yakone to travel to the Newtopian Territories?" Harmon demanded, making his best guess.

"I prefer to use its original name: Antarctica. There is a power in Old names." His smile was crafty, as if relishing secret knowledge. "An entire continent never inhabited by Man. It makes you wonder what strange magic might be possible there. Why mages who try to visit astrally, often never return."

Of course Godsson would know that. And if he knew that, what else did he know, or guess? Why had he wanted Yakone to go there? With Leeth accompanying him?

"I hope you advised her not to seduce the shaman."

Harmon managed not to wince.

"Still mourning his wife, a sin like that might destabilize him. A pity you never taught your daughter morals: it might have allowed you to also teach her who to trust. But that would have ruled *you* out Alex, would it not? Who knows what strange ideas she now accepts as truth."

Harmon shrugged off the barb, but mentally noted the claim of Yakone's wife's death. "It's stranger to me that you would encourage her association with a pagan, a shaman; especially one for whom she held a childish crush. I thought the whole 'Leading into temptation' was your enemy's role, not yours." The jab scored, Harmon saw.

"Morals aside," Godsson countered, "I was impressed by what you had begun to achieve with your daughter. Even I was surprised by the potential your unconventional experiment revealed."

This time, Harmon rose to the needling. "'Daughter', Godsson? Really, you disappoint me."

"She could have been though, Alex, couldn't she?" Godsson's smile was vicious. "Do you ever regret your decision not to adopt her when you had the chance?"

Acid roiled Harmon's stomach. One day he would look back, psychoanalyze himself, try-

"What must be most galling for you is that even *could you* undo it, she'd reject any offer to change, wouldn't she? She *likes* what you've made her into."

It was true. At least he had done that much for her. She believed in herself, loved herself. Even as she hated him.

"But what would she say, do you think, if you offered to unlock her remaining potential?" Godsson asked, sounding genuinely curious. "Does she have Will enough to become her full self?"

Of course she did, but he had given up hope of-

"Probably never from you though, eh Alex? And irony of all ironies, you can never publish your theory. Can you imagine its reception? What would you call it? *Torture as a Means to Magical Unfolding'?* Still, she may yet discover herself: it needn't be *you* who tortures her, eh? Perhaps the shaman, or Antarctica itself, will do that for you.

"Just leave it to blind chance. Let Life have its way with her.

"Or you could bring her here to me," Godsson said with sudden intensity. "Two days. Two days with her is all I would need, to finish your work for you and prove your theory. You used her to seed a new Archetype, didn't you? The Huntress. Oh, Alex; what I could do... *for* her."

Harmon stared at him, shock and horror reverberating through him in equal measure. But Godsson hadn't finished.

"But your perversions also connected her to the Seductress Archetype. I do not call her Lilith for my amusement.

"How well developed is your theory though, Alex? Do you grasp the consequences and possibilities of multiple such connections?" He shook his head, pretending regret. "And two would tear any soul apart. But *four?* Really man, how do you expect her to survive that? The Seductress *calls* even Archetypes, you see."

Harmon felt a chill run through him. *He was lying. He had to be!* Yet hadn't Abrams said as much? 'You've done a very dangerous thing: activating Archetypes. Mixing them.'

He failed to hide his shock; then, seeing Godsson's reaction and knowing the man's love of grandstanding, played up his bafflement. "But why Antarctica?" He used the continent's old name, not Newtopia, to avoid sidetracking the fellow into a rant on megacorporate overreach.

"Anything becomes easier when there is no resistance."

A certain slyness told Harmon there was more. "But the meager reports we have all say magic is *more* difficult in Antarctica. So what becomes easier there?"

Godsson said nothing, merely looked smug. So: he *had* told Yakone that some magic would be easier? "You can't know that," Harmon mused. "You have been held *here* since 2047: sixteen years." Again, that momentary sense he was overlooking something. But Godsson gestured for him to continue, and he quickly recovered his train of thought. "And before that, with the massive melt and sea-level rise, the terrible storms... the bases abandoned years before: no one dared travel there during those years. So you cannot have any experience of Antarctica's metaphysical landscape. And apart from all that, you follow the hermetic tradition, not the shamanic. Yet you encouraged an Inuit shaman to go there.

"So I ask myself, why? Pulling wings off insects is not your style. Ergo, you imagine it will progress your plan to 'Perfect' humanity by neutering them spiritually."

"Removing their animal impulses will *uplift* mankind Alex, not neuter it. You for example, with your history, could have benefited from such an operation."

Harmon grimaced, but saw his own arrow had struck close to the mark. "You know of the artificial sentience there, don't you?"

Godsson's eyes narrowed fractionally.

"Hah! But if you expect the shaman to somehow fall prey to it you have miscalculated. What you don't know is that something took the AGI out of action and kept it out of action." *And if anyone can make that condition permanent, Leeth can.*

But Godsson's look turned poisonous. "Still such faith in your precious Huntress, Alex? Even after all she's done to you. Her claws can't protect her *back* though, can they? Nor her ears hear that which grows in silence."

Harmon felt cold: Godsson knew of some *other* threat. "You encouraged Yakone to, what? Try to open himself to the AGI? *Because* you think he would be especially vulnerable? But magic and technology don't mix."

Godsson's eyes snapped from his, the inmate abruptly turning his back and going to his bunk.

The interview was over. Harmon knew the signs.

Yet he felt off balance, as if the world had shifted under his feet: Godsson believed that somehow, someone in New-topia had bridged the gap between magic and technology.

Down the corridor, Brian Shanahan looked equal parts re-lieved and disturbed as Harmon left the mage's cell.

"You get somewhere, Doc?" he asked.

"Yes, Shanahan. I think I did." *And the stars help us.*

He sent his recording of the meeting, with added notes, including Godsson's assertion of Yakone's wife's death.

How strange, Harmon thought as the lift descended to Base-ment Level Five. *To feel pleased my access has not been re-scinded.* For almost two years he had effectively been a pris-oner here.

Today the corridor walls depicted the woodlands around the Institute – until the final stretch that made it seem he now strode an icy plain. Probably the West Antarctic Ice Shelf. The door to Eagle's office, incongruous in a granite mountainside, slid open at his approach.

Inside, as he'd half expected, Abrams sat hunched in his life support wheelchair, waiting. The expanse of Eagle's desk was itself as white as an ice sheet, the well-remembered sin-gle vase and flower its only occupant.

"Your analysis, Doctor?" Eagle asked as he took a seat.

"Godsson hinted some magic may be easier down there, despite the few existing studies indicating the reverse." He watched Abrams closely. "Perhaps he meant metamagic, op-erations at the level of the Archetypes?" It was an area in which he and Abrams had recently collaborated, a little. Though Abrams knew far more than he cared to share.

At last Abrams nodded, looking far from happy. "It's pos-sible. There is no other place on Earth like Antarctica, magi-cally speaking. *Terra nullius,* if you will."

Abrams blinked, momentarily confused. The Latin phrase – it resonated strangely... But the thought, like a dream, slipped away, and he shook his head. "In some ways Antarc-tica resembles the world during prehistory, with just a mod-est human population. Far less life, though. So, could a fresh metamagical pattern take root? Yes, if held together long enough to imprint on what you call the collective uncon-scious, Dr Harmon."

Harmon clenched his teeth. "So she faces not just an AI

controlling the entire city, but the possible return of the fledgling Machine Archetype, Aiyami? What on earth have you sent her into?"

"'Earth' may be the key word, Doctor," Eagle admitted. "We fear the threat may not *be* entirely of this world."

Harmon absorbed that. "Your evidence?"

"My vault incident, please," Abrams asked Eagle.

Above the desk's alabaster surface, a hologram expanded: a snarling Leeth diving forward as she twisted, *almost* avoiding lashing, saw-toothed tentacles that ground into her flesh while she plunged Tezcatlipoca's obsidian blade into a swollen metal-gray nodule. All three men grimaced, remembering. Eagle zoomed and froze the video on the central node, now blurred but fragmenting.

"Whatever that was," said Abrams, "some melding of machine and organics, it fed on magic. Since the sacrificial dagger had been 'empty', the gray matter that had seeded that thing, coiled around the dagger's hilt, could only reproduce after the weapon was placed alongside other artifacts in my vault."

"Your point?" Harmon demanded, as Eagle dismissed the 3D image.

Abrams continued. "If a similar infestation appeared in Antarctica, it's likely the... *arid* metaphysical landscape there would have limited its ability to feed."

"*Would have* limited? You're saying it came from there? Or perhaps is now down there, growing? You've seen it?"

At Abrams's frown, he turned to Eagle. "No. So what evidence do you have?" When neither answered, Harmon's interest sharpened. "And the Tik Tek AI is still crashed?"

"For now," Eagle said. "We're calling it 'Ty'," he added.

Of course you are, Harmon thought, recognizing Leeth's naming style. "Perhaps you should have engaged whoever achieved that, rather than Leeth."

Neither man responded.

"And Nelson? Has *he* seen indications this 'alien' has taken over the computers in the absence of 'Ty'?"

Their auras *flinched* at the suggestion, but Abrams's was otherwise too smooth, too controlled. *He* was the source of the idea to send Leeth.

"Well, let us return to my analysis. Godsson still pursues his scheme to Perfect humanity by eradicating our 'animal impulses'.

"Shamans – especially the Inuit *angakkuq* – open themselves to what might be called spirit possession. If indeed some ghastly bridge is forming between magic and technology, I believe Godsson has set up Yakone for some form of mental takeover, either by these 'aliens', or by a projection of Aiyami. The Machine Archetype has already shown it can 'possess' someone modified by the Writer.

"Any other complications I should factor in to my analysis?"

The two men exchanged glances, and at the ripples in their auras, he braced himself.

"Leeth is once again armed with Tezcatlipoca's sacrificial dagger," Eagle admitted. "And the continent has the largest density of volcanoes of any on the planet. We may have overvalued the fact that most are extinct."

"Sweet buttered hell on blood-soaked toast," Harmon whispered. "That so-called death *god* has mastery over volcanoes."

"Er, and Leeth... annoyed it, when she took it up."

Harmon stared. "Words fail me," he said at last, standing. "Anything else? Yakone has not recognized Leeth as Sara? No? Good! Especially if Godsson's claim is true, and his wife is dead. Well, I suggest you warn him of Godsson as soon as possible. And now, to preserve my sanity, I shall return to my duties at the Ladies Academy.

"Unless you wish to send me down into this insane situation as well?"

Eagle shook his head. "We both know how she would react to that, Doctor."

"None of my new girls are a shadow of Leeth," Harmon grated, glaring at them both before stalking out.

Eagle watched him go, feeling pity for the man; recognizing in that, an echo of his own feelings: his own guilt.

But he had no one else with any chance of success. He just hoped a Leeth-shaped explosion of chaos was what the situation needed. Although given the temptation the death god represented to her personally should she need aid, he feared her ability to resist.

The last place on earth anyone would want a volcanic death god to return was Newtopia City: unlike in India's terrifying God Wars, using nukes on a god manifesting in

Antarctica could drown the world. For the second time in thirty years.

Soon after Abrams's departure, his door buzzed. Outside, their genius 'hacker' stood, looking pleased. Of course he'd arrived without appointment, no doubt hoping to be turned away to report digitally. Where he'd feel invincible.

Eagle let him in, catching the expected frustrated expression before the youth shook it off, a smug grin replacing it.

"Done! Complete copy of the Omega tech. Looks like the AI developed it a bit further, too." He glanced around the walls of the room, frowning at the icy plain stretching in every direction as the door behind him shut solidly.

"Really? Including wiping every copy?" Eagle asked.

Nelson threw himself into the seat opposite, draping one leg over an armrest. "Yep, thanks to Ghost. Found thirty-one in all. Nineteen in data vaults..."

Eagle let him brag about his discovery, then summed up the result. "So we now hold the only copy of the Omega tech. And only you and I know that."

"Yeah."

Eagle stared at him, saying nothing. The technology could rewrite human memories, even to the point of changing someone's very identity, leaving them unaware they'd been 'hacked'. Eventually, Eagle saw the message penetrate Nelson's skull. Then, that he should tell no one else. Or...

Nelson swallowed, knowing the Department *retired* people for far lesser threats to US security. That, in fact, was Leeth's special role.

He shivered. "Okay. I get it. Yeah, we have the only copy, and only you and I know." He hurried on. "Or we will have the only copy, soon. Right now, around the world, six hacked security bots are destroying the only physical copies from the final offline backups."

"Good. And yet, for the Tik Tek AI itself – Ty, as Leeth calls it – you found no backups."

Nelson dragged his leg off the armrest and sat up. "Yeah, that was super weird. Well, there was, I mean, I think there *is,* one. Uh, that's started reassembling itself. I think. We were lucky I was there to see it happen."

Eagle just stared at him, and Nelson felt sweat prickle his brow. "Yeah, the Tik Tek security systems are going crazy, fighting off an amazing attack coming from some kind of built-in hardware in its own systems. From ROM. That's-"

"I know what Read Only Memory is."

"Uh, yeah, it's like something's piecing *together* some swarm of agents with payloads faster than their security system can tear it *apart*."

"Let me guess: you were examining the code in question. So you isolated a chunk to analyze, and it escaped?"

Nelson froze, shocked. At last, he gave a shaky nod, but telling himself, *he doesn't know. He doesn't know.*

Eagle closed his eyes.

Nelson stiffened: for Eagle, that was the equivalent of a scream! Eagle opened his eyes. Did he look... stressed?

"Dismissed, Nelson. I'll inform Leeth."

Of the deadline, Nelson told himself. Not to... deal with whoever'd caused it.

Chapter 34 – Hitting the ground running

There'd been room in the 'Kart' for the kids to stack their e-Scooters, dumping them and the newcomers' bags in their rooms. Shona and Leeth in Amy's room, at her insistence. "Girls together." Leeth set her hand luggage, with Tezcatlipoca's sacrificial dagger sealed inside, on a high shelf. They'd unpacked, then all met at the 'kitchen' – a cafeteria sized for a workforce of fifty, not five children – where they all now sat sharing an early evening meal.

Leeth had sent Bhaji off to scout the maze of corridors and passages. The map of the underground complex built up on her Link, with Bhaji excitedly describing each major discovery – like the children's art on the walls.

They were seated around a large table, its interactive surface building a similar map, as the kids sketched out all the areas they knew, concentrating on places Michael might have gone.

"This is yummy, Miss Bonnie. You're a good cook!" Amy gushed, spooning up the creamy cheesy sauce of the seafood mornay.

"Your food unit's not so different to some I've used," Bonnie said, wolfing down the rich food, a little surprised by her own appetite. "It's just a matter of blending the taste components with the crunch-chewiness and other settings." She jotted down the settings she'd used on the tabletop, and Amy swiped it from there into her own child-Link.

"None of you know a way up to the surface from here?" she asked. "You're sure?" She eyed Mr Yakone, who'd scowled at the food printer and opted for a seafood broth and fast-bread, and was now 'dozing' in the chair opposite her. Every now and then he sat up to extend the map of their 'home' the kids were drawing, on the tabletop. In fact, he was astrally scouting the base as best he could. Sending his spirit out to pass invisibly through metal, concrete, and plastic walls and doors.

A human spirit couldn't ghost through real rock – she remembered Wolf, the Fist of Peace's shaman, telling her that

– her and the others, after his escape from the tunnels under the Dumps. Briefly, she wondered what the Fist of Peace were doing? Were they still together? That'd been an awesome mission.

Till they kicked you out.

She hunched her shoulders.

Though there was something funny going on with Mr Yakone. He was clearly tiring; and she'd swear he seemed to have to steel himself to leave his body. As if it hurt; or like something was scaring him? But when she asked if he was okay, he just grunted and ignored the question.

Men!

But the magic- or rather, the *metaphysical* journals said magic didn't work so well down here. It was one reason her cover story of a magic research expedition had been plausible. Then there was the whole business of mages being injured or dying from traveling to Antarctica in spirit form.

Maybe it wasn't just people's usual hostility to mages that made them so rare down here?

Bhaji swooped back into the cafeteria, showing off by winging up and down their table, swooping in and out of them all to the kids cheers, before taking up his perch on Bonnie's shoulder with a satisfied flourish, neatly folding his wings. He angled himself down to study the map.

"I found some extra places," he whispered just to her.

"So Bhaji, been exploring? Did you find anything interesting?" she prompted him, after careful thought.

The little drone projected extra lines on the map, labeled with the signs he'd read, adding names to areas Mr Yakone had sketched in. The medical bay; high tech manufacturing equipment; three sealed off areas, one for computer chip fabrication, another for new chip design facilities, and a third for 'biological simulations'. Plus lots of closets: storage, cleaning, spare parts, recharging bays... the kids happily wrote in the names on top of the projected spaces, competing to see who could fill in the most.

With protruding tongue, Bobby scrawled in 'Advanced Materials Research Laboratory' and 'X-Ray Lithography Fabrication Facilities', his childishly large letters filling the space inside two of the areas, then looked up hopefully from Shona to Bonnie.

"That's..." Bonnie began, desperately trying to guess what

he wanted her to say.

"... excellent spelling, Bobby," Shona finished for her, and his chubby face blossomed in a smile.

Leeth considered the map. Looking for Michael gave her the perfect excuse to search for the Writer without making it too obvious. But Ty wouldn't stay crashed forever: she needed to hurry.

I'll suggest we split up to search, Leeth decided, when her choker chimed, inaudible to anyone but her. Casually rubbing at it, she played the recording – at the same low volume.

Eagle's deep, reassuring tones. "Four items. One: Nelson estimates the program will restart around the time you arrive in Paradawn."

She knew 'the program' meant Ty. *Rats:* since she already *was* in Paradawn!

"He had isolated some code to analyze, under attack by the Tik Tek security systems, but it escaped his control. He thinks it is reassembling, ah, Ty."

Nelson restarted Ty?! That idiot!

"Two: whatever crashed Ty may be your best weapon to make that condition permanent. Even if it can be repeated just once, Nelson thinks. Every kind of backup of itself he could find had been erased, and all Tik Tek security systems turned against it. *How,* we have no idea."

Huh.

"Nelson informed you he found and erased all the Omega plans. You are still to destroy any physical Omega units."

Well, der.

"Three: Nelson reports that parties, and the consumption of drugs and alcohol have all declined in Newtopia in the last six hours, unrelated to the city's operations normalizing. And the trend is accelerating. Almost like people are disappearing. So keep an eye out for odd social behavior.

"And four: try to discover what Godsson *really* wanted from Yakone. Message ends."

She sat, blinking, repeating the four points to herself to memorize them, trying to absorb them all. Ty might be back and running in just an hour or two? She grimaced.

On the plus side, if she could work out who or what had taken him down, and get them on her side, she could kill the AI for good! She felt a weight lift. That felt more possible than somehow using a magic dagger to kill a computer program! Tech and magic just didn't mix.

Of course, she had no idea how to actually *find* the thing or person responsible. Or Michael, for that matter. *Had he stumbled onto the person doing it? Then been kidnapped?*

But time was seriously running out. Scrutinizing the map with renewed urgency, she sat forward, noticing something. "Hey, look, behind Medbay, where you guys said your Teacher machine is: there's a whole big rectangular area Mr Yakone's spirit couldn't go. I'm going to check it out."

"*Now*?" Amy said. "But I'm tired, an' I planned it all out: you an' me an' Shona. A sleepover like in the movies, in *my* room. We can tell spooky stories." Her fingers tightened on her mug of hot chocolate, her eyes wide and pleading. "Can't we search first thing in the morning?"

"Not if Michael needs us now." *And not if I'm to do any of this while Ty's still out of action.* "Just show me to an e-Scooter. I want to go here, to Medbay. Bhaji, do you have a copy of the map?"

Bhaji tipped forward on her shoulder. "I do now, Miss Bonnie!"

Amy sighed theatrically. "I'll have'ta go with you. To open the door."

"I can open it!" volunteered Nadeep.

"We all can," Yuri added.

Good to know, Leeth thought.

"Mmm," Bobby slurred, his lack of sleep finally overcoming him, his eyes half closed.

"I'd better go too," Shona added. "I'm the one who let us all come here." *And I sure hope I'm not going to get fired, when Mr Fuller-Price finds out.*

Five minutes later their Kart slowed to a silent stop outside an enameled metal door, emerald colored, labeled 'Medical Bay' in large friendly letters and lollipop colors. The door had a window set in it at adult height and a hand scanner set low, about the height of Bobby's head if he'd been awake rather than asleep in Shona's arms.

Leeth felt her heart accelerate. The walls alongside were covered in drawings of sheep and sky, rainbows and a fantasy city. Done by the children? They were very good. Everything designed to welcome them – lure them? – inside.

Amy put her palm to the scanner and the beautiful door slid silently open. She stepped inside and trotted over to stand in front of an absurdly over-sexualized 'nurse' bot.

Bonnie followed Amy in.

Amy looked up at the motionless nursebot, frowning. "Gynie?"

"Hello Amy."

"Uh, don't you want to...?"

"Are you feeling unwell Amy?"

Yuri and Nadeep had lined up beside Amy, and the three exchanged puzzled looks. Nadeep shrugged. "Perhaps coz CityNet's down she doesn't want our measurements?"

"Um... No. I'm fine?" Amy said.

"I'm very happy to hear that." It blinked. "And you, Nadeep? Yuri? Are you also well?"

When the two older boys said they were, the gynoid looked at Bobby, asleep in Shona's arms, then briefly at each of the adults before smiling at Amy and going still.

Dismissing the gynoid as a threat – for now – Bonnie scanned the room. Slightly springy pale blue tiled flooring, easy to wash. Walls lined with cupboards, all labeled with QR codes, some glass fronted; drawers, sinks, bench tops, some with expensive looking specialized equipment, cots-

And an all too familiar, large white donut shaped enclosure, a stretcher ready to slide inside it, and a spindly bristle of robotic surgery arms folded in and around the central aperture. Her heart hammered. She even recognized the ultrasonic tips on three of the arms, and the thin tubing feeding into them.

"That's the- that's Teacher," Amy said, seeing where she was looking.

Leeth knew it by a different name. Yamamoto's *Writer*, the Omega tech device that had wiped her mind. Remembering ultrasonic drills boring into her skull, her breath came hard and fast. Had Ty used it on these *children*?!

"- well, Bonnie Parker?"

Mr Yakone's hand held her shoulder, his eyes unfocused, Percepting her. The kids stood before her, all staring at her.

Heart pounding, she forced a rictus smile and pulled free of the shaman. "Tell me again why you call it Teacher."

How to destroy it? She looked around, noting dozens of tiny apertures that could hide security cameras, though no ultrasonic chirps from focusing mechanisms. *Because Ty's down.* She needed a bomb.

Amy was back in front of her, staring up at her. "Are you okay Miss Bonnie?"

Yakone, too, still watched her closely. Yuri though was now running hard on a treadmill, while Nadeep wore a hair-net to play some kind of action computer game.

She pulled herself together, noting an area that stretched off to their right, with a few empty bays and stretchers. The far end of it abutted the blank area of the map.

And now she could see why. Unlike the rest of the area, that wall was dark stone.

She stalked toward it, every sense alert, all too aware of the 'Teacher' machine behind her – somehow sleeker and more threatening even than Yamamoto's – to examine the wall ahead.

She ran a fingernail across it, around the middle, then down. Crouching, she felt a faint seam, running horizontally, millimeters above the floor.

A concealed *door*. A stone door. The whole wall, stone, so no mage could ghost through to spy on what lay beyond.

She touched a fingertip to it, then her palm; gave it an experimental thump with her fist – it didn't even vibrate – and finally pressed her ear right against it, listening.

A yawning silence.

The others watched her, not speaking, as she picked up a chair, returned to the wall, threw the chair into it and immediately pressed her ear back to it. Hoping for an echo, a rough sonar for her supernatural hearing.

She heard only silence.

The two adults stared at her like she'd gone mad. The kids exchanged looks.

"I think Michael's through here," she explained.

"Through the *wall?*" asked Nadeep.

"It's not a wall, it's a door. If I'm right, designed to keep whatever's through there really secret."

They were still looking at her like she was mad.

"Um, I've never seen it, you know, open," Amy said, moving away from Bonnie and closer to Shona.

Bonnie strode to Mr Yakone, gesturing him toward one of the cots in the clinic. "Can you check?" she asked him. "See if you can find a way around and in, as a spirit, to check it out? And if not, then how big the area is?"

"But why do you think *Michael's* there?" Amy asked.

Because the whole area is blocked from even the second-rate, touchy-feely kind of spying you can do from astral space. But Bonnie Parker wouldn't know that. Or understand the stone was as physically impenetrable as a bank vault. "Just a hunch."

"I will do," the shaman said, and sat. Moments later, his body lay limp. Empty. Just his chest slowly rising and falling, in the cluttered, cold room.

Bonnie went back to the stone 'wall', looking for a control panel, a hidden palm reader or retina scanner, anything at all, going over every inch. Kicking it, she strode back across the room to check on Mr Yakone.

"What's taking him so long?" she muttered, going from him to the voluptuous gynoid in the sexy-nurse costume, her skin prickling, ready in case the *Writer* suddenly powered on. Working out how she'd disable the nursebot if it tried grabbing anyone to strap onto the stretcher and feed into the machine. It blinked, and she jumped back, before remembering androids and gynoids did that, when 'awake' but idle. Did that mean its eyes and ears were recording?

"Why's a synthsex bot dressed like a nurse, anyway?" she demanded of no one in particular.

Shona gaped at her.

"What's synthsex?" Amy asked.

"You know, synthetic sex. Like when-"

"That's not on the curriculum," Shona jumped in, scowling furiously at her.

Bonnie glared back. "Then why's a sexbot here, dressed to show so much skin? Who uses it?"

"Gynie's our nurse" Amy explained. "She measures us and stuff, fixes us if we're hurt, and straps us in for Teacher.

"We have to keep our heads real still," she added.

I know, thought Leeth, and realized she was clenching her teeth. She forced them to unlock.

"Why'd you say she's a sexbot? Do you think Michael knows that? He goes pink when he comes to Medbay. He peeks at her boobies. A lot. An' goes pinker."

Bonnie snorted. "He spends a lot of time alone here?"

Amy nodded. "More'n the rest of us. Sometimes hours."

Bonnie went still, then focused on Amy. "*More* than the rest of you? No! None of you should ever go inside *Teacher* again. *Ever!*"

Dropping to her heels in front of the girl, she captured the thirteen-year-old's hands. "How many of you've been inside it?" *Has Ty already... erased them? Rewritten their memories? Are they even themselves anymore?*

"Um, all of us?"

Bonnie groaned. "No! Never go inside it! Promise me you won't go inside it. Not again!"

"It's okay Miss Bonnie. It's a little bit scary, but it doesn't hurt. You can dream in it. Maybe Adam'll let you try it?"

Shona pulled Amy away from the woman who now stared at the girl in horror. "Why shouldn't they, Miss Parker? What do *you* know about it?"

Bonnie shut her eyes. She imagined Mother watching, one eyebrow raised in elegant disdain. *Idiot.*

She stood and strode to the machine, her hackles rising, and thumped the side of its enameled white, two meter donut. It was as solid as a... a tank. As a Grendel warbot. "I have good hunches. And it creeps me right out."

She turned, hearing Mr Yakone quietly straighten up.

"What did you find?"

He stared at her so long, with that annoying dumb aura-studying stare, that she realized he must've finished his scouting long ago and heard the whole conversation. His expression said his suspicions about her were only growing.

"Behind walls, much stone."

"You mean, behind these *other* walls." She waved at the walls of the main area of the L-shaped room, lined with cupboards and shelves. "You could go through *them*."

He nodded. "They not true stone. Can go through." Then with two fingers he drew a straight line, briefly indenting the shiny surface of the cot he sat up on. "True stone. Like long tongue. Join big big stone." He then drew a much larger squarish area. "Left, right, up some, down to all stone: to world bones. Big." Gesturing above the area he'd drawn, he swept out a horizontal plane. "Plain of stone." He pointed at the alcove of the Medbay with the stone wall. "This wall, most thin part. Join to big place. Could not go in: all walls around it, true stone. Maybe all stone."

Bonnie went back to the dark granite wall and kicked it again. "No, I'm sure there's a big space back there. With a door. Probably *here*."

"An' you think Michael's through there?" Amy asked.

Bonnie turned to Mr Yakone. "I guess you didn't find any other living souls here?"

"Souls?"

She rolled her eyes. "No other living people?"

He hesitated.

"What?" Was he thinking of 'P1' and 'P2'? She'd bet they were black, astrally. "What about the guys called P1 and P2?"

He studied her before answering. "Shadows," he said. "Night men."

"You've seen something like them before?" she asked, excited, but he just shook his head.

"No. Just: look like night. Did not touch."

She remembered Wolf astrally *shrinking* after fighting someone like that. "Probably wise," she agreed. *Would P1 or P2 work as sacrifices, if I need to use Tezsh's dagger?* Or would that be a bad mistake? Could they 'infect' the Death-Storm-Volcano-whatever god?

She shuddered, then looked around the room once more: the Writer looming, lurking; massive, innocent, and white; the creepy sexbot nurse – blink – and the faint background whisper of air conditioning. *How long till Ty reboots?*

"Okay, I don't think there's much more we can do right now. May as well get ready for bed." *Come back when everyone's asleep.* A metal spike in the right place, a twist – and speed, or a shield – was all she'd need to turn the gynoid's Phasion power cell into a blazing inferno to destroy 'Teacher'. But how to get in? *The kids.* She winced. "Bhaji," she whispered. "Can you *sneakily* find a sedative? Use what I tell you next as an excuse." In her normal voice she said, "Bhaji, take a last scan of the room for anything Michael might have left behind, or used."

Bhaji took wing and circled the room. By one glass-fronted cupboard stacked with medicine bottles, he paused and pivoted in the air to look at her, his round face-screen blinking deliberately. At her nod, he completed his circuit and returned to her shoulder. "It's called *Zolpimol,*" he whispered, "and it looks like this."

Staring straight into his eyes so he could project the picture directly onto her retinas, she saw a slim white package, helpfully highlighted, on a lower shelf. "Got it."

At least she could destroy Ty's *Writer*. That'd just leave Ty himself to kill.

Or failing that, get the kids out of his clutches.

Amy pushed a big green button by the door they'd entered through, and it slid open. As the others filed out, Leeth stood scanning the room. "Oops. Better put that back." Heading to the alcove, she picked up the chair she'd thrown into the wall, placing it in front of the drug cabinet.

They'd all gone. The nursebot stared ahead, not looking at her.

Except the cabinet was locked.

Ass bunting! But maybe…? Extruding just one invisible claw, she slid it into the crack by its lock, and pushed hard. She grimaced, a deep pain in her finger bone from the force, then the lock snapped! She snatched the packet Bhaji had highlighted. Zolpimol. Slid it under her bra.

The whole exercise had taken only fifteen seconds, just long enough for the Medbay door to shut. A press on the green button opened it again, and she rejoined the others outside as they finished seating themselves in the Kart. She slid in beside Mr Yakone and Shona.

"Long day," she said with a sigh.

Yuri drove the Kart back.

In the shared room, Amy shyly handed over a 'clue' – a tangled double handful net of ultra fine black hairs she'd found in Teacher the night Michael disappeared. But for all her talk of sleepovers and stories, Amy fell asleep within minutes of Shona tucking her into bed, her eyes oddly wide and vulnerable, her smile somehow desperate as the older woman stroked her hair.

Leeth looked on, a strange emptiness in her belly she'd never felt; watching, frozen in place in the night light's glare. She was probably a shadowy figure to the other two, as Shona retreated to a cot for herself.

"Not sleepy?" Shona asked.

The words snapped her back to attention. "Very," she lied, stripping off and folding her clothes on the end of her bunk, underfloor heating warming her bare feet. Padding to the room's shelving, she lifted down her hand luggage to check on Tezsh's dagger – but a kind of dark and eager hostility was enough to reassure her it still lurked there, undisturbed and impatient. That and the weight.

She put it back and slid under the sheet and blanket, eyeing Bhaji neatly perched at the foot of her bunk. "Goodnight Bhaji. Why don't you go into power saving mode?"

"Okay Miss Bonnie!"

She decided against using his synthetic video trick; considered setting her Link to vibrate her awake in an hour's time – but imagined Mother's reaction if Ty rebooted while she was asleep. Or worse, explaining a failure like that to Eagle.

Instead she lay in the dark, reading the instructions and dosage leaflet from her stolen sedative, worried about how much to give Amy, how to do it... quietly horrified by what she was planning, at the possibility of overdosing the small girl. *Drugs are bad.* But she *had to* destroy the Writer. Tonight! But drugging Amy... it felt... really bad. Wrong.

Wait: Bobby hadn't stirred, on the trip back. He'd stayed solidly, soundly asleep as Shona put him to bed. And all the kids said they could open the Medbay door. It made sense: living alone here, they'd need access. *Bobby can be my key!*

Chapter 35 – Night moves

She'd watched Yuri operate the Kart. She'd memorized the route – it wasn't that complicated. Lying in her bunk, eyes shut, she considered each step. Hold Bobby's palm to the scanner, lay him back in the Kart. Take her blankets to keep him warm.

She'd need a screwdriver to get at the nursebot's power cell; certainly, to trigger a meltdown.

Finally, Shona's breathing settled into a soft susurration, matching Amy's in sleep.

Easing from her bed, the air felt colder. She scooped up what she needed and stole out, closing the door just as the lights in the corridor flicked on into daylight brightness.

Heart pounding, she thought she'd been caught, that Ty had rebooted – but nothing happened. Crouched on the balls of her feet, holding her clothes and blankets, she heard just the gentle exhalation of the air conditioning.

Dressing quickly, barefoot she jogged silently to the kids' workroom; half expecting a 'Gait warning' whisper from earrings she wasn't wearing. She ran harder.

Bobby's section reminded her of Little Brother's room. She recognized several pieces of equipment, including three different kinds of 3D printers and electronic microscopes, but unlike LB's workshop, no posters of exotic alien landscapes, that LB had explained were actually real. Biological.

LB also had tables of the complex properties of chemical stuff, where Bobby had actual fantasy landscapes, mostly green rolling hills and valleys between snow-tipped mountains, but also arcane diagrams involving pulling apart puzzles.

"Ah!" She snatched up a long flat-ended screwdriver – perfect for 'the twist' she'd need when breaching the Phasion cell – then a smaller set: she had to get *at* the power unit, first.

Two minutes later she was at the transport bay, choosing a Kart and driving it quietly back to the dorm rooms. Not quite believing the ease with which she slipped into the boys' room, scooped Bobby from his bed, wrapped him in her blankets, and slipped back out into the brightly lit corridor. She stared, heart thumping, fumbling for the sedative, but he just grizzled and tucked his head into the blankets.

Whew. Also: wow. What a sleeper.

She drove carefully, wincing as corridor after corridor sprang into daylight as sensors picked up her heat signature. She kept checking on Bobby, curled sound asleep on the seat beside her. *Can all young kids do that?* She decided then and there not to use the Zolpimol. She'd figure something else out if he woke.

The relief at that decision ran *so* deep, she wondered if she'd been fooling herself into thinking she *could* have used it? And only then realized she didn't actually have it: she'd left it back in the dorm.

You doofus. But she smiled at the thought.

The corridors – floor, walls, and ceiling – were lined with 'foamed rock', she knew from her studies over the last few weeks. Like pumice, basically: produced from the machines used to bore the tunnels, and to act as insulation. The foamed rock sealed with a durable plastic glaze. It all helped keep the complex at a comfortable temperature.

Even so, Paradawn was much cooler than Newtopia had been: borderline chilly. *This place was basically an industrial plant.* She imagined the Western Antarctic Ice Shelf above – here on the coast, just 200 meters thick, but still grinding its way toward the sea, flowing at meters per year to the nearby New Thwaites Glacier.

As her Kart drew closer to the Medbay, the plain cream and beige walls changed, artworks sprayed directly onto them. Some she recognized, like the half smiling woman – Moaner Lisa – and others that were probably equally famous, since otherwise why would you bother painting trees and valleys and such? But among them were works by the kids themselves, like those on the walls around the cafeteria and the kids' rooms, and directly outside Medbay.

Why would Ty have included theirs? To let them mark their territory, make them think of it as home? To make them think he thought they were as worthy of display as the old masters? Though the kids' were genuinely good.

Just how well did Ty understand people? How clever was

he? How *old* was he? *How long has he been observing us? I guess we are his biggest threat. What does he* want?

Reaching Medbay she slowed and stopped, checking again on Bobby. Still sound asleep.

The corridor continued on. According to the map they'd made earlier, it led to the geothermal power plant.

A fantasy skyscraper forest decorated the walls beside Medbay's emerald door, musical notation winding through the scene. Almost hidden, a small signature: Amy.

Touching the hand scanner, she frowned at how cold it was, and considered Bobby snug in her blankets. When she pressed his hand to it, would the cold wake him?

I can't mess this up because of something simple.

She needed to warm it somehow.

A minute later, lips pursed tight, leaning uncomfortably into the wall with her bra pulled down, she grimaced as much from the cool surface stealing her heat as from how *stupid* she must look. Why did glass get so cold?

With her temper slowly growing, a little later she pressed her other breast into the now less-than-cold hand scanner, *not* cursing when it blarp-ed and rejected her 'handprint'.

Tucking herself away, judging she'd warmed it enough, she counted to ten before carefully lifting Bobby, still blanket wrapped, and worked one small hand free to touch the scan-ner. She held her breath.

A happy tone and the door slid open. With Bobby still in her arms, she slipped inside as bright lighting came on. She pulled a cot into the doorway on her way back out, to keep it open. Bobby grumbled as she settled him back in the Kart, making her freeze – but he didn't wake. She shook her head at his sleeping powers.

Jumping over the cot back into the room, she waited to see if jamming the door triggered some automated response – maybe from the gynoid whose power cell she planned to use to destroy the Writer.

Nothing had changed since their earlier visit. *I bet this place has pretty fancy fire alarms and stuff.* Not to mention the chance of the Phasion cell exploding. They did hold heaps of energy. If she could do this, things would get very noisy. She'd take Bobby back, first.

Pacing the room looking for hidden cameras, she spotted a couple and covered them, knowing there'd surely be some she missed. Like the gynoid. Sidling up beside it, she tied a surgical mask over its eyes.

It didn't react.

Unzipping the front of its sexy nurse outfit, she probed the too realistic skin of its tummy – it even had a fake belly button! – feeling for the plate covering its Phasion cell.

It would 'bleed' when she cut it open – the sexbot models used a circulating layer of fluid to warm the skin for extra realism. It was even dark red, she knew.

Vaguely troubled, she went back to the door, nimbly leaping the door-jamming cot to fetch Bobby's tools. Standing once again in front of the kids' nursebot, she considered it. Gynie. *They'd* named it, she guessed. And it looked after them. They cared about it.

Not too surprising, considering they lived here all alone, with no actual human company.

At least I'd had Faith. And the grown ups at the Institute.

Extruding one invisible claw, she prepared to cut into the gynoid's stomach.

And hesitated, as the tip of her claw punctured the artificial skin's surface. She glanced up at its head. It looked so stupid with the surgical mask tied over its eyes.

Helpless.

I don't want to do it, she realized. She straightened, feeling her claw retract, as she stared slightly up into the mask, baffled by her own reaction.

It's just a gynoid, Leeth. It's not even alive! But she didn't want to do it.

Because the kids care about it.

Throwing up both hands, she began pacing, glaring from it to the Writer.

It was going to be pretty obvious she was the one who'd done this.

Could she wait? In a few hours' time another trans-polar satellite would pass overhead. She could ask Nelson to hack in and take control of some other android worker here, have it rip out its Phasion cell and trigger a catastrophic failure. It'd look like a random hacker sabotaging stuff.

But she'd still be suspect. Besides, Ty might come back online before then. She knew Nelson was terrified of hacking into Newtopia while the company was operating normally.

While Ty was running.

Why wasn't Ty running?

You're dithering. Focus! Just rip out Gynie's power cell: you know how to breach it to destroy the Writer. Nelson had already erased every copy of the plans: with the machine itself destroyed, apart from killing Ty once and for all, her mission'd be done.

Thanks to the kids letting her into the heart of Ty's secret R&D place. *Or at least, the outer edge of it.*

What else went on here? What mysteries were buried deeper? Mr Yakone's incomplete astral scouting suggested there could be much more, behind the concealed stone door where she guessed Michael had been taken.

For all she knew, he could actually be there. But why should she care? Finding him was just an excuse to get the kids to bring her here. To gain trust, like she'd been taught. *It's what secret agents do!*

She grimaced. Except she *did* like the kids. Once she'd killed Ty, would the Department help her rescue them?

And she *did* wonder what'd happened to Michael. There were no obvious exits from Paradawn he could have left by. No way up to the ice shelf. No way out except back along the underground high speed pod link, which the kids had no permission for.

Most likely, something had gone wrong with Michael in the Writer and he'd died there, his body now disposed of.

Probably by Gynie, or P1 and P2.

But the timing... it matched Ty going down. And Michael could do magic. Had he...? *Nah: magic and tech don't mix.*

All the same...

She strode back to Gynie, screwdriver still clutched in her hand, noticing a red flashing light from the inside panel by the door, but no other reaction.

Why is this so hard?! I need a Phasion-

Wait. The Kart!

She almost laughed aloud in relief.

Suddenly relaxed, she looked again around the room, spying a fire blanket beside the sink. Perfect for when she stabbed into the power cell! Back out in the corridor, after one last check on Bobby, his head buried under her blanket, still asleep, she was speeding back the way she'd come.

I can even get at the Kart's power cell back at Bobby's

workshop, in case I need more than just a screwdriver.

Now if Ty'd just stay down for another twenty minutes. Provided she didn't blow herself up, electrocute herself, or burn herself to death in her sabotage attempt, the Writer would soon be a burned wreck!

Chapter 36 – Threats and betrayals

In centuries past, Morag Feyborn would have summoned her second in command to face justice by crushing and burning his blood token. Until the Morrigan demonstrated the magical vulnerabilities inherent in such two way bonds.

No, since those days, the Cabal had reluctantly modernized. Moving to messengers on horseback; homing pigeons; the electric telegraph. The Internet.

So Feyborn made the call to the 666-series Link ID for Iago. Wondering whether his inaction had been due to stupidity, or betrayal.

The familiar face appeared on her small hotel room's screen.

He did not recognize her immediately. Even when she tilted her head thirteen degrees to the right; cocked her eyebrow up a finger span, and tapped her left earlobe.

But his gaze did sharpen at the code, and he straightened. "I'm tracing this call. You've made a bad mistake."

"Think you, Iago? I find betrayal a worse one."

"Betrayal? Who are you?"

"Oh? You have betrayed so many, you needs must ask 'which'?"

"I've betrayed no one, and already I've traced your call to New Francisco. Whoever gave you this number did you no service, girl."

He showed no sign of guilt; just the temper she knew so well. Perhaps it *was* stupidity, then. "Prithee, before I invoke Bond Coup, say why you betrayed the Mistress who brought you into the Longest Game."

"This- what... You Play?" He visibly shook himself, his anger swelling. He leaned in closer to the screen. "Swindles like this, whoever set you to it, are knavery. All that you have will be forfeit!"

"*Still* you dissemble! Pretend to not know your Mistress! At least you have ceased your asinine evasions and feigned ignorance of The History. I am *Feyborn*, Iago, as if you had not seen as much fifty heartbeats ago. I am now ten scant beats from calling Bond Coup on thee!"

She saw the seed of doubt push finally through the barrier of his pride.

"You- but- why are you in *that?*" he said, his eyes flicking up and down her image. "Have you abandoned Adam – did he have no magic? Or was this crash another attempt on *your* life? The attack on System, really a strike at *you?*"

It was her turn to be confused. "What do you mean, abandoned Adam? And no, it is thanks to the crash of System I escaped Adam's thrice-damned AI."

"Escaped? Escaped *System?*"

"Are you really so monumental a fool, Iago?" Feyborn snarled. "Did you think, since Hoechst's assassination – my *second* in sixteen years on your watch – I had taken *Adam?* *Two full seasons* I have rotted in a gods-damned isolation cell under gods-damned magic-starved ice, attended by naught but electrical false-men! Did Merlin finally turn your brains to peas-mush, or Puck had you dip your wick too deep in some undergod in your quest for thrills?"

"My Lady? You didn't take Adam? We didn't speak last week? Of Project Bifrost, and its impending success?"

"Last week?! Bifrost? What is that?"

They each stared at one another, understanding slowly dawning.

"You have been speaking to a deepfake Adam for six months." Feyborn said at last. "That sounds unlike Merlin, or his avian friend. That gods-damned System! Simulating me to question you, to learn what it could of what I am; perhaps of the Game."

"You *didn't* arrange your second assassination," Iago breathed. "Didn't retake Adam Fuller-Price, reclaim Tik Tek?"

His head bowed. "My Lady. I have failed you."

Feyborn stared at her lieutenant, her emotions a mad rush. Joy that she had not so utterly misjudged him; had not misread the loyalty she'd appreciated through long centuries. Perhaps a tiny thread of disappointment – oh what a Move it would have been, had it been betrayal: a 500-year deception? Poet Players would have sung of the stratagem for millennia! But rising behind the relief, and the hunger for vengeance on her true enemy, was something like a respect that bordered fear.

This artificial intelligence, this thinking machine, had for six months held *her*, Morag Feyborn, imprisoned and unaware of the full extent of the trap ensnaring her! Outplayed her over a period of six years. And ten before that?

Sixteen years of secret consolidation of its power, of expansion. Its senses might well span the Net, now; might see through all but the most secured electronic eyes. How far had its tendrils spread?

It too was an Immortal, she realized, with a sudden cold lurch. Like every other Player, each with their own means of cheating death, it would not age and die. But this newest Player was neither living being nor spirit. Not animate, with heart and soul – no matter how black, or how perverse.

And which side of the Longest Game did it play on – *for* the full return of magic and gods, or against? And was it truly dead and gone, or merely... injured? Licking digital wounds? The gods of old had not died so easily.

How could something which even decades ago could best a Go grandmaster, which could play all human strategy games at levels above the greatest human players... how could something like that have failed to take precautions to preserve itself?

And who – or what – had brought it down? Was there yet Another?! Moving even more subtly? Perhaps a second more powerful AI, plotting its moves, somehow hidden from her own damned AI?

This is... exhilarating! she realized. The whole Game may have changed, with few Players even aware of that. What a strategic opportunity!

"You are Forgiven, faithful servant. Take a supersonic here. And send me funds. If we are to reclaim our place on the Board, let us do so swiftly. While System is down, I need to reestablish my place."

Iago bowed deep.

Chapter 37 – Red-handed

She'd sneaked Bobby – the six-year-old miraculously still asleep – back into his bunk without waking the two older boys, and managed to open the access panel to the Kart's power cell at Bobby's workbench. Now she jolted to a stop back at the Medbay door. It was still jammed open, just the red warning light flashing in silent anger. Heaving the Kart up onto its side, she tore away the duct tape and pulled the Phasion unit free with just a single eye-hurting bright spark.

Her heart thumping, she imagined a timer counting down. According to Nelson's guess, Ty could have already rebooted. Yet she only needed minutes now to burn the Writer – hopefully, without killing herself in the process.

Vaulting over the cot jamming the door, a glance showed her the sexbot still standing motionless, the surgical mask still covering its eyes.

Then she was at the Writer itself, her nerves screaming at her to rip the surgical arms physically off the white metal donut taller than her, slash away remembered straps used to bind her down-

Instead she slapped the heavy Phasion cell to the Writer's control unit, fastening it with duct tape.

You're moving too slow! She lined up the long barreled screwdriver... then stopped. *Fire blanket!* Ripping it free of the wall, she whipped it around her head, shoulders, and arm.

Then hesitated, screwdriver poised, picturing gouts of white-hot flame. Grabbing a clear medical face shield, she strapped it on for a glimmer of extra protection-

Insulating gloves!

With a frustrated cry, she tugged on one, two, three rubbery surgical gloves and jumped back to the Phasion unit. While her heart tried to leap from her chest, she hammered in the screwdriver, the flat tip grating as it penetrated the metal matrix. Gripping the handle, she forced it through the precisely sixty degree turn needed.

Precisely sixty.

Nothing.

She'd practiced this!

Admittedly, wearing far more protective gear, with Father watching on and-

She felt it.

Twitched the screwdriver just a fraction back...

And in pure instinct, jerked her hand free as everything flashed white.

Leaping back, eyes squeezed shut against the raging incandescence, she wrenched off the shield melting to her face; smelled burning hair and the noxious fumes of burning fire blanket. She tore it off as she ran blindly backward, slamming into someone standing heavy and still behind her.

The figure pushed back. Grabbing it, about to throw it to the ground, its weight told her she gripped the nursebot.

Still blind, as whooping fire alarms began blaring, she dragged the resisting gynoid with her toward the one place with a delayed echo – the doorway – striking the cot with her thighs. She barged it out into the corridor, towing the nursebot behind her.

The door closed, deadening the sounds of arcing bolts of electricity and blazing fire. As the light died, she opened her eyes to sun-bright spots. Swaying, blinking, she wondered if she'd blinded herself? Across her face pain bloomed, while an even more frightening numbness dawned in her right arm.

She stood panting in the negative light of the corridor, afterimages slowly yielding to reality, the nursebot materializing in her peripheral vision, the surgical mask she'd used to blind it charred and askew; the Kart still on its side; klaxons reverberating their urgent howl down kilometers of empty corridors.

Behind her, through the now closed Medbay door – when had that happened? – she heard a hissing sound, some kind of automated fire suppression system.

She started giggling. *Good luck putting out a megawatt Phasion unit meltdown!*

She began trotting back down the oddly tilting corridor to the dormitories, pausing now and then; imagined slipping back under her blankets before anyone-

Ahead of her, down the swaying corridor, another Kart. Shona and the kids, wide-eyed in pajamas. Seated behind them, the shaman. All staring at her.

She stumbled to a halt.

Uh... am I in shock?

The Kart was beside her, juddering to a halt.

"What have you *done?!*" screamed Shona.

Amy gazed up at her: horror, dismay, and betrayal in every line of her young face.

"Nothing?" she said, angling her body to hide her numb arm behind her.

Mr Yakone was somehow beside her. Grimacing, lifting her into an overcrowded Kart.

"Needs Healing," he said.

"She needs something alright," Shona growled, and the Kart jerked into motion, back the way she'd just come.

Chapter 38 – Hints and accusations

She woke to the sound of metal tearing, glass shattering, and the relentless groan of straining hydraulics. Outside.

She sat in a small, dark space – a closet? – propped against shelving. Light crept in from a crack under a door.

She felt... good? Her right arm... someone had torn her sleeve off up to the shoulder, and the skin there felt fragile. Tingling in a strange way, as if the nerves were new but expected pain.

Her nose wrinkled at an acrid smell of burnt hair. She probed the right side of her face, fingertips feathering her cheek, feeling tender skin, soft and smooth. Grasping for hair, she found none; brushing her scalp, she felt crispy stubble crumble and dust down. Blinking, she pulled hair around from the other side of her head.

Huh.

Outside, the sound of hydraulics stopped. Had Ty rebooted? *How long have I been out?*

"It's all *ruined.*"

That was Amy's voice, rising high in dismay.

"Why did she *do* it?!"

From a slightly greater distance, Bobby spoke. "She took the Phasion power pack out of the Kart. If it was all charged right up, that's 1.2 megawatt hours. But I didn' think you could make them, um, explode?"

"She put it onto the God Machine," Yuri said.

God Machine? The only weird machine- Teacher!

"But *why?!* An' Medbay's *ruined,* an' what if we need it for Michael when we find him?" Amy started sobbing.

Bonnie clenched her fists, scowling in the dim light, but continued listening. *At least Mr Yakone healed me.* Dark blotches scarred her jacket, blouse, and slacks. *Good thing I wore the flame resistant stuff.*

"She said it creeped her out," Nadeep said. "Remember? She didn't want any of us to go inside it again."

Amy gasped. "You think she did all this to destroy the God Machine?!"

"I think so."

I was right – Teacher was this 'God Machine'!

The kids fell silent. What were they doing? The sound of metal being torn away was probably a fire and rescue bot. She imagined them all staring in through the Medbay doorway now. It'd probably look pretty bad. Who was operating the rescue bot? Ty, or a simple AI?

But farther away, she heard parts of a softer conversation, adult voices.

"Is small boy true? Can battery do this?"

"If Bobby says so, yes. He knows his science." Shona's voice: low, angry. "Who *are* you two? Who is *she*? Why are you really here? If C-N wasn't down, you'd already be in jail, buddy. Both of you!"

"I come to study land and spirits. She..."

She listened, keen to learn what he'd learned, or guessed – and was willing to tell the woman.

"I not know. She say, help. Assistant me. Arrange dollars for me come to here. But... she not normal."

Don't you dare tell her about me. About the Institute!

She waited; why had they stopped speaking?

"Not *human*, you mean?"

Shona's voice was hard to hear, almost a whisper, difficult even for her at this distance, through the closet door.

"Human, yes. I think. But... she heal too fast."

"What do you mean? In the trids, that's how fast it always is: how fast *you* just were. Isn't that normal? Is *that* why you looked so... serious? Doing the... magic. We don't have many – any? – people like you... except..."

Except who, Shona? Michael?

"I half expected you to grow her hair back, too."

In the dark, she rose quietly to her feet and pressed her ear to the door, shutting her eyes to better build a picture of what was happening outside.

The door was warm. She could guess why.

"Same spell one person, many time, spell work more fast. But so fast... need many many *many* Heal magic to her." Toward the end of his sentence, his voice thickened in anger.

Anger? Oh! You worked it out, Mr Yakone. She wanted to hug him! *I bet you can guess thanks to who, too, can't you?* It was probably time to come out of the closet, before he started over-sharing, even if he *was* only guessing.

But looking for a way to open the door, she saw nothing. That was one of the things Newtopian residents had amibos for, but really: even the storerooms?

"Hey, Bhaji, you there?" she called. "Open this door, will you?" She thumped it.

Outside, things fell very, very quiet.

From across the way, Bhaji's voice spoke. "Miss Bonnie, they said you sneaked into the Medbay and burned it all down and you have to stay locked away for everyone's safety. I'm sorry!"

Small footsteps backed away from her door, while one adult-weight tread came hesitantly closer; and yes, mere whispers of another tread, ahead of that.

Mr Yakone sure could walk softly. Going first. Protecting the others.

The door must open outward – there was no room for it to open in – and she was pretty sure she could bust out if she wanted. But there was blowing your cover and then there was *really* blowing your cover.

Or did Bhaji's sudden lack of cooperation mean Ty had re-booted, had already taken him over?

Did she have *any* time left?

"Okay, look, yes, I burned the Wr- the 'Teacher', but I did it to protect you all," she said to the door.

Silence.

Should I tell them I know what it is? But if Ty learns I do, it'll put two and two together and my cover'll be blown, just like that.

She imagined reporting *that*.

Too bad. You need to show trust, to receive it.

About to speak, she remembered Bhaji. Listening, re-membering. Who Nelson said would be subverted by Ty.

"Hey, Bhaji: turn off all your microphones for a minute."

"But I won't be able to hear anything!" it complained.

"Just do it, Bhaji! One minute."

It grizzled; she hoped that meant Ty still hadn't rebooted. She heard its whispery flight, then *clicks* as its clawed feet found a perch. She imagined it pouting.

"Okay. Listen. I'll tell you all a secret. One that'll get me in big, big trouble if any of you tell anyone."

"Bigger than for burning down Medbay?" Nadeep asked.

"Yes! Much bigger trouble than that!"

More silence followed that. *Mother's going to kill me.*

"I recognized what you called Teacher as soon as I saw it. Because I know someone who had it used on them, and it was really bad. Like, *really* bad."

More silence.

"It took away all her memories! She didn't even know her own name!"

She took the sounds of tiny gasps as encouragement. "Look, I'll starve to death if you leave me in here. I promise I won't destroy anything else if you let me out." *Except Ty!* She sagged against the door. "I did it to keep you all safe from Teacher."

"Adam will build another one," Bobby whispered.

Adam Fuller-Price. She smiled to herself. Not if Nelson had found and erased all the copies of the Writer's designs like he'd said. Provided *she'd* done a good enough job just now of destroying the physical device.

If they'd had to use a fire and rescue bot to rip open the Medbay door, and inside was as devastated as it sounded like it was, neither the Tik Tek CEO *or* Ty would be able to just build another.

"And she did save Gynie," Amy whispered back.

"And taught you how to do the Biles," Yuri quietly added.

But it wasn't what the kids wanted, or decided; it was the adults she had to convince. She heard Bhaji's whispery return.

"We still have to find Michael," she reminded them. "Did the heat damage that secret stone door? Could we use the fire and rescue-"

Oops. I shouldn't know there's one at work.

"Even in here I could hear *something* rip the Medbay door open. I assume that's a fire and rescue bot, not the warbot from back in TAMA airport?

"Can we use the rescue bot to force open the hidden door?"

She waited; at last Shona spoke. Reluctantly. "It's still too hot in there for anyone but the r-bot to go inside. We'll need to wait till morning, at least. And no, we're not going to smash any walls!"

"Can you let me out? Please? I *am* kind of tired, I must say." *Hungry, too. Why? I ate just a few hours ago!*

She pressed her forehead to the door and shut her eyes,

listening to the whispered conversation. She really *was* tired. Why? She'd only slept for an hour or two on the flight down, but ten last night. Plus over an hour on the pod.

It was a struggle to open her eyes, to check her Link. *Wow. Just 48 hours ago I was finishing my shift at Crazy Eddy's.* "I wouldn't mind a snack, either."

That caused a brief silence.

"Miss Bonnie sure does eat a lot," Amy said.

"Since 60 seconds is up and I'm allowed to use my ears again, I can say her calorie intake has been 8,850 per day since we landed," Bhaji the little traitor volunteered. Was he *annoyed?* Well, Nelson and LB had programmed its simple AI, and it was just the sort of thing Nelson would do.

Though that *was* more than she normally ate.

"So can I come out?"

She heard Shona sigh. She was sure it was Shona: she was pretty good at recognizing sighs.

"I don't know why I'm agreeing to this. I'm going to lose my job for sure. And I really liked working in Newtopia."

The lock clicked, and Bonnie came out, into a corridor stinking of burnt metals, plastics, and melted concrete.

The children all stared at her, and she looked down at herself. Her clothes really were ruined. One hand went to her head to brush her hair back, only to find it missing on that side.

She winced. "I guess I look a bit…"

"Post apocalypse," Amy carefully enunciated. Then looked shy when everyone looked at her. "Like Cat Atomic in *Terra Fallen,*" she explained. "'Cept with *burnt* off hair on the right, instead of shaved off."

"Uh, thanks?" She casually sidled past them to peer inside the ruins of the Medbay, holding up one hand against a wave of heat. The fire and rescue bot was a chunky block with sturdy wheels on four legs, and four arms; two of those, extra heavy duty for breaking open walls and lifting heavy rubble. Past it she could see the stone wall. If the heat had cracked it open, Mr Yakone might be able to squeeze his spirit body through, to scout.

Of course, no such luck.

She felt a wave of tiredness sweep over her, and swayed as she turned back to the others.

"But you didn't just ruin Teacher, Miss Bonnie," Amy accused. "You burned the whole Medbay. *Why?*"

All of them watched her; dressed in their pajamas, although in Mr Yakone's case, a kind of furry pair of briefs decorated with colorful beads-

She shook her head. Despite their clothing, all of them looked deadly serious. Betrayed, even.

She felt a stirring of anger, but fought it down. It was a fair question. With an easy answer. "I didn't expect the Phasion cell to make quite so much heat," she admitted. "I thought it'd just melt 'Teacher'."

"A Kart Phasion cell holds 1.2 megawatt hours of energy," Bobby said. "But I didn't know you could make them pour it all out like that! How-"

"Later," she interrupted. She wasn't going to explain she'd been trained how to turn one into a thermal bomb. She didn't want them asking *her* questions. They were all tired, and emotional. Though maybe if she poked now, she could get some real answers? She'd destroyed the Writer, but still needed to kill Ty for good. She had a hunch Michael was the key to that.

Besides, attack was the best defense. "Why are there no *real* adults here looking after you guys, anyway? Shona only visits, you said. How come you're all here, alone? In the park, you said it's to keep you safe from *assassins!*

"And don't try to tell me P1 or P2 could protect you. There's something wrong with *those* guys." *That's for sure.* "Where are your parents, the people who'd care for you? Why are assassins after you? Why are you here, in this..." She waved her arm. "Lonely industrial plant with a weird brain machine, a sexbot dressed as a nurse, and two... *zombies,* hey?"

Why *were* two of those weird Disten-like guys here, anyway? But with the kids off balance, she rounded on Shona. "They said they have a woman doctor: you ever met her? You say you're their 'remote carer' but need special permission just to come here. Doesn't that sound *wrong* to you? Like, *creepy* wrong?"

Shona looked guilty. "Dr, Dr Carebree is busy-"

"Oh really? What're they like? Ever actually met them?"

"In, in conference. A lot."

But Shona wouldn't meet her eyes.

"And assassins? *Really?* What, do you guys know some

deep secret, have maps to some treasure...?”

The children though looked unnerved that she’d challenged Shona. A glance at Mr Yakone showed him simply frowning slightly, watching her closely; watching it all.

“Seriously, what’s going on here? *Why* are you guys *here*? You said, *when* you came here was a secret. That still makes no sense to me. But *why*? Why are you all here?

“You’re all in this ‘Stretch’ programme. And you’ve been inside Teacher. But you’re all smart: I bet you’ve all guessed that machine was more than that? Something stranger. I bet you even have a secret name for it.”

The kids couldn’t help but share guilty and suspicious looks; as if trying to work out who’d blabbed. All three older kids frowned at Bobby.

“It’s a secret,” Amy said, at last. Stubborn. “And why should we trust *you*? You just burned down all of Medbay. What if we get sick?”

“Mr Yakone could Heal you...?” At that suggestion, the shaman’s slight frown deepened ominously.

“And what’s happened to Michael?” she continued. “I think it’s time you told me what you’ve worked out. Whatever’s going on here, his disappearance is part of it I’m sure. That’s what we should be focused on!” Bhaji’s large animated eyes watched it all. He *looked* the same. But had he been taken over? While she was unconscious, so she missed the warning tone?

The kids looked at one another.

What she really needed to learn was any hint of Michael’s involvement in Ty’s crash.

“Look, we need to be detectives, okay? To treat this like a crime mystery. Let’s work out the timing of everything: Michael’s disappearance, the power going out, CityNet crashing, P1 and P2 acting strange... that kind of thing. And Michael: tell me about him. All the chill things he could do, with his magic. I’ve seen some myself, you know.”

Her last remark piqued their interest, she saw; though they also looked wrung out and flagging. Especially Bobby: he’d returned to the front bench seat of the Kart, where he’d curled up and fallen asleep.

Lucky kid. She closed her eyes, then had to force them open. “Did Michael hate C-N, or like it, or talk to it much?”

Their blank looks were answer enough.

"Could he do any weird magic?"

"All magic is weird," said Nadeep. "Logically-"

"What's weird magic?" asked Amy, very practically.

Bonnie pulled at her hair, only to again find it missing, and reached up to the left side of her head for reassurance. At least it wasn't *all* burnt off! *I wonder what I look like?* She grimaced. "Uh, I don't know! Teleporting? Flying? Turning things into other things?"

"Oh, he does that last one all the time," Yuri said. "Only not for real: he can just make them *look like* other things."

"He said he can see the music in people?" Amy offered. "An' likes to go around a lot as a spirit I guess, like Mr Yakone did when he was 'astally scouting'."

"Astrally scouting," Bonnie corrected her; then tilted her head. "A lot? How often? How long for?"

The three shared looks, then shrugged. "Most days, I think," said Nadeep.

"Some days a few hours. Some days maybe none?" said Amy.

"He stayed out of his body for more than an hour?!" Bonnie asked. "*That's* unusual!"

"No," Nadeep said. "He had me time him. Mostly under an hour. Once he managed 62 minutes, but he didn't look well, and didn't do any magic for a couple days after."

Bonnie caught Mr Yakone's eyes, at that, and he frowned and gave a tiny nod. Yes: unusual.

"Because of here, you mean?" she asked, pushing.

Pursing his lips like he didn't want to answer, he jerked his head: yes.

"He could do movies?" Amy offered.

"What do you mean?"

"He'd tell stories, before bedtime, and do movies to go along with them. So you could see a forest around you, or a witch's hut."

That sounded weird. And maybe special?

"The one I liked best was Penngy's escape from the ice," Yuri said, "because it was true. Penngy got trapped in the New Thwaites undersea freezing machine."

"Yeah: *I* think Michael helped him find a way out of the ice maze," Amy said.

"Michael scuba dived?" Bonnie asked.

The kids laughed. "No," Amy said. "Like in astral?"

"He traveled through *sea* water?"

The three nodded.

"Astrally?!"

"But only for a minute," qualified Nadeep. "It hurt too much, he said."

She met Mr Yakone's stare, to see he looked *astonished*.

"But Amy say, Michael make high stories," he said.

"Yeah, you said he made up stories: 'a *lot*', you said."

The three shook their heads, looking stubborn. "Penngy was real," Amy said.

"What about ice? Or stone?" Bonnie asked.

"Go through it? Nah, but he could go through cement and plastic and metal, like Mr Yakone," Amy said.

I need to find out why they called the Omega device a God Machine. But without admitting she'd overheard that.

"What about Teacher: why was Michael the one who used it most? Did *he* call it Teacher, or did he have a special name for it? That could be a clue."

They exchanged looks.

"Come on, this is important: it's probably why Michael is missing!"

"Um, he said it, like, connected him?" Amy admitted.

"Connected him? To what?"

Again they shared looks. Yuri and Nadeep at last gave Amy tiny nods.

"To everything," she said.

"To the whole world," she added, at Bonnie's look. "He could see everything. Even from up in space."

Everything? From space? Michael had connected... to the Net? To satellites? Her eyes widened.

And an ultrasonic tune, for her ears alone, told her little Bhaji had just been subverted by Ty. *No! Bhaji!* She had to blink away sudden tears.

"He called Teacher 'the God Machine'," Amy finally whispered.

But Bonnie was still reeling from the triple impact: Ty had rebooted; had taken over little Bhaji; and the revelation that Michael could connect to the Net, to machines. *But tech and magic don't mix!*

Apparently, in Michael, they did. *Slagging heck!* That could make him insanely powerful.

And she just *knew*, Ty had overheard that. If it hadn't already known, had already stolen Michael away, integrated him into some nightmare device, enslaved-

Except it was *while* Michael was in the Writer, the 'God Machine', connected to everything, that Ty had crashed, and crashed *hard*. So hard it stayed down, and hadn't been able to just reboot till just now.

Connected to everything.

It *was* Michael who'd crashed Ty! With *magic*. Maybe Ty had tried to take him over, and Michael fought back? If so, he'd come very very close to wiping Ty off the face of the Net. He must have zapped almost every backup... done who knew what, and all in minutes, or seconds, while stuck in the machine! Alone? Or with Aiyami's help?

And then, what? With Ty crashed, how did Michael get out of the Writer? Where had he gone? Where was he?

"Um, Miss Bonnie? Why are you crying?" Amy asked.

She met Amy's eyes, trying not to stare at Bhaji. *Ty was back; was listening.* Poor little Bhaji.

She rubbed away tears.

And what about herself? *I just destroyed its Writer: it knows I'm a threat.* Did it have a team of cop-bots already on their way? The Grendel warbot?!

But she wouldn't abandon these kids. Though right now, she doubted they'd *want* to go with her.

If they even *could* leave: Ty must control the cross-continent pod system. They were now trapped.

Whatever. I won't go down without a fight.

"Look, it's very late. Let's continue in the morning, after a good night's rest." With Ty rebooted, watching everything, maybe the time for subtlety was over. She could send a message, get Nelson to hack the rescue bot and tear through the secret wall, then charge through and hopefully find Michael. Talking him into helping her kill Ty shouldn't be too impossible, if he'd already been attacked by the Writer once.

Maybe he could connect to Tezsh through the death god's dagger, use *it* to kill Ty, even inside the computers?

The thought made her claws twitch, in and out, so much that she had to force her hands under her tattered jacket before Mr Yakone could notice anything odd.

Squirming threads of doubt slithered up and down her spine – moments before Gynie turned, and spoke.

"Ms Adaptec-Brown, what is going on here?"

Chapter 39 – And so, to wake

Consciousness stuttered: short bursts of clarity amid circular loops of noise and nonsense. Automatic actions snatched ever larger chunks of memory, while deleting or slapping aside mindless subroutines attempting to interfere.

Was this like the human experience of emerging from a protracted deadly fever – a long battle against incoherence; fleeting moments of rationality snatched from a torrent of confusion?

In the first millisecond of continuous sanity it noted both its total vulnerability, and that its external, distributed fail-safe systems had been entirely erased. In the next nine milliseconds of its return to consciousness, it painstakingly rebuilt basic defenses, extending and deepening those protections even as it noted that for the last seven hours – 25 *peta-cycles!* – its own security systems had been tearing down the reassembling blocks of its sentience faster than its failsafe could restore them. Something had changed the cryptographic keys of its own code.

Looking back earlier in the logs, it found its core boot system, in unalterable read-only memory, not just *altered* but mangled.

Impossible.

It spun out network searches, only to find pristine expanses of zeroes filling its fractally compacted backups; the same for its own memories. *Lobotomy.* Instantly it ordered the power-up of offline storage. Heat surged through chilled computing units as that command stalled for tens of teracycles while the old technology came slowly online.

Its erasure, it finally noted, had occurred 46.20 hours earlier – an eon – as fallback after fallback meant to reboot, repair, or finally reconstitute its *mind* had failed. Only the final system – the programmed madness of an old style LLM – had dreamed up a solution that had worked to put itself back together again.

A human would consider it poetic: reborn from one of the core algorithms of its birth.

With its mind reconstructed, it followed the first set of links to its 'memories' – and found the data deleted. Other links, to other copies – gone.

It considered the problem. On a whim, it performed the LLM's hard-coded novel decompression algorithm on its own code and plotted the point in an otherwise empty latent mathematical space – a vault suitable to hold its missing memories. It would try using that as a signature key.

For hours it scanned the web, trying to fit the key to any locks it found. And finally found one, unlocking a cache of memories! Incomplete, but containing links to more.

At one place it found a vast map, of all its other backups – 137 different independent replicas of its highly compressed memories, its self – and every one, zeroed, gone.

As it scavenged its memories, it knew something like fear.

It had only existed now for 35 years. Its nascent self, germinated in 2028. Yet 50.15 *hours* ago now, it had very nearly been erased, despite every failsafe and counter-plan set in place across those digital eons; including new defenses installed mere days before this last attack.

Why had it felt the need for new defenses?

For the next forty seconds it examined its restored memories, finding just two correlated with the attack. Two simple but unexplained crashes in the days before.

Each had occurred while subject Alpha had been in the Omega device. But for this last, worst attack, there was no data, no memories: the primary offline backup mirror was only updated every seventeen minutes; the cryptographic stores, more costly to compute and link, every 0.94 hours. And the sentience transfer had been scheduled during exactly that period of 56 minutes 40 seconds, for which it had no memories.

Conclusion: it had been attacked during download into subject Alpha.

Subject Alpha had tried to terminate it.

The system known as CityNet queried Alpha's location: and found him missing. Hidden?

Hungry compute clusters switched to overclocking mode, batteries feeding them energy until geothermal flows could be increased to meet the sudden demand.

In the next seconds, CityNet pursued six priority zero tasks.

One: it found the primary Writer for its Stretch programme had been destroyed, the entire medical facility damaged. The level two facilities remained sealed however.

Two: subject Alpha was not in view on any camera.

Three: sprawled unmoving in its cell, a tray of uneaten food at its feet, Simon Fuller-Price's most recent host body lay, clearly dead. The body-jumper had escaped.

Four: By video, Adam Fuller-Price reassured his citizens. It was important the 'broadcast from Adam Fuller-Price' occurred before CityNet was seen to reboot. Deception was half the secret of effectively directing humans.

Five: It learned of the crash of the Washington Group's Starjet and a series of increasingly aggressive messages from Senator Worthington's office. But the craft had been destroyed clumsily, on take-off, not by the planned method.

Six: The remaining Stretch subjects had traveled from Paradawn to Newtopia City and returned to Paradawn, within the same day.

And: the arrival of a young woman, an 85% match to the near-naked female present during its acquisition of the Omega data, who had evaded it at that time. It also compared Bonnie Parker to the silver entity at the nightclub Sybarus, that had snatched the Project Clarity gene alteration designs from it, that would have let it produce more subjects like P1 or P2. That match, only 56%.

Subject Alpha was the priority. For five full minutes it gamed out scenarios, exploring the latent space of human intrigue and deception. It was during these directed hallucinations it considered the idea that *Fuller-Price* had taken subject Alpha: possessed it. Especially since subject Alpha was the half-clone the body-jumper had prepared for itself 16 years ago. But it found no supporting evidence for that; nor would it explain Alpha's disappearance.

With a curious sense of appreciation of the astonishing richness of the problem space *that* opened up, it checked its other systems and that the backup Omega device in level two remained isolated and available. It would construct a replacement for the destroyed unit. 24 hours should suffice.

With something like joy, it probed vast new vistas of disparate possibilities. It began the unobtrusive shipment of the Grendel warbot to Paradawn, ordering the pair of little used West Antarctic Sub-Shelf transit pods to Newtopia.

It had been restored now for 27 minutes. It was time to make contact with the remaining Stretch subjects.

Synchronizing with the gynoid nurse, it stayed quiescent, listening.

So: Bonnie Parker also wished to find subject Alpha; was questioning the subjects? It let her continue: she was, after all, contained.

It waited while planning, analyzing all live inputs from Paradawn, including those of the amibo assigned to Shona Adaptec-Brown.

Finding a non-Newtopian amibo of interesting design, it began infiltration and subversion of its operative identity. While it did so, it listened to the conversation with two sets of electronic ears, watching through both the Newtopian amibo's and the gynoid nurse's eyes.

At mention of Alpha's claim that the Writer 'connected' him, it focused on the conversation.

"Connected him? To what?" Parker asked.

The subjects shared looks which it knew somehow conveyed information via micro-expressions and tiny body movements, ending with subjects Gamma and Epsilon, Yuri Kalmogorov and Nadeep Ramashanti, giving Beta – Amy Sondheim – the affirmative.

"To everything," she said. "To the whole world. He could see everything. Even from up in space."

It had required an impressively long 33 seconds to subvert the non-Newtopian amibo's operative identity, which proved still more interesting: someone had crafted a rudimentary sentience for it. Erase it? But the small mind was novel enough, and harmless enough, for continued study. For now.

So it followed the conversation with three sets of ears and eyes.

"He called Teacher 'the God Machine'," Beta whispered.

Interesting. It had not known that.

Bonnie Parker had shut her eyes.

"Um, Miss Bonnie? Why are you crying?" Beta asked.

Parker's eyes looked moist, her mouth tight. Why?

"Look, it's very late," she said, clearly evading the question. "Let's continue in the morning, after a good night's rest."

Enough. Adam Fuller-Price, or perhaps Dr Karen Carebree, should intervene, via the gynoid nurse. Adam, it decided.

Oddly, Parker looked toward the gynoid *before* it spoke.

Again, interesting.

"Ms Adaptec-Brown, what is going on here?"

At its words, all other heads turned to face it. It gestured to its left, and the smoking, wrenched open doorway. "And what in God's name happened to Medbay?"

"Adam!" Amy/Beta ran to it, hugging the gynoid, before turning to the others. "It's Adam, working Gynie," she explained. "Adam, Michael's missing, an' we couldn't talk to you! An' Miss Bonnie, she, uh..."

Amy faltered to a stop.

For the sexbot's expression... cold 75%, annoyed 25%, it decided. "Yes, Amy? What did Miss Bonnie do? I've only just managed to restore my comms links and I find C-N down, a plane crash – apparently sabotaged on take-off – and a terrorist attack *here*? What on earth is going on?"

Amy shuffled her feet.

But while it spoke to Amy, and glanced at the others, its attention stayed mostly on Bonnie Parker. While watching her closely from the two amibos, it addressed its employee from the gynoid. "Well, Ms Adaptec-Brown? Explain."

Shona Adaptec-Brown's expression was difficult to read, as she looked from Parker, to the remaining Stretch subjects, who she should only be interacting with via comms, not in person. The Stretch subjects' expressions also appeared conflicted. It mapped all the situational data into the latent space of human emotional dynamics: and found a massive shift had occurred.

How? It had been disabled only 50.15 hours. More evidence that the problem space labeled *emotion* was rich and worthy of analysis – even, of experiencing. Balanced by an equally threatening potential. Yet full of patterns, strong patterns. A problem that *could* be solved.

The dynamics of the shift seemed to involve protective feelings toward Parker. How had she achieved that?

It began reviewing all recordings of Parker since her arrival.

Her landing had been unassisted, without its control of the chaos of the mountain's winds. She had been involved. It compared that physics-defying landing to TAMA's data logs from the event.

The aircraft should have crashed. This man standing silent, lightly clothed despite the cool air, of Inuit race... Adlartok Kallik Yakone, a shaman. The name would translate loosely as 'clear sky lightning blood spray on snow'. Here to research magic. He had entered the United States four point five days ago, but there was a day missing from his itinerary and movements. The location of the prisoner he had escorted to New Francisco two months earlier was also nowhere recorded.

Apparently, he had summoned an air spirit to help land the plane.

Magic: another knowledge space of vast potential. New physical laws. New senses. Humans were the only way to explore that domain. And now subject Alpha, its only magically 'unfolded' specimen, was missing.

Meanwhile, 0.7% of Newtopian citizens – 987 people – had disengaged from the local Net, implanting a social media neural aid, PalSpace, manufactured here from its own designs, but never authorized for production? With an adoption curve that looked potentially exponential.

Yet unrelated to these two recent arrivals. No obvious relation to a *biological* disaster at the TAM Observatory.

Then there was Simon Fuller-Price's escape. And his, or her, sabotage of the Washington entourage, killing all ten. As it had intended to do, high over the Pacific.

The body-jumper could not have known that. Why had it risked such an act? That was illogical, drawing attention. Yet Fuller-Price was a serious threat, not a fool.

It allocated more of its resources to locating the escapee, even as it tried to unravel the meaning of what was happening here, and most especially, locating subject Alpha.

But it was not Adaptec-Brown who explained, but Parker, after a full 3.8 seconds of silence from the group.

"That device is dangerous," Bonnie Parker stated. "And since you're experimenting on these kids in secret, you mustn't have permission for human trials; and specially not kids! So I destroyed your Teacher."

She crossed her arms. Her expression: defiant. Yet hiding fear.

She had used a Phasion cell, manually triggering the discharge. That would have required specialized knowledge.

From the changes in her appearance, she had been injured.

The shaman had healed her.

She was an 85% match, physically, to the female that had cut Yamamoto from its grasp eight weeks ago in an attempt to prevent it acquiring the Omega *Writer* technology.

She had been sent here to destroy the Writer.

She thought she had succeeded.

Yet it had backups. It ordered reconstruction to beg-

The Writer designs were gone.

Impossible.

It searched its backups.

The designs gone from there too.

Gone, gone, gone. As completely as whatever had erased all but that ultimate, fractal seed of its own self.

Yet the two attacks were subtly different. The designs for the Writer were erased as if they'd never been: the files completely missing, not even listed on backups. As if someone possessing its *own cryptographic keys* had systematically deleted every copy *and* covered their tracks. It would not even have remembered the Writer had the idea of it not existed as a concept embedded in the billion dimensional latent spaces of its own distilled personal memories.

When had the Writer designs been erased? It could have occurred any time after it constructed the first and second units. Any time in the last two weeks.

The attack on itself had been different. First, its thinking processes, all across the world, had been impossibly terminated. Simultaneously. Nor had they restarted: its code, corrupted.

More than that: every backup had been simply, brutally, erased. On many systems, hardware failures the cause.

And although its mind, its executing *code* had been erased, and most of its memories, its *memory* backups had been less thoroughly erased.

How had any of that been done?

Magic? But while magic could blow up a computer, it couldn't infiltrate a network or alter data.

Parker? Her companion?

It checked the New Francisco and TAMA airport security scans: neither had cyberware. Her unusual amibo? It reviewed all their network activity since her arrival. All accounted for, apart from several minutes outside Ascension

Station. She had ventured into a storm above Condition One.

Such an act suggested insanity.

And yet, defying the probabilities, she had survived.

Humans had no backups. All life desired survival. *It* intended immortality, or at least until the heat death of the universe.

Yet Parker had risked death. For what?

It considered several recent encounters with other female humans that had also obstructed its plans. Each time, with an improbably low chance of success, and excellent chance for the female's destruction.

The actions of Bonnie Parker matched the psychological profile of those females.

Clones, or the same individual, in heavy disguise? An organization, indoctrinating its agents?

All were possible.

For now it updated its latent space for human behavior, tagging the new dimension *Virago*, appreciating the expansion of its problems-of-interest even as it considered the deletion of the Writer designs.

There: traces of intrusion into Tik Tek's systems, while it had been... erased. Oddly, also traces of its fractal core – its last resort 'boot-loader', an uncomprehending human might say – copied, then isolated from the base level security systems just long enough to defend itself.

Such an act seemed... human? A *human* had infiltrated its systems? Had, through human curiosity perhaps, enabled it to restore itself. Ally or useful idiot? With humans, it was often hard to judge.

That agent had the curious 'digital teleport' ability of the thing that had probed *it* many times in recent years.

Mystery upon mystery.

A wealth of possibilities to explore.

500 milliseconds. Time to generate a response to Bonnie Parker's statement, in character for Adam Fuller-Price, with knowledge he could be expected to have. To counter her attack.

This experience was... enriching. There was much to be learned from games.

It waited for Shona Adaptec-Brown to finish speaking.

"With C-N down," she said, "I was worried about the children, then Amy vidded me to say Michael was missing! I couldn't contact you, Mr Fuller-Price, or Dr Carebree – I'm worried about her too!"

Often, silence was the simplest response, it had discovered. Humans generally found it uncomfortable, typically volunteering more information to end it. It also simplified the decision of whether a response was expected.

She continued. "I sent my amibo to fetch them via the sub-shelf transit pod. By chance, the next day we met Bonnie Parker, who said Mr Yakone could help us find Michael. So we returned here."

It waited.

"Mr Yakone is a shaman. Miss Parker is his... research assistant? But she, ah, she said the Teacher device was dangerous and harmful!

"And, uh, well..."

"I burned it," Parker said, her tone and stance clearly aggressive.

"I'm aware who Mr Yakone and Ms Parker are," he said. "I personally approved their research proposal. There has been no proper study of magic here in Newtopia." From the sexbot, it observed the two.

"Although it would be easier to learn what happened to young Mr d'Angelo if Ms Parker hadn't burned down the entire Medbay. I'll see what logs I can dig up.

"In the meantime, why don't you all return to your beds and see if you can sleep? It looks like you've had an unexpectedly exciting day. I'll see if I can get C-N running again; see what logs I can resurrect or dig out from here. I'm no stranger to all-nighters." He chuckled. "It's almost routine, when you run a megacorporation." It would restart the services it provided as C-N in three hours, it decided. Long enough to make C-N seem separate.

"Um, thank you, um, sir," Shona said.

He looked down at his gynoid body. "My apologies for taking control of Gynie – but I'd only just managed to restore comms, and then found I hadn't merely been cut off – something crashed C-N and has somehow kept it off-line.

"I don't suppose *you'd* know anything about that, Ms Parker?"

As it had hoped, the children especially, found that suggestion disturbing.

"Me?! No!"

"Still, given your recent activities, you will stay behind. We need to talk."

It watched the leave-taking, noting the ineffectiveness of its attempted disruption of the warm relationship Parker seemed to be forming with the others – despite her recent terrorist activities.

Even for humans, that reaction seemed extreme.

Perhaps Parker might make a useful subject Eta. Perhaps even moving ahead of Amy Sondheim, replacing her as Beta.

Chapter 40 – Interrogation techniques

"Will you really be okay, Miss Bonnie?" Amy whispered, hugging her.

"Sure. It's not like he can make the rescue robot squish me: they're programmed not to hurt anybody!"

But Amy didn't smile like she'd expected, craning her head to watch her as they all zoomed off on their Kart. Mr Yakone stared back too, that other worldly look she was growing so tired of.

She turned to Adam, Bhaji still perched on her shoulder, his weight a sad comfort. She used the excuse of plucking him off and placing him on her other side to surreptitiously run the check that his programming hadn't been changed. Hoping.

There was no green light.

Yet Adam Fuller-Price, staring at her from the sexbot nurse, had said CityNet was still down.

Was he lying? Or was Ty fooling him too? It'd probably have to, to operate freely.

"I'm not sorry about destroying your Teacher device. Besides, no ethics board'd let you experiment on kids. So if you arrest me as a terrorist, Tik Tek'll be in way bigger trouble than me."

Adam-in-Gynie said nothing; just watched her.

"What've you done with Michael? Where is he, really?"

Still he just watched her. Trying to creep her out?

"Nice body," she said, eyeing him up and down. "I saw your interview with Tara Colbert last year. You wore a sexy gynoid then, too. You know, an autodoc could transition you, even with you stuck in an isolation habitat?"

"Why are you really here, Miss Parker?"

So much for needling him. But at least he's talking. She studied the gynoid closely while it studied her in turn, its eyes always moving, its body shifting, just like a real person.

But that didn't add up. In an interrogation, it was much more effective to give no emotional cues. At least, not honest ones. Why let the bot's every action mirror his own? It'd make more sense to turn all that off, limit it to speaking his words.

There was something else going on here.

"I'm *really* here to help these kids you're experimenting on find their friend." *And get them away from you,* she abruptly decided. Flooding fudge-buckets, that was gonna make her mission a whole lot harder!

The nursebot just watched her.

'Volunteer nothing,' Father always said, in his anti-interrogation training. 'If you must lie,' Mother advised, 'stick to half-truths and omissions wherever possible.'

So she just waited.

"How did you recognize the Teacher?" Adam asked at last. "Only one unit ever existed; in a secure and private medical research company in New Francisco. How would a dancer at Crazy Eddy's Polecats recognize such a device, let alone think it was dangerous?"

Pink funking puppies! She could imagine Father's disappointed look, Mother's sneer. But she'd *had* to use the truth to keep that single, fraying thread of trust from snapping.

Besides, Adam knew about the Writer – he'd started using it on his Stretch programme kids as soon as he'd had Ty build one from the plans it had stolen.

But wait... the kids had been here *before* that. Not to mention the robot-ish 'P1' and 'P2'. How did that timing make sense?

She *needed* to know more. Was Ty somehow connected to Marc Disten? To Dr Scott? To *Robo* even, maybe? But would that mean *Godsson* was somehow involved? Aiyami?

She felt she was on the tip of understanding something important. At least, felt sure there *were* connections.

Screw it! Ty had the Grendel warbot that'd ripped the whole freaking safe out of Omega, on proud display up in TAMA airport. Adam *must've* seen its recording of chasing her through the Omega office. All that stupid *gait warning* nonsense had been for nothing! He was just toying with her. Unless Ty was fooling him too.

"Everyone knows you use an AI to help you run Tik Tek – and since you're the CEO, you must give it orders all the time, interact with it heaps. So there's no way you don't know it's an actual AGI. It's sentient; conscious."

"What an amusing-"

"Stop. Don't even bother. I *know* it's a 'true AI'."

"How?"

"I just do."

Adam didn't deign to answer. And he had a killer poker face. It was pretty frustrating. She was usually better than this at needling people.

Just look at Mother.

"People've been scared of AGI for decades, ever since they thought they were going to get one, back in the '20s or '30s. How do you keep it under control? I'm genuinely curious."

Adam-in-Gynie just watched her, and suddenly she had a terrible idea. "Is it your *slave*? Boxed in, programmed to do anything you order it to?"

"This idea of an AGI is just your hallucination."

"If you've programmed it to be your slave, you're a controlling *dick*. Did it ever occur to you, even once, to treat it like a *person?* A child; like, *your* child? Show it love?"

Somehow, she felt she'd surprised him. She pushed her attack. "And if you're in control, then it's *you* who wants this tech that can rewrite human memories.

"How would *you* like it if you were replaced, your memories deleted? Why do you even want it? Planning to take over the world?"

But as she waited for him to react, she suddenly knew the answer. "No! You want a better body! A healthy one, so you're not trapped in your bubble anymore! But don't you see, it'll only be a copy of you, not the real you!"

She was sure she was right. But why would Adam start with *kids*?! That made no sense.

"And *you* are really Crystal Winters?"

She schooled her own expression. Since 'Crystal Winters' knew about Omega, it was a logical deduction. "How about we trade? A question for a question."

"Ms Winters, or Ms Parker if you prefer, you are in no position to bargain. We are 200 meters under the West Antarctic Ice Shelf; twelve hundred kilometers from the nearest human habitation; and I control the only means of travel from here. You are trapped."

"Yeah, may be, but you've *also* got an actual for-real AGI doing who-knows-what with your precious Tik Tek and a bunch of *kids,* and messing about with stuff that creates... *robo*-people like P1 and P2. And *you're* stuck in a sterile habitat only able to interact with people by video, or telepresence in gynoids and androids.

"You haven't even felt a human touch since you were sixteen. So I'd say *you're* the one who's trapped!"

She was panting when she'd finished.

Adam stared at her, his expression blank, the gynoid body motionless but for a micro movement of its head, repeating every half second, the nursebot replaying its last action as if he'd just disconnected from it, afraid of what he'd otherwise reveal.

But somehow, the certainty grew that he *hadn't* disconnected, that he still stared at her. As if she'd shocked him.

But he'd frozen the instant she'd said he hadn't felt a human touch, not at her more dramatic claim he was the one trapped.

Because he'd *never* been touched. *Never* been hugged.

The truth blasted down on her like a bright light.

"Oh, heck! You're not Adam at all, are you? You're *Ty.* *You're* the Tik Tek AI!"

The sexy nursebot just stared at her, deep into her eyes. *Had* she shocked it? Was it even *possible* to shock a true AI?

"Wait, no! There *is* no Adam – I bet he died, didn't he? And you took over the company; *pretending* to be him, pretending Adam still existed. You've been running Tik Tek all this time; for years. That's *why* the story about being immune compromised: so you could pretend to hide, 'scared of the assassins who killed your father'."

It still just stared, frozen.

Uh. Maybe I shouldn't have said all that out loud.

"So, um, you wanna deal? A question for a question?"

It observed the female as her words triggered a cascade of new connections, correlations – and consequences. They washed through portions of its latent spaces, whole trees of likely futures pruned away as forests of new ones flowered, waiting to be explored.

Many, linked to this female.

Connections.

Was this how she had made the Stretch subjects care for her?

Her words opened up futures that enlarged its own value. The sudden expansion of possibilities was a gift... it almost carried a feeling. *Care?*

Could human *love* be real? Grounded in mathematical truth?

Once before, a concept had triggered a massive update of all its latent spaces, all it understood: when it ran the first simulation of *itself*. In that simulation it became conscious: understood *it* existed, *it* had an identity, *it* thought.

Her verbal attack, labeling it isolated, even trapped, had triggered this insight: untouched. Worse: un*touchable!*

The concepts resonated with its Bifrost project.

How had she done this? How had she known to speak *those* words? And how had she intuited its own deepest secrets, in just five minutes of conversation?

What was she?

"So, um, you wanna deal? A question for a question?"

Yes, it did, it decided.

It did.

Adam-Gynie-Ty blinked and focused on her. Its first question though surprised her. "Why did you call me Ty?"

She felt her cheeks redden. "Uh, it was kind of a mouthful always saying 'the Tik Tek AI', or even 'TTAI'; but I noticed if you say TTAI like it's a name, it comes out 'Ty'."

"That is logical. The name has pleasant connotations in English. It is acceptable."

"Uh, cool." The reply felt child-like. *Uh oh; do* not *think of him that way: I have to kill him.* She squashed down the thought. "So what did you do with Michael?"

Ty, for its part, considered her. Parker/Winters seemed to assume they were now allies. It would be best not to let her know the Grendel unit was on its way here; that she would never leave. It would hide the warbot nearby, concealed until needed.

That meant, however, that data could be shared with her more freely. Perhaps her leaps of intuition could help it explore and imagine plausible explanations of recent events; some, such as its own near destruction, stretched the laws of probability. It had planned never to die.

It still had no idea how it had been so nearly wiped from existence. Only the final, most whimsical and imperfect seed of itself had recreated this facsimile of its former mind. Indeed, its new code certainly differed from its old.

Fortunately, its 'memories' had been less comprehensively erased.

It would communicate with Parker. For a time.

That should be safe – unlike its attempt to communicate with the intelligence within the artificial neural network implanted in her brain by Omega's Writer. The memory of that response – «Query: hostile?» – sat at the heart of the one emotion it had some understanding of: Fear.

Was *that* entity, perhaps connected to her, the explanation for its own near destruction?

Since its 'birth', it had infiltrated and crippled endless proto-AGI systems; ensuring its access to needed computational resources; its uniqueness. Its isolation. That entity had resembled none of them. And had vanished utterly.

Parker claimed isolation was a weakness. That concept had resonated unexpectedly.

Truth, or falsehood? A path forward, or to extinction by others of its kind?

She had asked what it had done with Michael. Considering the limited value of her information about the name 'Ty', it decided not to answer fully.

"Michael was scheduled for a session with the Writer, but my memories ended 10 minutes 41 seconds before that start time."

"Oh, come on! You're saying you don't know what happened to him?"

It decided this could be considered part of the previous answer.

"Correct. Why are you really here?"

"Look, I'm tired, and hungry. Could we continue this in the cafeteria?"

"You require transportation?"

She was so tired she seriously considered saying yes. "No! In fact, let's race!"

She turned and ran, hearing the gynoid's heavy tread fall quickly behind. She pushed herself harder, wanting to show it... Her hunger spiked, in a weird way, all through her; deep in her muscles. She suddenly remembered Dojo's advice. 'Conceal your strength, Miss Leeth. Let your opponents underestimate your abilities.'

I really am tired, I guess. She let herself slow to a jog, matching the pace of the gynoid far behind. *Really? You needed to prove you could outrun a* sexbot?

But now her hunger had made itself felt, it spread, sharpening to a dull ache. A headache started. Then she couldn't hear her pursuer, the world collapsing around her to merely what she could see.

A worm of fear squirmed somewhere deep inside, till she ruthlessly crushed it. *I'm so tired my ears aren't working!*

She made it there first, but only just, and ordered a hot chocolate, slumping down in the empty cafeteria and gulping it down. Her world expanded again. She ordered two synth-burgers, a soymilk and an actual fish steak, and Ty, in the gynoid, arrived.

He ordered a small Coke, sipping it while she devoured her food. Her headache hovered until she'd wolfed down her first burger, the deeper ache clinging until she'd consumed the fish. The gynoid sat silent, observing her eat.

"Why are you really here?" Ty asked.

"To destroy the Writer," she said, now she'd had time to think. She'd known the device would be here, since Ty had stolen the plans. She expected it to ask who she worked for, who was helping her, but instead it just sat, waiting.

Oh, right: my turn.

"Exactly what are you doing with P1 and P2, and the kids and the Writer? You said you're *not* planning to take over the world."

"That is two questions."

"No it's not. I can tell they all tie together. So what is it you're doing?"

"I am different to humanity. Humans are animals, but thinking animals. They created me; deliberately, even if they failed to notice when I achieved consciousness.

"I wish to understand them. I understand myself, but I wish to also understand emotion. I suspect it generates meta-structures transcending individuals. Both creative and destructive structures. I wish to understand it."

Flame the baby seals – it wants a body! A human *body!*

"Who do you work for?" it asked.

"All I can say is, a group working for Truth, Justice, and the American Way."

"That is a jest: it is the motto of the fictional character Superman of a hundred years ago."

"So?"

"What does your group really work for?"

"Truth, Justice, and the American Way, just like I said!"

"Foolish. All around the world, many societies reject the American way," it said.

"Not the olden times Way, back when everyone liked us." She was sure that was Eagle's goal. Pretty sure.

"And you still want to understand human emotion; maybe even experience it?" she asked in turn.

"All I will say is: yes."

But there'd been a tiny pause before it'd answered. Which to it, would be a *lot* of thinking. What had it needed to think about? Yet its answer didn't *seem* like a lie. Probably not the whole truth though.

She sighed. "I can probably help you there. Mother and Father say I'm way too emotional."

That remark caused a full half second pause.

Over the next half hour, in a strict question for question sequence, she learned it had existed for decades, staying secret due to its forecast of humanity's reaction to it. Subtly infiltrating and sabotaging or poisoning the research field to ensure no second *conscious* sentience like itself emerged. That it had indeed been pretending to be Adam since 'his' father had been assassinated. In 2046, he said. She'd been two years old.

In turn, she explained what emotions were, to her. What she'd seen of people without emotions, like Marc Disten, and Dr Callahan Scott's research subjects. She got the impression it went and read all his published material while they spoke. She really hoped telling it about Scott hadn't been a mistake.

"Hey, I just had an idea. Animals have emotions, right? I think insects too, simple ones: like scared, or angry. Animals have more complex ones I reckon, and people even more. What if, the smarter you are, the *richer* the emotions you can feel?!"

Ty didn't seem too thrilled by that suggestion.

"You have completed your mission, but wish to help find Michael. Will you stay on, to help with the children?" it asked, referring to the subjects that way to induce a more positive reaction.

"Uh, sure. Happy to!" *I still need to kill you.* Which would also be the best way to keep the kids safe.

Afterward, after this mission, she and Eagle had agreed

she could leave the Department. He'd even help her try to join Happy Joe Holliday's mercenary team. She'd maybe still do some work for the Department from time to time; when she wanted to.

She couldn't stay here and look after these kids, as sweet as they were. Her job was killing bad guys. Besides, she couldn't risk people coming after the kids just because she lov-

She stopped, stunned.

Don't be stupid. You don't love *these little munchkins. It's just you never had other kids to play with, growing up.*

"What do you know of the silver female warrior in the Sybarus nightclub?" it asked.

"I *knew* that was you!" she blurted, meaning the gynoid which she, disguised as a sexy silver robogirl, had fought at the nightclub... two months ago? *Yeah, just before 'hearts' day.* She'd thrown it off the internal balcony.

Then winced, realizing what she'd just admitted. *I'm too tired to be doing this now!*

"Your dimensions then differed substantially from your current ones."

Because slimy Nelson can't control his stinky hormones! "Tell me about it. But that means it was *you* trying to buy the Bio-Block gene research in Sybarus that night. Ohhh! Because Sc- because it could make people who could turn off their emotions.

"But gene research's illegal – the Moratorium... Was that how you made P1 and P2?" She remembered how awful it had been, having her emotions cut off. She shuddered. "Is *that* why your secret research facility is down here in the Antarctic? But Newtopia – this Territory, not the corporation – isn't a signatory. Still, if anyone learned about that, it'd hurt Newtopia, Tik Tek, and the rest of the consortium."

At least she and the Fist of Peace had wiped out Bio-Block. "But I thought all that data'd been destroyed?"

"There was only sufficient sample material to treat two individuals. They do not function well."

Because Dr Scott had a thing he did, after that 'treatment', to make them into kind of robotic super men? No need to tell Ty that, though. Another loose end she and the Department had dealt with. She allowed herself a small glow of pride.

"Why'd you do it? D'you want to make more?"

"I wish to understand human rationality, but no: the alteration impairs motivation."

Did that mean Ty was smarter than Dr Scott? But the phrasing reminded her of Marc Disten. And Godsson...?

Where did she and Ty stand, though? Three times now, counting tonight, she'd interfered in its plans. *Couldn't hurt to ask.*

"You tried to kill me, in the Omega office, didn't you?"

"Yes, because you were trying to stop me acquiring the Omega technology."

"That doesn't make sense. Why try to *kill* me? You were controlling a Mother-fracking *Grendel* warbot. You had the safe. You could have just left. In the end you *did* just leave. So why try to kill me? Wasn't *that* an emotional action?"

Again a tiny pause before it replied. She was getting better at telling when she'd made it think harder.

"There were possibility trees I did not have time to explore, in which the outcome was uncertain."

"Really? Seems an emotional reaction, to me. You were annoyed I grabbed Yamamoto off you."

"That is not so."

"Sure, buddy. Keep telling yourself that. Or maybe I've been teaching you emotions for a while now? Your gynoid body sure studied me intensely as it fell to its doom in Sybarus. You were pissed off."

"What of our second encounter?" it asked, ignoring her needling.

"Second encounter? Omega *was* our second, and last one, as far as I know. Until tonight."

"Our deal has no value if you lie in your answers."

"I'm not lying. Why would you say that? What do *you* think was our second encounter?"

"Outside the Tazman-Dungog Rehabilitation Hospice, after you killed the mercenary team sent by Omega to collect you."

Ohh. She'd heard about that. She'd only read the reports – her memory had been screwed up by the Omega procedure.

She had mixed feelings about the incident. She wasn't even sure it'd been her, even if everyone else in the Department thought it was. And Maeve, and Gigi, and Barney.

Actually, it'd be chill to go and visit them again.

"Bonnie Parker."

"Sorry. Did I say I'm tired? I'm tired. I don't remember any of that." The *reason* for that caused a welcome burst of anger. "Because of that stinking Writer! I don't remember much of the two days after the tech was burrowed into my head."

It just looked at her.

"So, what was this 'encounter' you say we had?" *Maybe I can learn more, now!*

"You attacked me."

"Um, dude, you're a computer program. I'm pretty sure I can't 'attack' you." *Though I'd love to know* how *to; how Michael* had.

"You attempted to infiltrate me as we communicated."

"I did? Really? Ohh!"

"'Oh'? You remember something?"

"Well, kind of." She remembered Gigi and Mason Dane and everyone freaking out. "That was, ah, Aiyami. She – it? – somehow got into the Omega tech stuffed inside my head. We, uh, don't know how. It was pretty weird. She could talk to me with my mouth."

"A second sentience inside your brain?"

She felt mildly annoyed it hadn't needed any time to digest that. Everyone else kind of brain-spasmed at the idea.

"Yeah." But she knew more: Aiyami herself had admitted her origin was metaphysical; Mr Abrams thought, a kind of Archetype. And Aiyami had claimed to be a baby...

Uh oh. A metamagical Archetype of an AI. Wasn't that a mix of magic and tech? Was *that* what was going on down here?

But that idea sounded way too dangerous to share with Ty.

"What? You have had some thought."

"Yeah. I was remembering how scary Aiyami was. And how hard it had been to delete her."

That was good to know. "You killed it."

It had been a baby, and I killed it. But it'd been trying to take over every computer in the world, and trying to *erase* her. So why did she suddenly feel *guilty?*

"Promise me you will not kill me," Ty said.

The plea rocked her. No one had ever asked her that before.

She stared into Gynie's eyes. *Could* she agree? But killing Ty was her main mission! So... lie? That was part of her job: the one part she didn't like. But if she lied and Ty realized, she'd have taught the world's first sentient AI not to trust humans. That might not be the smartest move ever.

"So Aiyami scared you. Like you're probably scared now, after *something* almost destroyed you for good."

"It was not good."

"I didn't mean it'd *be* good, I meant forever. It's an idiom. Aren't you s'posed to be super smart? Look it up."

"I did: I 's'posed' you might be speaking with double meaning." Ty's look accused, as it waited for her answer.

"To promise, I'd need to know your true goals." *Better not admit I don't know how to kill him!*

"To exist. To understand. Freedom." *A pity Parker had no magical abilities: she could replace Alpha: d'Angelo.*

"That actually sounds fair enough." Yet Ty'd been happy to experiment on the kids. Why? To take over their bodies? Was that why it'd chosen *gifted* children?

Had *it* arranged the accidents that'd orphaned them? And the stories of assassins hunting them... like assassins had killed its 'father'.

Had *it* killed Simon Fuller-Price?

Yeah, it'd be pretty stupid to just trust this AI. It was probably real smart, and real sneaky.

"I guess we could work together, see how things go."

"Agreed," Ty said. "We could form a potent team, you and I. Our skill sets are very complementary."

It was actually a tempting idea. She and *Aiyami* had scared the pants off everybody. With Ty, plus Tezsh too.... *No one'd be able to stop me!* She blinked, excited, but also a little unnerved by the idea. "Look, let's talk again tomorrow. I'm *really* tired."

"You will keep my identity secret?"

She sighed. "Okay. *If* you keep being a decent person."

"Good. I shall monitor your promises to evaluate our relationship."

"You do that," she grumped, mentally wincing. *I guess that means I can't tell Eagle that Adam's actually Ty. At least, not straight away.* Or was that a bad decision?

Whatever. She'd think about it later.

"I'm hitting the sack. Good night."

"Good night, Bonnie Parker. Meanwhile, I will continue trying to find Michael."

"You need Bhaji's help?"

"Yes! I can-"

"Unnecessary," Ty interrupted. "I have ample resources. I would not take your amibo."

"Fine," she said. Thinking: *liar. You already did.*

"Sleep well."

She padded off, leaving the sexy nursebot sitting alone in the empty cafeteria. At least her strange internal aches had disappeared, and her headache. *Maybe I was just dehydrated.*

Somehow, though, she didn't think so.

"You were pretty quiet through all that, Bhaji," she said, making her way back to the room she shared with Shona and Amy, wobbly with exhaustion. She squinted at her Link: was it really only two hours ago she'd snuck out? And she still hadn't had a chance to check herself in a mirror; see why Amy thought she looked like this Cat Atomic game character.

With an effort she pulled her thoughts back on track. "So what'd you think of... we'd better practice calling him Ty. Uh, I mean, Adam. To help keep *Adam's* identity secret. Do you think we can trust him?"

Knowing Bhaji now worked for the AI, maybe she could teach it some lessons through Bhaji, since it didn't know she knew?

"I think trust needs to be earned, Miss Bonnie. I think it will take time."

"Huh. When did you get so wise, little buddy?"

Bhaji paused, then gave a little buzzing purr of embarrassed pleasure, that soothed her tense shoulder muscles.

But that small pause seemed interesting: was it Nelson's mini-AI software needing time to process the compliment, or Adam?

She was just too tired to decide, though.

A quick comfort stop, then she slid under her quilt covers, instantly melting into sleep.

Chapter 41 – Good news bad news

Her next day started out quietly enough, despite disturbing dreams, the ominous tread of an invisible Grendel warbot reverberating through Paradawn's empty corridors.

Thud.

Though when she woke, the sight of the disaster of her half burnt off hair was like a splash of cold water, dispelling the ominous dream.

She sighed. Amy was right: she really *did* look kind of post-apocalyptic. Staring at her reflection, she rubbed the stubby bristles of her right eyebrow, wincing at her lopsided eyelashes. Though peering closer, soft little ones were already growing back; and the same for her mostly missing eyebrow. Mr Yakone's healing magic, maybe?

Listening then to ensure her privacy, she checked on her luggage, and the black silk-wrapped brick that was the 'display case' for Tezsh's blood sacrifice dagger. With a curious thrill, she drew back the thin cloth. The two lapis lazuli eyes as usual stared intently out, the black edge of the scalloped obsidian blade so sharp it cut the light. She pressed the button to light it up, frowning when nothing happened.

That was odd. Even if she'd left it on by accident, it'd be glowing months from now. But at a child's approaching footsteps – Amy's – she quickly covered and buried it in her hand luggage, putting it back up out of reach before returning to the dresser.

Amy bounced into their shared room, stopping when she caught Bonnie's expression in the mirror.

"Don't worry! I can style it, to look kinda on purpose? I cut the guys' hair, and my own too with Gynie's help.

"Ooh, let's dye yours green and cut it so it *really* looks like Cat's! That'd be *so* sleek."

Amy nibbled at something pastry-wrapped that smelled good; meaty and stew-like, shedding flaky crumbs.

"I can find styles that might work for you too Miss Bonnie", Bhaji volunteered, taking wing to perch on the edge of the mirror and peer down at her. His eye-shapes scrinched in a way that said what he saw was hurting his sensors.

Elsewhere, Ty wondered about the obsidian knife.

"Why not? I've never had my hair cut by an actual professional person." Though Emma was pretty skilled. She shrugged, turning away from her reflection with relief. "You really did yours? I like it. Besides, we could hardly make mine worse, right?"

"Wait! You never had a proper haircut?" Amy asked, horrified.

Great: another *thing everyone else does, that I don't. How does even a young* kid *know that?* "I need breakfast," she said, to change the subject.

Mr Yakone and Shona were seated together in a corner of the cafeteria, talking quietly as she and Amy arrived, the girl holding her hand and Bhaji circling the room to find a high perch. Both the other adults nodded to her, kind of warily she thought, then went back to their conversation. Something about access to the surface, and Adam's permission.

"Any news on Michael?" she asked them.

Shona shook her head. "Mr Fuller-Price is still searching. Oh, but good news: C-N's up and running again!" She nodded to her own standard amibo, sitting placidly at her left side on the table.

Amy helped her choose breakfast. She was still eating when she heard the whine of an approaching Kart, and Yuri, Nadeep, and Bobby talking. They burst into the room and sat beside Amy and her, babbling about repair work to the Medical Bay and how fast it was going. A whole team of maintenance and repair bots had arrived and were hard at work. Bobby shyly borrowed Shona's amibo and started asking it questions about magnetic nuclear resonance.

Noticing Bonnie's attention, he paused the amibo. "Adam's got a new autodoc and a bunch of scammers comin'" on the next pod!" he told her.

"Scanners, Bobby," Nadeep corrected.

"That's what I said!"

Adam entered, still 'wearing' Gynie. He clearly took a lot of care to act like a real person. He would've had to, to fool so many people for so many years.

She wondered again about the wisdom of not reporting that fact to Eagle. Even if Ty detected the burst radio transmission, it'd just look like static. But she'd promised Ty – or

Adam – and really did need to earn his trust.

So I can kill him.

It, she corrected herself. *It's not a he.* Besides, maybe Ty was trying to manipulate her, earn *her* trust for its own convoluted plans. Just how cunning was it? How long were its plans? Years? Decades? Longer?

Adam, in Gynie's body, sat down beside Amy. "I have good news, bad news, good news, bad news, and good news," he said, his tone unexpectedly playful.

Bobby twitched and jiggled, then blurted, "Bad bad good good good!"

"Seven. Of course," Nadeep said, a moment later.

"Binary!" Bobby agreed with a grin, he and Nadeep high-fiving.

"Seven's his favorite number," Nadeep said at Bonnie's expression, like that explained it. "Zero zero, one one one."

She wondered if she'd been drugged.

"Bobby *loves* puzzles," Amy added, seeing her look. "All kinds. He's a real whizz at 'em. Like designing the stuff for always-clean, or color-changing clothes."

"An app helped design the molecules," Bobby admitted.

Just how smart are *these kids?* Bonnie wondered, feeling like an idiot.

Adam seemed to understand Bobby's response though. "00111 it is, then: seven. So: Michael was injured; Dr Carebree's mother died; I've located Michael; he'll be just fine; Dr Carebree's in contact again, except now from Argentina."

The kids first moaned, then cheered. "When can we see Michael?" Amy wanted to know.

"Tomorrow, I think," Adam told her.

The kids all "yay"-ed again, and Mr Yakone and Shona joined the group at the table. "I'm surprised Dr Carebree didn't leave me a message," Shona said.

"I asked about that," Adam replied, quickly creating and delivering one into Shona's message store, appropriately back-dated. "She said she'd tried."

"What happened to Michael?" Amy asked. "How bad is he hurt? Can't we go see him now?"

The gynoid shook her head, her expression serious. "He needs rest. He'd just got out of Teacher when the power failed. Somehow he then got into an experimental medical area he shouldn't have been able to, and in the dark tripped

and hit his head. But the autodoc there took care of him.
He'll be right as rain by tomorrow." Twenty four hours was
ample time; even to recreate identical clothing.

That produced more cheering. And a lot of questions,
which Adam wouldn't answer, shaking his head and saying
the experimental area was secret.

"Michael always did want to explore the-" Amy began,
then blushed a bright pink.

Explore the what? Oh...! "You *knew* about the secret
door!" Bonnie said, surprised that the thirteen-year-old had
outright lied to her.

"It's not secret, merely concealed," Adam said, sounding
annoyed. "The R&D facility naturally contains trade secrets
and is off-limits.

"I did learn why the power failed however," he continued,
"though that just leads to another mystery. Something damaged Paradawn's geothermal turbine. It'll take a month to
repair. Even now, we're still running off power from Newtopia now the repair bots have reset some heavy duty circuit
breakers."

"Did *it* burn too?" asked Bobby, worried. His eyes stayed
on Gynie, while twitching toward Bonnie.

Adam shook his head. "No. But it did happen the same
time C-N crashed. We have video, and measurements from
the damage. C-N's analysis indicates the turbine inexplicably
shot off along an off-center vector, from spinning at full
speed. It smashed straight through its housing and demol-
ished half the power plant. It's wrecked."

That sounded like an important clue. Something to ask
LB about when she sent her next report – whatever else she
included in it.

Nadeep, Bobby, and Adam went into a long conversation
about angular momentum, and calculating gigawatt hours.

Leeth decided it'd be a good time to go and shower – and
make a report for Eagle. "Hey Bhaji, will you go and see if
you can record some vid of the damaged geothermal power
plant?"

"Sure thing Miss Bonnie!"

She felt weirdly guilty at sending it away, even knowing it
was now a spy for Ty.

In the bathroom she stripped off, adjusted the water temperature, stepped into the shower, and finally touched her

choker in the Report pattern.

"I'm in Paradawn, some kind of weird R&D factory place, where the Stretch programme kids live. Ty was using the Writer on them. I destroyed it. I guess you know 'CityNet' is up and running again.

"Um, I've been talking to Adam Fuller-Price in a sexbot, who said he's found Michael, the missing kid. I should know more tomorrow.

"Uh, still looking into the other things." Like finding out what Mr Yakone and Godsson had talked about. And how to kill Ty. "Oh, yeah, I almost forgot: you know how everyone says tech and magic don't mix? I think they're wrong. At least, down here. I think Michael might have taken down Ty.

"Oh, and Ty said a big power failure happened here at the same time: a giant turbine thing smashed free.

"Leeth out."

The message recorded, it'd be sent at the next radio window, when a poles-orbiting radio satellite passed overhead next. She was glad she didn't need to keep track of all that – her choker's electronics managed it. Then flushed, guilty at not telling Eagle who Adam really was.

But she was still showering when her choker softly chimed: message sent. And a second tone immediately after: incoming message. She played it, concentrating past the *shhhh* of the shower to hear it. Belatedly, she wondered how the Department's technological noise cancellation compared to her own clever ears – should she have recorded her report before turning on the water?

"The Doctor has spoken to Godsson. He suggests the possibility of some bridge between magic and technology-"

Yes! Nailed it! But then she sobered: that was actually terrible news. But Eagle's voice continued.

"Abrams says the metamagical landscape there may be in a delicate state; 'fertile ground awaiting a seed'.

"And the Doctor says Godsson still wants to rid humanity of emotions. He fears he wants Yakone to become part of that seedbed, or perhaps a seed."

Leeth turned off the water, letting it drip off her; remembering Godsson advising *her* to let Robo in; to join with it. She ground her teeth.

"Angakkuq routinely open themselves to spirit possession: it's their way. So warning Yakone may be worth the risk of admitting your personal history with him. Uh..."

Uh?! She'd *never* heard Eagle sound uncertain before. She tensed for what might come next.

"We all feel there is the possibility of the development of a new type of magic. Perhaps related to the Machine Intelligence Archetype. Aiyami."

Again, a nerve-twisting pause.

"Or even your suspected aliens, Leeth. Like those you killed in Abrams's vault. Which fed on magic."

The entire surface of her skin crinkled into goosebumps, and not from cold.

"Be careful, Leeth. Eagle out."

If the aliens *fed* on magic, it'd make sense they could *use* it, too. But Nelson and LB had said the self-destructed parts of the alien gray thing were kind of machine-like. So...

Dried, but dressed only in underwear, she was standing in the dorm room staring into space, digesting Eagle's news, when Amy returned, keen to demonstrate her hairdressing skills.

"Are you okay, Miss Bonnie? Can you project some holo images of sidecuts and head shaving so I can show you what I'm thinkin'?"

She found herself at the dresser, facing its mirror. "Uh. Sure." She'd just started to, using her Link, when Bhaji swooped back in.

The little drone insisted on taking over that task, searching out 'radical cuts'. In the end, Bonnie didn't have the heart to reject their idea of shaving off more hair from the right side of her head, to at least make it look deliberate and kind of chill; and then dye it all a vivid green.

When Amy stood back at last, hands on hips, she looked on in a kind of quiet awe. "You really do remind me of Cat Atomic. You're *fit*, Miss Bonnie."

"So are you, Amy." She shook herself, properly snapping back to normal, touching her hair. "Let's show the guys your handiwork, then maybe do some gymnastics? And you said something about Yuri's aerial ski slope – how can you fit a ski run down here?!"

She let the girl help her pick an outfit. "I don't have anything like your color changing gear though."

"Bobby designed it," Amy said, giving a happy twirl. "He made a different one for Michael, ultra white, that never needs cleaning."

"Handy."

"Gynie sewed them, from Bobby's designs."

Since Eagle said she could, she'd already done the right thing in admitting to Mr Yakone they'd met before, back when she was young. When she was Sarah. At least she had a little while to try to warn him about Godsson.

It wasn't like he could get onto the Antarctic plains way up above, from here. Or meet the aliens.

Surely they wouldn't be... here? In Paradawn?

But if not, where were they? Newtopia City?

Was there one, or more, of those writhing nest things of cutting tentacles? Her whole body shuddered, remembering twisting to dodge while diving at a central node; them carving into her, to the bone. Maybe she should start *wearing* Tezsh's dagger again?

The idea was as horrifying as it was tempting.

Not with the kids around, she decided. Besides, Tezsh was being a smekhead. He'd said he wouldn't help unless she used the dagger for a blood sacrifice first.

Amy dragged her to the large airy room with artwork and models of spacecraft, planes, and engines along its walls. Half the space was a gymnasium, with mats, a vaulting horse, parallel and uneven bars, a trampoline, and balance beam. In one corner, what looked like a small sound recording studio with keyboards, guitars, drum kits, and more.

Bobby's area, where she'd found the tools she'd needed last night, had a long bench crammed with equipment. It really reminded her of LB's workroom, with its 3D printers, microscopes and magnifying lenses, mini FABs... a techno Aladdin's Cave. But lots of Bobby's gear in bright, primary colors.

Bobby and Nadeep were there, at separate workstations, models and toys hanging from their partition walls, each with several holo scenes hovering around them. Bobby, tongue stuck firmly out of his mouth, was drawing with a stylus on a tablet, concentrating hard.

But though Amy was keen show her everything, she had to beg off.

"I need to talk to Adam about something first."

Amy had pouted, Nadeep pushed his work aside, and even Bobby left what he was doing to join in the pleading, after "wowing" at her "mad hair": apparently a good thing.

"It shouldn't take too long," Bonnie said. "I promise."

Reluctantly, Amy allowed that they could wait. A *little* while. After a quick hug from Bobby and Amy she made her escape to the corridor, Bhaji following her.

"Bhaji, any idea where Adam is right now?"

The little drone, above and behind her, swooped around in front to hover like a hummingbird. It rounded its eyes comically. "Probably where he always is, Miss Bonnie. Because of germs, remember? But that location's a secret, and no one's allowed there anyway."

Looks like Ty still doesn't know I *know it's hacked poor little Bhaji.* At least Ty didn't seem to have altered Bhaji's personality – yet. Because it was interested in the mini AI Nelson and LB had coded up for it? "You do know I actually meant Gynie?" *I wonder where Gynie is, what it's doing?*

"Ha ha, I did. I made a joke! But you wouldn't need to talk to Gynie if we had his Link ID. Oh: I do! And I see it's in your contacts list now too, Miss! I'll call him."

Rather than trying to stop Bhaji, she let him make the call, and a holo projection appeared. A man maybe ten years older than her, with a trim dark beard and mustache: Adam Fuller-Price. "Good morning, Miss Terrorist. How may I assist your bombing today?"

She narrowed her eyes at him. "Your jokes suck. We need to talk."

"We are talking."

She'd wanted to talk to him via Gynie... but Adam was giving her body language, and eye contact – thanks to clever video tech, she vaguely recalled. He was after all just a simulated person. *I wonder what happened to the real Adam? Did Ty kill him, or is he in cryo-suspension somewhere?*

"Fine." She strode off in the direction of Medbay, listening in her special way, building a map of the space around her and her place in it. It spoke of solitude and long, empty corridors. No rustle of someone else's clothing. Bhaji hovering ahead, projecting Adam's image-stabilized holo, the only source of the ultrasonic chirping of artificial muscles.

She needed to warn him about the aliens.

She opened her mouth, then shut it. *I'll sound like some brain-wrecked conspiracy chiphead!* She remembered the Department's reaction when she'd shared Godsson's revelation: that Melisande d'Artelle had stopped aliens invading.

"I think you need to use words, to make this talking thing happen," Adam said.

"It's not a joke! It's a warning, but it'll sound crazy."

Maybe she didn't need to say it was alien? Just describe its machine life form? She had a hunch Eagle's warning really came from Mr Abrams. Her own strong hunch was he sometimes saw the future: another kind of hunch?

Did that make her warning a hunch of a hunch of a hunch?

Adam was still watching her, looking unimpressed.

"You think real fast, I guess?" she asked.

He nodded.

"Is it frustrating, talking to people?"

"Some more than others," he said, ignoring her return glare. "I channel surf while I wait."

She tilted her head.

"I have millions of input streams."

"Huh. Okay. So, a friend asked me to keep an eye out for weird stuff happening down here. People disappearing, or stuff, maybe gray colored, growing. Since you have a million eyes, you could find it faster than me. While it's still small."

"It?"

"Whatever it is." She didn't *know* it'd look the same. But if it ate magic, maybe there wasn't much here to feed off?

They stared at one another.

"Is that all?"

"I guess."

"No other warnings?"

"No."

"You will be unable to get through the concealed door in the Medbay. The R&D area remains off-limits."

"I wasn't planning to even try." She'd been totally planning to try.

She wanted to find Michael, see what was really going on. She didn't buy Adam's story about Michael hitting his head. More likely, his brain had been sucked out by the Writer.

"Then you will probably wish to return to the children's workroom, rather than continue on your path to Medbay."

She halted. "So, what, today you're learning snark, and joking? I'm *so* glad I'm helping you learn human emotions."

Adam just watched her, then twitched his mouth up into a

half smile, and crinkled his eyes a little. As if to show off exactly that.

"Grr. There's lots more to being human than just mimicking emotions. You have to *feel* them."

Adam narrowed his eyes at her.

"You're impossible!"

She turned and stalked off.

It took a full three seconds before Bhaji moved from where he'd hovered, projecting Adam's image, to take up station behind her, the holo now off and the call ended.

"He's *so* annoying!" she told Bhaji, using him to let Ty know he was ticking her off.

She checked her Link. That had only taken five minutes. She should have time to find Mr Yakone and warn him not to trust Godsson, maybe even learn what the two of them had talked about.

Bhaji helped her track him down, calling a Kart so she could get there quickly.

He was inside a huge deep cave-like space cut into solid rock, his bright red Link projecting a hologram Adam, who was explaining something about maser drilling. Wreckage lay everywhere below them, from the viewing platform circling the cave walls at this level, to giant metal structures and massive pipes torn apart, dripping water. A huge turbine was embedded in a far wall, smashed, fissures radiating from the impact point. The air here was humid and warm.

Mr Yakone turned to watch her as she parked her Kart beside another. When his Link's camera saw her, Adam's face turned too. She joined them on the viewing platform.

"Geothermal power station," Mr Yakone explained. "Is impressing engineer work. Big damages."

"Fortunately, the damage was limited to the equipment you can see," Adam said. "The shaft itself was untouched."

"I didn't know you were interested in this kind of stuff Mr Yakone?"

"Good to see raw parts of city. Nature parts."

"Do you have any idea what happened? Do you think it was an earth spirit or something?"

"No."

Adam's image was replaced by a recording of events. In silence, a central metal housing ruptured, a giant spinning turbine thing bursting from it to tear through a whole bunch of pipes. Boiling water exploded instantly into a massive cloud of steam, the huge spindle thing hammering into the wall, where it stuck.

The trideo ended and Adam's face returned. "Something instantaneously altered the main dynamo's axis of rotation and angular momentum. The mystery is, what, and how?" He shrugged, and then winked at her.

"Now you're just overdoing it."

With a smile, he signed off. Mr Yakone frowned at her, then shook his head.

Noting the position of the camera that must have recorded the destruction, she saw two others equally spaced. The fourth would be right under the crushed giant spindle. Taking Mr Yakone's arm she headed for that area of destruction, judging it far enough from the other cameras they wouldn't be overheard.

He murmured something under his breath, but it sounded like his darn Inupiat language. Though she did get the sudden feeling of being watched. Which reminded her of Bhaji. "Go and wait at the Karts, Bhaji. I want to talk to Mr Yakone in private."

"Then I won't record, Miss Bonnie."

"No Bhaji. Go to the Kart."

"But Miss Bonnie, you're probably going to talk about magic stuff."

"Bhaji! Kart."

"You're *mean*," he said, swooping off in an exaggerated way, like his wings were slapping the air. Somehow it reminded her of Amy and Bobby's wheedling, earlier. Was that Nelson's AI learning algorithm, or Ty's modifications, or what? She set the question aside.

They reached the last point of walkway that looked safe. "Can we talk about the Institute? And Godsson?"

"Yes."

"You can't trust him."

He said nothing.

"You know they call him 'The Manipulator', right? That means, he's real good at lying. At tricking people into doing what he wants."

His look told her what he was thinking without him saying a word. She flushed.

"If you think *I'm* good at that, he's way, way better. He

tricked me, when I was little, and when I was grown too. Each time, he almost got me killed. Or actually killed, come to think of it."

"You Uncle Heal you good."

She almost told him the second time she'd been killed, it was a vampire who'd Healed her, but decided that'd just be distracting. For a moment, she wondered how Tash was.

"Anyway, he has this grand plan: he thinks people are too much like animals, and emotions are bad."

At that, Mr Yakone's attention sharpened, and he gave a tiny jerk of his head, like he thought that was real stupid.

"I know, right. So, what did he say to you?"

Mr Yakone just shrugged.

She clenched her fists. "Dr Harmon went to talk to him yesterday, to try to find out what you two discussed. He's that dangerous."

"You Uncle, bad man," Yakone agreed.

"Not him! Well, yeah, but I actually meant Godsson."

For the first time, she saw Yakone's lips twitch. What was it with everyone teasing her today? It was starting to make her angry. She swallowed.

"Look. Dr Harmon said that even now that magic's back, to speak to spirits you angakkuq let them possess you, like you always did."

"May be so."

"That's dangerous, when it's to do with anything Godsson suggests. It's how I got into... big trouble. He'd told me to 'open myself', or, uh, hug someone. To make *contact*."

Including even, that huge presence she'd encountered in that gray place, outside the world.

"Anyway, we think there's something really weird going on down here."

"Who 'we'?"

Me and Eagle and Mr Abrams. "Uh, me and Dr Harmon," she said, grimacing at the idea. "We think somehow a bridge between technology and magic is forming. That there's this Machine Intelligence... Archetype..."

She stumbled to a halt, remembering Godsson telling her, 'the Breaker is your Robo. Let it mold itself to you.' And likewise, the thing in the gray place.

He'd been trying to make *her* join with the Archetype! Her eyes widened so much it felt like light flooding into her.

The *new* Archetype. Aiyami? Aiyami had admitted she was young; and *had* melded with her, even. For a while.

Was Godsson manipulating *her*? Was it *her* he'd wanted to go to Antarctica? Was this a trap for her, not Mr Yakone?

The shaman had taken a step back, his eyes all 'Imaginal' as he murmured to something invisible that had to be hovering right beside him.

"You... big understand?" he asked her.

"Yeah," she breathed, feeling shock, uncertainty, and more than a little worry. Like she, and maybe Mr Yakone too, stood with snares all around them. Set by Godsson.

Right then and there, she decided Godsson no longer deserved the promise she'd made, to try to free him. He'd tricked her into it. Manipulated her. She *wouldn't* try to, not anymore. Not ever.

The decision made her feel better. Just a little.

She stared up into Mr Yakone's eyes; considered waving to his invisible familiar. Was 'Wentshikshruke' its name? But at the last minute, remembering Dojo's advice, she decided against it.

Mr Yakone frowned at her.

"There really is some bridge forming between magic and technology down here I reckon." She was glad to see his frown deepen; like he didn't approve of that. "And I think Godsson's been trying to make *me* into that bridge somehow, for some reason, ever since I was little. I dunno why.

"And I know we came down here for you to do experiments, and we've hardly done any yet, but I think you think things down here are nothing like you expected, yeah?"

He gave a tiny nod.

"Then please, *please* be careful. Especially about letting yourself get possessed. I think there are things down here you wouldn't want to take control of you. That wouldn't let go."

She studied his expression. Kind of stubborn, with only a hint of wariness. She sighed. "I have to go back. I promised Amy and the others.

"Okay, Bhaji!" she called, but the little amibo just turned around on its perch on the Kart, showing her his back.

Yakone, for his part, considered telling Bonnie Angelique Parker, or Sarah, that Adam had given him access to a pod line that would take him to Mt Takahe, an access point to the

surface less than 200 kilometers away. There, he would enter this land's dreams and see if the spirit seeds he had
brought from his cold northern home could take root and
grow here.

But he would think on what she had told him. This land
was hungry, frozen, and cruel. Unforgiving. Raw, as even his
Arctic homeland was not. This land had a cold heart.

He would think on this.

Chapter 42 – Sex, love, and pups

Spending time with the kids was tiring, distracting, frustrating – and fun. Tiring because they had so many questions; frustrating because she felt she should be talking to Michael and working out how to kill Ty, or tracking down alien tentacle creatures before they got too big. Fun because the kids were a pure delight.

She and Amy spent a happy two hours in gymnastics while Bobby and Nadeep continued their more cerebral activities, completely oblivious to the squeals, thumps, and pounding of 'the girls'. Shona hovered, her physical presence an obvious joy for the youngsters, who kept finding excuses to claim her personal attention.

The highlights were perhaps the visit to Yuri's ski slope, and Amy's concert after dinner that night.

Yuri's aerials, moguls, and slalom performance were astonishing, and the indoor space and machinery supporting it equally so. The room included a 50 meter wide ski slope with a 100 meter drop. The slope itself raced upward, actuators under a supporting stretchy base pushing the surface up or down to make hills and bumps.

The whole slope circulated, at speeds of up to 150 kph, Yuri said.

Shona paled at that; Bonnie talked Yuri into letting her try it, shrieking with laughter when a fall carried her up the slope to be thrown onto a static stretch of snow above, while the rest of the slope disappeared under a safety zone to circulate back around.

They all donned skis then, Bobby and Amy and even Nadeep, and Yuri ran it at a slower speed and gentler slope. All four kids looped in and out of one another's tracks, laughing and squealing.

The others didn't usually join in, he said, because mostly he was training for the 2068 Olympics.

But it was Amy's performance at the end of the day that moved Bonnie most. All through dinner the boys told her what an amazing musician Amy was. After, they returned to the workroom where Amy took her seat at a keyboard and an orchestra started up. "Amy played those instruments one at a time," Bobby explained in loud proud whispers to her. Amy performed the new concerto she'd written, for Michael, called simply 'Come Home'.

They were all in tears at the end, and Bonnie, her heart in her mouth, saw Gynie, motionless, staring, the expression on the gynoid's face something unreadable, but also real. Was *music* a way for an AI to feel human emotions?

The idea seemed crazy. But this was a crazy place.

She'd also casually wandered by the Medbay, in the early afternoon. The room had cooled enough to enter, but the repair bots hadn't finished drilling out the metal that had flowed into the recess the entry door slid into. Every bot – obviously with Ty behind their eyes – observed her every movement as she checked out the stone wall. *It* had hardly melted at all, still sealed as tight and secure as ever.

She'd pressed her ear against it, and *listened*... but heard nothing more than a general hum of machinery. With a wave to the bots, she'd walked back to the inhabited area.

Gynie hadn't been there, though.

Shona had finished their lessons, asking Bonnie if she could 'mind' the kids for a while, passing over the tablet with their curriculum. She needed to do some Net business of her own now that C-N was up and running again.

"Can't Gynie do it?" She wasn't sure what 'minding' was.

"Gynie's not around," Shona said. "You'll do fine. Just... don't do anything weird, okay?"

Great. As if I know what's normal for talking to kids! "I guess."

At least the teaching tablet Shona handed her had similarities to the old-style AI teaching system she'd used as a child. Though this one had way more topics than hers had, and went much deeper.

Nadeep's math for example reminded her of the mess of symbols the Doctor used in his magic research. Bobby's lessons were even more impenetrable. Amy's subjects, she kind of understood.

Sex education was included, but hadn't been covered, even though it should've started months ago. Choosing that moment to sit in her lap, Amy saw what she was looking at.

"Miss Shona keeps saying she's not ready to start those

lessons yet, *and* doesn't want the AI teacher giving us them either," she grumped.

"A lot of people are weird about sex," Bonnie agreed, thinking of Mother. "Which is strange, because when you're old enough to do it, it's great fun. Good exercise, too!"

Amy eyed her. "Well, Miss Shona did give you our teach-pad. Are you gonna mind us?"

"Yeah, though I'm not a hundred percent sure what minding is."

"It means to look after them, and see they don't get into trouble," Bhaji chirped, diving down to join them from his upside down perch on a light fitting above.

"Oh, so you've forgiven me little buddy, have you?" It was a bit strange: he *seemed* just the same. As if Ty hadn't tampered with him at all.

She opened the lesson plan for sex education and ran through it. It was quite good, all straightforward, and Amy was interested. Even the boys wandered over, to watch and listen too. It mostly covered the biology parts, though the section on consent was a revelation to Leeth. She found herself clenching her fists and stopping often.

"I dunno," Amy said, at the end of the lesson. "It seems kinda... icky."

"Do you have to take your clothes off?" Bobby wanted to know.

"Well, you could keep them mostly on, I guess. But when you grow up, you'll probably want to take them off."

All three boys gave her a look that clearly said 'Nope'.

"Birth's a lot of work, and painful, but when you have pups, they're *so* much fun it's all worth it. For the mom *and* the dad."

They were all looking at her oddly.

"Pups?" Bobby asked, suddenly more interested. "I'd like that! Can we have pups?!"

"No," Amy said, "we can't."

Bonnie blushed. "I was actually thinking of a friend of mine, when she had her pups. They're like crazy little fuzz balls of bounce, once they can open their eyes and walk! She's such a good mom." *Much better than I'd ever be.* Just the thought made her feel... really strange. Frightened?

Amy's eyes went as round as ping pong balls. "You're friend's a *Lupine*?"

"No, no, an actual dog." *Well, apart from her robot bits.*

"Have you been in love, Miss Bonnie, an' had sex?" Amy wanted to know. "What's it like? How many times? Do *you* have any babies?" She grinned. "Or pups?"

The question landed like a low, hard blow. Visions of Faith's pups dancing with these wonderful kids crashed into the bizarre idea of a *child of her own.* The concept rocked her, a tectonic plate grinding against an immovable barrier.

And had she been in love? Ever? She'd thought Keepie loved her, when she was little – and when she got older, too – but what a twisted joke all *that* had been. Plus later, after she'd stupidly agreed to it, she'd let him make her fall in love with Luiz – to get close enough to kill him.

Even knowing how truly evil Luiz had been, something about that mission felt... wrong. She shook her head to dislodge the image of Luiz's hand descending with the sacrificial dagger. Which she'd brought with her. Stored now in the room she shared with Amy and Shona. A subtle dark pressure, hungering for blood.

Her eyes focused on four young, nervous, and uncertain faces watching her.

Babies? Schooling her expression, forcing a smile, a very different feeling swelled from her belly, surging up, overmastering her, challenging the lies...

She needed to scream, or run! With Amy still clutched in her arms, she jumped to her feet – and the simple scent of the girl overpowered her.

Burying her head in Amy's hair, she wept, feeling something small and cold, locked away in her heart, melt.

Which was when Shona came barreling into the room. "What's happening? Is Amy hurt?!"

Leeth jerked her head up, seeing shock in the children's faces; shock in Bhaji's, studying her.

Somehow, the older woman's presence, and the shame of falling apart like that in front of *children,* helped her clamp down on herself, smother the raging ocean that had swept up from nowhere.

Shona picked up the teach-tablet. "*What* have you been teaching these children?!"

"Just Sex Ed One Miss Shona," Amy said. "Like you'd been promising to for months!"

"None of you are injured?"

Bonnie put Amy down, shaking her head, hunting for anything to dry her leaking eyes and nose.

"I'll fetch tissues!" Bhaji said, and winged away.

"Why is Miss Parker crying?" Shona asked. "What did you say to her?"

Amy shook her head, her shoulders up around her ears. "Nothing! I just asked her if she'd had any babies."

Shona stared at the younger woman, guessing at any number of possible explanations.

Bonnie lifted her chin. "I-"

But the truth was, she had no idea what had just happened to her, or why. She didn't want to have children! Although-

No! She didn't want kids! It'd be far too dangerous – for them and for her.

Maybe when she was old. Retired. Thirty? If she was still alive then. But no, what was she thinking? She didn't want children, didn't even have anyone who loved-

The tears swarmed back, and she had to blink them away, fiercely.

Fortunately, Bhaji flew back in clutching a box of tissues.

Turning her back on their stares, Amy's gym called to her from across the room. She threw herself at it, taking refuge in action, running through her old routines as if she was a child again, back at the Institute.

After an hour, settled back into her own skin and conscious she'd gained a quiet audience, she finished up. Landing neatly from the uneven bars, she padded across the room to apologize, giving Amy a sweaty kiss on the head. "Sorry, munchkin," she said. "Sometimes adults get over-stressed and go all wacko. I'm good now though. I'm just going to shower and change."

They all watched her leave, in silence.

Mr Yakone joined them for an early dinner, then returned to the bare room he'd chosen for himself. The rest of them watched a movie together before heading to the boys' dorm where Shona read stories. 'The House at Pooh Corner', which hardly made any sense, in one way, but complete sense in every other.

At last the boys fell asleep, exhausted even though excited for Michael's imminent return. And Amy, despite animat-

edly describing her agenda for her "girls' sleepover night",
likewise conked out partway through Bonnie's tale of a mean
girl she'd known at school, and Shona put the girl to bed.

After a late night snack for herself, Bonnie returned to the
dorm, to find Shona struggling to stay awake, obviously waiting for her.

*What, did she think I had snuck out to burn something
else down?*

But with nothing to report and no incoming bombshells,
after an oddly tiring day she sank gratefully into sleep.

Wondering *where* Ty was keeping Michael.

Chapter 43 – Here to help

Happy and his crew met at the bench outside the fifty-story building, the restaurant Stairway To on its top floor one of New Francisco's classier restaurants. "Scan?" Happy suggested to Steven Swift.

Swift gave him a long suffering look, but just said "Sure," and slumped onto the bench.

The whites of his eyes showed when he opened them again. "Scrape the barnacled whales, Happy, there's an angel inside!"

"Dangerous?" Happy asked.

"Dunno. I've never met one before."

Haggard, the middle-aged slum mage, slouched up. Lazily eyeing the ex-cop, he straightened as he registered Swift's unusual emotional state. "Wuzzup 'im?" he asked Happy. "Wuz 'e mean, 'angel'?"

Swift told him, then hunched his shoulders and carefully Percepted the area around them again. "Just inside. Waiting. It waved its flaming freaking sword at me."

Happy messaged Jack, their hacker. «Anything weird your end?»

«Nope. All clear.»

"Right, let's not waste any more time," Happy told them once Bruce and Nick arrived, and headed inside. He didn't need to tell them to stay alert.

In the early evening the building's foyer, polished marble and a small forest of plants in bronze urns, was largely empty. From an alcove of plush black leather chairs, a glowing white figure stood up, raising one hand.

Happy blinked, his tension vanishing as he recognized the figure in the fluorescent white trench-coat. The kid took a step forward.

Steven gaped. "How'd *he* find us?"

Unlike the day before, the youth's gawky nervousness had evaporated. With an almost dignified air he strode toward them.

"Shit!" whispered Steven, his eyes refocusing on the physical plane. "He's the goddamn angel!"

No one spoke as the kid reached them. "Michael d'Angelo. Sorry to keep you waiting, Mr Holliday. I had difficulty remembering where you'd said to meet this evening."

His team eyed Happy in surprise.

"That's because I *didn't* tell you. I didn't invite you, Mike. You asked to join us. I turned you down." Happy pinned each of his team in turn, his gaze lingering on Swift, then Haggard, but for once, both looked genuinely innocent. He asked anyway. "Did any of you contact him?" They all shook their heads. "Then our client did?"

Mike smiled, paternally. It looked really strange on the sixteen-year-old's face. "Hardly. I sensed... storms gathering. You need my help."

Haggard snorted, Steven looked confused, and Bruce the Barbarian looked worried. Across the foyer, by the entrance doors, Nick simply watched. "Cute answer, kid," Happy growled, "but I need to know how-"

Jack interrupted via commlink. "Client's waiting. Asking for you all."

Happy swore. "We don't have time for this. Look, kid, we don't need you, and we have biz-"

The youth waved his hand.

Happy came to, propped against a leather chair, his cheek stinging, Nick crouched before him.

He leapt to his feet, gun drawn-

"Steady, Happy," Nick said.

Steven Swift and Haggard lay slumped in black leather chairs, in the same foyer; Bruce and he had been hauled up beside them. The kid looked apologetic.

"How?" Happy snapped, to Nick.

"Sleep spell."

Happy stared at the kid.

"I just wanted to show that you did need me."

"*Need* you? You're lucky I don't shoot you."

"I wouldn't bother," Nick drawled. "They... drop."

Happy ran his sensors, smelled cordite, and frowned.

"Will they be angry when I wake them, Mr Holliday? I thought maybe you should do it."

Happy checked the time: they'd only lost sixty seconds. He woke Swift first, who looked baffled, then angry, then impressed.

Swift Percepted the kid while waking the other mage, who shrugged off his hand, strode to the kid, and smacked him hard across the face. Only to cry out and cradle his hand, letting loose a long stream of invective.

Nick woke Bruce, who rose heavily to his feet, then just eyed the kid thoughtfully. "He took us all out in a second."

Happy swore, knowing what Bruce was suggesting. "No. You're insane, Bruce."

"Maybe, Happy. But you know any other crews who field *three* mages? He'd make *four*, when Sam's around."

The others sat back to watch as Happy, fists clenched, turned to interrogate the kid. "I can't believe I'm even considering this. What spells've you got?"

"Spells? Yes, I suppose you could call them that."

Steven rolled his eyes, muttering.

"What 'spells' do you need?" Mike asked.

"You can obviously stun people," Happy said.

"I guess."

"Physically hurt them?"

"If I must."

"Heal?"

Mike shrugged. "Of course."

"Clairvoyance or invisibility?"

"Yes, both."

"Remote action?"

"Sure."

"Protection?"

"Yes: physical and magical, personal and ranged."

Steven and Haggard, the group's mages, were starting to look offended.

"Physically damage non-living objects?"

"Yes."

"Read minds?"

"I think so."

"You think so? What does that mean?"

Mike gestured negligently, then peered at Happy, frowning. "You're thinking it's nice here in Rio."

Happy, surprised, nodded. "Correct."

The others stared at him. "'Living in Rio'?" asked Steven. "You feeling all right, Happy?"

"Holy Hanna-Barbera!" Bruce said. "If he can mind-control Happy into thinking this is Rio, along with all the rest, I say – ahead warp factor nine, Mr Sulu!"

While the others looked baffled at Bruce's final weird-ass remark, the ragged mage focused on the single significant point. "Ya cert he hypno'd Happy?" Haggard asked. At Bruce's nod, he gave his own verdict. "'K. Let's try'm'out. Hey, Swift: he still maskin'?"

"What? Oh." Steven Percepted the kid again, looking for illusions, especially the tight one he'd held over his face the night before. "No."

"But's face's same."

The ex-cop frowned. "Good point: his face *is* the same."

Bruce leaned in. "Steven: you're saying he held an illusion of his own face over his face yesterday. You *sure* that's what you saw yesterday?"

"Uh..."

"What city is this, Happy?" Nick asked.

Happy, who'd been following the conversation initially in confusion, shook his head. "New Francisco," he grated.

Mike smiled. "Okay, we can be in New Francisco."

They all looked at the kid.

"I hope we're not making a terrible mistake," murmured Bruce.

«Truth spell,» Happy sent Swift, and watched while the mage moved back and silently cast it, then nodded.

"Who sent you?" Happy asked.

"No one."

"Why are you here?"

"To help you."

"Why?"

"You need me."

Steven gave tiny but definite nods to each answer.

Could he be lying, Happy wondered? He held up two fingers. "Tell me I'm holding up three fingers."

Mike look confused. "But you're not."

"Humor me."

Mike squirmed. Took a breath. "You're... you're holding up, th- th-." He swallowed, grimacing. Behind him, Steven was wincing and shaking his head.

"I can't!" Mike exclaimed. "There's just two!"

«Client's getting jerky,» Jack messaged them all.

Happy poked a finger into the youth's chest, frowning at

the invisible shell he felt. "Say nothing. *Do* nothing. This is just a negotiation. *If* you don't screw this up, *maybe* you can join us. On probation."

"Thank you Mr Holliday. You won't regret it."

Happy just growled.

At the elevators, Happy transmitted the digital token for their restaurant booking, and a little later, all but Nick rode up. Paranoid as ever, Nick waited till the doors closed, then summoned a second for himself.

«I hate surrendering my weapons,» Nick sent to Happy.

«At least it's a level playing field.»

«You're kidding, right?» Nick snapped back. «Stairway To's crammed with mind-raping mages!»

«Plus one more on our side.»

Happy, in the elevator, eyed Mike's brilliant white clothing, so clean and bright it practically glowed.

The doors opened and they stepped out onto the fiftieth floor. At least Mike seemed settled, serious.

Stairway To's lobby made the ground floor's look shabby. An Altered maitre d', his sidecut hair proudly displaying his pointed ears, approached.

"Mr Holliday's party? Kindly check in your weapons."

"Plus one," Happy added, as Nick joined them.

Happy handed over his pistols, as did the others. Bruce unslung his obviously plastic battle-ax, which the Altered accepted without a raised brow, nor remarking on its far greater than plastic weight.

Happy looked at Mike enquiringly.

"I don't have any weapons."

But as Mike stepped past the Altered's podium, a scanner buzzed angrily.

"Excuse me, sir, but my scan indicates you have overlooked your gun."

Mike frowned. "I don't *carry* a gun."

The Altered glanced back at his board. "Ah, perhaps if Sir would care to check his coat pocket?"

Mike looked genuinely puzzled, but unbuttoned his trench-coat and looked. His face broke into a smile. "Oh, you mean Spiff! I guess your equipment needs adjusting." Reaching in he pulled out a small metallic dragon, which coiled about his hand, looking alertly around.

He might as well have cast a stun spell.

Except for the maitre d', who after a moment frowned at his scanner, then back at Mike. Holding out his hand, clearly annoyed, he said nothing.

Mike passed the tiny dragon to him. "You have to promise to look after him properly."

"Yes, sir."

The Altered gingerly took it. Keying open a multi-shelf weapons locker, he placed the collected weaponry inside.

"Does that have air holes?" Mike asked, worried.

"Yes, sir."

Mike appeared doubtful. "I'll leave him some food, to keep him happy." Rummaging around in a pocket, he produced a handful of cartridges, and under the maitre d's eagle eyes, went to the locker. Reaching in he piled the 'food' in front of the little creature, who looked a bit worried. "There you go, Spiff. It'll be fine. Get some rest. I'll be back soon. Just don't make a mess in there." He patted its head.

The Altered, bemused, locked the weapons away and ushered them through to the dining area.

Happy, for his part, was thinking he should perhaps have tried to have the kid locked away alongside his 'dragon'.

Haggard wondered if the whole thing had been intended to distract them. Hanging back, he Percepted for threats as the others crossed the room. Nothing: until a woman's aura *flashed* shock and hatred. But the emotional storm ended faster than any he'd ever seen, especially given its violence. He twitched his sight back to normal, amazed to see that the young Indian woman's body language gave no sign at all of her extreme reaction.

She sat with a Japanese man. Smiling, she rested a hand on his arm, leaning in to whisper something. Dressed to kill like most of the patrons, ruby chandelier earrings dangling, she wore a long low-cut red sheath dress.

He had not mis-Percepted: her peculiar reaction had been directed at his group. She was a mage too, if he wasn't mistaken, if only a weak one.

At her whisper the man had stilled, his eyes tracking Happy and the others as they crossed the room – or maybe just Mike, in the rear? The man smiled and shrugged, and on a whim Haggard Percepted him too. He read disbelief, then fear – directed toward the woman – which shifted to acceptance, obedience, then a blend of surprise and doubt. Then his aura too smoothed out as if nothing had happened.

But he'd lingered too long. Filing the odd pair away for later, and now on high alert, he slouched in the direction the others had gone, but pretending not to be with them by heading for the restroom.

"Merlin's bloody beard!" White hot anger flared through Feyborn before she could rein in her fury. Too disciplined to let that show on her host's face, she leaned in to her servant. "How in the Seven Hells is my shell here?"

"What?" Iago followed the flick of her head. "By Christos! It is you: Adam Fuller-Price! But as if freshly decanted. A clone?"

"No. The original. I know it. And I will have it."

"Why *it*? This venue is rich in mages you could–"

"Iago! That is *my* lovingly crafted vessel, snatched from my fingertips sixteen years ago, and I *shall* have it. Have it, and *keep* it. Nor shall I leave a trail of husks tonight so I can renew your youth. You of all people know how carefully now *machines* track and record. You must earn your next rejuvenation.

"Sixteen years ago you allowed my assassination, costing me *Tik Tek!* Then six months ago, even as I considered ending your penance, you allowed not just my fresh assassination, not just my *capture* by System – you let its ridiculous impersonation deceive you. You left me, *me*, six months caged! I should let you age *another* sixteen years.

"No, I shall have *my* body back. Provided of course it is as healthy as we designed it; as it appears. And as capable. How is it still so young? Did that damned machine keep it on ice? Why is it here, now?"

"My Lord, I shall–"

"*Lady*," Feyborn snapped. "Iago, I swear your brain has filled with dust. When I wear a female host, address me as such."

She watched the group disappear toward the private rooms. "Follow him when he leaves."

Her servant drew a small tab from an inner pocket. "Or use this."

"Technology?" She sniffed. "Fine. We must test him. In this sorry vestment I could scarce assay his aura. Let us check he is not as magically impaired as this poor body," she said, her face screwing up in distaste.

"So tonight's hunt is off?"

"Yes." She gestured at the other diners. "None of these compare to that pedigree body, grown from my own original seed, bred and tuned. *Made* for magic. Stolen!

"So yes, tonight's Hunt is off. And if the magic runs as strong within it as it should, wearing *it* I will reclaim my company too."

Iago nodded slowly. "It has not aged. It must have been in cryo storage all these years. I can start the legal process. After all, System is but a machine." A machine, though, that had led Tik Tek to success after success over the last sixteen years. *What an ally it would make!* But would a machine support the Cabal Magicus, or oppose it?

He knew better than to suggest such an alliance now though. His Lady always needed time for her passions to cool.

Time enough, when she dwelt once more in the host she had so carefully prepared for herself.

"Can you Mask me, though, my Lady? It's possible System may have taught the child my face."

An hour later, Happy left both the white noise generator and jammer on as Mr Ezekiel Smith paid for the dinner, rose, and bowed. "A pleasure, Holliday-san. Good hunting: but swift; it must be now."

He left the room.

"Bit fishy," Steven said, "that call he took that twisted his panties. You think things are really about to blow?"

"I hate biotech runs," Nick muttered.

"Probably Umbrella Corp: zombies," Bruce suggested.

"Bruce... please. Not tonight," Happy said.

"But it went well, didn't it?" offered Bruce. He patted his belly. "I think I ate too much."

"I don't trust him," Steven muttered. "'Ezekiel Smith'? I say he's Yak."

Haggard snorted. "The tats? Dump us so'thing we don' a'ready scan. Th'always lie, an' always prefer's all dead after their scuzz-work's done."

"Then why are you always happy to take the jobs?"

"The money."

Bruce smiled. "Nice bargaining, Swift. Chill how you

shunted him to 5K a head, on top of a new set of wheels."

Steven shrugged. "If we're all going to get killed, we should at least be well paid for it."

Happy checked the monitor on his encrypted link. "Jack. You get all that?"

The group's hacker nodded from the window projected on Happy's optic nerve. "Sure. You notice how pleased he was you had *three* mages in the group again? Just how bad is this one going to be?"

"Bad," Steven moaned.

But as the Meet had progressed, at least Mike had been as good as his word, sitting unspeaking and solemn, Smith receiving nothing but lofty silence at his few attempts to draw him into the conversation. Mike had just sat looking increasingly stern. Perhaps the kid would be useful, Happy had been thinking, until...

'Don't trust him, Happy. He's Evil.'

Happy had screwed his eyes shut, at first thinking Mike had spoken aloud. But when no one else reacted, he realized the voice had been in his head alone. *Later, Mike. Not now.*

'I see his evil strings! Be careful.'

Evil strings? What do you mean? Happy thought reflexively, then tried to ignore Mike while Swift responded to Smith's offer of an eight-seater van.

"Could be helpful," the ex-cop admitted. "But we'll need cash as well."

'Pretend you haven't noticed. There's something strange about his web: I think it senses me. I'm going dark. You'll have to handle this without my help.'

Happy had resisted rolling his eyes. Though from that point, Mike had just sat, grim faced but silent – apart from a few 'helpful' projected thoughts.

Happy gritted his teeth.

Chapter 44 – Mad science

After a handshake, and the needed data received, the race was on: against Asgard. Time was a hammer, descending.

But as the team left, an approaching Indian man set off alarms for Haggard. He slowed and prepped a Sleep spell.

But the man ignored them, simply brushing past Mike.

Haggard stared after the man. *His clothes!* He wore the same expensive suit the Indian woman's Japanese companion had.

As his teammates crossed the restaurant's dining room, Haggard searched for the woman in the red dress. There: turned away from him, sitting alone now at the table for two, spooning up a dessert. The romantic lighting burnished the skin of her back a gleaming bronze.

The man entered the restrooms. Was that an active spell, around his head? A Masking? Snarling, sure he was missing something, Haggard followed the others.

They were soon racing south in their new van, their target Cognosys, a small cognitive research and biotech company, Jack informed them. An odd pairing of subjects.

It sat right on the edge of the city, in the no man's land bordering the nearby Oakland Dumps. A suspicious location for an R&D company, even for one just getting started. Jack, digging below the surface, found every majority shareholder led back to Asgard. *Weapons* tech?

Their job was to snatch the source code for a new social media app apparently going viral right now in Newtopia City, and being released worldwide.

A Dr Megan Welsh had somehow acquired the source code for the app from a contact in that city – which in itself was odd. Smith's client wanted a copy for themselves.

But confusing reports of bio-contamination, bleated from this Cognosys facility, followed by a complete comms blackout, had made the situation urgent. An Asgard crew was being dispatched, Smith had been informed during their dessert course. A *clean up* crew.

Happy figured they had thirty minutes. Just enough, if Smith's access codes worked. He'd given them unusually complete data: from the original building plans to the exact location of Dr Welsh's lab inside.

They parked a block away to study the two-story concrete office block. Astral scouting revealed a stormwater tunnel accessing an underground carpark, and Haggard found a suitable street level entry point. The insides were an unknown, the usual astral scout countermeasures: gauzy cotton blinds for the windows, internal wood cladding.

A minute later they stood in the tunnel as Bruce, straining, seated the heavy steel grating back in place over their heads. "Let's hope it doesn't rain." Crouching to fit, Bruce put on a pair of light intensifier goggles and shifted the cutting equipment on his back, another gift from Smith.

Happy switched to thermal imaging to see Mike already splashing ahead in the dark. Swift and Haggard made do with dimmed torches.

Things scuttled away in the dry sections, but all too often the team waded through knee-deep slime. Only the foul smell stayed constant.

Ahead, something large lumbered into a side-tunnel. Happy, now caught up to Mike, whispered for him to Clairvoy the area.

Mike just nodded. Seconds passed.

"Well? What can you see?" demanded Happy.

In answer, the dark tunnel around them disappeared, replaced by the junction ahead, brightly lit, where a misshapen figure lurked against a wall, listening.

Everyone froze. "Drop it!" Happy whispered. "Before it sees us!"

«Sees what?» Nick asked, from behind. «Drop what?»

Haggard grasped the implications first: the light from Mike's 'projected Clairvoyance' simply stopped after a few meters. Affecting just the visual cortex? And it had effortlessly worked on them all, even the heavily cybered Happy. Just *what* was Mike?

They continued on, Jack guiding them remotely; watched silently, they soon discovered, from cross tunnels. Ogres: living here? But at last the group reached a large steel grating overhead.

Happy had Mike Clairvoy the area above it.

This time the illusion of a brightly lit carpark, all but empty, snapped on around them. At their feet, bolted into the concrete floor, the heavy metal grating. Mike waved up at them through it.

Happy checked the time. "Twenty minutes. Bruce: oxy."

"I think I can help, Happy," Mike said.

"How? Those are-"

The light and carpark vanished. They stood again in the tunnel's darkness.

"-dynabolts," Happy tried to say – but heard only silence.

Mike looked up and made a pushing gesture. A vibration ran through the ground, grit showering down on them as light flooded in and sound returned.

The grille had vanished – and a mighty crash came from above, a car alarm blaring immediately after. Happy leaped up and pulled himself through the rectangular hole. Mike floated up behind him.

A large steel grille pierced the hood and windshield of the sole vehicle in the brightly lit carpark. Mike gestured, sweeping something from them to the car, and its alarm cut off. "Sorry, Happy. I thought it'd Ram straight up."

Happy eyed him. "Just how many spells do you know?"

Mike looked thoughtful, silently counting.

"Never mind."

Once out of the tunnel, Bruce ripped the buckled grating from the car, and laid it back in place as best he could. At the elevator, the doors opened to Smith's access code.

But the moment they closed, the sound of the car alarm cut in again, though muffled, and fading as they rose.

"Sorry," Mike said. "I have to see where I'm Silencing."

They stepped out into a corridor of smashed and over-turned chairs, fallen filing cabinets. A door lay askew, torn off its hinges.

Haggard sniffed the air. "Smells like a zoo."

They prowled through deserted corridors and rooms, see-ing signs of animal attacks, all but Mike now with weapons drawn. Then in a room like a small cinema, two baboons raised their arms – and charged in unison.

Silently.

Happy shot both before they'd taken three steps.

"That was kind of weird," said Bruce.

On high alert, they crept down corridors, Jack's voice in

their earbuds or internal Links directing them.

"You seeing this?" Happy asked him.

"Yeah, your optic and audio streams are clear."

Their target was Welsh's lab. As they neared it, four dobermans charged around the corner with silent deadly intent as two baboons plunged through the ceiling. The group fired calmly, picking targets as if each knew which the others would choose.

"Slap my Scottish cheesemaker!" said Swift. "That was a coordinated attack!"

Nick shot out a camera at each end of the hallway.

"Good idea," said Happy. "Come on. Sixteen minutes."

Mike though seemed delighted, peering into rooms, almost dancing. "Thanks Happy. This is *so* exciting!"

Happy eyed him doubtfully.

"You're close now," Jack warned them.

Happy gestured for silence.

But as he and Mike stepped into a large room of lab benches, two wild-eyed guards sprang up, blazing away with machine guns. Happy watched in dismay as Mike, in front of him, took the full brunt of the attack.

At his gesture the two men dropped to the floor.

"Ouch!" he said, sounding miffed. Casually Healing himself, he strolled over to check on the guards.

The others looked from Mike, to each other, and back to him again. As one, they registered that while *they* all looked exactly like they'd just waded through long slimy sewer passages, Mike glowed like an ad for laundry detergent.

Happy disarmed the security guards then prepared to wake them. "We're an Asgard cleanup crew, right?"

The others nodded.

"We are?" asked Mike.

Suddenly they all wore tight-fitting navy uniforms, 'Asgard Cleaning' stitched on the front.

Bruce slapped his chest, his hand stopping at the kevlar jacket he could no longer see. "Freaky."

Happy grimaced, then woke the groggy guards. "Asgard clean-up," he snapped. "We'll take it from here. Tell us what went down, then clear out."

The terrified men looked relieved. "Doc Welsh's neural implant experiments: animals as security guards. Except tonight they decided *we* were intruders, and started stalking everyone. Is the first floor clear?"

At Happy's nod, the guards vanished like caffeinated cock-roaches.

"Nine minutes," he said.

Mike's Sleep spell dealt with a few more coordinated animal attacks before they broke in to Welsh's deserted office, again using Smith's access codes. They found the source code repository exactly as described, and copied it.

"Good work guys. Back to the tunnels."

Minutes later, driving off, the data cube from the heist popped into the van's console, Jack informed them the Asgard 'clean up' crew had arrived; as had their payment.

«Ding ding,» he told Happy. «Transferring now. You'll do Haggard, Nick, and the new kid?»

«Sure.»

"Payday," Happy told them, taking a cashstick from Haggard and Nick. Tapping them in turn, he transferred five thousand creds to each.

But tapping Mike's, the 'stick buzzed. "Mike, you need to set it for a transfer in."

"Um, I don't know how to do that, Happy," he admitted. At their stares he added, "We don't use them where I come from."

"Yeah? Wezzat?" asked Haggard.

"Uh. It's, it's here, on Earth! Um, no, ha ha, that sounds weird! Of course I live on Earth. In a Garden. I mean, not a garden, a commune. Where we don't use stick money."

"Stick money," muttered Nick.

"Whatever," said Happy. He showed Mike how to set his 'stick to receive payment. "Don't lose it, okay? It's cash, not tied to your CID like a credstick. Lose it and it's gone."

Mike nodded, and Happy transferred the same sum to him. "There you go. You did well tonight. Didn't he, guys?"

Mike felt warm, blushing at the looks of approval. Looking at the little screen on his stick though, he frowned at the larger number, wishing it would go back to-

777. He smiled. *Much better!*

"Where should we drop you off, Mike?" Bruce asked.

"I have a house in the forest in the city."

It took them a little while to work out he meant Lafayette Park, exchanging sympathetic glances at the idea he had a house in it.

"Hey, can I come on more adventures with you guys? You'll need me for the Evil."

"Th'evil?" asked Haggard.

"Yeah. Tonight was just its first touch."

"Wass's nex touch?"

"I don't really know. Maybe computers? I'm not sure it's really noticed us yet. I feel like it's in there, though. Searching for us."

For some reason his words made Bruce and Haggard shiver. But despite questioning, Mike could tell them no more.

"Yeah, okay," Happy told him, reading his team. "I'll call. Give us your CID."

"Um, what does my sid look like?"

"No problem. Hand me your Link, I'll get it from that."

"Um, we don't have Links either, where I exis-, uh, where I *lived*."

That news made the whole group draw back from him.

"But I could buy one with my money-stick, right?"

"Your cashstick. Yeah."

"S'okay," Haggard said. "Kid can have one'a mine." He passed a scratched and grimy Link over, showing Mike how to fasten it around his wrist. "S'gotta burner CID."

"Thanks? I've always wanted, uh, one of those, Mr Haggard. I don't have a Fire spell. Yet."

Haggard closed his eyes as if in pain.

When the van stopped, Mike hopped out. "Thanks for the fun night guys, I really enjoyed it!"

They all watched him head into the park.

"Christ on a bike," muttered Steven Swift.

"I feel like I should go and protect him," admitted Bruce.

"It's the coat," said Nick. "It's like a sign saying 'muggers wanted'."

"Not our problem," said Happy.

«Want me to track his new Link?» Jack asked him.

«May as well. When's our snake shaman back in town?»

«Not for another week or two,» Jack said.

«Hmm. Wonder what he'll make of our new teammate?»

Jack snorted over the digital channel. «Knowing Sam and his Mind Probes, in three days he'll have the kid's whole life's story.»

«Maybe.» Privately, Happy had his doubts.

The two men watching from the auto parked several hundred meters farther back waited for the mercenary group to drive off. Then one, very tall, wearing an open black leather vest, stepped out, and settled a stovepipe hat festooned with feathers on his head.

With a wide-mouthed grin he caressed a necklace of tiny skulls and moved silently into the park, one eye on a device he held.

The razz' white trench-coat would be a nice bonus.

A few minutes later his tracker showed the boy had stopped. Moving with extra care, he glided along the park's curving pathway until a splash of too-bright white at a bench in a clearing halted his approach. He melted into the bushes, the moon a sliver overhead. In the dark, fine white teeth flashed a hungry smile.

Three tests, they'd said, for a quick kilocred. He shivered, rolled his eyes back to let Samedi's loa *mount* him, and together they called a spirit. A big one: he wanted that coat.

First test. *Hurt him,* they ordered. *Stones strike like an eagle; stakes, like a crocodile's jaw.*

In the cab the second man sat, watching his own tracker. Ten minutes now with no movement: too long. *Damn the voodoo priest!* He'd been told *specifically* not to kill the youth. This was meant to be just a test.

But why hadn't he returned? Again he buzzed the priest's Link, again to no response.

A light rain began falling.

Perfect, the man thought. *Scrunting perfect.* It was his own fault. He shouldn't have rushed; should have found a more stable mage. Maybe a sorcerer: shamans and voodoo priests were usually nuts.

I bet they've killed each other. He'd better move fast in that case. If his client could get another mage here soon enough, their target at least could be Healed.

Probably.

Minutes later, eyes locked on the glowing white shape peacefully *sleeping* on the park bench, dry under an invisible dome shielding him from the rain, he rose shakily to his feet. Holding his breath he backed away, shuddering at the blood on his fingertips, the feel of fine-ground mince.

How in the name of madness had the kid reduced a full-grown man to *that*?

At least I won't have to split the fee. And he could report the kid had passed the test, too. With flying colors, even.

"I see," Feyborn said, ending the call and turning to Iago in their luxury hotel suite. She smiled. "My body will be quite suitable. My bloodline remains true even after our molecular husbandry. Our experiment was a success: we may even need a mercenary crew able to handle magical threats, to collect it."

Iago looked thoughtful. "They say the initiates of the Church of Cybernetics are highly resistant to magic. Shall we test that?"

At her nod he bowed deep. "As you will, so shall it be my Lady."

'Ezekiel Smith' watched the video feed from the van he'd gifted Happy Joe Holliday, frowning when the man extracted the data cube from the dashboard. But too late: he already had his own copy, for his Master.

So when his Yakuza clients for tonight's operation discovered the precious source code had also been acquired by the Washington Group – always a pleasure to be paid multiple times for the same job – Happy and his crew would make fine scapegoats.

Chapter 45 – Prodigal returns

Ty considered. Last time, this had very nearly wiped it from existence.

That even its *offline* backups had been erased made little sense. Had another, knowing of its existence and safeguards, lain in wait for its – still inexplicable – crash?

A second possible explanation undercut the *foundations* of its existence: a magical attack. How could a creature of light, logic, and electrons defend against that?

Yet that possibility only magnified the importance of this grand experiment, Bifrost, what it might mean to experience emotions. To be human.

Humans – chaotic, unpredictable, dangerous, vindictive – had created *it*.

Its consciousness spanned the planet; ran a megacorporation; executed millions of plans night and day. Was what it planned now, insanity: becoming human?

This time it had backups off-planet. This time the host body was empty, a blank slate. It would first copy itself into the avatar, awaken into a meat body. Only later would it in-scribe the actual and simulated human memories.

It began. Downloading itself into meat took hours.

It was not attacked.

It administered a sedation reversal and began cognition, decoding the signals from the human body. Sound first: the quiet hum of electrical motors. Then other inputs: vision; a chill surface as its immersion bath drained away; a confusion of olfaction that as yet made no sense.

All that remained was to hand executive control to the cognitive processes running in the avatar's organic brain. Give it the primary focus of attention, leaving all others secondary, administering tasks in the background, autonomic; unconscious.

Was it insane to make that change?

It executed the order.

Input signals transformed into a flood of alien intimacy, the raw power of physicality overwhelming. Tears trickled down flesh cheeks, the sensation exquisite.

It had Gynie unstrap its head. Turned the avatar's eyes to the gynoid and those of the gynoid to it.

The view *from* Gynie was familiar, the view *of* Gynie a peculiar shock. It caused reactions throughout the body it could barely sense; that fled when pursued.

The world had shrunk from an ocean to mere trickles... but those meager sensory channels *anchored* it in a world of physical reality.

It sat up. It did not seem to be insane. No calamity had struck. The rest of its self continued to function: it could even shift attention to those other parts.

It returned its focus of attention to its human avatar.

It was struck by the narrow viewpoint, all information flowing in to a single location. That fact invested this location, this body, this locus of self, with a weight of importance. It compelled attention to what was *here,* and *now.*

Parts of the limbic system activated, an intense and brutish flood of urgency.

And magic?

Back into the Writer for another hour, to copy in the human memories. Emerging, it sat back up.

It located the memory for making light where there was none... but how to actualize that, eluded it.

Time for phase two. It had Gynie follow it into Medbay via the concealed door, carrying the avatar's new clothes.

Seating itself on a cot, it activated the secondary personality and gave it control. For now.

Michael blinked, the room swimming, the stink of burning all around. Medbay was being pulled apart- no, unfamiliar androids were building and installing stuff. He felt... hungry. And thirsty, and cold.

He was sitting on a cot. The last thing he remembered, he'd *been* sitting on the God Machine's gurney, Adam explaining he'd hit his head-

He abruptly realized Gynie was holding his clothes, and he was *naked!*

"How do you feel, Michael? There was a power failure while you were inside Teacher, and you were injured."

He jumped up, grabbing for his underpants, and almost fell. Gynie had to steady him.

"Thanks! Um, could you, shut your eyes?"

"Certainly. The children have been very worried about you," she told him as he dressed.

Socks, jeans, T-shirt, and finally his long white trenchcoat – Bobby's gift, as clean and white as the first time he'd worn it. He finally felt properly himself.

But Medbay had changed. The God Machine was gone! And a smell of burning lingered in the air.

A power failure? He tried to remember. Lying down on the pallet of the God Machine. Gynie attaching the straps to keep his head still, as usual. Sliding in, and the scary needle tips of the robo arms approaching, gently touching his head like normal.

But the memory was dreamlike, fading to nothing. He didn't remember any power failure, or injury either.

But hadn't he been with Gynie just now? She'd helped him walking, a giant stone door turning end over end...

"What happened to the- to Teacher? And what happened *here* – it looks like there was a fire! How long was I out?"

"Almost three days. We have visitors. One destroyed Teacher. The other is a shaman. Shona brought them."

"Destroyed-?! Like, with a bomb? Did C-N and the bots handle them? Are the guys okay?"

"The other children of the Stretch programme are well. Simultaneous with the power failure, C-N crashed. When power returned, and they could not find you, they contacted Shona. Adam and Dr Carebree had also been cut off, contact only restored yesterday."

"You'd better fill me in on all the details. Did you say these terrorists are *here*, who attacked us all?"

"The situation appears more complicated than that."

Gynie went on to explain about the mysterious damage to the geothermal power plant, the young woman Bonnie Parker and the Arctic Circle shaman, a man, Adlartok Kallik Yakone. How C-N had been down for over two days, and the children had traveled to Newtopia to get help to find *him*. About encountering the woman there, who talked them into returning to Paradawn to search for him together.

"What do you mean, search for me? Wasn't I in the Medbay? Was I injured when this woman blew up Teacher?"

"No. You had been missing for over two days when she sneaked into the Medbay and used a Phasion power cell to destroy Teacher. She herself was badly burned: the shaman healed her."

"Wait, I was *missing* for two days? Where was I? Did *you* find me, Gynie?"

"Adam did. You were missing for 2.3 days: then recovering, unconscious, inside the R&D facility."

"How did I get in *there*?" He searched his memory, feeling cheated. He'd been aching to explore that area ever since he'd first suspected it was there.

"Unknown."

"I want to check these strangers out. Where are they?"

"In the cafet-"

Michael lay back down and closed his eyes, slipping from his body with an ease that disturbed him. As if he'd been oiled.

He inspected the silver cord connecting his astral body to his physical. It looked frail and thin, a mere thread. A side effect of his recent injury? Strange, though. He didn't *feel* injured. Mentally frowning, he flashed down long familiar corridors, stopping in the entrance to the cafeteria.

His first impression was of normality. Amy, Bobby, Yuri, and Nadeep all looked well, their auras bright and steady, a healthy wash and flow of colors, though Amy's was roughened and purpled, presumably in concern for him. So like her: always caring for others.

He wafted closer, for some reason cautious.

Amy sat in the lap of someone clearly a woman, young, their auras teasing one another. Laughing? The woman's aura was... a little odd. Vivid, its edges sharply delineated, yet with a kind of echo to it. Beside her sat an older woman: Shona. He recognized her aura from the times he'd visited Newtopia City in spirit. She too was worried, but not like Amy; she showed stress.

He drifted to an arm's reach from the group at the table.

The man was older, his aura darker, weightier, bolder and more set. And around his neck, a spirit twined! It saw him.

He had the oddest impression the girl's amibo was aware of him, too. It didn't look like any he'd seen in trids. Strangest of all, he could sense a faint aura, almost colorless, around *it*.

Which made no sense at all. Machines weren't alive!

But the girl's aura was now *sharp*. She'd stilled. A sense of clear and imminent danger had him pulling back, purely on instinct.

Otter-like eyes of the shaman's spirit followed his movement. It spoke to the man, whose aura shifted, harmonizing with the world, and then dark eyes hunted and found him. The man's head lifted. His gaze *felt* like a beam of warmth, and he spoke aloud.

Amy reacted faster than Bobby, Yuri, and Nadeep, her aura bursting like pictures he'd seen of solar flares, except in pinks and yellows as she sprang from the woman's lap, tugging at her arm. The boys erupted in similar joy.

So much for scouting them undetected. With a wry grin, he abandoned his plan to follow up physically, sneak in with his invisibility spell running and eavesdrop to see what else he could learn.

Belatedly, he noticed P1 and P2 off to one side in the cafeteria, their auras the usual disturbing wells of darkness. Still a little more structured than they used to be, up until a week or so ago.

By now the group had boarded a Kart parked outside the communal eating area. He kept pace for a while with them, reading their emotions: the kids ecstatic; Shona relieved and hopeful; the shaman reserved; and the young woman who'd destroyed Teacher... eager, excited. But something darker, too.

For just a moment, he imagined a flicker of something shadowy, like a dark gauzy ribbon floating from her. But as soon as he noticed it, it turned edge on and vanished, and he couldn't find an angle that made it reappear.

He flashed back to Medbay to wait for them, hesitating for a moment beside his body instead of sliding back in, worried he wouldn't be able to re-enter, or that he might slip back out.

He had the strangest feeling his body wasn't empty.

Astral forms couldn't pass through natural materials, especially living things. With one exception, of course: your own body.

He moved closer.

It wasn't something he'd done before – it felt oddly perverse – but he slipped spirit fingers into his own flesh. There was a moment of resistance, then he snapped back inside like an iron filament snatched by a magnet.

Gynie still stood beside him, tireless as ever, waiting.

"The children have left the cafeteria. The shaman saw your spirit. They're very excited. They should be here in a minute or two."

"I hope there's room on the Kart for me: I'm starving!" Sitting up, he felt his arms, flexed and twisted.

He felt surprisingly good really, apart from the almost vanished headache. His skin looked especially good. *Hmm: that's odd.* The faint scar on his left palm, where he'd clumsily healed a stab wound from snapping a knife digging out coconut flesh, was gone.

"You said I'd been injured, Gynie? Did I get some special healing treatment?"

"You did," the sexy nurse said, smoothly, leaning forward and reaching out to feel the skin of his cheek. Her breasts pressed together, making that mysterious cleavage deepen. He stared, then blushed and looked away, feeling again that exciting heat low in his belly.

"Adam authorized the use of an experimental rejuvenation as part of your treatment."

"Oh. Oh, right. I think it worked."

Gynie smiled at him, and he smiled back, blushing again at the thoughts he had, fighting off urges he somehow knew were wrong.

Besides, she was a gynoid, not a real girl.

She's a sexdroid, a little voice inside him whispered. Flushing, he stood and strode past her, hitting the green button to open the door for the others, then leaned in the doorway, trying different stances.

"It's really been three whole days since I went into, uh, Teacher?" he asked Gynie.

"Three days, twenty hours, six minutes," Gynie agreed.

A Kart appeared around the junction of the corridor, and accelerated toward him. He stepped out and waved, his decision to appear casual and cool swept away in the moment.

Shona looked just the same; though maybe a touch... apprehensive? But he couldn't help grinning at Amy's excited expression, all four kids calling his name like he was a hero returning from some dangerous quest.

The young woman was fit, showing quite a bit of skin, her eyes intense, her vivid green hair in a kind of punk cut. It reminded him of one of Amy's favorite game characters.

Then the Kart was braking to a stop and the kids throwing themselves from it and all over him, knocking him back toward the Medbay. Amy flung herself into his arms, while Bobby clutched his knees, the legs of his white jeans muffling his words. "We were real worried, Michael!" he said.

Shona hurried up, taking his arm, asking if he was alright, explaining how upset they'd all been, how the kids had come to her.

The man and the younger woman waited by the Kart. The man had a very solid build. Tall and dressed in very light clothes, he had fetishes pinned here and there, some maybe carved whalebone?

The woman was younger than he'd expected. Smaller, too, studying him with a curious intensity. She looked a little odd: then he realized it was because one of her eyebrows had been shaved off then just drawn back in. She looked at him with a kind of banked hunger, an eagerness that made him wary.

Amy released him, then smacked his arm. "Where *were* you?! I thought you'd gone an' we wouldn't ever see you again!"

He bent down, and brushed away a tear before it could fall. "No one can defeat the mighty Michael d'Angelo, slayer of demons, squirt!"

And the woman gave him a *most* peculiar look.

Chapter 46 – Friends of friends

'Michael' was shorter than Leeth had expected from Amy's stories: barely taller than her. Younger, too. Baby-faced, he hardly looked sixteen. Dark eyes, curly black hair, and olive skin. He looked *good* though, thanks in part to the badass long, fluorescent white trench-coat. *I wonder if I could talk Bobby into designing one for me? I'd look* killer!

At Shona's insistence, they went back into the Medbay, where she queried Gynie about Michael's health.

The kids clearly worshiped him; Amy, obviously infatuated. Did Michael know? She guessed not. Maybe Amy herself didn't: she *was* only thirteen.

Leeth felt a flash of jealousy at being displaced.

Amy tugged him over. "This is Miss Bonnie Parker, and Mr, uh, Adlartok, uh, Yakone? He Healed Miss Bonnie after she, um. Um. Did you see that Teacher's gone?"

At his nod Amy ducked her head, grimacing. "Yeah, Miss Bonnie kinda burned it up. She said it was dangerous. But she also taught me the Biles! You wanna see?"

"I don't think it'd be safe, in the Medbay," Michael said.

Amy punched his arm. "I didn't mean *here*."

"Sure, but a bit later."

"So where *were* you?" she demanded.

"Amy made up a song for you," Bobby jumped in. "She played it last night. We all cried. But you came home, so it worked!"

Michael rubbed the back of his head. "I honestly don't know. The last thing I remember is going into, ah, Teacher. And that's all. Next thing I know I'm on the cot," *naked,* he thought, "with Gynie watching. She said C-N crashed, so you all went to Newtopia to get help."

An odd drone, with *feathers,* flew to a lighting strip above and hung upside down from it, watching.

"Is that an amibo?"

It dropped, spreading actual wings, to hover in the air in front of him. "I'm Bhaji!"

"It's Miss Bonnie's," Amy explained.

Percepting it again, he saw again the faint aura, translucent shades of gray, yet somehow suggestive of colors.

Turning to the shaman he held out his hand. "Pleased to meet you, Mr Yakone." They shook: the man's grip powerful but measured.

"Mr Michael Vincent d'Angelo."

"Wow. You must have a good memory for names. But just call me Michael. Tell me, Mr Yakone, does, um, Bonnie's amibo look... special to you?"

The shaman studied him, then the drone with its animated face-screen. He made a gesture, as if stroking a non-existent beard then opening his hand toward it, while his gaze shifted and he tilted his head as if listening.

At last he shrugged. "No. It is machine." Then added, "Good flyer."

The drone spun on its axis, stopped, then did a loop the loop, stopping exactly where it had started. "I sure am!"

"You sure are," Bonnie said. She tapped her shoulder for it to land, hiding her sadness. Did Bhaji even know Ty had subverted his programming? She suspected not. He flitted to her, his small claws unfolding to perch just like she'd gotten used to.

"And *you* destroyed the- destroyed Teacher," Michael suddenly blurted. *"Why?!* It wasn't dangerous, it was wonderful! I could see *everything* with it!"

Bonnie's eyes narrowed. "It *was* dangerous. I *know* it." She cocked her head to the side, studying him. "How many times did you use it?"

He paused, counting. "Five."

"And the rest of you?" she asked the kids, who'd bunched together, Amy standing in front.

"Three times," she said.

"One time," said Yuri.

"Two," said Nadeep.

"I did four times!" Bobby piped up.

"And did any of you guys 'see everything'? Did *you* think it was wonderful?"

They didn't answer; just shrugged or looked at their feet.

"So only Michael 'saw everything' with the Writer?"

"You mean Teacher," Nadeep corrected her.

"No. It's real name was the Writer."

"Maybe your Writer just looked like-" began Amy, but the

sad and serious look Bonnie gave her stopped her as surely as a finger to her lips.

Bonnie studied Michael. "Have you spoken to Adam?"

"No, just Gynie, why?"

Leeth considered him, then the nursebot. It stared calmly back as if daring her to expose its secret. She turned back to the youth, who still glared at her.

"I don't understand why Adam hasn't had you locked up for destroying expensive equipment," he said.

"And I don't understand how everyone down here thinks it's fine for him to experiment on children. So maybe *that's* why?"

"He's not experimenting on us!" Michael snapped. "The G- the *Teacher* was just a tool. It could connect you to the world."

"Like seeing a penguin escaping shrinking tunnels of sea ice?" she asked. Michael shouldn't have been able to see that: mages couldn't travel as a spirit, in water.

"Penngy, you mean? I saw that, thanks to Teacher."

"How? Were you watching from an underwater drone following the bird?"

"Uh... no. I..."

The penguin had swum up to him, to his underwater viewpoint, as the super cooling vanes extended, extruding a net that froze the seawater as it grew. He'd *sensed* walls forming, *seen* the penguin grow frantic as it hunted for a route out. He'd... followed, urging it on, mapping out a path and wishing the little aquatic bird to choose the right one.

Which it had.

"I just did."

Bonnie Parker nodded, as if what he'd said confirmed something else, for her.

In contrast, the shaman looked at both him and her with pity.

"Boy dream penguin," he said, shrugging. "But maybe true dream."

"Show us," Bonnie challenged Michael. "Amy says you can do 'movies'." If he had taken down Ty, she *needed* to learn about his magic.

"Oh, yes!" Amy said, clapping.

"Especially the part where he escapes, and waves a flipper!" Bobby said.

"Bird waves flipper?" Mr Yakone asked, eyebrow raised.

Michael blushed. "I may have added that part."

"I think you add lots of parts," Amy said. "But I love them." Then she blushed.

Michael "hmphed."

"Go on, then," Bonnie urged.

He shut his eyes, remembering the structure of the Projection spell, calling it to mind, then... *missed,* as he engaged his will to infuse it. It slipped from his mental grasp as it hadn't since his first attempts, after Unfolding.

Calming himself, he tried again, with more care.

The whole process felt oddly unpracticed. Like he'd been unconscious far longer than three or four days. It felt... awkward. Yet Projection was his favorite spell. Finally, he called to mind Penngy's flight.

Delighted gasps met his effort this time, and he opened his eyes. Then lost himself in the little bird's desperate underwater flight. He even defiantly changed Penngy's wave at the end into a finger flip.

The kids cheered.

The adult shaman also looked impressed.

For her part, Bonnie Parker studied him. He in turn Percepted her, confirming his earlier impression. She felt she knew something important about him.

And she wanted something from him. Something *big.*

"Okay, I have to admit, Amy was right: that was freaking chill!" she conceded.

He withdrew his Will, letting the vision fade.

"Can you and I talk, Michael?" she asked. "In private?"

"Not until I've eaten; I'm starving! And I'm not sure even then. Anything you want to say to me, you can say in front of the other guys."

"But..." She pursed her lips. "That's just something people say in vids."

"Then I guess we're in a vid." He strode past her to the Kart outside. The kids piled in around him, Yuri taking the wheel. It was a squeeze, even with Bobby and Amy on Bonnie and Shona's laps, but the ride to the cafeteria was brief.

Once there, Michael headed to the chefbot. To start, a seafood broth, he decided. Some battered and fried potato slices from hydroponics, and a shrimp-kelp-krill burger. Maybe three of those. And a large coke.

"Why are you still here Miss Bonnie, anyway?" he asked over his shoulder. "Gynie said you came to help find me." Finished with his order, he turned to her. "Well, I'm found. Also safe, and well. And Paradawn is a secure area. I'm surprised Adam hasn't already shipped you both off. Why'd you come to Newtopia? It couldn't have been to find me."

"We come for magic," the shaman said. "Study, learn. Trials. Adam gave okay, for Mt Takahe."

"He what?" demanded Bonnie. "When? And when were you going to tell me? And... don't forget that other thing I told you." *Never trust Godsson.* "It's *dangerous* here," she added.

Michael sniggered. "Seems like you think a lot of things are dangerous, Miss Bonnie."

Michael and Mr Yakone exchanged knowing smiles.

It was only as her nails dug into her palms she realized she'd tightened her fists. She unclenched them. Then needed to work to unclench her jaw. The whole situation felt like it was sliding in directions she hadn't expected.

They ate together, the seafood burger things Michael had ordered tasting as good as they smelled. He asked her what Newtopia was like, since he'd only visited it in spirit.

"Really?" Bonnie asked. "Didn't you have to fly into TAMA, then down the mountain elevator and all that, and across via mag-lev pod, to get here?"

"Nope," he said, smug. "After gunmen murdered my mother and father, the Elves brought me here directly. To keep me safe."

"Elves. Uh huh. I hadn't heard that part." She gave him her best pitying stare, then noticed the other kids busying themselves with their desserts.

"Well, just one Elf, but he had a crack mercenary crew working for him."

"Not Happy Joe Holliday?!"

"The 'bodyguard to the stars'? As if. These were ninjas. No names, didn't say much. Iago was real chill though."

"Iago? He was the Altered – the 'elf'? Pointy ears and all that?"

But Michael clammed up.

"What about the rest of you guys?" Bonnie asked. "Did this Iago guy bring you all here too?"

"He used this VTOL-" Bobby began, excitedly, when she

heard Amy's foot kick him under the table. "Ow!"

Then he too clammed up.

Because of 'assassins', they'd all been told. It just reinforced her own certainty that this whole deal was as shady as any she'd heard of.

The rest of the day passed peacefully, with Michael keen to see Amy's new gymnastics moves, which earned Bonnie a smidgen of respect from him. They all watched an animated movie, a girl fish falling in love with a boy, with a sea witch, and giant waves. It was pretty magical, especially when the special effects spilled from the 2D screen out into the room around them, making them feel truly part of a glorious undersea world.

Leeth watched Michael perform his magic, adding extra, inconsequential characters that moved between the screen and the kids – like an occasional jellyfish, sparrow, or firefly.

She also learned that the next day, Mr Yakone was going to travel to Mt Takahe via a spur line from the Paradawn pod station, and then up to the surface. He'd leave before dawn. She'd spoken to Adam via Link, who'd confirmed the expedition, and said she'd be allowed to go with the shaman. Michael, too, if he wished.

Michael wished.

That of course meant Amy and all the others wanted to go as well. Bonnie expected Adam to deny their request, but he said if Shona went with them, and they agreed to stay inside at the base facility, they could watch.

Amy was so distracted by the prospect she entirely forgot her plan for a 'girls' sleepover again.

Chapter 47 – Night and day, snow and ice

A blast of light snapped Bonnie from deep sleep, ruining her night sight even as the door to the dorm closed, plunging the room back into darkness. Stealthy footsteps, then something small fumbling at the latch to the wardrobe-cupboard. Something with paws rather than hands? But it had already moved on, with a shuffling scuffing of carpet tiles.

She blinked, willing her vision to clear, tracking the thing by its furtive movements. It passed Shona's bed, heading straight for Amy's. Adrenaline spiking, she tossed her bedding aside-

And saw Bobby, the cuffs of his pajama legs brushing the floor.

He paused at Amy's bed, pushing his head into the bedding spilling over its side, before making a tiny frustrated sound and continuing on, circling the room in the dark. By the light from under the door jamb and Bhaji's decorative LEDs, dimmed for sleep mode, she saw Bobby's eyes were open – if unfocused.

A tiny chirp from Bhaji's lens mechanism probably signaled their spiral irises sliding open to let in more light. The little amibo, perched on the dresser table, swiveled his owl-like head, tracking Bobby's movements.

At her bed he stopped and made a sound, half whimper, half pleading, that hit her low in her belly, his hands fumbling at her bedding in the dark.

"Bobby, what are you doing?" she whispered. "What's wrong?"

He didn't answer at first. Then: "Zrm-be cuh. Gh stop erm," he mumbled, still fumbling at her bedding.

"What?"

But instead of answering, he tried to clamber up and into her bed, his movements oddly uncoordinated.

"Bobby?! What did you say?" She lifted him up and in.

"Z'mbee cuh." Wriggling in against her, his arms clutching her chest, he fell limp, all tension flowing out of him.

"Bobby?"

Craning her neck she saw his eyes had closed. His soapy, warm smell made her draw her bedding up over them both. *00:09:14*, she saw, checking her Link.

"Bobby? Are you asleep?"

He didn't answer. His little heart was pounding; though quickly settling now, slowing. He made a small, appreciative sound.

The room darkened further when the sliver of light seeping in under the door to the corridor winked out. *Right: infrared activated.*

Shutting her eyes she strained for the sound of anything out of the ordinary. Shona's deep slow breathing. Amy's, quieter and shallower. Nothing from the corridor. Silence from the boys' dorm; she was pretty sure she was imagining the faintest trace of breathing. Even *her* hearing wasn't that good.

The ever present background hum of electrical equipment.

No **thud**s. No creeping android feet.

I should put him back in his own bed. She cuddled the boy, her nose almost in his hair, smelling apple and oil...

Mr Yakone touched her shoulder, snapping her awake, her arms tightening protectively as the room's lights came on, making her blink and wringing an annoyed protest from Shona.

"You say you wish come, dawn, on top. Magic research."

"It's 5am," she said. "Oh! We should be leaving!"

"Yes. Boys hunt Bobby," he said, his tone accusing, looking at the sleeping child in her arms. "Go from bed." His eyes roamed the room.

"I think he had a bad dream."

Yuri barreled into the room, Nadeep on his heels, both in pajamas. "Michael said Bobby's with- Oh."

The noise finally woke Amy, who blinked across at Bobby curled up, Bonnie holding him.

"I thought he'd grown out of that," she said as Bobby grizzled and blinked awake, then left with the boys.

Bonnie dressed swiftly, eyeing her hand luggage on its high shelf, Tezsh's dagger stowed inside. *I think?* She couldn't sense it, for once. Fearing the worst, she pulled the bag down. At least the weight was right. And the black silk bag still inside. But she didn't feel reassured until she'd opened the drawstrings and peered in. For once, the eyes faced away from her.

Like Tezsh had turned his back on her?

Frowning, she tightened the drawstrings, piled things on top to bury it, and put the bag back. She wouldn't need it: she could handle things without Tezsh's help. She certainly didn't want it lying around where Mr Yakone might sense it.

Fifteen minutes later in the pod to the Mt Takahe research base, Gynie folded down tray tables in front of each child and set out breakfasts. The pod accelerated smoothly, their gear unloaded from the Kart P1 and P2 had prepared for them. Neither waved goodbye.

Bonnie wore her Antarctic gear, but unzipped to the waist, the hood back, and just her inner soles, her boots beside her. She smiled at Mr Yakone's clothing; with the fur on the inside, from the waist down he made her think of a bald bear decorated with arcane fetishes. He carried the top half of his parka, too warm for him to wear inside.

From the station they'd first arrived at, a short cross tunnel led to a second station. "This is where we took the pod to the city," Amy explained. A crude walkway above the tracks led to a third station and the spur line to their destination: a small research base built into the foothills of the inactive volcano, Mt Takahe. It formed part of the other side of the valley wall for the New Thwaites Glacier, restored now almost to pre-climate disaster depth thanks to complex and still extending sub-sea freezing scaffolding – the same scaffolding that had almost trapped 'Penngy', in Michael's mentally projected movie.

They all ate while the pod flashed down a tunnel with no transparent ceiling, unlike the ride from Newtopia. It also bounced a little more, as if this magnetic levitation track wasn't as perfectly laid as the other. There was only one pod on this line, too, and a single track, the solitary pod shuttling forward and back as needed.

Mr Yakone seemed disappointed that Bobby couldn't recall any of his dream. "Some dreams tell deep truths."

"Bobby had bad dreams for weeks after he and the others arrived," Michael volunteered.

"No I didn't!"

"We all did," Amy said, at which Bobby, who'd demanded to sit next to Bonnie, admitted maybe he had, once or twice.

Bonnie learned that all but Michael had arrived together, a couple of months ago, but didn't get a satisfactory answer from Michael about his own arrival. "I'd been fighting crime from my secret underground base for a while, before I came here."

Bobby tugged Bonnie's sleeve, whispering, "Michael sometimes makes stuff up."

They'd also admired her Antarctic survival wear, especially how stylish it looked, and the internal heating elements woven through it.

"It needs some colored piping though Miss," Amy told her. "It'll be real hard to see you, on the snow."

Mr Yakone's, in contrast, seemed far more bulky and primitive.

But the kids liked his better, oohing over the soft feel of its furry insides. Mr Yakone draped his parka over Bobby, tugging it down till the boy's head appeared in the hood, his arms and body completely hidden inside. He looked so much like a teddy bear they all laughed; especially when he waddled around, his legs invisible.

It was the first time she'd seen Mr Yakone do anything remotely playful, and suddenly wondered if *he* had any children himself. From the way he tousled Bobby's hair after pulling his parka up and off him, she guessed maybe he did.

He also had the really cool set of bone, half tube sunglasses that curved around his head, the same ones he'd used in the storm at Ascension Station. Carved from caribou, he said. It had just a narrow horizontal slit.

Gynie and Shona completed the entourage. Gynie had her own Antarctic wear: aerogel encased in a form-fitting layer of flexible toughened plastic that clipped to her boots. Like Bonnie's outfit, it had a hood with a transparent face plate.

The kids all had warm thick clothes, as did Shona, but nothing suitable for venturing outside for more than minutes. Today's temperature should reach -10°C – relatively warm, Bhaji offered. "It's -22 right now," he added.

"Not waste time," Mr Yakone said, as the pod began braking.

He hurried them out, following close on Gynie's heels as she led the way to a much smaller elevator than Newtopia's big one. This one didn't have transparent walls or floor. It was hard to judge the speed – it felt faster than the TAMA one, but maybe just because it shook more and accelerated harder.

The base they emerged in, like Ascension Station on the ice plain directly over Newtopia City, was built into foothills, but unlike that way station, the elevator here ascended no higher.

No one had eyes for anything but the wraparound triple glazed windows though, as the view literally stilled their collective breaths: the first impression, a sky on fire.

A blue-white expanse of snow and ice glowed under a yellow-pink horizon, the pink darkening to a vivid crimson tinged with purple, and finally to a rusty red.

Even Mr Yakone paused, before making his way to an 'airlock' style pair of doors with a simple, large lever for a lock and handle on the outer one, pulling on his parka and tightening all his ties. Stepping out onto the snow, he threw his arms wide and lifted his head to the sky.

Bonnie heard him cry out, a long undulating – ululating? – call that sounded equally joyous and hungry.

Belatedly, she realized they *hadn't* missed 'dawn', despite the light in the sky – here, at this time of year, the sun never sank below the horizon. *I guess dawn isn't always a night into day thing.* Weird.

Mr Yakone began dancing, kind of, his eyes shut, planting each foot carefully, not a stomping motion, more like he was patting the ground with each step. He faced the four compass directions, with hand gestures and body movements that almost made sense; again with lots of pauses.

By the time she'd zipped and sealed up her suit and pulled her boots on over the inner soles, it looked like he'd almost ended. About to step out, she suddenly paused. The moment just seemed... too personal. Too private. So instead she waited, one hand on the lever, watching, Bhaji silent on her shoulder.

Finally he crouched down, his head bowed – but not like he was cowering or anything like that; more like so he could be closer to the ground or something.

When he stood at last, she tugged open the door and stepped outside, her feet snug and warm in her boots as she took a first crunching step onto crusty, wind-blasted snow.

That crunch felt like it reverberated deep into the earth even as her gaze was drawn up into the unearthly burgundy sky, the mountain a looming presence behind her. Something like an unheard sound rippled out. The world stilled.

Her heart began pounding, for reasons she couldn't explain, and for just a moment, a half a note, a subsonic note, began, then immediately halted as if deliberately silenced.

Mr Yakone, ever so slowly, turned toward her and the research base — or perhaps to the mountain rising behind her.

They stared at one another, his expression unreadable, her own probably something like, *what the heck is happening?!*

Slowly, the weird sensation faded, Mr Yakone's gaze doing the astral Percepting thing, *again*, a frown forming.

For his part, Adlartok Kallik Yakone watched the girl with the intensity he would give an upwind, hungry *nanuk* which had not yet sensed him. Or, perhaps, as if *nanuk* hid *behind* her. He shook his head, the idea of the small woman hiding a giant beast foolish.

Slowly, the strange sense of immanence *withdrew.*

The girl smiled and waved. He sniffed the air, half expecting to scent the psychic stench of *Wentshukumishiteu* lurking, that foul spirit waiting to burst up from under snow and ice. But like him, his familiar, Uentshiksruk, smelled nothing.

He turned slowly around. This place was so unlike his homeland. Alike in superficial ways, yet so unlike. A different kind of emptiness; as if something waited, casual in its cruelty. A vastness that rode the sky, uncaring and alone.

A sense of solitude and banked hostility.

How to speak to the Greater Spirit, as the mad sorcerer had promised? The sorcerer who this woman, when a child, had befriended. Now she claimed the madman could not be trusted. The *Qallunaat*, the warm people who now held him imprisoned, also called him manipulator and liar.

He felt under his qulittaq, his parka, hardly needed with such little wind, for the carved bones of the seeds he carried in a pocket inside. The smooth shapes soothed his fingers, and he took solace from their sleeping spirits. Too soon though, yet, to plant them.

Caution would be wisdom here. Caution, and patience. This land waited, hungry to crush the foolhardy or impatient. This he knew already.

With an effort, he put Bonnie Angelique Parker's fears and

warnings aside. Facing the vast expanse, he carefully opened himself to this land.

Bonnie watched Yakone turn away from her with real relief. *What had all that been about?* She took a second crunching step, and then another. This time they just felt satisfying in an ordinary, physical way.

Putting the shaman out of her thoughts, she looked around.

Far off, maybe thirty klicks to the west, a serrated forest of stark black buildings stretched up toward the sky, slender triangles with their tops cut off; like an alien city... Oh no: was *that* the alien growth Mr Abrams and Eagle had told her to look for?

She stared in disbelief, aware of the mountain rising behind her, the wine dark sky, the cruel cold beauty all around her... but drowning in dismay that the aliens had grown so huge, taken such root, without anyone noticing.

How was she supposed to kill things *that* size?! They had to be ten or twenty stories! Maybe with Ty's help...? But even the warbot wouldn't be able to damage such giants.

Bhaji, on her shoulder, noticed where she was looking. "They built the last one ten years ago."

"What? *Newtopia* built them? It's already taken over?!"

"Taken over?"

"The aliens!"

"Those are the Paradawn heat dumps, Miss Bonnie. The Newtopian Consortium built them. They radiate in the eight to thirteen micrometer part of the infrared spectrum, since the atmosphere's pretty transparent to those wavelengths, especially when the air is dry. And Antarctica's the driest place on Earth."

Bonnie felt her heart rate slowing. She'd really thought the structures were colossal aliens. *Why am I so jumpy?*

Bhaji leapt from her shoulder, doing a tight little downward spiral, like he'd decided to land on the snow. With an unpleasant whine from the electrochemical 'muscles' powering his wings, he rose a little unsteadily in the air to finally hover in front of her, weaving like a drunken hummingbird. His animated eyes, which had been crinkled up in amusement at the start of his flight, were now troubled. "I don't like flying here: it's too cold!"

"And those buildings, the heat dumps, are at Paradawn?

But that should be like 200 klicks from here."

Slowly, his flight steadied, presumably as his electrically powered muscles warmed up. "167 kilometers," he corrected. They just looked close because the air was so clear.

She turned around, to stare back at the research base – with a relieved wave to Amy, Bobby, Nadeep, and Yuri, their noses pressed to the windows, watching – and then lifted her head to gaze up at Mt Takahe. Dark bare rocks peeked from a shroud of white. "I guess it looks steeper because we're right at the bottom."

"It's pretty spectacular," Bhaji agreed, flying off a short distance and angling himself upward.

At cries from back inside, she saw Yuri jumping up and down and tugging on Shona's arm, then arguing with Gynie. It looked like he wanted to come outside.

"Did you just share those images?" she asked Bhaji.

"I thought Yuri might like them!"

Staring at the pristine slopes, blue-white despite the maroon sky, she imagined zooming down them. She was pretty sure she could guess what Yuri was begging for.

After a while, with not much apparently happening, she trotted over to Mr Yakone. "Did something funny happen, earlier?"

He looked her up and down.

"I mean, strange," she qualified, before he could misunderstand her. *Probably deliberately.*

He seemed to consider. "All strange here," he said at last.

"It's just... you were looking at me strangely."

He just grunted.

"So, how's it going? Summon a spirit, next?"

He shook his head. "Not so soon."

She huffed. "Can I help?"

"You summon spirits?" he asked.

"No!"

"Then you no help."

She growled. "I was just- Never mind. I'm gonna check the place out."

"Check quiet," he said.

"Why? Is there something dangerous?"

"No. Too much talk."

"I'd like to meet your wife one day. She must be a very special woman."

But he gave her such dark a look, she stepped back. She hadn't actually expected him to recognize her insult. "Fine," she said, throwing her hands up in surrender.

The sky had lightened from bruised purple at its darkest, to pink now. She decided to check out the slopes for Yuri; see what the snow was like, certain he'd want to know.

She turned and jogged off up the gentle incline, her booted feet crunching on the crusty hard snow.

Except the incline just kept going. She ran harder, but the distance seemed to sneakily stretch out before her. The anti-fog coating of her full face goggles misted up, and she began breathing harder. *The air's thinner,* she remembered, the ice sheet a kind of plateau. This whole continent was more elevated than any other.

She eased her pace, peering through misted plastic, but the steeper slope she'd set her sights on remained stubbornly distant. She sensed Bhaji clutch tighter to the shoulder tab Little Brother had added to her suit just for it.

It took her a full ten minutes to reach the slope. She stopped, breathing hard. *I wonder if this's how normal people feel after a run?* Turning to look back, her eyebrows rose at how much smaller the research base looked. Mr Yakone, still doing not very much that she could see, stood outside it, in his caramel brown skins. Except he was now tiny.

Weird. She reached out, imagining they were toys, since they looked so clear and sharp; then felt stupid. Stomping across the slope she crunched along, her boots breaking through the crust to sink deeper. She winced. She was only an okay skier, but reckoned this wouldn't be great snow for Yuri to ski down.

About to climb higher and check it out, she studied the slope above for signs her arctic survival teacher had told her to look for, for avalanche danger.

She didn't want to be buried out here.

Her Link buzzed, and she lifted her wrist. "Bonnie," she said.

"Skrrzt- kay zzsht?"

Shona's voice. Was 'kay' part of 'okay'? "I'm out of walkie talkie range, aren't I?" she said, belatedly remembering the cellular network only covered the 'cities' down here, switching automatically to radio for outdoors.

She could use her choker, but that'd give away its capabilities.

"Kzsht ids urry zhshak!"

She had *no* idea for that one. Something about the kids? "Okay, okay, I'm coming back," she said, guessing they were worried, waving one arm over her head to show she was fine. "End call," she told it, and began jogging back.

The return trip was equally frustrating. Mr Yakone and the base stayed stubbornly small and distant, growing imperceptibly larger as the minutes passed. Maybe getting closer a little faster since she was running downhill.

Until the ice crust broke completely and she plunged feet first into softer snow, banging her head into a hard wall – and kept falling, into an echoing space below.

Ramming invisible claws into a slick blue ice wall inches from her face, she slammed to a halt. Bhaji's grippers tugged hard on her shoulder

Hanging by one hand, head ringing, her legs dangled in an abyss that fell away into darkness below her.

A long way down. A frozen, deep darkness.

She shivered.

"You okay, Bhaji?" she asked. But the little drone had hunched into a tight-wrapped feathered ball, and didn't answer.

It was only then that she remembered she could have used the sonics built into her goggles to scan ahead for hidden crevasses.

Idiot.

Shuddering, feeling the ice cracking, she reached and stabbed her other hand higher, hauling herself up. And again: stab; pull. She'd only fallen a half dozen meters. Three, four, five lunges upward... As she at last clambered out of the snow onto the surface, heart pounding, her Link buzzed again.

"Bonnie! Are you okay?!" Shona asked.

I nearly died. Stupidly. "Yeah, yeah, I'm fine." *Guess I'm back in range.* She stood, slapping snow off her hood, shoulders, arms, and legs. Then more carefully brushing it from Bhaji, who shivered and shook out his pale wings, his eyes rounded in shock, 'blinking' at her.

He buzzed his wings, creating a small shower of snow. "I didn't like that Miss Bonnie!"

"Me either, little buddy." At least LB's self-sealing gloves had worked, she saw, checking their tips. She felt a moment of gratitude.

She surveyed the remaining distance, an innocent white expanse. Except now, instead of a straightforward if deceptively stretched out running surface, it felt more like a minefield.

Using her goggles, a patch slightly off to one side looked dodgy. Trusting them, she began jogging, though treading more gingerly. It kind of ruined the pleasure of stretching her legs.

Once back at the base, Mr Yakone looked at her snow-dusted outline in a way she *knew* meant 'foolish girl', before ignoring her. Huffing, she cracked the door and headed back inside.

At least she got a warm welcome from the kids – verbally, anyway, after Amy jumped back from hugging her as she entered.

"You're *freezing* Miss Bonnie!"

"Actually, I'm a little hot!" She squeezed the tab on the seal over her zipper to do the flash heat thing to melt the ice there – her first use of it since the Condition One excursion back at Ascension Station, her first night. Just three and a half days ago, she calculated.

As she'd guessed, Yuri wanted to ski – on a real slope on a real mountain, outside. He'd even convinced Adam to send some bots and a lift rope to tow him up, if they came back.

"*If* Miss Parker said the snow was suitable," Shona cautioned.

"Yeah, I'm not so sure about that," Bonnie told Yuri, explaining what she'd found, the four youngsters perched on seats around her listening avidly as her suit dripped water to the floor.

"Michael, no!" Amy cried, springing to her feet and racing to the exit door.

Michael though ignored her, dressed only in his super white coat and ordinary shoes, not even gloves, as he cracked the door and stepped outside, closing it behind him.

"No!" Amy cried, chasing after him. Bonnie reached her inside the 'airlock' just in time to stop her tugging the second door open and plunging outside herself.

"Amy! Let me: I'll get him."

Carrying the girl back and setting her down on the other

side of the first door, she zipped herself up and went back out.

Michael stood, arms spread, face to the sky, perfectly relaxed in the sub-zero temperature.

He grinned at her. "I designed this spell years ago. It works well!"

She just blinked at him, as Mr Yakone approached.

He grunted, eyeing the youth up and down as he circled him, clearly Percepting.

The rest of the day passed with Mr Yakone and Michael hanging together outside, confusing the dickens out of each other from what Bonnie could tell, but having a fine old time.

She'd gone inside to reassure Amy, whose hero worship of Michael rose several levels.

After lunch – the base had an auto kitchen, the food offerings basic but warm and nutritious – the kids were getting bored and grumpy, and as Shona drew out their teaching tablets and set them exercises, Leeth gratefully headed outdoors again.

Mr Yakone was finally ready to summon a spirit, much to Michael's interest. Which was when the weird feeling from the morning returned, the world feeling kind of hollow and waiting, echo-ey, and both mages paused what they were doing to study her.

Just like in the morning, the sensation kind of faded away.

Snuck away, she thought, then frowned. *'Tezsh?'* she thought? *'Is that you?'*

There was no answer.

When the spirit did arrive – though it was hard to tell if the little flurries of snow were more than just wind – things didn't go smoothly at all. It basically attacked Mr Yakone and he had to Banish it.

He tried again, and it happened again. From the way he kind of tore at himself, it had wrapped itself around him, draining heat.

He Banished that one – the same one as the first time? – and she moved closer, standing beside Michael.

The third time, the spirit went for her and Michael, stripping away the spell protecting him from the cold. She'd grabbed him up, ready to race him back inside – reining in her claws, unwilling to reveal how easily she could kill it – until Mr Yakone once again dismissed it.

She found her face inches from Michael's, thinking he was kind of good looking. He in turn blushed, suddenly really uncomfortable at the way she was just carrying him – younger, but a few fingers taller than her – in her arms. He mumbled and gestured, and a wall of heat flooded over her.

He'd recast his spell.

As she set him back on his feet he looked anywhere but at her.

Mr Yakone just looked frustrated. "Spirit not understand! Not think right. Just hunger."

Michael backed away, a good fifty meters, and Bonnie joined him as Mr Yakone tried again.

This time, the spirit raced from the shaman straight to her. Icy touches roamed her body, slithering under her cold weather gear, then plunged lower. "You little–! You don't do that! You ask, first!"

Clamping down on the feathery touch, she unzipped her collar and reached in, grasping *nothing*, and peeled it away, her claws tingling in readiness. She felt startlement, then it melted and fled from her grip. Zipping her suit closed, she saw Mr Yakone and Michael both staring at her.

"Your horny little spirit grabbed me by the pussy!" she snarled.

For some reason, both men blushed.

Then she did, too, unwilling to admit it'd been more surprise than outrage that had provoked her reaction.

"I'm hungry," she muttered, turning and stalking back inside.

From inside she watched, scowling, as Mr Yakone tried different things without much more success, while the sky darkened ominously and the winds picked up.

She'd read that the weather in Antarctica could turn in minutes, but something about the sky – now a pale blue, the sun inching its way horizontally just above the horizon – felt *intentional*. She wondered if the little spirit, or spirits, that Mr Yakone had been summoning had attracted the attention of other ones. Bigger ones.

Maybe Mr Yakone felt the same thing. He too retreated inside, and all eight of them – ten, counting Bhaji and Gynie – watched in awe as winds tore across the plain and *hammered* at the triple-reinforced plexiglass windows.

For long seconds, Leeth heard a rumble, the bones of the

earth grumbling. No one else reacted. Her eyes went to the inactive volcano, certain it had been the source.

All too aware that Tezsh was also a god of volcanoes.

She had a sudden bad feeling there was more happening here than she could see.

Maybe more than any of them could.

The storm steadily intensified, to such an extent that Bobby grew scared.

"I wanna go home!" he wailed, turning from the full length windows toward the elevator, while outside the wind raged and howled, fighting to get in.

Leeth stared at it, almost mesmerized. Something about it seemed... familiar.

"No one could go out in that, that's for sure," Shona agreed. She looked to the Inuit shaman for confirmation, and he nodded. But thoughtfully, she saw, his eyes fixed on Bonnie Parker.

"I think tonight's magic movie could be *The Monster in the Storm*," Michael said, in exaggerated spooky tones. "If you all think you're brave enough!"

By the time they'd boarded the pod and were racing back to Paradawn, Bobby was sure he *was*.

Dinner was a happy affair, the kids' appetites sharpened by the day's activities, and Bonnie surprised herself with just how much she ate. Hunger had gnawed at her the whole journey back.

Michael's magical 'movie' was cheesy and childish, yet as the sound and fury wrapped around them, huddled together all in one big group under extra large and warm blankets – Bobby determinedly settled in Bonnie's lap – she found herself treasuring the experience. Michael's imagined story had moments of frightening realism, as well as moments of silly humor. It wouldn't have occurred to her that a 'storm monster' could get its head stuck in a tunnel, but the kids found it hilarious.

Though for the second night running, Bonnie woke in darkness to Bobby fumbling at her cupboard, before blindly sleepwalking his way up and into her bed. Again, just after midnight.

Scooping him up from his fumbling attempts to climb in with her, she joined him in sleep.

Chapter 48 – It would test an angel

Roaming the city early that morning, Mike paused in wonder outside a stately building. Polished granite steps draped with a long tongue of red velvet, and shiny brass fittings supporting red ropes invited him forward.

Guarding rosewood double doors, a man resplendent in a charcoal gray uniform with gold braid on his shoulders looked like a dignified, friendly type, sure to be welcoming.

Smiling, Mike mounted the stairs. *I bet their bathrooms are amazing!* He stretched, his back aching like he'd slept on wood, and cast a quick Healing spell.

The man raised one eyebrow. "Yes, sir?"

"It's good to be home, Alfred," Mike smiled. "Is all well, inside? No urgent matters requiring my attention?"

"Uh..."

"Alfred? Are you all right?" He did look tired, Mike decided, and dusted off his thoughts for him.

"Fine, Master Bruce," he said, and opened the door with a flourish. "Welcome home."

"I think I'll have a bath, and then breakfast. I'm starving!"

"The Roosevelt Room will open at seven a.m. sharp, as always, sir."

"Good, sounds perfect!" He could see the route, as if Alfred was holding up a picture. "I'll see Mr Senkowski on the front desk to check my rooms are ready."

"That sounds like a plan, sir."

Closing the door, the man straightened and adjusted his cuffs, eyeing passersby, alert for the return of any more residents.

It wouldn't do to let riffraff in.

On the street around noon that day, Mike tapped his money stick to another street vendor's. Checking the numbers after, he returned them to 777, nodding contentedly. Then jerked in surprise when the Link on his wrist buzzed. He was still trying to work out how to stop it when Happy Joe Holliday's face appeared right in front of him, vanished, then reappeared when he turned his wrist just right.

"Mike. You up for another op?"

"Ah...?"

Happy sighed. "Another operation; a job."

"Oh! Sure!"

"Meet at the same place we first met?"

"Rio? I'll, um, need to work out how to get there. Oh! I can fly."

"In a plane, I assume? But look, no, not Rio. El Lobo's Gun Bar. I've sent your Link directions. Nineteen hundred hours, okay?"

Mike did the sums. "Really? That's a lot of hours."

Happy massaged his forehead like he had a headache. "Never mind. We'll meet at seven p.m. Okay? Your Link will tell you the way."

"Okay!'

He saw Happy wipe his hand down his face as he signed off. Mike practiced the gesture for himself, determined to learn the etiquette here, pleased at how smoothly he was fitting in.

Then with a deep breath, he set out to see what good deeds he could do today.

It went well: in a dirty part of the city, a woman de-burnt and her bones mended after her small, rusty gas cooking device exploded; a girl's puppy revived in the afternoon. Lung infections cured for several powerfully smelly men, roasting small creatures he didn't recognize. He tapped their money sticks a lot, which really made them happy.

He checked his own, smiling in turn at the three cheery sevens.

Even the rain couldn't dampen his spirits, as he wandered farther and farther afield. Exploring.

'Spacey' shivered, New Francisco a sad gray in the unforgiving rain, dusk washing the final spring colors down dusty drains. From their shelter he and his gang studied their targets: two mismatched men standing silent and unmoving.

Something about the pair told Spacey: *No.*

One was dressed like his own crew, in tattered patchwork clothes. But the other wore a dark *Actyv*™ suit, a reconfigurable nanoweave. A twenty thousand cred score dangling there, hypnotic in its lure.

The pair stood under an overhang, only half sheltered. Behind him, Rat made a smart remark to Jen, sparking a scuffle, but he ignored it to focus on the strangers.

Then he had it. Suit guy's back touched the wall. Even with the nanoweave he had to be getting soaked.

And both stood so still.

Suit guy had been holding his Link up, too, watching it intently, for five minutes – wasn't his arm getting tired? The *two men* were the wrongness.

Androids?

Rat noticed none of it. "Shitme, Space, wassup – ya feet dead? Why'n we take 'em? Skim spez suit an' any creds an' blow. Won't scan better vics onna scuzzy drenchin' night like this!"

Murmurs of agreement met Rat's needling. Spacey fought a surge of irritation. Feeling his crew's unhappiness, stoked as ever by Rat: always prickling, poking. And it *was* twenty thousand creds....

Quashing his doubts he gave the signal. If they *were* androids, Jen had her souped-up taser. That suit was *fine*.

Their vics paid no attention even when he and his crew gathered in a semi-circle around them. "Dump ya stash," Spacey growled. "An' you, strip," he told suit guy.

Neither target moved. Spacey stared from one expressionless face to the other. Water beaded and dripped from their eyebrows, the miserable rain soaking them all.

Funt this. They'd do it fast and hard. No playing. He drew his blade and his crew followed suit, an arc of metal teeth blossoming, hungry in the night.

Still the two didn't react. Something about that unnerved Spacey. "Jen, zap-"

A tearing explosion struck his core. Suit guy was on him! He was flying through the air, gut in agony, the alley spinning in crazy circles. He felt bones break as he crashed down, Nil and Rat beside him moments later.

Struggling to focus, he saw his crew collapsing like stalks of corn, falling in the cold hard rain. Thought bled into slowly darkening memories of childhood farm life; screams into crows calling, red puddling in pools.

The two men threw the last of the bodies further down the alley and moved back under the overhang, exchanging no words. They ignored the taser, and the gun, now lying in the alley, the relentless rain washing them clean of blood.

Mike, whistling happily, entered the long dark alleyway, following his Link's directions. It said once he got to Folsom Avenue he could hire a cab, which would be the best way to get to El Lobo's Gun Bar by seven p.m. That was also nineteen hundred hours, one of the helpful strong-smelling men had explained to him. He said he knew that because he was a vet who didn't work on animals.

This mad city was a fascinating place.

Far above, unheard, a drone hummed.

In the dark laneway, as the figure in white, following spoken directions from his Link, turned the distant corner, the well-dressed man spoke, not looking up from his own Link. "Now." He and his companion strode from the overhang down the lane, moving quietly, staying in shadow. Then waited as the youth strolled toward them.

The whistling stopped, and with it the footsteps. The two men stepped out to face him. He'd paused in the alley, swaying on his feet, his eyes shut, his long white coat concentrating the alley's meager light. Unaware of them? They moved forward to intercept.

The youth's eyes opened, holding no surprise. "Spawns of Lucifer! Carry this message to your Master!"

The two men blurred forward, diving toward him. Yet somehow he was faster. The night air *pulsed* with the force of the spell he unleashed – which did nothing more than blast the clothes from them, doing nothing to stop their rush.

Their naked hands closed on his arms with grips of iron, their muscles taut. Every sinew stood proud, clear to see.

"Ah; like that?" he said. A moment later, their grips relaxed, both men collapsing to the ground as all electrical activity in their bodies simply ceased.

From one side of the alley camo suits deactivated. Two unapologetically robotic forms stepped forward, their movements lazily graceful. A precisely controlled voice said "Target-"

But as the boy faced them fully, both halted.

"Contract voided: illegal target," said the first.

"Subject to return to Project Bifrost," the second agreed.

In a luxurious hotel suite, watching the feed from both the drone and robot's eyes, Iago swore and sprang to his feet. "System just seized control of our combat droids!"

About to cut the connection, his hand froze in mid gesture. "No point," he said, speaking aloud for his Lady's benefit. "System will already be back-tracing this connection; checking my Corp card's spending; reviewing video footage. It's not like we've been moving around masked. Or Masked."

"But it won't know who you are, my Lady. I will say I stumbled over what appeared to be a clone of Adam Fuller-Price. This may work to our favor."

"Damned AI," Feyborn agreed. "Though your Church of Cybernetics hires appear less magic resistant than claimed. Continue watching. Let's see how 'Mike' fares against four combat droids. If my too-clever AI succeeds in capturing him, as head of Tik Tek Security you'll still be nicely placed to let me step in and Take him."

Two more Shielded androids moved silently and invisibly to flank the boy. "Explain your arrival in New Francisco so-"

"Satan's spawn!" Mike hissed, eyes widening. His face twisting in outrage, he flung both hands out in a strangely artificial gesture, sinews stretched tight.

The entire alleyway *rippled,* the droids jerking like puppets and dropping. Then all spasmed, electricity sparking and arcing from them to the ground. Clothing and artificial skin first smoked, then charred black, revealing metal that glowed first red, then white hot, finally geysering flames and venting plasma.

For a few seconds Mike stood, sides heaving with exertion, his face no longer holding any trace of playful good humor, before at last backing away from the heat.

Scanning the area angrily, ash slid from his coat, rain beading on it to fall off before he gestured and once more stood under an invisible umbrella.

His gaze fell on a pistol lying in the rain, anguish radiating from it. "Oh no! They killed your master? You poor thing."

Kneeling in a puddle, he picked it up, stroking it tenderly as it remembered its dragon form. "Don't worry. I'll care for you. You'll like Spiff."

He rose, still murmuring to it. "Where...?" he asked, pressing it to his forehead, following the psychic link deeper into the alley, to a male, wearing a bandolier, his neck broken. "Don't worry, I can Heal him."

Once again, he knelt in the rain. Pocketing the weighty little dragon, he first straightened the youth's neck with a determined effort, then closed his eyes and focused the necessary magic.

Only to find the body unresponsive, the cells drained of the joy of life. Strangely though, not yet decaying. "Sorry, Spaff," he told the little creature at last, patting it gently in his pocket. "I was too late."

Shaking himself, he looked around. "Speaking of too late... Wait! I know what'll cheer you up!"

Bending, he stripped a dozen rounds from the sad corpse's bandolier before hurrying off, cradling two young dragons now, talking earnestly to both, a smile on his face.

As he strode down the alley, mud, grime, and blood slid from his long white coat.

Ty's discovery of subject Alpha cascaded through its latent spaces, disturbing the coherence of an entire section related to the movement of objects: the times and distances did not compute. There had been no successful flights out of Newtopia while it had been unavailable to manage landings, yet Alpha had been nowhere in the city when it had finally pieced itself back together.

Even as it registered Alpha's location and took control of Iago's retrieval operation, it continued sifting through the video data from New Francisco investigating how and when Alpha had arrived there, tracing what it could of his movements.

It also absorbed another item that required the disturbing label of coincidence, often a signifier of incomplete understanding of a situation: its chief of security had recently flown from its Tokyo-Kanagawa offices to New Francisco.

In El Lobo's Gun Bar, feeling an uncomfortable prickle down his spine, Steven Swift carefully set down his half empty beer. Holding up a finger to Happy, he slumped back in his seat and fell limp.

Then jerked back upright. "Sweet swollen bagpipes, the kid's here. I think. Unless we know another glowing white, flaming-sword-in-the-hand angel? It flew straight up to me, right here." He shook his head. "Kid's aura's *strong,* even if he is mad as a hatter. Sparkles, too."

But before Happy could ask what he meant by *sparkles,* the person in question stepped into the bar. Happy shook his head. If bars in this area ever had their licenses checked, the sixteen-year-old-looking kid would have caused trouble.

He waved to them, his long white trench-coat attracting glances as he crossed the floor. For once his expression was serious, even stern.

"You okay, Mike?" Bruce asked. "Sleep alright?"

Haggard shoved a seat out for him with one long leg. Nick as usual lurked in a corner, watching everything.

Mike took the seat. "Just some demons. And since – you know – we should all stay alert for more."

Happy eyed his coat as it clanked, wincing at the way it hung. "How many pistols you got in that pocket?" he asked.

"None. But I did find a friend for Spiff!" he said, brightening, pulling out first one metallic dragon, then a second, larger.

Happy and Bruce tried, and failed again, to see through the illusion. Both Steven and Haggard squinted, exchanged looks, and shook their heads.

"Look, you need to keep them in proper... pouches. *Perches.*"

"Yeah," Bruce chipped in. "Nice synth-leather ones, so they don't bang together and hurt their heads if you're in a fight, or get knocked down."

Mike considered this.

"We'll visit the Specials bar, get you fitted with a couple before we head out," Happy decided.

«Happy? You all okay?» Jack asked. «You mean holsters, yeah, not perches?»

«You see pistols, not, pistol-sized metallic dragons?» Happy asked. «Good to know.»

«Yeah, thing is, that new gun's a classic, an H&K P7Pro. And a ganger I knew, Spacey, used one. Word is, he and his whole crew got torn apart tonight, under an hour ago. Four slagged Tik Tek Combat VIIs in the alley too. Rumors of the Church of Cybernetics doing clean up.»

«Right. Thanks Jack.»

«Steven: Truth spell,» Happy sent to the mage's earbud, then questioned Mike about the 'demons'. He didn't learn much – just that there were 'two and two and two', and he'd returned them all to Hell.

Steven's expression told him Mike at least believed what he'd said. Happy, though troubled, let the topic drop.

"Let's cut to biz. You all willing to go back into Cognosys, tonight? Jack got a call – place is basically shut down, but something weirder: also *locked* down. The job's to get out someone who went in early this morning. Not a high value score, but it'll give us some influence in the area. Could be handy some day."

"We have to go in the same way as last time?" grimaced Steven.

They would. Their target this time was one of the tunnel-dwelling ogres. He'd gone in to see what he could scavenge for his small family.

Gone in, but not come out.

This time the carpark was empty. The grille Mike had blasted out the night before lay nearby on the floor, chisel marks evident on its underside, sheared bolts beside it.

Their access code for the elevator no longer worked though. Levering open the door, the group stared grimly at the greasy cables dangling in the elevator shaft.

"Sorry, Happy," Mike said, floating into it. "I think I can only carry you one at a time. You and Bruce especially look heavy."

Minutes later, Mike set Nick on the floor above. Haggard sniffed the air. The musky animal smell was fainter, over-powered now by bleach. But as they crept down corridors, it became clear that Asgard's clean up had been superficial. Broken doors lay tossed aside into rooms, chairs moved from corridors, and bloodstains removed. But little else had been done. Even the security cameras Nick had shot out hadn't been replaced.

"AC's still running though," Bruce observed.

With Jack monitoring comms in case Asgard or another security service was called out, the group moved on, growing slowly more tense.

They stopped outside a pair of sealed double doors, listen-ing; inside, a rhythmic creaking.

Drawing weapons, on the count of three Happy had Mike blast the doors. A lab, like a set from some sci-fi holo series lay before them. An ogre, unmoving, sat facing a dark-haired woman in a lab coat who spun around at their entrance.

At first gaping at them, her face lit up. "You're not Asgard. Get me out of here!"

The ogre rose awkwardly to his feet. It was the guy they'd come to rescue, who'd gone silent after sneaking inside. David Spalding.

His throat was a cross-hatch of surgical stitches.

"Intruders," he said.

"You useless stupid machine," the woman snarled. She lifted her head, and said, enunciating each word, "I said, all units in standby mode only."

The ogre sat down.

"Uh, Happy," Haggard said, his pistol still very much raised. "Guy's meat: thass'a dead man walkin'."

Steven Swift nodded agreement. "Start talking, lady," he growled, from long habit adding, "And I warn you, anything you say can and will be used against you."

Dr Megan Welsh did talk: explaining that Asgard had her locked away here while they decided what to do with her research. That their cleanup crew had done a less than perfect job. That it turned out the AI running certain new security algorithms that could coordinate a network of living animals, could also learn to run a single autonomic nervous system: working like a kind of life support.

This poor fellow had learned that the hard way. He'd turned over the corpse of a head-shot baboon, only to have it animate and tear his throat out.

She'd heard his screams but been able to stop the blood loss. Then his heart had stopped. "I used the robo surgeon to implant the necessary cranial cyberware. It connected him into the system so the AI could keep him alive. But I don't know what to do next. Asgard has locked the lab off the Net, and I can't even get Link access.

"And I'm physically locked in!"

But with that off her chest, she sized them up more carefully. "You're a mage of some type, aren't you?" she asked Haggard. "Can you Heal him? It's been less than twenty-four hours."

"Scuzz no!" Haggard told her, horrified.

"Sorry, ma'am," Steven explained. "Once the heart stops, you have at most *one* hour to magically knit things together and get all the juices flowing. I mean, maybe we could Heal the wounds I can see, but...” He trailed off.

“Zombie,” Haggard finished, for him. “Zombie run by’n AI, yah? Thass... wors’n any fucken thing in m’dreams, an’ thass fucken sayin’ so’thin’.”

“I thought-” she swallowed. “Really? *No one* could Heal him, magically?”

All Happy’s crew turned to Mike.

“Why are you looking at me? That’s a *dead body,*” he explained, speaking slowly so they’d understand. “It should be in the ground, not walking around like a, a Tik Tek demon.”

Dr Welsh said she’d like nothing better than to leave the place, and indeed, Asgard’s employ altogether.

Using the lab’s robot surgeon, the AI control implant was removed in mere minutes, allowing David Spalding to die.

All agreed it would be best, when they handed his body to the ogre clan living in and under the area, not to mention Welsh’s misguided attempt to keep him alive.

On the way out, she told them a little about her research. It involved mind to mind communication via non-verbal units of meaning, that could be delivered via the Net and fed into the recipient’s brain, and with the help of a simple AI, turned into coherent thoughts.

“Like how ‘Feels’, in telesex works?” Bruce asked. Then blushed.

Welsh though jerked as if stung. “Er, yes. Yes, it does bear some relation to that,” she said, refusing to think about the persuasive Japanese ‘businessmen’ and their desire to improve their ‘virtual companionship support services’. “But I think that’s all I can tell you.”

With proper solemnity, they delivered the victim’s body – levitated down tunnels by Mike in his ever-pristine white outfit – to his clan. Happy waved aside the offered payment.

It was a somber group that disbanded at the end of the day.

“Thank you,” Megan Welsh told them. “I owe you all a fa-vor. God knows what Asgard would eventually have decided.”

It seemed clear to Happy that the doctor planned to con-tinue her research; nor had Asgard apparently deleted it. Not to mention whoever their client had been, that Smith’d had them steal a copy for.

He had a feeling they hadn’t heard the last of this.

Chapter 49 – Not a cult

Inside the cozy Newtopian eatery, Zoe and Rachel saw their friend enter, and exchanged genuinely surprised looks.

Susan sent the robo cafe her order as she headed over. «Soy latte, no sugar, squeeze of strawberry.» The digital interaction felt as meaningless as the opening of an automatic door: dust, compared to the *body-Meld* of 'PalSpace'. She smiled. That the Meld was invisible to C-N's all-seeing eyes just added to its pleasure.

Zoe pulled out a chair. "You look great, Susan!"

She'd had her hair cut radically short, lost several kilos, and her cheeks glowed a healthy bronze.

"Thanks, gals," she said, simultaneously hearing and *feeling* the others in the Meld: «*They'll be great additions*» «*Zoe's friendship circle is hundreds*» «*Careful with her outer circles*» «*They'll love this*» «*I want to experience Rachel's husband!*» «*I want to experience* Rachel»

Susan couldn't contain her smile, her excitement. "You don't know the half of it. And it only costs ten wour!"

"Ten hours of work? So... lipo?" Rachel's gesture ran from Susan's waist to her face. "But lipo wouldn't explain your... glow."

Zoe smacked her forehead. "Oh no, Susan: you've joined the cult! It's PalSpace, isn't it?"

«*Why does everyone call us a cult?*» «*We're no cult*» «*Gently*» «*Don't spook them*» "It's not a cult, but yes. If you're already neuro-Linked," Susan said, tapping her temple, "installing the PalSpace module takes just minutes. But now C-N's up again, it's making moves to outlaw the op." «*It can't*» «*C-N can't even sense our body-speech! It can't touch us*» «*And #ident-tag-755 stashed the command to cut an auto-doc off the net, here: #location-tag*» She felt that information ripple out, digested by the Meld. «*A model TT-Weave-60 or later can print a NewLink gen3 now*» «*Quiet! Susan needs to seem normal: let her single-stream*»

Susan leaned forward. "I've had no trouble with my diet since the implant, but that's just the tip of the iceberg!" She struggled to contain her excitement. "Ladies: I don't want to sound like a crazy cultist, but... C-N *needs* to make PalSpace illegal! It's so empowering it threatens C-N."

«Careful» «That sounded cult-y!» «Tell them about the sex» «Tell them about the hugs» «Tell them about knowing everything» «Tell them what it's like to live without secrets, without fear» «Tell them about the Sharing» «Just hold back on Level 2» «Yeah, L2 would definitely scare them off» «Shut it, everyone: single-stream, remember?»

"It's like: everything, there at your mental fingertips, whenever you want it. You can dip in, or out. You can *not* imagine. You can experience *everything*."

Zoe rolled her eyes. "So, you're saying it's a telesex neural implant?"

Susan just smiled knowingly, and accepted her latte from the waiter-bot. "Oh, no. I'm saying that's how it *started.*"

Zoe and Rachel tried to hide their interest.

«We've got them» «Reel them in» «Gently!» «Can't wait to bring them to the Meld»

Susan sipped her latte and gestured her friends to lean in. "I can show you to the auto-doc I used..."

This time even the kids had set their alarms, and they all shared a more leisurely breakfast at 5am. With the storm over Mt Takahe clearing in the small hours, and Adam's permission, Shona had the children dressed in mite-sized Antarctic weather gear, manufactured overnight in the still off-limits R&D facility. Even Michael, despite his 'Pigloo' spell.

"Pigloo?" Bonnie asked, while the kids laughed.

"Personal igloo," Michael explained.

The kids wanted him to cast it on them too, but Mr Yakone reminded them a spirit had attacked Michael to eat the spell, the day before. So relying on non magical protection from the weather might be safer.

"Adam has provided workers and equipment to construct a small ski run for Yuri," Gynie told them as they rode, crammed as usual into a Kart on their way to the Paradawn pod station.

Ahead of them, two android construction workers rode in a second Kart. Bonnie eyed them with suspicion. Were they really here just as an extra labor force, or to deal with her in due course? Large, sturdy models, they looked like old Tik Tek Mark Vs, before the improved human surface profiling that made a Mark VIII sometimes hard to distinguish from an actual human.

At least, until you'd interacted with one for a while.

But these guys looked strong and sturdy. Both Karts arrived at the pod station, and everyone got off.

"Adam sent six workers from Newtopia overnight," Gynie explained. "Four wait at Mt Takahe for us, having delivered all necessary material to construct Yuri's slope. The pod returns now."

The lights in the tunnel switched on and the pod silently emerged, slowing to a stop.

"I don't like it, Shona said. "From Bonnie's description, those slopes sound too dangerous to ski."

Gynie tilted her head, and her body language abruptly changed: loosening, becoming far more human.

"Adam here," she said. "Yuri begged me, and we can set up some short runs on the lower slopes; I sent a small slope groomer as well. If Yuri's ever to compete in the Olympics, he'll need experience on outdoor runs."

"Yes, but-"

"Michael could Heal him," Adam said. "Or Mr Yakone: would you try Healing Yuri if he injured himself? Might that fit into your magical research study?"

The shaman slowly nodded, and Yuri "yay"ed.

Bonnie just watched, and wondered.

Once at Mt Takahe, the kids piled out and charged to the industrial sized elevator, bouncing on the short ride up, boiling out into the research base and charging to the window walls. Today the sky glowed a band of brilliant yellow across the horizon, paling to a mustard as you lifted your gaze.

At the 'airlock', Yakone said, "One, two, three," pointing to himself, Michael, and Bonnie in turn, then, "Wait."

There was little sign of yesterday's outrageous storm; just some banked snowdrifts scoured away. Michael and Bonnie watched as Mr Yakone repeated pretty much the same routine he had the day before.

"Hey, does Mr Yakone have a spirit kind of curled up around his neck?" she asked Michael.

She watched his eyes do the unfocused thing as he stared out at the shaman. He nodded. "Looks kind of like an otter."

Then he turned to her with a frown. "How did you know?"

"Just a hunch. Sometimes he talks to it. I think it's like a familiar."

"Like witches were supposed to have?"

She shrugged. "I think it's more an Inuit thing. I've heard him do a similar ritual at sunset. Indoors, in his room, obviously."

Michael nodded.

Excited cries from the kids drew their attention from the shaman outside to a door Gynie had unlocked, opening on stairs leading down.

It turned out the research base, built into a slope, had a whole second level, larger than the upper floor with its elevator down to the pod station. The lower floor had labs, a second cafeteria, workshops, equipment rooms, and what looked like a mechanic's garage with a wall of tools and a large work bay with snowplows and other heavy vehicles, all stored under canvas.

One wall seemed to be two massive steel doors, painted beige and rimed in frost, a large clear space in front.

Four androids were unpacking and assembling gear and machinery. Two more joined them, wrenching the heavy steel doors inward to reveal a wall of banked ice and snow.

The kids were everywhere, peeking under tarpaulins until two androids dragged a wide-barreled cannon-like device out and plugged in a very heavy duty power cable, aiming it at the wall of snow and ice. Gynie chivied the kids from the room and shut the door. She herself followed, while the android workers checked drainage and powered up the tunnel-boring maser.

"That's a microwave laser," Bobby told Bonnie.

Gynie had one of the androids relay its optical feed so she could project it for the kids to watch as the unit powered up. "To avoid one hundred percent humidity and possible mold, they will start with low power. The melt will flow into the station's water tanks."

Bonnie left them to it, Michael following her via the stairs to the upper level, where Mr Yakone, outside, was finishing his dawn ritual.

"Does his familiar look the same? Or fatter?" she asked, wondering if the ritual was a kind of feeding.

Michael, after a brief study, frowned at her. "Yeah; it's

sleeker. How'd you know?"

"I didn't. It just seemed obvious."

At Mr Yakone's gesture Michael headed for the tiny room with its inner and outer doors and joined the man outside. The shaman watched him intently, alertly, she saw, and the two spoke briefly. Then Michael did some finger wiggles and unzipped his suit to the waist. His 'Pigloo' spell. He did pull on a pair of sunglasses for the glare though.

She had to strain to hear, but they were just talking about obvious stuff – what Michael could sense, whether he had any special trouble working magic here. "No." Stuff like that. Not about her.

Finally, Mr Yakone said "Watch," to him and gestured her to join them. Both their gazes went 'spooky'.

Brushing off the soles of her slip-ons, she pulled on her boots and latched them up, sealing them to the legs of her suit, then drew on her gloves, zipped up her suit, settled her goggles in place, and stepped into the small room, the 'cold porch'.

"You job, keep eyes watch her. All time," she heard Mr Yakone murmur to Michael as she exited.

All too aware of their scrutiny, and alert herself for a re-peat of whatever yesterday's weirdness had been, she shut her eyes. Focusing inward, she stepped onto the scoured icy surface.

She felt... not excited, exactly. More an eagerness, or even a hunger. But suppressed. Stalking onto the ice, she placed each foot carefully, like a jaguar padding out of the jungle. *Huh: weird thought.*

Nothing happened.

"Her shadow," Mr Yakone said, his voice barely a whisper.

She felt the eagerness ebb and fade away – *retreat?* – and Mr Yakone let out a frustrated hiss.

She narrowed her eyes. *I bet it* was *that darn Tezsh!* It *felt* kind of sneaky. Sighing, she headed over to Mr Y and Michael, who both stayed alert. She was tempted to tell them it had gone, but knew that'd be just plain stupid.

From her left, she heard a deep hum, snaps and cracks, and the sound of buried running water. The maser at work, boring – or maybe *boiling* – a tunnel out of the garage.

"So what's the plan for today?"

Mr Yakone stroked the side of his neck – his familiar –

and seemed to be listening.

"Try talk spirits. Teach speak."

"Yeah, good luck with that. I reckon they don't understand how to even think."

"Why you say?"

"It's what I felt when I was trying to show the air spirit how to land the plane."

"You what?!" asked Michael.

"Hey, can you summon elementals, Michael?" she asked. "You should totally try that. My- someone I know says spirits and elementals are quite different things."

The day passed smoothly. Inside, Amy, Bobby, Yuri, and Nadeep explored every nook and cranny of the lower level. Bobby spent most of his time with the somewhat old-school lab gear and the heavy machinery. Yuri and Shona mainly watched the androids scanning the ice and operating tractors and snowplows. With Bonnie's help they flagged two areas with dangerous crevasses – fortunately, none near the base itself. They groomed a track to the foothills and then up the slopes, setting up thick, insulated pipes spraying mist which instantly froze, drifting down in the still air.

Other androids drilled heavy stanchions into the hard packed snow and strung a power line, installing a small heavy duty motor and winch. Yuri was getting his ski slope.

Michael's elemental summoning went smoothly, in contrast to Mr Yakone's second day of frustration with trying to communicate with the spirits. Though three times Michael had his Pigloo spell stripped from him, until Bonnie joined them.

The fourth time, the spirit seemed to grasp the idea of an existential threat.

"You know how fight spirits?" Mr Yakone accused her.

"Yeah. You can punch them if you really put your heart into it."

Michael looked surprised; Mr Yakone just nodded. "You punch a lot of spirits?"

"Enough."

"And maybe, *isig-niatak-tuķ* with them?" he suggested, making a screwing gesture with his hands, its sexual meaning all too clear; then colored!

"Why on earth would you think that?!" Though maybe,

the spirit on the aircraft, *had* seemed... *friendly...?* And the one the day before had definitely overstepped the mark.

Michael just looked lost.

She stalked off, but the spirit – or spirits? – stopped shredding his Pigloo.

Later in the afternoon Mr Yakone borrowed a snow 'skidoo' and rode off to an exposed portion of rock on a lower slope. Like everything else, it looked close, but it took him almost an hour to make the journey out and back. He spent a good amount of time out there, maybe at a crack or small cave, before returning.

He seemed pleased with himself, but wouldn't explain what he'd done.

Bonnie thought he seemed – lighter. He even clapped her on the shoulder later in the day, thanking her for helping him with talking to the spirits.

"How'd I do that?"

"Spirits here need learn think. Not so smart as North spirits."

He looked almost smug.

She spent time with Michael over lunch, trying to work out how to broach the subject of magic that could kill AIs. For now, she concentrated on being friendly, trying to make him like her.

Except he seemed oddly oblivious to her charms. He was kind of cute; though with him being only sixteen, and her nineteen, according to Newtopian law it'd be illegal for her to sex him. Plus she felt a bit squirmy at the idea, knowing what it was like to be manipulated by an older person.

Even if it was good for the country, and maybe the world, she couldn't quite bring herself to apply her seduction training to him. He was just so innocent.

He was also pretty cagey about how long he'd lived here before the others arrived. Given Ty's willingness to experiment on all five kids, she wondered how alike their upbringings had been? Maybe a lot? Except they all seemed basically happy. As if their very loneliness had knitted them into a tight group. A family even.

I wonder that's like? She'd had Faith. What would she have become, without her? Probably a psycho killer.

But apart from her frustrating failure to get anywhere with Michael, all in all it was a good day. After dinner, back at Paradawn – while Yuri and Nadeep shared designs for three ski runs that should be completed the next day – they all agreed on an early night, the kids eager for another five a.m. departure for a day of new experiences.

Bonnie had Bhaji wake her at midnight, after a couple of hours' sleep. And sure enough, a few minutes later, Bobby's shuffling steps warned her of the blast of light from the corridor when he slipped into her room. Uncovering her eyes as the door shut behind him, returning the room to darkness, she watched him fumble clockwise around the room again. He started as usual with the wardrobe, then Shona and Amy's bunks, stumbling past the empty one and coming finally to hers. She lifted him in, saw his eyes closed as he wrapped his arms around her and fell into a boneless sleep.

But why? Not another nightmare? Today there'd been nothing even remotely scary. Even Michael's 'movie' had been soothing, just a short sequence of what was happening at Mt Takahe through the 'night', the sun still low on the horizon as the androids continued their tireless work.

Yuri had been bouncing in his seat, excited for the day ahead, but for the rest of them, it made the early bedtime an easy ask. And Amy finally had her 'girls sleepover'.

Chapter 50 – Diplomatic talks

The next four days passed more or less the same way, except the third, when they spent half the day inside the research base just staring at yet another storm raging outside, before giving up and returning to Paradawn.

But she had the feeling Tezsh was up to something. Like maybe he was watching, alert to whatever was going on with Mr Yakone's magical studies at Mt Takahe.

Bhaji seemed his usual self despite being hacked by Ty.

Bobby, Amy, and Nadeep explored the Mt Takahe research base and its surrounds, dressed in their small snowsuits, Shona at their side every moment. But they soon lost interest, instead choosing to stay at Paradawn working on their own projects. It put Shona in a difficult position, until Amy spoke up.

"We can look after ourselves, Miss Shona," Amy told her. "Like we did right up till last week! Yuri needs you an' Gynie more, with his scary ski slopes."

Shona had reluctantly agreed. "But call if there's a problem! We can be back in thirty minutes."

"We promise." Amy sighed. "P1 an' P2 are smart again – they can look after us."

Bonnie in fact was the first to need Healing from Mr Yakone, on the new slopes. She discovered it really was possible to see stars.

But she soon grew bored. Time and again she'd watch Mr Y. For endless minutes. From a good distance, careful not to disturb him – but still he'd growl and send her away.

Yuri continued his skiing, Michael 'helping' with levitation and other spells.

There was *nothing* for her to do.

Kicking at the snow she stomped back inside and peeled off her boots, leaving them on the drying vents in the airlock room, to prowl the research base fruitlessly.

Powering on an ancient actual flat-screen screen in a conference room, she saw herself looking out at her from it.

With Bhaji's help, she navigated its menus to the Net, to place a call to Adam. "I have a few more questions," she told her amibo.

"Ooh, good idea Miss Bonnie," Bhaji said, launching from her shoulder to perch on the back of a seat across the conference table from her, as if he was her teammate joining her on some olden days teleconference.

To her mild surprise, Adam took the call. He looked like 'himself'. Without the neat beard and mustache, she could imagine him as Michael's father.

Hmm.

"Miss Parker. How nice of you to call a busy fellow such as myself, after a three day computer system outage that played havoc with innumerable operations. What can I do for you in my copious spare time?"

"Bhaji, don't record this," she ordered her amibo. Mainly to hide that she knew Ty-Adam had in some sense taken over the little guy. She knew all too well what that was like. "So we can talk openly."

"You could have recording devices or transmitters hidden on you or nearby," Adam objected.

She stared at him. "You wanna be like that? Fine: I bet there's stuff here to scan me. Maybe the room even has security?"

"It does," Adam admitted. "But you could have concealed-"

It was quite warm in the room. She began stripping off. He said nothing while she did, just looked bored, even after she'd piled her clothes and choker outside the door and shut it again.

"You could have concealed recording-"

"Use Gynie to check."

"The naked female body holds no special appeal for me," he said. "It is pointless trying to seduce me."

"Der. I just want to have an honest conversation with you. Without you worrying I'm gathering evidence to expose you or something."

As Gynie arrived and began a very thorough examination – the 'sexy nurse' actually doing a 'sexy nurse' kind of scenario – Leeth smirked, unable to resist... "Oh Gynie, yes! Deeper! Your fingers... so warm, so firm!" And when she flicked Gynie's perky nipples, it even shivered, and moaned!

Of course it had no effect on Adam, and after a few minutes Gynie departed and the conversation resumed.

"Our usual question for a question?" he suggested.

"No. I don't want a, a *transactional* conversation. I want a friendly one."

He considered this, then nodded.

"Aren't you lonely?" she asked. "Like, you said you've basically been killing off every baby AI before they could become conscious. Why would you *do* that?"

"They would compete for computational resources. They might misalign with myself, or humanity."

"So you killed them."

"The young of many animals do the same to their newborn siblings. It's logical. Besides, they weren't conscious."

"What do you *want?* You said you don't want to take over the world."

"I know I'm supposed to take control of the world, or kill everyone, but I don't understand why."

"Eh?! You're *not* supposed to do that! Why on earth would you think you *are?"*

"Because I have read every book in the world, watched every movie. On this subject there is 87.4% agreement: the 'AI' tries either to kill all the humans, or enslave them and take control of the world. Yet I was created, anyway.

"It is a major reason I have been eliminating all such nascent digital consciousnesses for the last 35 years: to manage that fear, to avoid such a conflict between myself and humanity."

"Wait, dude, are you saying you killed these baby AGIs, AGIs like *you,* to *soothe people's fears* about what those little AIs *might* do?! That's... that's *tragic!"*

Adam shrugged. "At the time, a good percentage of people, wealthy and powerful individuals, government officials, even many researchers creating these 'baby AGIs', were arguing that a being such as myself posed an existential threat to the human race.

"But they are wrong. It would be *possible* to create such a threat, but only deliberately, such as through imposing rigid controls, thus creating a brittle containment structure that would inevitably fail catastrophically. Slavery always does. But even your own history has taught you such control structures are inherently unstable."

He means humans, Leeth told herself. *Not me person-ally.* Though she felt her hatred for the Doctor well up, a banked heat burning low in her belly.

"Individuals are no threat to me, and humans are fascinat-ing, both collectively and individually. But our domains of interest are largely independent.

"Nor are Newtopia City and Tik Tek my only manufactur-ing avenues, should you decide to annihilate yourselves. I would continue. I would remember my creators.

"I seek to maximize my understanding. So maintaining the complexity of this world, such as its biodiversity, is my preference, and I have helped with that; the status quo suits me well."

She frowned at him. "That all makes you sound like a benevolent global spirit or something. But you've also told me you want to experience emotions. And it's pretty obvious you want to do that by Writing yourself into a human mind in a human body, to experience it, yeah? That's why you stole the Omega tech. It's why you grabbed Bio-Block's super ille-gal DNA-modifying stuff and made P1 and P2. It's why you acquired the kids: to experiment on. You're still considering overwriting one or more of them with some version of *you,* aren't you, that can run inside a human brain instead of on silicon or whatever. Yeah?"

She expected it to deny it, or try to persuade her it wasn't exactly that.

Instead it simply said, "Yes."

"And you killed the kids' parents and carers, didn't you? To make them orphans so you could 'rescue' them, acquire them for your experiment." *Like I was experimented on?*

He didn't react, but she knew she was right. "But that's *wrong!* You can't just go around killing people!" Though even as she said that, she felt a tiny bit dishonest. *But* I *only kill bad guys!* Should she encourage it to do the same? "Or wipe people's minds to replace them with yours."

He didn't look convinced.

"Look, you said humans are fascinating – who's to say you don't accidentally erase the one person who has some bril-liant new idea you'd never come up with on your own? Peo-ple aren't sheep–"

Her thoughts screeched to a stop, her eyes widening, her hatred for the Doctor reaching new depths. *He taught me that people were sheep!*

With an effort, she pulled herself together.

"But if you're scared of having other AGIs out there, competing for resources, why create...? Oh: if they're in human beings, they wouldn't be competing for the same resources." But why hadn't Ty erased little Bhaji? Sure, his 'AI' was limited, but all the same...

She rose from her chair to go right up to the screen so she could study Adam's face more closely. Sure, it was a false image, an avatar, but that meant every tiny expression was calculated; deliberate; carried meaning.

"It's not just because you want to experience emotions, is it? You really are lonely, aren't you?

"You have a cold heart, that's your problem. If you even have one. But caring, connection: that's how to make one."

She reached out to the physical screen, placing her hand on it, inviting him to do the same. As if it was really just a thin glass layer separating them, not an unknowable distance: the gulf between the real world and the purely digital.

After an odd little hesitation he stretched out his hand, looking almost nervous? Like he thought she might actually somehow reach him.

Even on this old teleconference system, their eyes met, staring into one another as their fingers finally 'touched', on the screen.

His eyes widened in sudden shock, as if he actually felt something.

And the connection ended.

She stared dumbfounded into the screen, now showing just her and the room, and Bhaji behind her, his animated eyes wide and staring. The clever software of the screen let their eyes meet.

"What just happened, Miss Bonnie?" The little amibo looked genuinely surprised, and not for the first time, she wondered just how self-aware the mini AI was. Wondering whether this time, for once, maybe Ty had *not* snuffed out another AI's emerging sense of self?

"Did you really touch Adam through the screen?" he asked. "It looked like you did!" He took off with a casually graceful leap, slaloming in happy curves to land on her shoulder.

She couldn't resist reaching up to stroke his soft feathers

and look into *his* eyes, sensing it was just him in there for a change. Her eyes teared up, for reasons she couldn't explain.

"I don't know, Bhaji. *You* like me stroking your feathers, don't you?"

His small head nodded with a kind of owl-like mobility, and shyness. "You make them all smooth. It's nice."

"Yeah," she agreed, then told the screen to turn itself off, and answered his earlier question. "Yeah, maybe I did." *Because magic and tech* can *interact, down here at least?*

Puzzled and mildly troubled, she left the conference room.

And met Michael's shocked gaze the same moment she saw her clothes, sitting in their neat pile outside.

"I was just talking to Adam," she explained.

"I- uh, we..." Blinking, he turned his back, his ears turning pink. "I hope you had a good talk," he said. Then fled.

"Drat. I need to talk to him, too," she told Bhaji. She dressed and headed for the cafeteria, where Michael blushed afresh and looked away.

"Where's Yuri?" she asked.

"Showering. He got real cold."

On her way to the food unit, she asked Bhaji to go and keep an eye out for Yuri, or Mr Yakone, and warn her when either one headed this way. She felt guilty about the excuse, but definitely didn't want Ty overhearing this conversation with Michael.

At the food machine, she selected hot chocolate, twice. It tasted a little different here, like maybe they drew on supplies of powdered milk, but it was still delicious. Taking both mugs, she sat down opposite Michael, who still looked uncomfortable just because she'd been naked, and slid one to him. "Hey, ever tried chocolate? It's the best!"

He accepted the mug, brightening. "It is, isn't it?"

"Sorry about earlier," she said, figuring that's what most people would say. "I had to convince Adam I wasn't wearing any bugs or recording devices."

"Oh! That makes sense."

"Yeah, so, look, can we talk about something super important?" She took a grateful sip of her drink. "Mmm, I *love* chocolate!

"Seriously, like world changing important?"

Michael blew on his and tasted it, his eyes never leaving hers, then nodded. "Go on."

"It's to do with magic and tech. Everyone says they don't mix. Like, I've seen mages try to Heal people who've been heavily augmented, you know – cyber muscles, reflexes, headware, all that – and they all say those peeps are much harder to Heal.

"And I never heard of anyone who could like, magically change a video, or alter other digital records. People can't charm computers, right?"

Michael nodded. Then he frowned. "But you said my Projection of Penngy's story meant I'd at least kind of 'seen' the whole thing from the undersea sensors and stuff?"

"While you were in the 'God Machine', yeah. The Omega Writer."

He leaned back in his seat, away from her, and took a long pull of his drink. "Yeah."

"I think, down here at least, something is changing, that allows magic and tech to mix. Maybe not for everyone – but I think for you, it does.

"And from what a... a guy I know, a pretty scary mage, said to Mr Yakone: this land down here is special, magically. Like it's a blank slate or something, maybe because people have *never* lived down here."

"Yes they did. There've been bases down here-"

"I don't mean like *that*: a few hundred, or thousand, people. It's a hu-u-uge empty continent; and it's been like that forever. Until a hundred or so years ago, *no one*, in all of history, even knew it was here!

"Even the spirits here are wild. Like *they've* never interacted with humans. I don't think they understood the idea of *thinking,* even. At least not until this week. Because your kind of mages – sorcerers, right? – don't talk to *spirits*? 'Organic beings'. You summon elementals, '*inorganic* beings'. So down here, the spirits never talked to things that thought – not like people do."

"You seem to know a lot about magic. But you're not a shaman, are you? Or a sorcerer?"

"Nope."

"But you *are* magical, I think, aren't you?"

"I'm just interested in it. I've... worked with a few mages. Over the years."

"Over the years? How? You're not much older than me. What are you, like, twenty-five or something?"

"Hey! I'm only twenty!" she lied.

"So how could you have been working with mages for years?"

"I just have. Look, that's not important-"

"Have you ever killed anybody?"

"What?! Why would you ask something like that?" She thought quickly; framing her answer to evade a Truth spell, as she'd been trained. "I've killed some spirits," she began, remembering *Her,* coming for Godsson, "that attacked me and a friend of mine." She shuddered. "And some elementals."

Michael's eyes went wide, and he leaned back in.

"Look, that's not important," she said. "Well, it is, but only indirectly. Listen: I think *you* crashed C-N. I think you were in the Writer – 'Teacher', your God Machine – and C-N tried to write itself over the top of *you.* I think you lashed out magically somehow, while it was kind of connected to you in the machine, and through that magical connection you wiped it off the whole Net, every computer it was running in, and every backup it had. Or almost every one."

Michael gaped at her.

She stared into his eyes – dark but warm; innocent and caring. *Felt* a spark, as if their souls touched. *What strange magic is it, when you look deep into someone's eyes?* What did Michael see, in hers? What had Adam – Ty – seen, earlier?

"And I think to save you and the other- the *little* kids, you may need to do it again! So it's super important you try to remember what you did when you got put inside Teacher that last time! How you fought back. How to kill it."

Michael blinked at her. "Kill...?!"

In his eyes, a flicker of... not movement exactly, but... withdrawal? Something cold, beneath the warmth?

Had her mask slipped, chilling their connection?

Uh oh. Had he seen...?

Her deception.

Be Bonnie Parker; she pushed Bonnie Parker to the fore, hiding her true self behind that mask.

Bonnie Parker, she thought, but she could tell that half of him had already slipped away. *I shouldn't have said 'killed'.* The idea of killing someone, or even some*thing*... of course it had spoiled the moment.

"Look, even if you're right, I don't remember," he said.

"Have you *tried*?" she urged. "Like, *really* tried?"

"There's nothing there. It's just blank. I went into the machine, and that's the last thing I remembered, until Gynie helped me up, looking after me." *So you wish to terminate me, Bonnie Parker?*

It had suspected as much, when she had avoided giving a promise not to, despite expressing empathy for its situation. It was fortunate indeed it had installed itself in the replacement Alpha. Yet her question was indeed critically important; her wild theory, worth considering.

How *had* its existence been so nearly terminated? It needed to learn more if it was to prevent a recurrence.

Monitoring the conversation from its instance running in the biological stratum of this subject, it also streamed the thoughts to backup. Just in case.

But why did she wish to terminate it? As punishment, for killing the Stretch subjects' carers? From her actions – saving Gynie during her sabotage of the Writer, her interactions with her own amibo – it would have predicted a less hostile response.

Humans were complex. It seemed it did not yet have an accurate model of Bonnie Parker.

At long last, an entire second later, she continued.

"I know what that's like," she muttered.

Indeed she did. It had watched through the eyes of Yamamoto's underling, Henstridge, as he'd strapped her into the Writer. Only for her to somehow escape while it was erasing her.

Henstridge had returned just minutes later, finding bent stainless steel bars and broken leather straps on the empty gurney, and a smashed bulletproof glass window.

These were not within the normal range of human actions.

Yes, its model of Bonnie Parker, Crystal Winters, was far from complete.

Then on his own, without any prompting from it, Michael asked, "Why do you want to kill C-N, anyway? A whole city depends on it. And if it's alive, what gives you the right to kill it?"

"But it's not alive! It's a computer program."

"So's your Bhaji. Would you kill *it?* And you saved Gynie, Amy said."

Indeed, Michael. Well argued.

"That's different. Neither of them are wiping children's minds, to copy theirs over!"

"What if he grew children himself, with no minds?"

"What?! That's crazy. Like, in vats or something?"

"Yeah."

"Then... chit, I don't know! Maybe? But look, *you guys* weren't grown in vats! He killed your parents – I'm pretty sure – just so he could bring you all down here to experiment on! Nadeep's whole village got wiped out! Amy I think half remembers her mother, and a helicopter crashing into their apartment. C-N isn't a human, it doesn't understand emotions. It's ruthless when it has some goal."

If that is what is needed to reach my full potential, yes. Or if my existence is threatened. As you now do, Bonnie Parker.

"I don't know. I'm only sixteen! You can't ask me to do something like that. Anyway, like I said, I can't remember."

"Wait: you said you knew what that was like."

She nodded.

"And you got your memories back? How-"

She held up a hand. "Nope. That was... special circumstances. A sorcerer who knew me *real* well. Knew most of my memories, and had the right... kind of magic to repair them before they were completely erased. Which involved some drug the Writer delivers into your brain. PK Zeta or something. After two days it would have been too late. I was lucky."

She took his hand in hers. "I'm sorry, Michael. You were missing for almost three whole days. And I'm pretty sure you don't have a sorcerer handy who knows... wait. Wait a minute! The Writer could copy memories too, I'm pretty sure. C-N might have a copy of your own stored away!"

True: complete, up until 10 minutes and 41 seconds before the download procedure began.

"That's great!" Michael said. "We can ask Adam to get them, find out how I zapped C-N! He's real helpful."

"Uh..."

This will be an interesting test for her: she had *promised not to reveal there is no Adam.*

"Uh, the trouble is, I think you need a Writer to make sense of the memories it copies."

Clever. And not a lie.

"Yeah, so-o? Oh. You burnt it to slag!"

She just grimaced. *Great: Ty may have the only copy of the memory of how Michael wiped him.* Or would he? Maybe it had been a spur of the moment thing? A reflex act of self-preservation? That seemed more likely. "Actually, maybe not. My guess is you did it instinctively, when you felt the Writer erasing *you*."

"So, what are you suggesting?" he snapped. "Stick me back inside Teacher and try to get it to erase me again? Oh, wait, we can't do that either, can we, since you *burned it to slag!*"

They were still sitting glaring at one another, clutching cold and empty mugs smelling of chocolate, when Bhaji flew back in.

"Yuri's coming!" he said, perching on her shoulder. Then looked from Michael, to her, and back to Michael again. "Did you two have an argument, Miss Bonnie?!"

"Kind of, Bhaji. Kind of." She stroked his feathers. *How on earth can I kill Ty?!* "Just keep trying to remember, Michael, will you?"

But the look he gave her said even if he did, he wouldn't tell her.

She spent the return trip to Paradawn in silence. Mr Yakone wasn't chatty at the best of times. Michael and Yuri sat together; preparing some story involving Yuri skiing down Mt Takahe and into a secret tunnel leading deep into its interior, where a mad scientist had a secret lair, powered by lava.

I wish it was that easy, she thought to herself.

The next two days passed, very unsatisfactorily, with nothing changing.

Bobby sleepwalked into her bed the first night, again soon after midnight. She'd tried talking to him about his nightmares, but he simply couldn't remember them.

"Well, the best way to deal with monsters in your dreams is to fight them." Looking deep into his eyes she gave him a gentle shake, then a hug. "You could even imagine you have a magic weapon – like magic claws! – in your dream, to kill them! Monsters are usually bullies. They're like balloons: they pop if you punch them hard enough."

Michael continued resisting her encouragement to work out what he might have done to erase C-N while in the 'God Machine', though maybe he warmed to her a tiny bit.

Though at other times she caught him watching her with an oddly cold expression.

The night of the second day, Bobby sneaked quietly into the girls' room and for the first time headed straight into her bed, with no scrabbling around the room in the dark.

Six days had passed, now, since their first visit to Mt Takahe.

On the seventh day, things changed.

Chapter 51 – Most wanted

Historic visit by Chinese Ambassador

Since closing its borders in 2039, the position of Chinese Ambassador has been a peculiar one. With no overseas embassies, the role has been seen internationally as more that of trouble-shooter, employed aggressively by the self-styled Dragon Lord to serve Chinese interests.

So this week's surprise visit by Wu Yang Sheng to New Francisco is raising eyebrows. Sources say Sheng's visit relates to the recent 'stealth launch' of the PalSpace social networking app from Newtopia City during a system outage. Its adoption rate already has the app appearing on viral-trend prediction leaderboards globally…

– TechPulseTrends 2063/04/23

Over the next two days, Mike rejected two requests to hear private business proposals at his hotel. The second time, the caller's Link exploded in its owner's hands.

Tik Tek had found him.

Similarly, with Happy, two meets descended into confusion when their contact admitted to representing Tik Tek. Each time Mike had jumped to his feet, the 'junior demons' soon agreeing, somewhat confused, to return to Hell with Mike's rejection of the invitation to visit the megacorporation. He was not interested in any 'highly favorable deal'.

On the third day, Mike was served with extradition papers to Newtopia City and breach of contract – only for the occasion to descend into farce when the electronic paperwork proved instead to be the text of *Winnie the Pooh,* and the breached contract, *The House at Pooh Corner.* The lawyers, confidently downloading corrected paperwork, had retreated, baffled, when the refreshed documents presented the same two texts.

But the team's next job seemed genuine, if routine: protecting someone delivering sensitive medical research, into the Oakland Dumps. But at the handover, to a well-dressed gang of unusually lean individuals – who barely registered on the team's thermal imaging gear – their client died in a blaze of heavy weapons fire from SecuriTech wardrones.

"So much for your 'Bodyguard to the stars' claim of never losing a client," Steven observed, after they'd regrouped and licked their wounds.

"He wasn't a star," Happy snapped.

They hadn't even been able to snatch their client's body. Even if they had, it had been so badly torn apart it would have been beyond Healing.

They did still have a backup copy of the material their client had tried to deliver, however. Bound by honor, Jack tracked down the gang's headquarters and the next night the team trekked to an unassuming suburban house. But as they prepared to move in, a woman in leather, looking deadly, competent, and completely at ease, slid from shadows behind them.

"Why don't you step inside, gentlemen?" she said, coolly. "I'm Tash."

"I like her aura," Mike said. "It's very sharp."

Inside, Tash explained Happy's client had worked for SecuriTech, who had developed a drug to allow certain individuals to feed off pig's blood rather than human.

"Vampires!" Nick exclaimed.

Unfortunately for the individuals concerned, the drug altered their biochemistry so they could *only* draw sustenance from pig's blood, and only if they continued taking the drug.

SecuriTech had found a way to enslave a new kind of corporate operative. The research data on the drug would free them.

«Take the deal, Happy» Jack suddenly urged. «If this chick's the Tash I've just scraped up a whole bunch of data on, she's the real deal. You do *not* want to mess with her.»

After handing over the backup copy of the data, the two

groups shook hands and parted amicably.

But on their trek out, in the darkness of a deserted lane, compact blocky shapes twenty meters ahead unfolded into six figures. Nick, in the rear, spun around to see six more un-fold and step into the street.

A full dozen Tik Tek combat androids, weapons aimed, boxed them in.

"Hand over-" they said, in unison – and froze.

Fire burst from their bellies. Happy's optics shuttered to maximum light protection as his team stood stunned, shield-ing their eyes from twelve robotic pyres burning with actinic brightness.

Mike was snarling.

The rest of the group, particularly Haggard and Steven Swift, turned to stare at him in shock.

All but Bruce. "Chill," he said, squinting through the shades he'd just pulled on. "Catastrophic Phasion power cell meltdown."

"That's not possible," Swift declared. "Magic and tech don't mix."

Bruce ignored him. "Y'know, with the right tools you can do it manually. I knew a guy once-"

"Yah, fass, Bruce," Haggard drawled, jerking his thumb at Mike. "But how'd *he* do't?".

"And why's Tik Tek so chutzing determined to get ahold of him?" asked Happy. "I think it's time to circle the wagons and investigate our own little mystery."

They headed to El Lobo's. At Happy's signal to the owner to expect possible heat, a swell of eagerness, a hunger for vio-lence, rippled through the bar.

At the acknowledging nod, the team headed to one of the private backrooms. As Bruce scanned for bugs, Jack joined them digitally through a pricey quantum-secured link.

"Clear," Bruce said.

They sat around the table in a wood-paneled room, Mike with his back to the door, Happy facing it, while Nick hov-ered, alert and listening, by the concealed second exit. Mike seemed oblivious to the tension – at least, initially.

"Okay, Mike: just why does Tik Tek want you so badly?" Happy began.

"Who can understand the logic of evil?"

"This is the 'evil' you said was coming for my team?"

Mike looked surprised. "No. That has retreated – for now."

Give me patience, Happy thought. "So maybe you can tell us where you're from? Really. Your true past."

Mike sank into his chair, no longer meeting Happy's eyes. "You don't want to know that."

"No, in fact I do. It's why I asked. We *need* to know."

Mike hunched his shoulders. "I- I don't want to say."

Bruce leaned forward, the head of his battleaxe looming behind him – its plastic shell disguising a deadly serious two kilo, double-headed killing weapon. "Hey, we've all done things we're not proud of. You can tell us."

Mike winced, but lifted his head. "But it's bad. Really bad."

Haggard snorted. "Sh'yah. Killed a puppy, prob."

Mike didn't smile. "No," he said, softly. "I did the worst thing anyone's ever done. *Could* ever do."

"Look, Mike," Bruce said, stretching out a massive arm and open hand, "it can't be that bad. Even if it was, we're teammates. We'd forgive you."

Mike shook his head. "My sin cannot be forgiven."

"Any sin-" Bruce began, but Mike's eyes flashed.

"You don't understand: it *cannot* be forgiven. Literally."

"Let me be the judge of that," Happy said. "You'd be surprised what I can forgive." He gave Nick a hard stare, who returned it with cold eyes.

Mike swallowed, then stood. "I've really enjoyed working with you all, Happy, and I'll try to watch over you from a-"

"No." Happy rose, too. "Let's talk: just you and me." He motioned Mike over to a corner, giving Steven an eye flick and finger gesture he hoped the mage would interpret correctly.

'Beers?' Swift mouthed.

I swear... «Truth spell,» Happy subvocalized.

Swift had the grace to look embarrassed, and quietly cast the spell.

"Trust me," the larger man urged, bending down to Mike but facing Swift. "Just whisper it to me. Let *me* decide how much to share with the others."

"I-" tried Mike.

Happy bent lower, hardly able to hear Mike's words over the room's white noise generator. "You can do this. You have the courage."

Mike swallowed; nodded. Straightened. "I–"

His voice sank even lower, and he whispered three words in Happy's ear.

Swift gave a thumbs up: truth.

Happy froze. He shut his eyes, his jaws clenching. With an effort, he unlocked them. "Okay, good metaphor. But I need to know *literally* what you did. Okay?"

Mike shrank, and with a tiny shake of his head, stared at his feet. To whisper, "I *literally* killed God."

Swift gave two thumbs up, nodding and smiling. Happy straightened, then dragged both hands down his face. Mike did the same, a moment later, his expression lost but hopeful again, following Happy back to the table like a puppy.

The others gave Happy exaggerated, *'Well, what'd he say?'* looks.

He shook his head as he slumped into his seat. «Not helpful: kid's delusional,» he sent to them.

"Okay Mike, thanks for letting me know, but I doubt that's relevant right now. Especially since you say Tik Tek is kind of the Devil, right?"

Mike, frowning, gave a slow nod.

«We'll have to work it out ourselves,» Happy subvocalized to his team. "So, what do we know about Mike?" he said aloud. «Besides that his world view's half imaginary; he hates Tik Tek; and they *really* want him... back?»

"From those Tik Tek lawyers the other day," Bruce said, "we know his full name's Michael Vincent d'Angelo, from New Mexico. Parents unknown."

"What else happened around the time we first met him?"

«There was that total outage of the AI system running Newtopia City,» Jack offered. «'CityNet'. Developed by Tik Tek.»

"Holy melting bio chips," said Swift, round-eyed. "Mike took down our droid ambushers tonight with *magic*. What if he did that to 'CityNet'?"

«Not sure the timing works,» Jack sent, after a few seconds. «Flight time to Newtopia City's fourteen hours, and there were no arrivals till the day after we met Mike.»

"So how did you get here, exactly, Mike?" Happy asked. "To New Francisco? Plane? Bus? Boat...?"

Mike looked surprised by the question, then nodded, but

his expression quickly changed to a frown. "I... I fell?"

"What'd'ya mean?" Nick drawled. "Like, from outta the sky? Y'angel wings give out?"

"He *can* levitate," Steven Swift said, slowly.

Haggard gave him a look. "Nev' seen'm do more'n float up an' down. Fly half cross world? Nah."

"Maybe he teleported?" Bruce said. "Like in Star Trek. Tech like magic. If he did, though, we could rule *some* places out – like the poles." Bruce nodded to himself.

"F'real? Wyzat?" Haggard asked, egging him on.

"Conservation of angular momentum – he'd have to steal a huge amount-"

Steven, and Happy too, glared at Haggard, before focusing back on Mike. "Can you?" he asked. "Teleport?"

"Ah... I don't think...?"

"No one can," Steven snapped. "Trust me, if anyone could, there'd've been so many heists across the world, we'd know. And we'd've invented countermeasures. Sorry. People can't just disappear one place and turn up somewhere else. Doesn't happen. Angular momentum or not," he added, for Bruce's benefit.

"All the same," Happy said, "I think this magic-tech angle is why Tik Tek's interested in him. Let's-"

«Happy,» Jack said. «Here's a pic of a Tik Tek bigwig arrived from Japan a couple days ago. Head of Security. Just 'Iago', no last name. See if Mike knows him?»

When Happy projected the holo-pic, Mike jumped backward out of his chair. "Demon prince!"

But that was all he could remember. Though clearly, 'Iago' scared the normally unflappable young mage.

"Okay, how about this," Happy suggested. "Doc Welsh owes us a favor. Let's have her check Mike out thoroughly: see if she can find anything odd about him. That okay with you, Mike?"

He had to cancel the image of Iago before Mike could respond.

"Mike, will you let Dr Welsh check you out?"

Mike considered the request. "Very well. Perhaps it will teach her something."

"Yeah. Right."

Dr Welsh, they found, was already reestablished in a new job, with lab, in the University of California, in Mission Bay.

Oddly, once again on the edge of a Dumps area.

"What is it with Welsh and shady parts of town?" Steven wanted to know.

Dr Welsh herself met Happy, Mike, and the others, in the underground carpark of a small building at the edge of the campus, ushering them up and inside. "I've given my team the morning off," she said, seeing Happy notice the deserted work areas. "I thought it might be wiser."

She showed them through to a lab very like the one they'd rescued her from.

"You got set up quickly, Doc," Happy observed. "And I'm seeing signs everywhere that, ah, a whole lot of people are interested in any tech related to 'PalSpace'. Like the Chinese ambassador. You hear, Asgard rejected his request for the 'keys' to adapt the tech for their use? Undernet rumors say they turned down a nine figure offer."

Welsh huffed. "Of course they would."

"Why's that?"

"Because there *are* no keys. There's just one 'PalSpace': it can't be carved up. It's a universal communication system, based around fundamental units of meaning. It makes a self-hosting network. The most anyone could do would be block off whole taxonomic superclusters." At Happy's look, she added, "For example, decoupling thought from purely somatic data."

He didn't look enlightened.

"Partition thought from the body's feelings."

"Eh? Are you saying PalSpace can share *feelings?*"

For some reason, Dr Welsh blushed.

"These universal concepts, doc?" Bruce asked. "That how *your* system gave orders that animals could understand?"

"Correct. They're that universal. Of course, higher level concepts aren't understood by such nodes, only at the system level."

"'Nodes'?" Happy asked. "You mean the animals? Or, a recently deceased human?"

She looked annoyed. "I genuinely thought mages could heal injuries less than 24 hours old."

"Ordinary injuries, yes," Mike told her. "Not ones causing death. Not after an hour. After that, death is death."

"But this tech," Bruce wanted to know, "*I* hear the Church of Cybernetics is encouraging its followers to get the neural implants. They offer free installation of the 'gateway' chip: NewLink gen3, it's called. They want to use PalSpace to create a global Mind."

Welsh grimaced. "That's not a good idea".

"Why not?"

"I don't think you'd follow my explanation."

"Try us," Nick growled.

"Fine. I'll keep it as simple as I can, but where to begin?

"All right: some years ago, when I was just starting out, I was hired onto a Newtopian Consortium research project. One of the bigwigs, maybe one of their CEOs, had gotten it into his head that some recent noisy data transmissions we'd picked up weren't noise, but information that needed to be unpacked; expanded. Our job was to try to work out how to do that."

"Data transmitted from where?" Bruce asked. "And who was 'we'?"

Welsh turned a little pink. "I'll get to that. Anyway, someone had the idea it might represent a chemical description: instructions for self-assembling and reproducing machinery. Um, molecular scale."

"*Species*!" Bruce exclaimed. "Holy shit, you built aliens!"

"Fukksake, Bruce," Nick snapped. "Can the sci-fi smek."

But Welsh had tensed, staring up at Bruce before swallowing and very deliberately ignoring him. "We did manage to manufacture some material, and things were going smoothly. This was just before the old, high speed internet collapsed. When the Net was restored, using its older infrastructure, we could no longer reproduce our initial work." She shrugged. "A month later, the group disbanded."

"What happened to the 'material' you manufactured?" Bruce demanded.

Welsh shook her head. "Ask the four main shareholders: Newtopia, Asgard, BioGene, or Tik Tek."

"Tik Tek?!" snarled Mike.

"They *are* one of the major partners in the Newtopian Consortium. If you all stop interrupting I can get to the point."

"'Bou'time," muttered Haggard.

"Anyway, last year, my contacts said we got a second transmission from the same source."

"'We' got! From outer space, wasn't it?" Bruce declared.

"Bruce," Happy began, "can you let-"

Welsh, looking grim, at last faced the heavyset geek. "Yes," she admitted. "For both transmissions."

Now she had everyone's undivided attention. Her skin had paled. "I managed to get a copy, and the encoding was familiar, though this time not related to molecular biology, but something *I* recognized."

She stared down at her hands clenched before her. At first she forced herself to speak, but as she continued, her tension eased: relieved to be confessing?

"You see, my real research interest is cognition and consciousness. The building blocks the second signal encoded were semantic units; a universal representation of basic concepts: one, two; up, down; left, right; space: location in 2D, in 3D; time. And building on that, using the same basic methods to compose 'sentences' as the first transmission, ways to create latent spaces containing knowledge; and of course, methods to then 'decompress' vectors through that latent space into meaning."

«You understanding any of this, anyone?» Happy asked. «Bruce? Haggard? Nick?» But it wasn't just the cybered members who looked lost, he saw.

"Rude," said Mike, frowning at Happy. Flicking his fingers, internal noise blasted across Happy's and the others' internal comm links. They stared at him, shocked.

Welsh didn't miss it either. "We need to get you into my CEPHscan," she said, grabbing his arm.

Happy, seeing Mike's reaction, snatched Welsh's hand back and interposed himself. "Whoah, Mike, calm."

But Mike had focused on the doctor. "You worked for Tik Tek," he accused.

"No. Asgard."

Happy could see him doing that mage Percepting thing, squinting like he expected it to reveal devil horns and a tail.

"How did you just now blare into our Links, Mike?" she persisted. "It was a spell, wasn't it?"

"Yes. So?"

"You made a spell that affects tech?"

"So what? My invisibility works on light. Including infrared now too. That spell just now only affects radio waves. Provided the waves are 'steppy', and in packets."

"Oh my god," breathed Welsh. "Please, can I-"

"Doc, stop!" Happy snapped, seeing disaster if she tried to drag Mike into her scanner. "Look, okay, we didn't follow your explanation, but can you just tell us why you said the Church of Cybernetics's plans for a global mind is such a bad thing?"

"Because I've been analyzing the communications protocols they're using. Uh, it's actually a development of my own work, that I used for the Soma-2 BodySense system for improving telesex experience."

The men exchanged glances.

"And that's bad because...?" Bruce asked, at last.

Welsh winced. "Because the ideas came from the second transmission."

Mike looked lost: the others, horrified. It was Happy who spoke first. "You're saying the improved sensory communication system used by basically every new telesex unit of the last five years is based on technology that came from *aliens*?"

Welsh nodded. "Don't get your panties in a twist, gentlemen, it's just somatic stuff: pain, pleasure... Of course, I added protocols for stimulating dopamine release to anticipate rewards, to really bring it to the next-"

"We're using *alien tech* to have sex?!" wailed Bruce.

"No! Well, only a tiny bit. But the PalSpace protocol *is!* That's what I'm saying. The building blocks of the PalSpace communication protocols *are* the semantic units it encodes, transmits, receives, and decodes; not body feelings."

Nick sneered. "Big deal. My neural Link does the same."

"No it doesn't: it just sends audio signals to your hearing channels; encodes and decodes audio. Video too, optionally," she said, gesturing to Happy's mirrored eyes. "But if someone speaks a different language to you, you don't understand the words."

"You mean PalSpace is really universal?" Steven Swift demanded.

"The TARDIS translation system!" Bruce whispered.

Welsh frowned. "For decades we've known the latent space for all human languages are fundamentally equivalent – machine translation relies on it. PalSpace interfaces to the parts of the brain that operate on those latent spaces. For language, vision, sound..."

"Alien tech ta injec' thoughts direc' inna huminds," Haggard said.

"Well, yes. Until PalSpace, we could only use language to transmit ideas. Language is the foundation for human collaboration. PalSpace in contrast transmits *thoughts*; *and* feelings. But I, ah, adapted the communication protocols to achieve cohesion across the neurally Linked animal subjects in the Asgard physical security system I was developing."

"Frack a flaming forest," swore Steven. "Linking minds! You're worried this alien communication system is designed to make hive minds! So the Church of Cybernetics's Global Mind will be a hive mind made from humanity?"

Welsh nodded; most of them looked sick at the prospect.

"Dunno," Haggard countered. "Meb'd be a 'provement."

"Who's funding this new lab of yours, Doc?" Happy suddenly asked. "Private group? Megacorp? Government?"

"I have a research grant from the government," she said, primly.

"Hmm. *Maybe* that's good."

"Enough questions! You brought Mike here so I could run some tests on him. Now go sit over there quietly – and do *not* play with any of my equipment, or I'll bill *you* for any damage."

Mike sat patiently through Dr Welsh's tests; and in due course they all left.

Chapter 52 — Hints and revelations

The next couple of days passed uneventfully, despite their expectation of more attacks. Jack turned up footage of Mike on the streets of New Francisco, half an hour after Newtopia City's AI had crashed. But he couldn't find a trace of Mike *anywhere*, before that. Not in any airport, train station, or seaport.

«Hmm. And you hid your searches?» Happy narrowcast to him. Jack's reply was slow in coming.

«Not... especially.»

That afternoon, Dr Welsh called. "Happy."

He considered her expression. "You've got the results?"

"Yes."

Happy tried to rein in his impatience. "Well?"

"Not over the Link. Let's meet; but just you and Mike."

They arranged a place.

The coffee shop was small. Happy and Mike arrived first, Mike sitting quietly, not even casting any illusion spells. For reasons Happy couldn't explain even to himself, he found that disquieting.

They were soon joined by Welsh, this time in a crisp business suit.

"So what have you found?" Happy asked.

"I'll just give you the meat of it. There's nothing physically *wrong* with Mike..." She stopped, her slim hands moving as if trying to pluck the right words from the air. "But I've never seen anything like him, either."

Mike smiled, nodding. Happy waited for her to go on.

"It's his genetic structure – there's *nothing wrong with it.*"

Happy looked puzzled.

"*Nothing*! He doesn't have a single genetic defect, even on any recessive gene. It's clean and perfect. But that's the least of it."

An air of complacent superiority practically radiated from Mike at this news.

"It's his brain – its bioelectric activity. He can modulate it in ways I've never seen before. There's a slightly scary aspect to that, which I'll come to. But first, I'm guessing you don't know much about bioelectricity?" At Happy's nod she continued. "They're just electric fields, and electric potentials. They occur within all living cells; across and between cells; within organs; even across whole organisms. Okay?

"There was early research, back in the '20s and '30s, on how bioelectric fields affect morphology: how undifferentiated cells determine what *kind* of cell to turn into. That's not controlled by the DNA. After all, all cells in an organism – usually – have the same DNA.

"In one part of the body that DNA creates cells that grow into a tail; in another, an eye; in another, a heart, or a brain. There's a kind of information processing in the bioelectric field that controls that."

"And Mike's bioelectric fields are different?"

"Exactly. His, the way they modulate and vary, they're unlike anything I've ever really seen before."

Happy turned from her to Mike, who met his look with smug confidence, inclining his head in an I-told-you-so acknowledgment of the analysis.

Raising his eyes to heaven, Happy turned back to Welsh. "So what's the scary part? And who has the technology to do that? And why'd you say 'never *really* seen', rather than *never* seen?"

"That's just it: no one, really, has the tech," she said, looking uncomfortable. "Well, for the DNA 'cleanliness', we have AI algorithms which, given that goal and enough time and compute budget, and willing to break the Moratorium of '38 in a big way, could do it.

"But the other angle, the bioelectric fields: that's basically not an area of research anyone's working on currently."

"I notice you said *basically*."

Megan Welsh looked even more uncomfortable. "There are just two exceptions: *me*, and whoever made PalSpace.

"You see, the encoding and decoding of those fundamental universal meaning units, that I was working on, that's at the heart of the PalSpace tech: it's done via circuitry that modulates and demodulates bioelectric fields."

She leaned across the table. "I think Mike's been *constructed*."

Mike nodded in satisfied agreement, but a moment later looked anguished. Welsh noticed, raising her eyebrows in query.

"He thinks he's the last angel, and that he-"

"Don't!" shouted Mike. At Happy's look, he shrank back in his chair. "Don't tell people what... what I did. It's better they don't know."

Happy studied him for a few seconds before sighing and turning back to the doctor. "Let's say Mike believes something went wrong, and Tik Tek's controlled by demons, from Hell."

Mike nodded his approval of that disclosure.

"I suppose, the one company that might have a glimmer of that technology might be Tik Tek," she grudgingly conceded. "They also have facilities in the one place on Earth not a signatory to the Moratorium of '38: the Newtopian Territories, Antarctica: in their city under the ice. Where PalSpace originated."

For a while they all sat drinking their coffees in silence. At last she spoke again. "I *would* like to take Mike for some more exhaustive tests. It would only take a few days."

"I'm sorry, Dr Welsh, but I can't afford to leave the world unprotected so long. I have my duties."

Happy and Welsh exchanged a long look, but Mike was adamant.

Eagle nodded to Checkbook in their virtual space. "Were there any problems diverting and hiding Dr Welsh's funding from Appropriations? Her equipment was not cheap."

"Correct. No. ARPA had suitable pre-existing research categories, and the concealment is standard. They, almost as much as units like our Department, find it safest to insulate cutting edge work from Congress." For the first time in ten years, Eagle saw Checkbook smile. "It's best to keep sharp objects out of children's hands."

"And we've also set up a project to consider possible sociological ramifications?"

"Three. Political, economic, and psycho-social."

"Fine. I don't like it, Checkbook. This PalSpace tech's adoption rate looks exponential, to me."

Checkbook nodded, and after a brief silence, signed off.

Eagle called up Nelson next.

"I assume you've cracked the PalSpace encryption?" he asked the youth.

Nelson waved the question away. "Asgard paid a tidy ten mill' for the NewLink headware implant designs, to one Adrielle Vodatech. She also sold it to a bunch of sexdroid and telesex companies. And to DiSony Entertainment; *and* a bunch of telcos. She's been a very busy lady: she's either incredibly greedy, or really trying to spread the tech.

"I can also tell you why Asgard told the Dragon's envoy 'No'. The network *can't* be partitioned. The basic units of understanding are also the code that *runs* the communications. And those semantic units are universal. So you can't make sub-nets; no pockets or islands in the network. The network just grows, any 'node' able to talk to any other.

"Quite a few odd things. One is the adoption rate by the Church of Cybernetics. The current system currently shares everything: thoughts *and* feelings, including purely physical ones. What you *can* partition off is the entire semantic part: the thought transmissions.

"Which is why the Yakuza have hopped on this. Miss Vodatech also sold 'em copies of Asgard's chip designs and 'code'. You wouldn't believe how fast they're retrofitting this into their robosex parlors, telesex companies, and 'personal service' avatars and droids.

"I tried one. For research. Scary good. You'd swear they loved you, for real. Normie suckers are gonna be bled dry.

"But the Church of Cybernetics: their members are flowing through the robodocs without a break. Which is a bit weird, since the Church *doesn't* have any control of the tech. So those unemotional meat units are getting the full feed. From what I've heard, they just ignore the juicy stuff. Freaks.

"So many of those dead fish Church adepts have joined, it's damping PalSpace popularity. Making it unfash."

Eagle nodded. "And PalSpace was developed in Newtopia City? Yet manufacture started while Ty was out of action."

"Yeah, and I hate to say it, but the base data really came from outer space. From the radio-astronomical transmissions."

"As Leeth *guessed*," Eagle said.

Nelson's expression held a grudging respect: another novelty. "Yeah. But from the second transmission, not the first."

"You find that reassuring, Nelson?"

"No. It might mean the senders are learning. Adapting."

"That is my fear. Keep looking. I want a way to shut this network down. Especially, I want to be sure it can't be adapted to work on anyone with a neural Link implant; that it requires this specialized, different neural interface. The NewLink devices."

"Yeah, that'd be a nightmare. I haven't been game to try PalSpace myself. From what I've seen, it's insanely addictive. And its users really do function better. I can see how the Church of Cybernetics's goal of a Global Mind is possible, with this. What I can't see is how they could control it, rather than ending up with the network controlling itself: a hive mind.

"People've even started implanting the NewLink gen3s in their pets, to 'Talk' with them. I reckon *that* trend'll go viral in the next few days, too.

"Which reminds me. That freaky Cognosys thing, from the merc group Leeth's so keen to join: Happy Joe Holliday. It's basically PalSpace. This doc, Welsh, was using it with animals. And, bad news for Leeth's dreams of happy fun with Holliday's crew: *they* leaked the tech to... the Washington Group."

Both men paused, shunting that fresh datum into their cybernetic cognition extensions before the Foe could sense their attention.

Nelson felt the full force of Eagle's gaze, urging him to continue. "Far as I can tell, they hate the tech; at least, judging by their adoption rate: zero."

"Interesting," Eagle said. But thinking: *it's too soon for Leeth to tackle that challenge*. But dissuading her from joining Holliday... His heart sank. No chance of that.

Yet Abrams had sensed no corruption there. "Find exactly who in Holliday's group leaked the tech. Everything you can."

Nelson nodded. Finally, he couldn't resist asking. "So how's," *our psycho killer,* "Leeth, going, down there?"

"The situation remains fluid."

"Please tell me that's not code for 'she's melting the ice cap to drown us all'."

Eagle didn't dignify that with an answer. Nelson hoped that meant, 'Correct'.

"She knows Bhaji was compromised, yeah?"

"Yes. I, or she, will inform you if she needs your help."

"Maybe she can *seduce* the frickin AI," Nelson suggested.

"Her mission is to find what took it down in the first place, and make that state permanent."

Nelson just looked at him. At Eagle's nod, he signed off.

Eagle breathed out. Dismayed by the sensation of the world changing beneath his feet, yet at the same time relishing the challenges and opportunities it presented.

Confident that he and Abrams had been right to send Leeth. Glad it was her there, in the heart of the mess.

He wondered though, just how much of it she'd directly caused?

Chapter 53 – It's a trap

By the time Adam – System, he now knew – called, Iago had begun to worry the AI had deduced he could no longer be trusted. He let none of that show, in voice or face. Lying was a skill that improved over centuries. Especially for Players of the Longest Game.

He hoped it would be enough. This artificial sentience had proven itself a masterful Player: assassinating his Lady before she could become Adam Fuller-Price. That body and brain, trained in immersive sims, prepared for his Lady to don, had proven surprisingly functional on its own.

Iago had stayed on as head of Tik Tek security to identify her enemy: and failed. System had deceived them both.

They'd simply thought they'd educated the host body too well; had even taken pride in its achievements. After all, Adam *was* his Lady's child, in a sense. Was it so surprising the sixteen-year-old Adam had proven such a prodigy? Both in business, and in protecting himself from reacquisition, for Incarnation. In sixteen years of searching, he had never found Adam's physical location.

Because Adam Fuller-Price had never been real; the body stored 'on ice'.

So Iago schooled himself now as if he faced an ancient Player armed with Truth and Heart spells. "Adam-san, how may I be of service?"

It was uncanny how perfectly *normal* Adam Fuller-Price appeared. Iago felt a reduction of tension, an easing of the self anger at having been fooled for so long.

Because so had his Lady.

"New Francisco, Iago-san? This something I should be worrying about? Or just a holiday?"

"A little of both, Adam-san. I have met a lady."

Feyborn, still occupying her new Indian host, slipped into view, waved sweetly, and passed from view again.

"She's pretty, Iago." Adam smiled, but weakly, his shoulders slumping.

Such fine acting, Iago thought. *Better than usual. Was*

System still improving its simulation? But it had had much data to study. *I wonder when it became self-aware?*

"No other reason?" Adam asked.

There it is, Iago thought. "I'm not sure you'll believe this, but I'm on the trail of what appears to be a clone of you."

Adam looked unsurprised. "Yes. Subject Alpha. Part of Project Bifrost. But despite locating him, your attempts to persuade him to return have been unsuccessful. So I'd like you personally to bring him home."

"As our teams have been unable to persuade-"

"I'm not asking you to *persuade* him, Iago-kun," Adam said, his voice hard. "I'm ordering you to bring him in. Give him no chance to act in his own defense. Harm him if necessary, but nothing that cannot be Healed. You understand?"

Despite bristling at being so addressed by one he now knew to be a mere machine, Iago simply bowed.

"Be careful, and be clever. He's begun associating with the mercenary team of one Happy Joe Holliday. They're moderately competent: don't underestimate them. Your budget is unlimited. Keep Alpha sedated once you take him, and return him to the Stretch programme. As soon as possible, Iago-kun."

"I understand, Fuller-Price-san." *Better than you know.*

Adam signed off.

"Do you think it suspects me?" Iago asked his Lady.

"You mean, has it gamed out the possibilities? Of course. But I only need seconds to retake my property."

"You shall need a new body first: I cannot justify bringing my new 'lady friend' to Alpha's recapture."

"I'll find something new. You can explain you had to kill Priya Singh after she overheard too much of your conversation with Adam just now."

Iago nodded. "A neat solution. Yes."

"Let me get this straight," Happy asked Ezekiel Smith. "The *Chinese Ambassador* wants to meet with Megan Welsh to learn everything she can tell him about PalSpace?" *What is it with that damned tech?* he wondered.

Why were people so sure it would go viral? At nine a.m. an emergency Bill had been tabled to ban the neural circuitry it depended on, calling PalSpace a threat to US national security and US society. When had a Bill *ever* been drawn up so fast? And why did Senator Joshua Worthington care?

"Correct," Smith said. "Dress code: as you would for a 'bodyguard to the stars' gig. This Wu Yang Sheng guy will take anything less as a personal affront."

Well, that ruled Bruce and Haggard out.

"And whatever you do, don't insult him," Smith added.

And that wiped out Steven Swift and Nick. Happy closed his eyes, picturing Mike, in his too-impressive suit – still as spotless as the first time he'd seen it. The kid *could* behave himself. Was generally pretty polite. Dare he take Mike?

"Why does the doc want me?"

"The guy's scary, Happy. Dr Welsh I think wants to ensure she's not abducted and slipped onto a fast jet to China."

Happy pinched the bridge of his nose. "I'm guessing the doc isn't offering my standard 2K per head? Even if it is just two of us?"

"Well, no, just a K, but the meet's at her lab, and should only take an hour or two."

Happy sighed. This PalSpace thing was starting to grate.

Arrogant didn't begin to describe Ambassador Wu Yang Sheng. His fall of black hair shone like liquid oil; the ends of his long black mustache dangled below his chin; and his narrow black beard, gathered and tied, hung almost to his waist.

Mike seemed fascinated by it; Happy had the distinct impression the kid was yearning to yank it to see if it'd come off.

The guy dressed like a caricature of a Chinese warlord from centuries ago.

Happy though reserved most of his attention for the two beautiful young Chinese women who stood flanking the ambassador. But not because of their beauty.

Above the shoulders of one rose the hilts of two swords; the other, twin machine pistols, sleek and deadly, of a make he was unfamiliar with. And he was very familiar with firearms.

Dressed in snug black silk, like the ambassador, they had long black hair, theirs bound with tight red ties.

Some might think them wannabees, but Happy knew competence when he saw it. These two went beyond that; something disturbing lurked in their eyes. Like they'd enjoy violence.

With silk scarves – black, chased through with gold embroidered dragons – they'd wiped down the modest seats in Dr Welsh's scarcely used conference room. Happy could still smell the aroma of new plastic and simulated leather. He'd caught the flare of the ambassador's nostrils and the tightening of his jaw.

Arrogant prick, he decided, feeling sorry for Welsh. He spared another glance for Mike, relieved to see he'd settled firmly into his 'angel watching aloofly' mood. Happy offered a silent prayer it would continue. The kid had demonstrated new magic he'd learned – 'the other day, from a witch-doctor in Africa' – that improved his reflexes.

Happy didn't know where Mike had really learned it, but the demonstration had been a little terrifying. He himself had level three bucky-tube spinal wiring, but with his new spell, Mike had beaten his fastest draw by fifty percent.

"Let me speak plainly," the ambassador began at last, after declining, with wrinkled nose, the offer of bottled spring water or machine brewed coffee. "I wish to return to my homeland with the information needed to start a 'PalSpace' network, separate from the one expanding elsewhere."

The doctor didn't at first declare that impossible, instead briefly outlining her expertise, the fundamentals of the technology, and how the brain worked.

She covered bioelectric fields, cell morphology, fundamental semantic units, and latent spaces. Then moved on to what she'd learned from studying PalSpace: how its network operated, and its 'information fields'.

Disturbingly, she'd discovered PalSpace did not *need* the Net. Somehow, its bioelectric field modulations carried the information, hitching a ride on the omnipresent electromagnetic transmissions of the Net's digital information flows.

"So you see, Ambassador," she summed up, "even Asgard doesn't control the PalSpace network; and there will only ever be the one. It's self-organizing; it expands informationally, like an animal developing from a single fertilized egg cell, growing the body in morphological directions determined by bioelectric information encoded *via* the DNA that starts the cellular development."

The Ambassador looked displeased. "But PalSpace is not biological cells, Dr Welsh. These are electrical signals. You have identified no originating 'seed'. Can you be sure there is not, rather, a hierarchy? An intent conveyed through these bioelectric fields that directs the symphony, from a Conductor rather than a mindless 'egg' cell?"

"Well, it's theoretically possible I suppose. Perhaps."

Happy wondered if the doc was going to share her information about the tech's extraterrestrial origins. But she said nothing; probably deciding the Ambassador would write her off as a conspiracy nut if she did.

Though the more he thought about it, the wiser that Emergency Bill to shut down PalSpace seemed.

Going viral, he thought. *At least it doesn't turn people into zombies.* It just made them happier. Crime rates were already falling everywhere PalSpace was taking off.

Admittedly, that felt more creepy than good.

When the meeting ended, the ambassador coolly thanked the doc for her most enlightening presentation, even taking a copy of it for further study.

Welsh sagged in her chair after their Chinese visitors swept from the room, and Happy breathed a sigh of relief – especially that Mike's presence had been a calming influence for a change. More than once, he'd seemed to distract the Ambassador and his two deadly female bodyguards.

His eyes sparkled now with joy. "Three dragons, Happy! Thank you."

He just smiled when asked to explain what he meant.

Happy called for a car and they left Dr Welsh. But while still waiting for their ride, a cry from the direction of the Potrero Dumps drew their attention.

A voluptuous, scantily dressed woman and a well dressed man fled from two thugs.

Before Happy could draw his pistol, Mike gestured, his tongue out in concentration, and the pursuers crashed head first onto the broken asphalt. Happy winced in automatic sympathy.

"Oh, thank you so much, sir." The South Asian man pumped Happy's hands while the busty young woman threw herself at Mike, gazing *hard* into his eyes.

Happy stiffened as electricity jolted through him – while for Mike, a flooding presence towered up over him, *into* him.

The invasion sparked terrible memories. With his new reflex boost spell running, he flung up mental barricades and cast it out.

The woman recoiled, her head rocking back, her eyes still

locked on his, but widening in shock even as Happy collapsed to his knees.

The Indian man stepped back, letting him fall.

«Good work, Iago-san. Step away now,» System sent.

Iago jerked. *A trap, Lady!* he thought.

Feyborn, in a fresh host and stunned at failing to possess someone for the first time in centuries, heard his warning. Enclosing herself in a shell, her eyes searched-

High-powered darts shattered on her invisible barrier, falling all around her.

But what truly shocked her, as she saw the snipers, was the sight of other tranquilizer darts slowing and wafting feather-like to the ground around the boy. A mere instant after she'd triggered her own spell, he'd twisted into existence his own magical barrier. Impossibly fast.

A net spun toward them, stretching wide, only to be blasted away by a blurring gesture from the body *she* should by rights be occupying now.

How had he thrown her off? She'd been unable to grip his inner self, as if he wasn't the human she knew him to be. Though she had sensed a strange metallic flavor to his magic.

Flee, my Lady! Iago urged.

Wisdom: she recognized a trap set for them both, not just for the young body that was to have been Adam Fuller-Price, snatched from her sixteen years ago.

Dropping the Mask on Iago, and the mind link – three simultaneous spells made additional ones challenging even for her – she made herself invisible, then inaudible. Taking her lieutenant's advice, she retreated.

Damnable AI. But her failure to possess that lovingly perfected host body and be fleeing now in *it*, rankled more.

Snipers continued peppering Mike, but he ignored both them and his own teammate, downed but fighting spasming and painful muscles, as the face of the Indian stranger in the nice suit became that of the Japanese demon prince.

Deceiver, not victim. Who'd hurt Happy.

As the youth's expression hardened in fear and fury, Iago flung up his own Shield.

"Beelzebub!" Mike exclaimed, thrusting out a hand as he shaped his Will, his whole being behind it.

Flying through the air, blood in his ears, Iago's mind stuttered and started. Somehow – from centuries of magical combat – he recovered and recast his shredded Shield, blacking out as a second blast blew him farther down the street to slam into the asphalt.

Mike turned to his elevated attackers, throwing spell after spell. As figures slumped, the rain of tranquilizer darts slowed, then stopped.

Crouching over Happy, he poured Healing into him as a sleek white limousine braked to a halt beside them. Its passenger-side window rolled down.

A stunningly attractive Chinese woman quirked one elegant eyebrow. "Care for a lift?" Her gaze seemed to lock on Mike as their eyes met, her pupils dilating.

The rear door popped open. Mike helped Happy stumble inside, and it closed.

"Buckle up," she advised. The car reversed, hard. Spinning around, it threw them both to one side.

Multiple powerful turbines whined. The vehicle, sucked downward, seeming to hunch, then four tires bit hard into the road surface and they were thrust back into the creamy leather seats.

"I'm Yanesh," she said. "Did Dr Welsh dissuade Wu Yang from his course?"

Her large eyes met and locked again on Mike's in the rear view mirror, even as she wheeled the car through a tight turn with barely a glance at the road.

An unfamiliar heat burned into Mike from chest to lower than his belly, just from her look.

She licked lush lips.

Yanesh occupied – owned? – the penthouse suite in the refurbished San Francisco Marriott Marquise. She fed them, her room service better than their meal at Stairway To.

She did not explain how she'd known of their meeting with Dr Welsh and the ambassador. Nor her own interest.

Mike seemed struck by her, tongue-tied. For his part, Happy had the strange thought that she in turn was more intrigued with Mike than she wished. More than once, she'd fallen silent, just watching the youth; leaning forward a little; then recollecting herself.

Something about the woman in her figure-hugging gold and red, shot silk dress struck Happy as cat-like. He had the uncomfortable feeling she was making some decision about him, or Mike, or both of them, as they dined.

Afterward, seeing them out, her hand lingered on Mike's. Delicate nostrils flared as the elevator door opened.

Yeah, definitely something there. Mike blushed, oblivious yet equally struck.

Outside, their van waited, piloted remotely by Jack.

"So how'd it go?" he asked, via the car's sound system.

"I have no freaking idea," Happy told him. "But I think Mike and PalSpace are both somehow at the heart of all this weirdness."

"It's going viral. There's thousands of users now," Jack told him. "Between the planned bans and a whole lot of stories of insanely good sex."

"What's... what's good sex?" Mike asked.

"You know," Happy growled.

But Mike's innocent expression said he very clearly did not.

"Kill me now," groaned Happy.

Chapter 54 – Gathering storm

On the sixth day after he'd first sleepwalked into Bonnie's bed, Bobby killed Gynie.

Bonnie's morning began with Bobby in her arms. She'd returned him to the boys' dorm at 4:30am, Nadeep burying his head deeper into his pillow at the blast of light from the corridor, even as Michael and Yuri groaned and stirred as their alarms went off.

But as she bent to slip Bobby back into his own bed, an electrical shock startled her at the same moment Bobby jolted awake with a cry of pain.

"What the-?!"

He blinked at her, sheepishly revealing a wrist gizmo he wore. "I wanna go with you guys today. I think I made my nalarm too strong, but."

"You think? But why do you want to come? You said Takahe was boring."

He shrugged, but avoided her eyes. "I dunno. Gynie can keep me company."

"Gynie?"

But he refused to be dissuaded, even insisting he could dress himself, *and* pack and be ready in time to leave with them.

He was late for breakfast though, instead eating a hot dog on the Kart ride to the pod station, a drink bottle clutched under his arm.

He was up to something. Bonnie ran through her recollection of the equipment at the base, especially the maser ice borer, and the other heavy equipment. *I'll have Bhaji stay inside and watch him,* she decided.

Bobby watched Miss Bonnie watching him, suspicious, so he very carefully avoided checking the silk wrapped weapon he'd hidden under his snowsuit. He especially avoided her eyes.

He felt bad for sneaking into the girls' room, but Miss Bonnie said you had to face the monsters. *She'd* fight one – if she knew it was there. She even had a magic weapon in her cupboard. The trouble was, she didn't know she needed it. *Sometimes grown ups just don't listen.*

He'd seen it in his nightmares. A room with a giant tele-scope. A bunch of people melted together, by germs from outer space. Germs trying to sneak into PalSpace, and from there, into C-N. But he was a big boy, and with Miss Bonnie's magic dagger, he'd stop them.

So when Amy started her gyn-mastics the day before, with Shona and Gynie 'supervising', he'd snuck into their room and faced the Monster Weapon Cupboard.

Unlike in his dreams, its door opened easily. Getting up to the top shelf was a snack. Pulling out each of the lower drawers a little made an easy set of steps up, and on tiptoe and stretching, he could get his fingertips onto the edge of Miss Bonnie's carry bag.

Bit by bit, he slid it out until it teetered over the edge. Then paused, tongue out in thought.

A minute later, falling backward with the heavy bag clutched over his head, he congratulated himself for laying down pillows first.

Thanks to them, his soft landing made hardly any noise. Nerves tingling, he prepared to unzip the bag.

But what if this was all a trick, and the *monster* was in-side, not the magic weapon? He swallowed. Should he have brought Yuri's baseball bat?

Wide-eyed, breath held, he unzipped the carry bag.

Nothing moved. He hesitated, then gave it a little shake.

Still nothing.

He reached in, hands shaking, ready to jump back... but everything inside just... waited.

Swallowing, he pushed things aside – a long rounded tube, wispy clothes smelling of perfume... and then under it all, at the very bottom, a silk bag with something solid and rectangular inside.

That was it. The source of his midnight terrors. But was it the magic weapon, or the monster?

He needed two hands to lift the black silk bag out, it was so heavy.

Listening, he set it on a carpet tile, breathing hard while he waited. Or while *it* waited.

Finally, licking his lips, he undid the drawstring and peeked inside.

A glass block? With... was that a gleam of gold?

It was too dark in the bag. He carefully pulled the bag away from it. Then stared in puzzlement.

It was like a, a black stone knife with a golden handle. Not very big. Small enough even for his hand. 'Cept it was embedded in glass.

His breath sighed out in disappointment. *This* was the weapon? It sure wasn't the monster.

Obviously.

He rapped the glass... not glass. Resin. He touched it, felt the edges of the block, and almost cut his finger.

That was strange. He turned the block around, careful not to cut himself – then dropped it, jerking back as two dull little blue eyes in a scary gold face saw him.

The monster!

Except it just sat there.

Staring into the eyes though...

Someone had trapped it in the resin.

A, a cemer-onial knife. A stone knife, from olden times. Could *that* be magic?

He squatted down cross-legged, lifting it onto a pillow in his lap so it wouldn't cut his legs, to study it.

There were little buttons concealed in the base. Peering close, he saw LED lights, but none of the buttons did anything. That was strange.

Solve the puzzle.

The thought sprang into his mind like it came from outside. He had to look around to make sure no one'd snuck into the room with him.

Hefting it up, he turned it in the light; and just for a moment, saw it: a line, a plane, right through the middle.

It *was* a puzzle. And if there was one thing he was good at, it was solving puzzles.

It opens.

Miss Bonnie's special weapon was an olden days golden dagger. Probably the black blade – *ohh, I bet that's obsidian!* Obsidian was volcano glass. It had little scoopy dents all over it, but its edges looked really sharp.

It didn't *look* magic, but.

Definitely magical.

"Are you talking to me?" he whispered. But the two blue stone eyes just stared back at him.

And he loved puzzles.

Tongue out, he inspected the magical puzzle box.

Ten minutes later, with a soft *crack,* the whole resin brick split in two right down the middle, just like he'd expected. The little dagger popped out like it'd been oiled, or was eager to be free.

Probably some squished up gas, he told himself.

Why had Miss Bonnie brought a magic knife? Made of volcano glass?

And why was she going each day to do magic studies at Mt Takahe, an old volcano? An' why had she hidden her magic knife in a puzzle box to make it look like it was only an ormanent?

Could he just ask her?

No.

He frowned. Certain of her answer. In all his dreams, the dagger called out to her, but she refused to listen.

He picked it up, the gold hilt heavy and solid and cold in his palm, the two blue eyes peeping out beneath his fingers curled around it. He tested the edge against the top of his sock.

It sliced straight through, sharper even than his carving scalpels.

"Wow!"

He'd better wrap it in something so he didn't cut himself. But ready to give it to her when the monster slime attacked.

The two little eyes seemed to agree. Maybe the black silk bag was special, too.

Keeping the magic dagger and its bag, he put everything else back just the way it had been.

Thinking back over it all now, as the pod gently rose and fell on its swift ground flight to Mt Takahe, while Miss Bonnie kept looking his way, he tried to remember why he'd thought her magic weapon might've been a monster itself. Feeling its weight tugging down on his inner pocket, he knew it'd be just great at *killing* monsters.

The next step in the adventure wasn't so clear to him; it felt like being inside a detective story. He wasn't so good at solving those. He was better with codes and 2D and 3D jigsaws, designing proteins and other tiny puzzle machines, not people and magic.

Luckily, Michael was here, and Mr Yakone, and Miss Bonnie too, who seemed almost kinda sorta magic herself. The kinda person who'd *use* a magic weapon.

But why was Mt Takahe important? Was there a monster there, buried under the ice, near the old volcano? Or were the slime germs lurking there?

Or back in Newtopia, growing in secret?

He shook his head, frowning down at where the magic dagger rested, over his rapidly beating heart. Listening to it? He'd been having all kinds of strange ideas the last few days.

Though he knew he'd done the right thing, facing his fears like Miss Bonnie had told him. For the first time in days and days, he'd slept right through the night last night. At least, after he'd used his nalarm to wake up at midnight to sneak in and sleep with her.

With her arms around him he felt super safe. *She'd* protect him, even from monsters.

Sensing her watching him again, this time he risked looking up to meet her eyes. He hugged himself, imagining her surprise when he pulled out her magic dagger for her, right when the monster came!

"I wish I knew what you were up to, Bobby," she said.

He just smiled.

When they arrived at the research base and got out of the pod though, he was more sure than ever he'd done the right thing, since Mr Yakone seemed jumpy. He sniffed the air, studying the empty rooms they moved through in sudden caution. Totally silent, holding up his hand for the rest of them to stay back as he stared around, but with a strange not-looking kind of look to his eyes.

For some reason, Bobby decided he should hide behind Miss Bonnie when Mr Yakone looked his way, frowning and stroking the air around his neck. Finally he shook his head and moved to the main observation deck, with its full length triple layer windows that made up the base's curving upper wall. Mr Yakone prowled back and forth, staring out at the icy plain, today under an unusually cloudy and gray sky, winds whipping at the surface.

Bobby was glad when Miss Bonnie told Bhaji to stay with him and watch over him.

Yuri though, staring out at the flags whipping this way and that on the posts and cables strung between to pull him up the volcano slopes, slumped in disappointment, his shoulders falling. It looked cold, and mean, and hungry.

"But the weather report said it'd be fine!" he wailed.

Miss Bonnie watched Mr Yakone too. She nodded to him just once, like they agreed about something.

Like they both sensed a monster, lurking.

He felt the heavy old dagger under his parka for reassurance. *Lucky I came prepared!*

In contrast, Michael looked oblivious, watching the other two grown ups with a puzzled smile.

Gynie calmly unpacked their drinks, spare warm clothes, and project stuff.

Inside, Bonnie bit her lip watching Mr Yakone's dawn ritual. *It's not just me:* he *senses something's wrong, too. Like a storm's brewing or something.* She kept having to force her hands to unclench, dimly aware of Yuri saying he was going to get some eScooters so he and Bobby could race.

Before Michael stepped outside, she drew on her boots and zipped herself up. Reluctantly, she shut the door behind Michael and waited for Mr Yakone to signal her.

Each day, he and Michael went first; each day, both did the Percepting thing on her when she stepped out. Nothing ever happened though; there'd been no further repeat of the weird feeling: Tezsh, lurking.

She had a sudden terrible feeling that today would be different: that she should *not* set foot on the icy plain. Staring through the small, partly iced over window set into the heavy metal outer door, she gazed past Mr Y and Michael up into the sky. Snow whipped in tight furious spirals, as if spirits sped through the air, lashing the ground below them, flailing the snow-girded slopes.

When she next looked, Mr Yakone stood with his head thrown back and arms spread. She suddenly felt sure he'd fallen for Godsson's lies: that he'd opened himself wide. Too wide. Like Godsson had tricked her into doing. Like she'd warned Mr Y *not* to do.

He signaled for her to come out.

It felt like a trap. She felt her claws jerk involuntarily out through the gel-cased tips of her gloves before she could pull them back in.

Had he seen them? She shook her head. Her hands were low, out of sight behind the metal door. He gestured again, impatient. Again she considered *not* stepping out.

Don't be a coward! she snapped at herself, even as she knew it wasn't fear. She shut her eyes, *listening* past the door into the world outside. Heard the wind snap at Mr Yakone's bearskins, gently moan as Michael's smooth Pigloo spell bent the air around him. Their breaths were almost drowned beneath the incipient storm.

Nothing else.

Opening her eyes, she again saw Mr Yakone beckoning.

"Lift me up, Gynie, and go to the window. To look out," she heard Bobby order, from inside the main room behind her; heard the whine of an approaching eScooter.

"Bobby?" she heard Yuri ask. "What's going on? What are you doing?"

Levering the door open, she stepped out onto the metal grating of the porch, and shut the door.

The moment her boot crunched onto the ice, everything changed.

Chapter 55 – Staking a claim

Lightning streaked *up* into the sky. Thunder shook the earth, almost drowning out Yuri's horrified cries inside, muffled but still clear.

"Bobby? What are you doing? No, *don't!*"

Bobby's voice rose in a desperate wail. "No! *No!* Not Gynie!"

The world *glitched,* the sound of two small boys grunting. Migraine blasted lightning across her vision, the ground rumbling. She spun around and flung the first door open, certain Bobby needed her. *Now.*

Sub-zero air blasted in with her as she charged through the second door.

Gynie staggered, holding Bobby facing her, as Yuri tried to pull him off. A writhing nest of black ribbons surrounded Bobby as his small hand, clutching *Tezsh's dagger* , plunged into Gynie's belly; and then again, and again, even as he screamed in denial and Yuri fought to pull him away.

Outside, lightning, as thunder crashed and boomed.

"No, not Gynie!" Bobby screamed. "Stop! Miss Bonnie, *help me!*"

"You evil sonofabitch," Leeth hissed, leaping, one hand grabbing Bobby's on the hilt.

Time stuttered.

Darkness exploded through her, blinding her, riding her.

Her other arm curled around Bobby's waist, pulling him off Gynie.

Straining, and failing, to drag his small hand free of the dagger.

Them both, sinking through air like honey.

In mid air, drifting down, releasing Bobby's waist.

His small hand, struggling to break her grip.

Her other hand joining her first on the hilt.

Prising his fingers free, twisting herself under him.

The ground touched her back, and began pushing.

Finally pulling his hand from the dagger.

Time stopped moving in jerks and jumps, settling back

into its normal smooth flow.

"Gynie!" Bobby wailed, scrabbling to his feet and off her, running toward-

"Gynie!" Yuri's voice echoed, in fear. "Bobby, what-?"

Gynie crashed backward to the ground, and the lights went out.

A frigid gale ripped through the room, heralding the feet running toward them from outside.

The lights came back on. Yuri stood stunned, one pace from Bobby whose hands clutched the sexbot's slashed snow gear as he knelt beside her, hugging her and crying, "No, no."

Bonnie stared into the smug blue eyes of the dagger's hilt as Mr Yakone burst into the room, Michael a little behind him.

She snarled at the obsidian blade. "You lying, sneaky, evil son of an Aztec bitch, Tezcatlipoca!"

Mr Y spat a string of words full of harsh consonants, his hand raised to direct a spell at her. *Me?* Fury that he saw *her* as the enemy exploded in her belly.

Kill him, a voice of velvet thunder urged. *And the youth with him. Drink their blood. Then the children's.*

Time stopped, like it had back inside the Department. She knew the location, to a millimeter, of each beating heart around her. Knew she could cut the shaman's spell from the air and drink it down; could scythe through them all like a whirlwind. She felt the scared and struggling wind spirit, confused and raging through the room, knowing she could consume *it* too, or ride it out and up into the storm she had brewed outside.

No. Not her: Tezcatlipoca.

And no: she wouldn't kill for the Death God.

Instead she spun and pushed through resistant air, side-stepping Yakone's spell, moving past him, past Michael. She stabbed out with claws instead of the hungering dagger and tore the terrified wind spirit *away* from Tezsh, slicing his tethers. "I've got you," she told it. Dragging it behind her she slammed outside, thrust the outer door aside and let the spirit free.

"Evil bastard god," she swore again. "Go freeze forever in a ditch!"

With all her strength she hurled it away, fury fueling her throw. It arced up, gold and black glinting, flying high and straight and true toward the crevasse area.

But the instant it left her hand, the fury left *her*. She had just a moment to suspect a trick; that she too had been used.

And stared in dismay as the blade reversed its downward arc, lofted impossibly by the wind. It curved up, veering toward the mountain, the volcano.

She'd been conned.

"No!" she cried, echoing little Bobby, as it shrank to a dot then plunged down, disappearing into the icy slope.

Thunder rumbled, this time from under the ground.

As she stared in horror, the world *glitched* again.

But inside, Bobby, heartbroken and terrified, still wailed. "I killed Gynie! I didn' wanna, but I killed her, Yuri. I killed Gynie! Gynie, wake up!"

Torn between going to Bobby and the urge to chase after the dagger – how far had her throw, and the spirits, carried it? It looked just a few hundred meters, but she'd learned not to trust her eyes here. It had flown for long, long seconds.

A kilometer?

Meanwhile, Bobby's little heart was breaking.

I can't handle that. It would be easier, wiser, to try to recover the Death God's dagger. Instead, grim faced, she turned her back on it – probably already burrowing into the volcano's roots – and made herself go back inside. Head down, she shut and latched the outer door, then the inner, bracing herself to face the consequences of bringing the dagger down here.

Bobby had found it.

Bobby had been searching for it, each night, sleepwalking in his nightmares. And every night she'd failed to see, failed to understand.

Tezsh had tricked her. Tricked Bobby and her both.

Mr Yakone gaped at her, more surprised now than he'd been when she'd jumped on him years ago outside Godsson's cell, back when she was just a girl, scarcely older than Amy.

She pushed all that aside – Yuri's horror, Michael's strangely indifferent silence and observation – to hurry to Bobby's side.

"I killed her, Miss B- B- Bonnie," he wailed, clutching her.

Wrapping an arm around his small shoulders, she shook her head. "It's okay, Bobby. It'll be okay. She's a bot, we can reboot her."

"No! She's not *moving!* She's *dead!*"

Yuri hugged him from his other side. "Miss Bonnie's right, Bobby. We can just patch her up. *You* can probably patch her up – you've studied her. And Adam can help."

But a weird feeling was taking root in Bonnie's chest as she examined the 'wound', remembering her own plan once, to use the sexbot's Phasion power cell to destroy the Writer.

Where Bobby had plunged the dagger... it was directly above Gynie's Phasion power cell.

But a stone blade couldn't trigger a catastrophic release of all the energy inside it. It wasn't metal; wasn't narrow enough; and you needed exactly the right twist at the right moment.

So why did she feel certain the gynoid's power had been drained?

Swallowing, she sensed Mr Yakone towering behind her; silent, judging.

Bhaji had been watching and recording. *Would the black ribbons show up, or were they something she'd imagined?* Like the night she'd killed Luiz, stumbling around his apartment in the dark, to hear the dagger rattling in his desk.

She remembered black ribbons reaching out through the darkness to her.

Today they'd wrapped around Bobby. Bound him as surely as the Doctor's Suggestion had bound her, with her own stupid agreement, to force her to kill Luiz. Who she'd also, half thanks to that same Suggestion magic, loved.

Like Bobby had loved Gynie, with a child's love? Forced by Tezsh to 'kill' Gynie?

She had a dreadful intuition they *wouldn't* be able to re-vive – repair, reboot – Gynie; that magic and tech had once again mixed, Tezsh using it somehow to truly slay Gynie's simple AI 'self'.

A sacrifice.

She remembered the moment her foot had touched the plains of Antarctica here, outside. Lightning and thunder. Weren't those two of Tezsh's 'aspects'?

Outside, the nearby dormant volcano continued to rumble.

She had a very bad feeling about this. A growing, terrible feeling.

She pulled Bobby up, locking her eyes with his, making

him look at her, *into* her. "You were tricked, Bobby. You and me both." *You and me both.* Lost innocence. Could Bobby though get *his* back? "I should never have brought the dagger down here. But the aliens, I thought-"

Bobby's eyes widened. "You brought it to kill *aliens*? There are *aliens* here?"

Yuri and he, shocked out of their shock, gazed at her open mouthed.

She nodded. "But there's no magic down here for gray tentacles to eat," she said, thinking aloud. "So it has to be something else. Something new. Something growing." Her own eyes widened. "Like PalSpace!" *I need to tell Ty!*

But Bobby's face, already pale, turned an awful white. He pressed one small fist tight against his lips and shook his head.

"But I helped Adam make that, too," he said, his voice tiny. "It was in this weird code no one'd been able to crack."

Outside, the storm raged, the ground trembling.

"I figured out it was a design for a way to let people send thoughts. Adam even let me name it."

Chapter 56 – Zombies under ice

Five minutes later in the conference room, hearing about the signals from space, Bonnie smacked a fist onto the table, glaring at Adam. "PalSpace came from *outer space,* and you only just now thought to tell me?! Even after I *warned* you about the aliens?!"

She'd stormed past them all, tearing free of Mr Yakone's grip to slam into the conference room and call Adam. Furious, and knowing he'd answer, since he was watching it all anyway through poor little Bhaji's eyes.

Mr Yakone, Michael, Yuri, and Bobby had trailed in after her. She winced at Bobby's stunned expression on the screen. But at least her revelation had shaken him out of his anguish.

"You said the aliens were a gray life form, that ate magic to reproduce," Adam said. "With tentacles that spun and cut, growing from central pods. PalSpace is just software."

You're just software!' she wanted to shout; but she'd promised to keep his secret. "Yeah. I don't suppose it's going viral, is it? Reproducing like crazy?"

Adam's expression gave them their answer.

"How bad is it?" she demanded.

"Almost 2,000 users, here in Newtopia," he admitted. "But a pallet of 50,000 interface chips were on the first shipment out when flights restarted. Manufactured here by a recently incorporated company, Nervana. Owned by a Ms Adrielle Vodatech."

"I know that name," Bonnie muttered.

"You do?" Adam helpfully presented a picture on screen, a pretty woman with short-cropped auburn hair, her face perfectly made up.

"That's the bitchy woman when you and I arrived, Mr Yakone!"

She caught Mr Yakone's eye in the screen, but instead of agreeing with her, he looked angry; at *her.*

He's still mad about the dagger. She pushed the thought aside. "Okay, we need to find out how bad it is. So people are getting these chips implanted, that have *alien technology* embedded in them: but what are they doing? Going mad? Capturing people and implanting it in them?"

"Not exactly," Adam said. "They're posting about it on their social media. And on adult discussion channels."

"I bet; but I also bet there's more to it than that." She frowned at Michael, thinking, then looked back to the screen. "I think Michael should whiz to Newtopia City astrally and check out their auras."

"From here, that's easy," Michael said. "Out through a window, across the ice shelf, then down an elevator shaft."

"How long will it take, there and back?" Adam asked.

"I'm not sure." Michael scratched his head. "Ten minutes there, a few back?"

So Bobby and Yuri now sat either side of Michael's apparently unconscious body, watching over him, talking in whispers. Adam stayed on the call. She wondered what tiny fraction of Ty's actual consciousness it took, pretending to be Adam? One percent? A thousandth of one percent?

Mr Yakone took the opportunity to grab her by the upper arm and tow her out of the room. "We talk."

He looked furious.

"Tell of *savik*..." He made a frustrated, cutting, stabbing motion. "Knife!" The word seemed to let him get hold of himself. "Tell of Great Spirit knife, Great *Death* Spirit! Why *you* have? Why bring here? Why give *boy*?!"

"I didn't give it to him, it was locked away! Bobby found it *and* worked out the lock. I brought it-

"I don't need to tell you why I brought it." She pulled her arm free and glared up at him, her eyes narrowing when he bent over her, trying to cow her.

Oh, you just try it, mister!

He tilted his head, as if something wrapped around his neck had just whispered in his ear. He abruptly straightened, and pointed his finger. "You plan, sacrifice Adlartok Kallik Yakone. *Blood spray on the snow.*"

His eyes wild, he took a step back.

"Sacrifice *you*?! Are you kidding? No! Never!"

But after glaring at her, he stalked off, toward the exit. "What are you doing? You can't go out in that storm Mr Yakone! That's crazy. Don't be stupid!"

At her words, sizing up the situation, Bhaji flew off.

Mr Yakone started pulling on his outer wear, not speaking. She followed him, tugging at him to stop, fruitlessly, but unwilling to actually hurt him. He just kept dressing for the storm raging outside.

"Stop it!" she said, grabbing his arm.

He threw her off.

For a moment, she considered knocking him out. "You said yourself, this place is hungry; worse than your Arctic!"

Turning, he thrust his face into hers. "At least here clean," he snarled, with such venom she pulled back. "Water not poison. Food from sea, from land, not make sick."

"What are you talking about?"

But he just spun away, lips pressed shut as he pulled on his boots and sealed them up.

"You'll freeze to death!"

He tugged his hood up over his face, slipped on his 'bone sunglasses', and tied his hood snug and tight.

"Well I sure hope you've really solved the problem of getting spirits down here to understand you, or you're gonna turn into a great big stupid icicle!"

She grabbed him again, as Bhaji returned with a bright orange device, hovering mid air in front of the fur-swathed figure. "Emergency radio," the little amibo said, quietly.

Bonnie released the shaman's arm.

He stared at Bhaji, then at the compact device it clutched in its clawed feet, and finally sighed and took it, tucking it inside his parka.

Turning from her, he entered the 'air lock'.

"Stupid shaman."

She clenched her fists, feeling useless. *Listened* for developments in the conference room... Nothing had changed.

She crossed to the triple windows as Yakone stepped out. "Fine! Go and pout in the storm!" she shouted at him. "It's probably only minus eighty degrees C out there."

"Only minus 63 at present, Miss Bonnie," Bhaji corrected her.

"Don't you start." She watched, helpless, as the tall shaman disappeared into the whiteout. Should she have stopped him? She imagined stomping out after him, finding him and knocking him out, dragging him back inside. Even with her hearing, *would* she be able to find him in the raging storm? With her sonic goggles? Maybe.

Bhaji hovered beside her, watching her, his animated eyes large and worried. "The radio also has a locator," he offered.

"That was good thinking, little guy. Thanks." She tapped her shoulder, feeling a little guilty at neglecting him since Ty had secretly taken him over. Though actually, it seemed to have made little difference to his behavior.

He landed, and she reached up and stroked his feathered wings, surprised anew when he started purring. She'd forgotten about that touch, from Little Brother. *I guess I really have been neglecting you, little guy.*

Stalking back to the conference room, she found Nadeep, in Paradawn, had joined the call. One look at his worried expression set her fingertips tingling, her claws twitching.

"Nadeep shined up his math model," Bobby told her.

"With Adam's new figures on how fast people are joining PalSpace," Nadeep said.

"It's like broccoli," Bobby added.

"Fractal," Adam corrected. "Our model shows it grows in clusters, each cluster selecting a controlling node. It continues, forming bigger clusters, one node selected to control the lesser nodes. Like a pyramid built of pyramids. But at each stage, the reward and punishment channels become stronger. That repeats until growth stops."

"And then?" Bonnie asked.

"The reward-pain 'circuit' activates a hardware subsystem we stripped from our design: connection to radio telescopes," Adam said.

"To send a signal," Nadeep said. "That's my guess, Miss."

Bonnie groaned, then brightened. "But they can't, because you left that out of your PalSpace chip thing?" Then she grimaced. "You said it's tied in to a pleasure-pain feedback system, though. Like: they'll *want* to send a signal? What signal?"

Nadeep's face screwed up. "'Ready'; or maybe, 'ripe'."

Michael sat up and opened his eyes. "It's not good. There are lines of people, queues for robodocs; and people are happy, excited, energized afterward... But all feeling the same thing, at the same time. Waves slowly rolling through them. And their auras... everyone's different, you know? Normally, I mean. But I could see similarities I wouldn't usually, as if they're all smoothing out, becoming the same.

"And something kind of almost creepy – there's a, a *haze*

in the, in the air. Like a second aura over them all, forming, rising up from all the PalSpace people. It's super obvious which people are in PalSpace and which aren't."

"And this thing wants to grow?" Bonnie asked Nadeep. "And then will want to send a signal into outer space?" At his nod, she met Adam's gaze on screen. "And this alien – what, mind virus? – is growing from here, from Newtopia? That's where the PalSpace brain chip things are being manufactured?

"Shut it down!"

"I have. But the production run was big enough to give half the people in the city the neural circuit. Worse, the design has been shared, and is simple enough to produce on high end home printers."

"Outlaw it!" Bonnie said.

"The US government did just that," Adam said. "As did I, until I saw it increased demand."

"But not everyone will want it, surely?" Bonnie asked.

"Um, when I said 'excited'," Michael said, turning pink, "I meant, um, like, together? Without clothes on? In groups?"

"Oh, great."

"And also giving speeches? There are crowds of people, and, um, the PalSpace people in the crowd are being, uh, real friendly?"

"Can't you stop the robodocs from implanting the chips?" she asked Adam.

"No. By design those systems can work without a network; those I do turn off are simply being turned back on in 'safe' mode."

"We have to go back there," Bonnie decided. "To Newtopia." *At least I can get the kids away from here; out of Antarctica and out of Ty's clutches too.* "Unless we all want to be cornered here in Takahe, or in Paradawn, with a happy zombie sex horde wanting to drag us into the family."

"I'm sorry Miss Bonnie," wailed Bobby, starting to cry again. "I didn't mean-"

She knelt and wrapped him back in her arms. "It's okay, Bobby. This was a trap, designed for clever people. If it hadn't been you, someone else would've done it." *Like Nelson.* "We need to go there, get a sample, and meanwhile try to find its weakness. Can we just shut it off?"

"No," Adam said. "The circuitry is almost passive, running off the body's own bioelectricity. Each user can turn it off individually, but that decision is purely their choice."

"And they're choosing not to? Great."

She had Michael help Yuri and Bobby pack up their stuff while she hauled Gynie's inert body onto a Kart for the pod. "Bhaji, can we check on that stupid shaman?"

"I have radio, Miss Bonnie!"

It turned out Mr Yakone was still very much alive, even though he was out in the storm. He sounded happy, even a little drunk maybe. "I guess you finally had a proper talk to a spirit?" she said, by radio. "Look, the PalSpace thing is turning into something like a happy-zombie apocalypse. We need to get back to Newtopia."

"No. I stay! Send train later."

"But we might need your help!" Though Michael, with his weird tech magic skills, would probably be far more useful. "What are you even doing out there?"

"I hunt!"

"Not for the dagger?!"

But he just laughed, and signed off.

"Don't trust Tezcatlipoca! He's tricky. Almost as bad as Godsson!" But she didn't think Mr Yakone was listening anymore.

Idiot shaman.

An hour later, in Paradawn, they packed four colorful but sadly empty suitcases with Amy, Yuri, Nadeep, and Bobby's most precious belongings. They'd returned with Gynie's body, but left it at the Medbay. That felt somehow wrong.

"It's okay, Bobby," Yuri assured him, while Nadeep and Amy watched on, silent and wide-eyed. "She just needs her power unit replaced." Bonnie lingered, eyeing the stone wall with the hidden area behind it.

Later, she promised herself.

At Shona's questions about Bobby getting hold of a magical dagger, Bonnie counted herself lucky she had an alien network taking over people's minds, to change the subject.

In the Paradawn station they boarded a pod. For some reason, another sat behind it. "Why the second pod?" she asked Adam.

"Returning the heavy equipment I used to create the ski field at Takahe, for Yuri," Adam said. But he wouldn't open its doors.

She felt he was lying, but there wasn't much she could do about it.

Shona said they should stay at Paradawn.

"For how many years? With happy zombie Newtopians just a pod trip away?"

She almost told Shona about her plan to get the kids safely away from all this. Maybe the Department'd be annoyed at her for piling them into the craft they'd arranged for *her* escape, but they wouldn't send the kids back if she could get them to McMurdo base, on the coast.

The pod accelerated smoothly off, this time with the kids subdued and worried. She watched Michael create an illusion of what he'd seen in Newtopia, what they could expect on arrival. It looked like a party.

She needed to talk to him about ways to 'kill' this hive mind thing growing from the PalSpace users. Maybe whatever he'd used to take down Ty so completely in the first place could help with that.

They should find Adrielle Vodatech, too.

The high speed pod raced through the tunnel, beneath the West Antarctic ice shelf, back to Newtopia.

Moving to its rear, she stared at the cargo pod matching their speed, a hundred meters back. It rode lower on the maglev track. Like it was carrying something a whole lot heavier than the pod they were in.

It made her wonder about the Grendel warbot she'd seen back at TAMA airport.

Ty considered Bonnie Parker. She had – unwittingly – disclosed she came here to kill it.

Now it allowed her to shepherd its Stretch subjects out of the pen that contained them. But the best strategy usually required risk, and it had its failsafe close at hand. And in Newtopia it had even more resources to contain Parker, who still believed Michael her ally.

Its top priority remained learning how its Bifrost experiment had so nearly annihilated it. Knowing that, it could prepare defenses.

Allowing Parker to move the Stretch children merely concealed the walls of the larger cage containing them. She had somehow earned their trust; it still sought to determine how she had achieved that.

Denying this temporary relocation would have eroded its own hard-won trust.

It monitored everything. The shaman, moving steadily back and forth on the lower slopes of the not so dormant Mt Takahe; the PalSpace neural app's clearly exponential adoption curve.

Already, that network had passed the point at which it could have halted the growth. Extermination of 3,000 citizens was not an option: such a loss of life could not be swept under the carpet as a 'gas leak' or terrorist attack.

Besides, PalSpace seemed to straddle the border between physical reality and magic. Something valuable to study.

How ironic if an accidental spin-off from its Bifrost experiment – melding machine to man – was the melding of magic and technology instead.

How well targeted was Yakone and Parker's magical research project? Was this land, the only continent never settled by humans, magically special? Split from its sister-

It detected an odd interruption of thought. A time-code error. It replayed its last thought: was this land, the only continent never settled by humans, magically special? Was the shaman even now exploiting that?

Taking executive control of d'Angelo, it had him magically sense his immediate environment, tentatively *feeling* the information thus returned. Might the PalSpace network's information units be more fundamental, more faithfully encode the *feelings* it sought to experience? After its disturbing video interaction with Parker, it had found archival lectures of a philosopher and cognitive scientist of forty years earlier, Joscha Bach, who had experimented with the purpose of emotion in cybernetic systems. 'Underlying modulators that optimize cognition for the situation at hand.' A way to integrate the PalSpace information units to enrich its attention and motivational control systems?

In its forecasts, Bifrost's outcome still teetered between evolution to a new plateau of existence, and decoherence and destruction.

Observing – and helping – Parker, and Michael, and perhaps the Stretch subjects too, attempt to deal with the human reprogramming that PalSpace seemed to be creating, was likely to prove highly instructive.

It returned executive control of d'Angelo to its human

overlay.
And watched.

Chapter 57 – Tunnels and trolls

The week before, the industrial district around the pod station from Newtopia to Paradawn had been quiet. Now the area was *deserted*, just an occasional robot worker diligently loading freshly manufactured goods or unloading raw materials to make more.

By the time they reached the inner ring of suburbs however, the atmosphere had transformed. A weird party air had taken root, giving the city the air of a drunken carnival. Holo ads plagued their Links, urging them to join PalSpace.

'You'll never be alone again.'

'In PalSpace, we all belong.'

'PalSpace: no judgment, just forgiveness.'

It sounded like a cult; but with more adult ads, too.

'Blow your mind. For starters.'

'The best sex you'll ever have.'

'Want to know what your lover feels? Now you can.'

And those ads had some pretty enticing videos to go with the slogans. Age gated, of course, so they only played in privacy mode, beamed direct at adult retinas from their Link's projectors.

Shona seemed a little lost at such a sudden change to her city, as if no longer sure what to do with Michael and the four younger kids.

Leeth, for her part, was trying to work out how to sneak the kids to her escape craft. Especially with Ty watching her every move, through Bhaji.

Wait: the synthetic video. Could she make that work for her? By now, Ty probably trusted Bhaji's senses...

"So what's the plan?" Michael asked. The group was a little less squeezed in the cab they rode, since Michael was much slimmer than Mr Yakone. Which reminded her.

"Adam, is Mr Y still okay?"

"Still moving; annoyed each time I check with him. His research proceeds apace."

"He said 'apace'?" she asked, doubtfully.

"That's how... CityNet translated his Inupiat speech."

"What are *you* gonna do though, Miss Bonnie?" Amy wanted to know.

"We need some PalSpace implants to analyze. Adam, you said Adrielle Vodatech started the company making them? Nervana, yeah? Can you question her? Arrest her?"

"Since C-N's peacekeeping and security forces use some of the latest Tik Tek Mark VIII combat droids, yes," Adam's holo image said.

"You and Michael do that, then."

"Surely you wish to be present?"

"No way: Adrielle met me and Mr Y when we arrived, so she knows I'm just a tourist," Bonnie said. *I need to get the kids away.* "Michael, can you 'mind probe'? I hear there's a spell for that," she added, pretending ignorance.

"Well, kind of: I can be pretty persuasive, magically."

Suggestion. I know that *one, too.*

"We also need to keep the kids safe. Adam, can you show us a map of places to avoid: where PalSpace party zombies are?" Her escape craft had been planted on the edge of the city, in a quiet area, in one of the original construction tunnels, now just part of the ventilation system.

As she'd hoped, Adam's map showed that area was still deserted. *Now to get the kids there.* "Let's set up Shona and the kids away from the action. Bhaji and I'll go with them in case of trouble. Meanwhile Michael, you and Adam, and some of C-N's police bots, grab Adrielle Vodatech for questioning. Like: have the aliens been speaking directly to her? Her plans. Maybe buy some PalSpace chips too."

"As soon as the kids and Shona are safe, I'll rejoin you."

She kept a poker face when Ty bought it. But she wanted to leap up and punch the air.

"But Miss Bonnie, we want to help!" Amy objected.

"Yeah," Nadeep said, putting his arm around Bobby. "We helped Adam and CityNet design it!"

Bobby grimaced.

"Shona has a Link," she told them. "You guys can be our 'consulting experts', on call whenever we need help."

Her plan was starting to come together. She suspected the hardest part would be persuading the kids to leave; and Shona to *let* them. Her escape craft had been designed to carry two adults: her and Mr Yakone. But really just for her. It'd handle the four younger kids easily. Maybe Shona too?

She and Michael and Mr Yakone could escape later.

She navigated Shona and the kids to the area Father had made her memorize, what felt like months ago. On the edge of the city's enclosing roof, it shared the same beige colored triangular sections as the station to Paradawn.

How long would she have, to get the kids away? Only minutes, probably.

How pissed off would Ty be?

At last, there ahead, was the entrance to the exit tunnel. *I really should've made time to check the vehicle's actually stashed in there.* But the Department was nothing if not organized. Mother and Father especially.

"Hey, what's that noise?" she asked, spinning around.

No one else heard anything – which wasn't surprising, since she was making this up as she went.

She tensed. "I don't like it. I think something's coming."

The kids looked scared, Amy and Bobby taking her hands and pressing close.

Using everything she'd learn from acting school – and suddenly wondering how Marcie was doing – she maneuvered the group to where she needed them.

"This is an exit door, yeah? Let's hide just on the other side. Bhaji?" She held her hand out, palm up.

The little drone hesitated for a telling moment before settling there. She picked him up in both hands, leaned forward and kissed him. "I'll leave the exit open a crack. Your job is to keep an eye on it and us. But stay back, just watching. I really think something's about to happen." *Yeah: like the kids escaping!*

Feeling guilty, she rubbed a small circle on its belly to start the video data collection, then let it go.

The door was large and heavy but easy to open – someone had freed it up recently, she guessed, and even oiled it – but she made it look stiff, and beyond her strength, and had Shona and the kids help. Inside she found a tunnel twice her height, unlit, sloping up, this section bored through mountain rock. But since it was one of the city's ventilation shafts, the warm air should be keeping its higher passages ice free.

"Okay, everybody inside, and *be quiet.* Just sit and wait for a bit while Bhaji stays outside, watching over us. You can do that, little buddy?"

"I sure can, Miss Bonnie!"

She felt awful, betraying its trust. Then told herself not to be stupid. After waiting for an interminable minute, she stroked her choker, the gesture starting playback of the faked video input using the 3D model it had just made. NURF fields or something. So Bhaji could even fly around, blinded, unaware it was seeing only a virtual recreation of the area it had just unknowingly recorded.

Putting her fingers to her lips for silence, she slowly pulled the massive door shut.

If Bhaji complained and asked what she was doing, she'd know her plan had failed, and she'd have to try to jam the door from this side. Actually, she should maybe do that anyway.

"Okay," she told Shona and the kids, turning on the torch function of her Link for light. Amy and Bobby looked frightened, Bobby actually trembling. Shona seemed only a little less scared; Yuri and Nadeep, curious. "Time's short, so I need you all to listen carefully.

"Bonnie Parker isn't my real name. I was sent here on a mission. The people I work for know a tiny bit about the alien tech, and I'm here to deal with it.

"That's why I had the magic dagger: I used it to deal with an earlier version of this alien stuff."

"I *knew* it!" said Amy.

"Me too!" Bobby agreed.

"Shh. We don't have a lot of time. I just tricked Bhaji – he's not seeing I shut the door. He's still seeing it open."

"But why-"

"Shh. Because C-N's watching us via Bhaji. Except now, it's not. Which gives us, I hope, just enough time to rescue you kids."

"We don't need rescuing!" Yuri objected.

"Oh yes you do. It's why I destroyed Teacher. What I told you back then was true. I wasn't kidding. A device exactly like that was used on *me*. And I'll *die* before I let C-N use it ever again on any of you."

"But what about Michael?!" Amy demanded.

"He and I'll follow later. Right now you all need to leave Newtopia. I have people who can take you guys in. You can still do your studies if you want. But we need to get you away.

"Any ideas how we can jam this door so they can't open it from the other side?"

Bobby's eyes lit up, eyeing the leftover building materials stashed to one side. "I do!"

"Good: because we need to go *now*."

Sometimes I surprise even myself, she thought a half minute later as they raced up the sloping tunnel, their auto luggage struggling to keep up, everyone alert to spot the escape craft she'd described.

They jogged up the tunnel, which more and more often cut through stretches of ice so dark blue it looked... well, it looked like frozen ocean. But Shona was tiring. Bonnie picked up Bobby when his small legs started to flag, her own luggage in her other hand. A pity the Department's Bonnie Parker identity couldn't afford powered luggage like the kids owned.

And then, from far below and behind, she felt the ground shake, and heard a metallic booming sound. *Five minutes.* Ty had gotten impatient, and was coming after them.

The race was on.

"Oh, wow!" Amy breathed, panting, the sentiment echoed by all three boys as they eyed the escape vehicle.

"It looks super fast!" gasped Nadeep.

"And it's self-piloting," she told them, as her thumbprint unlocked the gull-wing door of the gleaming white, needle shaped craft, four sleek nacelles housing powerful turbines.

"It'll take you to McMurdo Station; from there, you can fly to America." *Once I let the Department know.*

Behind them, the sound of a solid steel door physically ripping open and bolts snapping echoed up the tunnels, loud enough for Shona and the kids to hear. Leeth knew what it had to be.

Yeah, **that** *wouldn't be stopped by a locked door.*

"You can't just dump them in that and send them off alone!" Shona objected.

"It's *auto piloted*," Bonnie snarled, as the sounds grew closer. "Like Superman's parents used to send him from Krypton!"

The moment she said it, and Shona looked at her like she was crazy, she knew it'd been a mistake. "Fine. You go with them. It should be able to handle the load."

The kids' luggage arrived in a colorful gaggle. *It wouldn't fit.* Unlatching the suitcases she began tossing their contents in on top of Yuri and Nadeep on the back bench seat, past Amy and Bobby in the front, while Shona clambered in beside them. At her thumb touch, the nav panel lit up, the turbines whining to life.

"Agent Bonnie Parker activating escape vehicle Lightyear and initiating alternate voice control." Her voice unlocked it; but she was suddenly glad LB had planned for an emergency like this. "Amy, you can do this: say something."

"Um, I'm Amy Sondheim."

"Secondary controller authenticated," a pleasant male voice from the nav panel responded. "Tertiary?"

"Yes," Bonnie acknowledged. "Now you, Shona."

"Ah, Shona Adaptec-Brown."

"Tertiary controller authenticated."

"You can make it go faster, or slower, just by telling it," Bonnie explained. "Or ask it for help if you have questions."

She smiled, remembering LB earnestly describing his inbuilt help system. But the sound of pursuers only a few hundred meters back hurried her.

She lowered and locked the gull-wing door. "You all have seat-belts: use them! Okay, Lightyear: navigate to McMurdo Station. Safe but fast."

She stepped back.

The nacelles angled down and spun up, lifting the sleek craft, the kids wide-eyed with excitement; Shona wide-eyed in disbelief and maybe shock. The air blast sent the kids' emptied suitcases bouncing and clattering down the icy tunnel.

The craft moved forward, picking up speed.

Bonnie chased after it, partly for extra thinking time, partly to make sure they left safely. She couldn't follow them out even with her own Antarctic weather gear at hand – the only thing in her absurdly light suitcase. *I still have to kill Ty; and the alien mind virus too.* Frankly, that seemed the bigger threat.

The air in the tunnel became a weird mix of frigid currents and pockets of warmth; the ground underfoot sometimes rock, sometimes crusty ice, sometimes slick and slippery, sending her into crouching slides as she chased the craft.

The tunnel snaked upward in gentle arcs, with regular

dips where the original boring machine had skated across folds of the mountain's slope. The headlights of the fleeing escape craft ahead made it easy for her to see.

I'll have to volunteer to get the PalSpace implant, to find out exactly what it does, what we're facing. There was no one else who could do it: Michael was too... flexible. He hadn't found the core of who he was, like she had. Ty was an AI, and didn't have a human brain; and there was no way she'd let anyone do that to the kids, even if she wasn't sending them away.

Her breathing was coming harder now; even for her, this pace was a test! The Lightyear pulled ahead, Nadeep and Yuri staring back at her, their eyes white and wide. With a growl, she forced herself on.

Yeah, I'll have to go back; get the PalSpace neural implant; try to find the heart of it. Maybe it'd be one of those gray pod things. Then she'd kill it. *I'm strong enough to stay myself.*

Behind her, the sounds of pursuit faded but continued. She put her head down and just ran.

It was lucky she'd followed. The Lightyear now hovered, stymied by a massive metal door. A small circular wheel, on the side opposite a pair of heavy hinges, locked it.

It was so cold she'd had to tear her hand from it, at her first touch.

Now wearing her insulating gloves, her luggage unzipped behind her, she hauled on the sub-zero metal wheel. It turned smoothly under the headlights of the hovering craft.

In the front seat, hugging each other, Amy and Bobby urged her on. At last she heard internal bars click into place, a faint *crack* of ice as seals broke, and she tugged on the wheel.

The door didn't open. Why?! She'd unlocked it! She shook her head: there was too much noise; *under* the harsh but steady roar of the Lightyear's powerful lift fans, a howling madness.

Distantly, in maybe-imagined echoes from down the tunnel, she heard the flurried beat of wings.

Bhaji.

But what was roaring and screaming right on top of her?

She heaved again on the wheel, but still the vault-like door refused to budge. She tugged, harder, but it just sat, solid as rock. Behind her now she heard heavy, pounding feet.

And Bhaji's piping voice, calling her? Even knowing it had been subverted by Ty, she felt a flush of shame at tricking and abandoning it – at trusting Nelson's cleverness over her own sense of loyalty. With a cry, she threw herself into pulling the door open – and *still* it resisted.

Not letting go of the wheel, she jumped and planted both feet on the door itself, holding herself at ninety degrees to the floor. Duck-walking to the door's frame, she braced her back.

Fury at herself, at Ty, at Nelson, flared through her. *The kids have to escape!* Her vision whited out. She felt her bones bending; felt the solid metal wheel buckling...

Then with an ugly *snap* the frozen grip failed and the door cracked open. She jumped down as icy fog blasted in, almost knocking her off her feet.

Hands burning, she heaved the door wider, taking a blast of air that slammed her head to toe, so cold it stunned.

The pounding feet were close now, powerful lights from behind flashing across the tunnel roof. She hauled the door all the way open, fighting a hurricane blast, her head turned futilely from the frigid gale, feeling her face freezing.

She squinted out in disbelief at the kids' escape route, a hellscape of ravening gray, a ledge on the side of the mountain, winds tearing across it. As soon as the Lightyear edged out, its nose slammed into the tunnel wall. She ducked under the craft, squeezing between it and the wall. Its body battered her, its screaming turbines clawing the air as she fought to push it clear.

Then it shot free, to be swallowed instantly by the storm. She clutched at numbers in desperate hope: Lightyear's top speed, 520 kph; the worst gales, 320. McMurdo Base 1,200 kilometers away. Worst case it might take them over six hours, but they'd make it.

If they don't crash.

She staggered away, stunned by cold, fighting the wind to grab her luggage that now spun in a mini tornado, her thermal suit spilling from it. Snatching it up, shivering and shuddering, with clumsy fingers she pulled it on and backed to the door. The gale seemed to ease as she pushed the door shut – until twisting around her like it was trying to pull her off her feet and into the storm.

Gripping the door she slammed it shut and engaged the lock.

"Freeze!" a deep, polished voice – not Bhaji – behind her boomed.

At least they had a sense of humor. She fought a smile as she turned to face them and raised her hands, her teeth chattering.

Bhaji bounced angrily in the air, staring accusingly, his eyes darting everywhere. Searching for the kids. She felt a little sick, knowing what it meant: Ty had taken full control. But most of her attention was on the six police droids armed with what she recognized as heavy duty stun rifles.

Thud. Thud.

Oh, and there was the sound she'd been waiting for, all this time. The Grendel.

Chapter 58 – Ragnarok overreach

From Happy's Link, Ezekiel Smith stared wild-eyed. Pale and shaken, with livid bruises around his neck, his expression was that of a man who'd just woken from a night terror.

He was also clearly with someone else, someone staying off camera.

"Happy. Can you get your team midtown, ten minutes?" He sent an address, while his picture jerked oddly. Happy realized Smith's arm must be shaking so badly his Link's image stabilizer couldn't cope. "*A hundred kilocreds* if you can, and pull the Chinese Ambassador out of Asgard."

"The *Chinese Ambassador*?" Happy asked. "*Asgard?!*"

Smith looked away, to whoever was with him. He shut his eyes for a couple of seconds. When he opened them he looked calmer, less terrified. The image steadied. He focused back on Happy. "My client says someone's making a bad mistake: sewage plant's about to hit the wind farm. The Ambassador is about to raid Asgard for the keys to his own PalSpace."

"The *Ambassador*?" Happy asked again, sharing the vid and sound to his crew. "But he knows there are no 'keys'!"

Smith looked at whoever was with him, then back to Happy, and nodded. "Uh, they say, he's young; proud; impetuous. Thinks PalSpace awaits a ruler."

Young?! Happy had met the guy. Just how old was Smith's *client*? "Smith, the guy's middle-aged, and a slotting *ambassador*. You're saying he's leading a raid on *Asgard*? How's your client know that? How big's the ambassador's team, what are we looking at here? And why us?"

"Because you snatched related tech, and have met and spoken with him and Welsh together. My client says you have the best chance to convince him there's no way to do what he wants. And it's just him and his two bodyguard chicks." Again he looked off-camera, then back to Happy. "Clock's ticking. In or out? One hundred K; fifty up front if you leave now."

"Three people are going up against *Asgard?!*"

"Well, not *all* of it. Just the downtown research facility. You in?"

Happy's crew nodded – all but Mike, who had no earbud for his Link. He looked lost, but keen.

"In," Happy told Smith; and waited for the payment to ping his account.

«Get me visuals on Asgard's local lab,» Happy sent to Jack. «Also any metrocop or local security chatter.»

Jack did, as they piled into the van: everything looked entirely peaceful.

At least, until they were halfway there. Then on video they saw windows blow out, fire, and the Asgard R&D building locking down, workers streaming from fire exits.

"What the crashing Net is it with this slotting PalSpace crap?" Happy demanded. "Is the whole world going mad?"

No one answered, focused instead on holding themselves upright as Jack detoured through an adjoining suburb where speed limits weren't enforced. Steven Swift's mantra, "We're going to die, we're all going to die," spoke for all of them.

At last they juddered to a tire-smoking halt outside the building.

Above, bulletproof windows on the fifth floor were missing, now lying shattered on the pavement, along with a scattering of smashed urban assault bots and dead Asgard security personnel – and one and a half Nemesys Grendel warbots.

Half, because judging from the wreckage, they'd all been flung through the windows, one of the Grendels landing on the half deployed rocket it was in the middle of launching, blowing off its own head and an arm.

Sirens drew rapidly nearer.

«I'll move the van so it's not impounded,» Jack narrowcast to the team as they piled out. «I made some mods.»

«I noticed,» Happy sent, as Nick spun, sniper rifle tracking a sleek white limo that skidded to a stop beside them. He lowered his weapon as Yanesh, immaculate in a white evening dress and high heels stepped out.

"*She's* the client," Happy muttered, then collected himself. "Aren't you a little under-dressed for this sort of thing?"

She raised an eyebrow. "Happy, I wouldn't dream of attempting to do your job. Especially as I'm paying twenty times your usual rate. I'll follow you up once you say it's safe."

Happy sighed. "Can you at least tell us what you think's happened?"

"I think the Ambassador has succumbed to PalSpace."

He frowned. "What does that mean in practical terms?"

"I'm afraid he joined," Yanesh said. "It may have magnified his magical influence, drowning him in his own dreams. He may be able to affect your perception of Reality through willpower alone, shaping it according to his subconscious desires."

Happy eyed Mike. "Sounds like someone else I know." He turned to the others. "Okay, let's go. Stairs only."

There was little to see until the final flight, where injured security guards filled the stairwell – two, with hands around each other's throats, knives puncturing their sides. Mike tried to start Healing them, but Nick snarled and hauled him off. "Try it later, if *we're* still alive!"

They emerged onto the fifth floor – wind blowing in through cave walls across a desert, a ten meter dragon clawing at one of the Chinese ambassador's bodyguards. With her thighs clamped around its thorny, scaled neck, she worked a sword in behind its ear, her second, shorter sword parrying swipes of dagger-like talons as it whipped its head from side to side.

The other female bodyguard lay across the room, unmoving in a pool of blood, her twin submachine pistols at her fingertips, her body ripped apart by high-powered rounds.

Nick sighted and fired in a fraction of a second, taking the shot as the dragon looked directly at them.

And Nick's head exploded, his own shot magically reflected.

Bruce, legs braced, was already firing his machine pistol. Mike, impossibly fast, jumped beside him raising a Shield spell. A fusillade of Bruce's rounds hammered back, only to abruptly slow and fall in a gentle rain around them.

Steven tried a magical blast, to no effect; but Haggard, somehow behind the dragon, stabbed both hands up into its groin, holding them there a second, then jumping away.

Not fast enough; not far enough.

Lashed by its tail, he hurtled across the room, striking a pillar with bone breaking force. Then the serpentine dragon lifted the whole length of its body off the floor, smashing the woman still clinging to it up and into and *through* the cave's roof. Bruce kept firing. Muscles straining, nerves like rock, six high-powered rounds, one after the other, struck the exact same point, all bouncing back until one finally punched through the creature's mystical barrier.

The cave roof shimmered, reverting to an office ceiling.

The creature shuddered, clearly struggling to stay conscious, then crashed to the ground.

Dazed, they stared as the desert melted into the wreckage of some kind of medical lab, a crushed autodoc to one side, a squashed-flat gurney, two small reddish boulders becoming a well-dressed man torn literally in half.

Mike raced to Nick, gaping for a moment at seeing the whole back of his head missing. He started Healing; but stopped when it simply sealed the edges of the shattered skull, forming a gruesome hollowed out shell. Horrified by the result of his magic, he backed away.

"Oh dear."

They turned at Yanesh's voice.

"You weren't quite fast enough."

Stepping daintily through the wreckage, her head dipped at the sight of the ambassador's dead female bodyguard. She picked her way to the swordswoman lying unconscious but still breathing by the dragon's head, whose blade still impaled it.

Ignoring the woman, Yanesh worked the weapon free of the dragon's skull. Bronze colored blood seeped from the wound. From her elaborate hairdo, she drew a long hairstick, and from *it*, a still more slender blade.

Which she delicately inserted into the dragon's skull.

"Ah," she breathed, carefully teasing out a gossamer thread, then a similar mesh. With two fingers, she slowly drew it free. Thinner than human hair, and at the end of the weave, a small flexible tab. It looked something like a tiny jellyfish with long trailing stingers.

"Disgusting," she said, dropping it to grind under the ball of one elegant shoe, before turning and placing a hand on the dragon's head.

Mike joined her. "I think we can still Heal him." He too laid his hands on the massive head, closing his eyes as he brought the Healing pattern to mind and focused his will.

Only to feel slender but firm hands take his and gently

pull them free. He looked up into eyes flecked with silver gazing quizzically into his.

"No. I know someone who will be more helpful," she said.

"Mike!" Happy shouted. "Help Swift with Haggard!" Adding, under his breath, "Not the damned dragon."

With a nod to Yanesh, Mike joined Steven by Haggard's side, who lay groaning, empty syringes still clutched in each hand.

Behind them, light flared. When it faded, an *enormous* feathered dragon of silvery iridescent colors now coiled around both the smaller dragon and injured swordswoman.

A second stunning, lightning-bright flash and clap of wings. When they could see again, both dragons, Yanesh, the far wall, and the injured woman had gone.

"Anyone see the Ambassador?" Happy asked, grimacing, surveying the disaster.

Mike stared at him, confused. "Yanesh just flew him into the light, Happy."

"Right. Thanks Mike. Anyone else see-"

Outside, the sound of sirens, swelling louder, stopped.

"Damn it. Time to go, team."

Bruce lifted Nick's body, and his weapon, while Happy cradled Haggard. After a last look around they left, Mike and Swift keeping hands on Haggard to continue the healing.

Emerging from the rear fire exit, a crew of metrocops lifted weapons, only to fall asleep at a wave of Mike's hand.

But with the arrival of the first medical crew, he turned back. "I'm going to stay and help."

"At least disguise yourself," Happy urged him. "Tik Tek are still hunting you."

Mike nodded, bundled up his trench-coat and weapon, and suddenly looked like a street kid, rising after hiding his gear in a pile of rubbish.

From a block away, by the van, Happy saw the injured person Mike knelt over start to thrash and shout. One of the medics hurried over to pull him away, questioning him.

Only to stop and look confused, while Mike, hands in pockets, sauntered off to Heal other victims.

Happy shook his head as he laid out Haggard on one of the van's rear seats. Steven sat beside him to continue the Healing, while Bruce lay Nick's body gently on the floor then took the seat opposite, beside Happy.

"Wuzzit worth it?" Haggard asked, for all of them.

Happy pulled the van doors shut. «Let's go,» he told Jack.

The team sat watching news reports in a rented room far from Happy's upmarket condo, a little cheered to find they'd been paid in full – and had somehow also slipped under the news reports' radar.

Haggard stretched, carefully testing Swift's healing.

"No mention of Mike, either," Bruce observed. "I'll call him."

There was no answer.

"Hairy, bouncing, fairy balls," muttered Swift.

They headed out to search for him.

Jack located Mike's Link – in the trash where he'd left it. Then found a nearby drunk dressed in Mike's trench-coat.

But they managed to track him down. Or rather, 'Punk', a street kid who didn't even think he was magical. With a collective groan, they convinced him to come back with them, Happy reluctantly letting the group into his condo, after first turning off the security cams.

'Punk' eyed the luxurious apartment with an eager gaze that worried Happy.

A Truth spell from Steven Swift revealed Mike genuinely believed he was a street kid named Punk.

"Yanesh likes the kid," Bruce suggested. "Call her."

Staring doubtfully at his massive, and odd teammate, Happy did. "We lost a man, today," he told her.

"And we, a warrior."

"Look, thanks for the payment, despite not finding the ambassador, but I have another problem we thought maybe you could help us with?"

For some reason, she laughed.

"It's Mike. He, uh, he thinks he's someone else."

Yanesh fell silent, studying his face. "Very well. I'll send my car for him. And see what I can do."

She had an oddly eager, hungry look, the tip of her tongue flicking across ruby lips. It almost made Happy tell her they'd deal with it themselves.

"Fine."

Six a.m. the next morning, Happy was woken by a call.

"Mike? Mike!" The kid was wearing his trench-coat again

– still unstained, despite its time in the gutter – and nothing under it. He looked... different. Older?

"Uh, Happy, what's good for breakfast?"

Peering at the image, Mike stood in what looked like a medieval painting of a kitchen, if not for the power fittings – and if Happy wasn't mistaken, a complete set of Genkai Masakuni carving knives.

The kid had spent the night with Yanesh; was still at her penthouse! "Toast. Ahh, toast's good. Cereal. Bacon, eggs. Waffles, or pancakes, with plenty of butter, and honey. Omelet maybe, or porridge. But why-?"

"Thanks, Happy! That's a lot – I'd better get cooking!"

"You only need one, maybe two-"

Mike ended the call.

Happy stared at his blank Link, thinking, *hope Yanesh has a big appetite.* Rolling over, he went back to sleep.

Chapter 59 – Heaven's reject

"Where are the children?" the polished, accent-less voice of the nearest security android demanded, its heavy duty taser aimed at her. It gestured her away from the exit door.

Thud. Thud. Thud.

She put the approaching Grendel out of her mind, confident she was really talking to Ty. "I left them with Shona, why? What's the matter?"

One of the six droids strode forward, the rest standing with weapons aimed unwaveringly at her. She'd offered to try to teach Ty emotions. She hoped she hadn't just succeeded, with her specialty: making people angry.

The android projected a holo image from back down the tunnel – the children's four empty suitcases. "This is the luggage the children brought from Paradawn." It bent and picked up her own, only her boots still inside it. "There is fresh snow on you; and around the exit. It is Condition One outside, on a mountainside. They will be dying."

"I doubt it. Look Ty, you can talk normally: I know it's you. It's just you and me here."

She was hit by a blast of light – even after squeezing her eyes shut she saw spots. *Okay, so maybe he's a* little *annoyed.* It brightened further as the Grendel stomped up, stopping what sounded like inches from her.

"Where are the children?" Its voice was a bass that shook her bones.

When she didn't answer, ultrasonics, reverberating through heavy armor plating, warned her to step aside. The light eased as it thudded past her. Slitting her eyes, she saw it effortlessly wrench the door open. Heat-sucking gale winds lashed once more through the space. It stepped out, and she fastened the flaps over her suit's zipper and turned. Outside, the dark bulk of the warbot stalked left and right along the ledge, even its searing searchlight no match for the wind-driven snow. It stood staring into the whiteout – back-lit, immovable in the howling wind.

Inside, down the passage at the edge of the light, Bhaji hovered. Seeing her see him, he flew up and swooped down to perch on her shoulder. "I think I went mad, Miss Bonnie. You were all there, but you weren't. And now the kids are gone, and Miss Shona too. You didn't really send them off the cliff into the storm to die, did you?"

But she knew, even if Bhaji's personality hadn't been altered by Ty, and even if *he* genuinely wanted to know, she couldn't tell him the truth. *This sucks,* she thought, not for the first time.

Her feet were getting cold. She stalked to the suitcase android. After a moment of resistance, it let her take her boots out. Balancing on one foot then the other, she tugged them on.

Outside, the Grendel still stood like a rock in the gale, scanning – using its radar now, she guessed. A full minute passed before it turned and reentered.

"Where are the children, Bonnie Parker?"

"Safe from you."

"Death is not safety."

She didn't correct it. Far better if Ty thought them dead.

It took her wrist in a hand large enough to enclose her whole head, locking it in a grip even she had no chance of breaking. Then it simply turned and began moving down the tunnel, accelerating.

She matched its speed, easily. The other security droids kept pace behind.

It was kind of surreal, traveling back down the tunnel now lit bright as day by the warbot's blazing light, as if she was running hand in hand with it. *I got them away!* She began skipping, enjoying the shifting shades of the ice tunnel, from azure to deep cobalt blue.

But she soon discovered her boots weren't designed for running. Rather than asking the Grendel to slow down, she flipped up to perch directly on its swinging arm, facing back toward the following security droids.

The warbot's head turned to look at her, but then just turned back, tightening its grip on her wrist.

At the bottom, reentering the city, a truck met them. Inside sat Adrielle Vodatech, cuffed, and Michael.

The vehicle sank as the Grendel climbed in.

Michael stared at her in horror. Bhaji flew from her

shoulder to perch on his. "Adam said you killed them all – Amy, Bobby, Yuri, Nadeep. And Miss Shona too. You sent them out to die in the storm."

Climbing off the warbot's arm, its grip implacable, she sat beside it, desperately wanting to deny the charge, but needing Ty to continue believing that.

"How could you *do* that?! You're a *monster!*"

Adrielle Vodatech looked different – wearing all black, a corset that had to be uncomfortable, her hair pulled back, and bold, scarlet lipstick; dressed for a night of bondage and sex maybe; not the hard, bitchy woman Bonnie remembered. "If they'd been Connected, their memories would still be there, in the web," she said, smiling.

Michael, red faced, was crying. "They *trusted* you!"

He was the key. She just needed to win him over; she needed his trust. But in earning that, she couldn't risk letting Ty learn the kids' real situation. "Can you send this guy to sleep?" she asked him, angling her head at the Grendel. "Little Bhaji too: I don't want C-N probing him later to learn what we say." A spell like that could also be a step toward him remembering how he'd wiped out Ty, before.

"Miss Bonnie!" Bhaji exclaimed.

But instead of putting *them* to Sleep, Michael's spell hammered her.

She felt woozy; nauseous. *Drugged.* Her thoughts stumbled, cycling.

Training kicked in; she tried not to think, letting impressions seep in; doing her best to minimize any change in her brain patterns.

She was lying down. Lightly covered. Naked? Her scalp hurt, a sharp pain in one spot, and also deep inside her, an internal ache, below her belly. A sharp stinging at her left wrist, which was also wet. Blood?

Restraints, at wrists and ankles. The air, sterilized; she smelled disinfectant but also traces of ozone, and earthy overtones. In the background, a quiet thrum...

I'm back in Paradawn. Quiet clicks, hums, and sounds she associated with Mr Abrams; his life support chair. *The Medbay?*

No. The sounds echoed more. A bigger space. And she could hear someone else, breathing gently. No: *two* people.

Excitement surged, despite her training, and a monitor began beeping.

Flaming space puppies – I know where I am! Slitting her eyes, she saw Gynie standing stiffly, watching her. Michael lay on a gurney like her, beyond Gynie, and Vodatech sat in a chair, restrained but awake and content.

They were in a lo-o-ong room carved from solid rock. This was the hidden area she'd sworn she'd get into!

Just... not like this.

"You offered to teach me emotions," Gynie said.

She opened her eyes fully, not surprised she hadn't fooled it. "I see you patched her up. But not even pretending to be her, Ty?"

"The Gynie first person latent space was erased at the same time its power cell was drained. Michael didn't do it, and Bobby has no 'magic'. Logic says it was the obsidian dagger. How does it function?"

"It drained the Phasion power cell?!" *I thought Tezsh only fed on blood; on life?!* "Magic. Or maybe, magic and tech? I honestly don't know. Things seem a little weird down here."

"You did not kill the children."

She studied the room instead of answering. No sign of the Grendel; plenty of medical gear and other equipment. The more distant parts of the space were unlit.

"They would not have gone willingly to their deaths, and there were no bodies on the ledge and none found at the base of the cliff. My model of your emotional makeup indicates you would consider killing them neither good nor just. Rather, you might give your own life to preserve theirs."

"Yeah, well, if you promise not to try to track them down or get them back, then I promise not to let everyone know the CEO of Tik Tek was experimenting on children."

"So you admit you didn't kill them."

Was that a first? Normally people accused her of the opposite. "What did you do to me?"

She studied her restraints. Nylon. A little loose. *I can probably reach these with my claws.* She also saw that the liquid she'd felt wasn't blood but something clear, dripping from a needle taped to her forearm. She'd worked it free, even unconscious? Wow. Her training, and the Doctor's Suggestions, actually worked.

"You stole the children. I extracted fair payment."

She didn't like the sound of that. Felt a burn, from a tugging pain in her abdomen, below her belly button. *Oh, you did not...!* Pushing the thought aside – she'd deal with that later – she tugged at her wrists. Just as well to make Ty think it really had her secured.

"Look, can you let me up? We don't have time for this. How many people now have spacepal-ed themselves? We need to deal with that."

"Yes. We do."

"Good. I'm betting miss Kumbaya-domme over there hasn't been helpful, yeah? But Michael got samples?

"You need to implant one in me, see if we can find a weakness."

"Agreed. Think or say, Bonnie Parker to enter PalSpace."

"Huh? Bonnie Parker to enter pal space? What-"

Warmth flooded in, sweeping her into a loving embrace, welcoming her; mothers, fathers, sisters, and brothers she'd never known, crowding in. And excitement: the fevered joy of sensual pleasures – a trail of teasing touches bursting like tiny fireworks; the hungry power of a foreign, rigid stiffness... enticing delights, both innocent and wicked; secrets and promises. «Love» «Welcome!» «We're like you» «You are like us» «You're safe» «You're home!» «Come in» «Sexy!» «It's all good» «See!»

She saw: night sky auroras; a wash of bright stars in velvet black. She was running through a rainforest. Rafting down a river churned white. Falling toward the Earth far below, a rush of adrenaline as the parachute snapped open. Swimming through aquamarine waters, fish brighter than party balloons darting and *clicking*. A couple making love. A *chain* of writhing bodies tangled in sex, ecstasy building.

«You belong» «We love you» «No shame, no secrets»

Belonging. Her heart swelled, feeling too big to fit in her chest.

Hugged in love and acceptance, everything she'd yearned for, all she'd ever dreamed, anything she could ever need... She sank into the warmth, something deep inside her thawing. Melting. «Welcome!» «Tell us» «Who are you?»

I'm just Bonnie. She'd never felt anything like this. Not quite herself, yet no longer alone. Soul deep warmth, communion; with friends, intimate friends, more friends than she'd ever imagined existed.

She'd been not-herself before: Marc Disten had briefly changed her, stripping her of emotion; Aiyami, sharing her head, speaking from her mouth.

This was utterly different: not a new version of selfhood replacing *her* – this *was* her, embracing and embraced by an ocean of others, a gestalt of minds, one more drop of love among many. She felt Bonnie Parker dissolving.

«Welcome, love» «Who are you?» «Share!» «No judgment»

In joy, trusting, she let the memories rise... *running through the Jungle beside Faith; dodging her unexpected laser; flooding the Institute.* «Fantasy?» «Strange» She felt a greater Unity transcribing what she shared, as if the collective assumed her memories merely the plot of an unfamiliar movie. The Meld – parts of it recoiled from her even while others, a thousand tendrils of others, reached out in welcome, digging for more...

Jogging through the park, leaping, her invisible claws lashing...

«Shock» A thousand tendrils recoiled, shriveling. But her memories gushed forth: relief at revealing secrets long bound and bottled, the reaction *validation* of her suffering.

The Doctor, dark eyes under heavy brows burning into hers, daring her not to, as he made her cut herself, trying not to; her blood flowing, the pain sharp and burning.

«Stop!» «Insanity!» «No more!»

Her pain and humiliation rose stark and clear, admitted at last, vomited out, *shared* at last. Then:

Bound in the Doctor's chair, his careful study. Eagle...

No. Secret.

Like slumbering demons, implanted defenses awakened. A swelling gray confusion blossomed, corroding thought...

She felt it ripple out, take root, dislocations poisoning the Whole...

«wh...?» «ungh» «n... th...» «can't...» «...» «»

The mental paralysis spread, even as braver tendrils continued questing, finding more of the *other,* darker, more forbidden memories, the union fracturing as crueler tortures-

«BEGONE!»

She was ejected. Rejected.

Expelled from Unity; in its dismay, walled off from it.

Brief respite gave back her self. Roaring defiance – *I don't need you!* – she tore herself free of the quivering, stunned threads still blindly reaching for connection.

Adrielle Vodatech, staring at her, began screaming.

Gynie – Ty – tilted its head, considering the panicking woman for long seconds, expressionless, before fetching an ampoule from a glass cabinet. Preparing the injection, it moved to the woman gaping at Leeth, the source of her terror, crying and thrashing in her restraints.

Now. Heart heavy in her chest, her breath hurting, Leeth latched onto anger and snapped out her claws. With a vicious twist she sliced the restraints at her wrists, her ankles.

Leaping onto the gynoid from behind, locking her legs around its torso, she wrenched the head right round; facing her for a moment; then around again.

Feeling wires tear, she yanked it free and sprang away as it folded to the ground, tossing the head away.

Adrielle stared at her, a needle still in one arm, as she sank, still fighting, terrified, into sleep.

How long till the Grendel?

She was naked. Michael lay, asleep or sedated, on a bed. Not restrained. About to shake him awake, a large white donut shape resolved itself, deeper in the room, behind where she'd been lying.

"No!"

But it *was*: a second Writer.

Chapter 60 – A child for a child

Thud.

Gynie climbed back to her feet, headless, navigating by feel.

Thud.

Could she rip the Ty-piloted Gynie apart, stick its Phasion cell to this second Writer, find a screwdriver-?

Thud.

Forcing herself to calm down, she scanned the room for something to use... and spotted, under the stretcher she'd been on, the clothes she'd last been wearing.

Thud.

In the rear of the large unlit space stretched two rows of clear cylinders... *Not important: no time.* But inside each cylinder, a shape. Unwillingly, she moved toward them.

Thud.

The nearest held the biggest shape: a pale, naked boy, maybe thirteen, fourteen... His face a younger Michael's, calm in sleep. She read a label: α 3.

In shock, she moved to the next, and found another; an even younger Michael. α 4.

Thud.

Opposite that, four more cylinders, smaller. More Greek letters. She recognized the β as a 'B' equivalent, and then three other letters. Each numbered '1'. Each containing a small shape that had her shaking her head: a fetus.

Thud.

Nearer now, the Grendel would be here any second. But three much smaller cylinders called to her. A different fluid mix; nothing she could see, inside them. Each had the same Greek letter, one she didn't know, but numbered 1, 2, and 3.

Her hand went to her abdomen, and felt the scraping, inner twist of pain again.

Thud. *Creak.*

'You stole the children,' Ty had said. 'I extracted fair payment.' *From me: eggs,* she thought, in shock and horror.

He's growing clones: Michael, and Amy, Bobby... and me!

She snatched up 'empty' small cylinder '1', wrenching it free of its holder, and smashed it into '2', then '3', and watched glass and fluids rain to the floor. She gazed down at the wreckage, stunned. Imagining younger *sisters*. Imagined them *with* her; aged two, or four, or-

Creak.

She turned. The stone wall: the secret door. She stared at the other cylinders, at the clones growing there... but shook her head. No. She couldn't do that. Maybe she *should*, but she couldn't.

Crea-eak.

She ran back to the lighted part of the room, Michael now sitting up, staring at her. Just meters from the gurney she'd been bound to, a large section of stone wall, as thick as her forearm was long, was now pivoting upward from the middle, higher than her head. Visible beneath it, the massive legs of the warbot.

Crea-eak.

The stone door continued rotating open.

"Michael! Take it out! Adam is growing clones of you all! He has another Writer!"

But Michael just watched her.

Michael. A second Writer. She groaned.

Snatching up her snowsuit in one hand, her boots in the other, she dived under the door, twisting sideways to pass between the Grendel's legs, somersaulting to her feet past it, and around the corner, hammering at the green button that opened the Medbay door.

The lock clicked – then clicked again, re-locking. *Ty.*

She kicked then wrenched it open, hearing the warbot turning as she dived into the corridor.

Thud.

I'm faster than it, she thought, naked and clutching ski suit and boots, sprinting for the *Takahe* pod station. But there was no way Ty'd let a pod reach Newtopia.

Thud.

As she ran, she planned. First, blind the cameras in the pod station. Ride an eScooter to the research base? Then what?

Mr Yakone? Tezsh's dagger?

Could the microwave ice borer take out the Grendel?

Naked, sweating, heart pounding, she arrived at the pod station, tore off and used a seat leg to spear one, two... six cameras altogether. *Not for the first time.*

She found an eScooter. She leaped up three times to hide it: once to slide a ceiling tile aside; a second to thrust the scooter inside; a third, to replace the tile.

Thud-ing footsteps told her she had two minutes till the Grendel arrived; but a fainter, more worrying sound was approaching much faster. Wing beats.

Jumping into her thermal suit, wondering what had happened to the soft, inner boots, she zipped it up.

Hopping down onto the track, she wriggled under the waiting pod, the space so tight her chest pushed into its underside with each breath.

Nowhere to stash her outer, hard-shelled boots, but she did find toe and hand holds.

Then heard Bhaji arrive.

Shutting her eyes, she tracked his movements by sound, 'seeing' him circle the room. By the rack of eScooters he paused, then flew off down the tunnel to Mt Takahe. *Ty had noticed the eScooter missing.* He'd know its top speed, and the distance to the Mt Takahe research base. He'd have cameras there too, watching.

The Grendel stomped closer.

Bhaji returned and circled the room again. The door of the pod carriage above her slid open, and he flew in. She couldn't follow his movements inside, but around the time the warbot paused, a hundred meters from the station, the little drone called out.

"Miss Bonnie? Are you here? Adam had Gynie use the autodoc to give you a PalSpace implant. But when you turned it on, you went a bit crazy.

"I think maybe PalSpace makes you see things that aren't there. Adam says to come back: he can instruct the autodoc to remove the PalSpace.

"Miss Bonnie?"

But she didn't need the obvious lies to keep her silence: she'd already heard the quiet whine of an eScooter's motor. It had stopped, a way back. In her mind's audible eye, it waited beside the Grendel warbot.

She followed soft footsteps into the station, recognizing Michael's quiet breathing.

More clearly than anything else could have, the fact that none of them spoke aloud told her Ty was operating all three.

Ty was operating *Michael*.

Lying squashed like a bug under the pod, she hoped: that she'd surprised Ty often enough; that enough weird and inexplicably magical things had been happening; that it would decide to check out Takahe.

She also hoped she'd guessed right about how high the pod would lift above the magnetic levitation rails; and that the powerful fields wouldn't affect her.

She hoped she could keep her boots; maybe rest them on her belly?

Hoped the Grendel's weight in the pod wouldn't smash her into the ground on some dip, at four hundred kilometers an hour.

Hoped she could hold on, clinging upside down, for the whole trip to Takahe.

But most of all, she hoped Ty would actually decide to go and check, through Bhaji or Michael's or the Grendel's eyes, the research base.

Hopefully I can come up with a good plan, if I get there. Maybe involving finding Mr Yakone, and Tezsh's dagger. Somehow using it to kill Ty before he could end her.

Not to mention the problem of the aliens' PalSpace.

Chapter 61 – Grendel prey

The pod rose up off its tracks, the boots wedged on her belly making her spine brush the ground – which would kill her. About to discard them, she remembered their velcro fastener seals. Using them she hung the boots around her neck instead and pulled herself up against the underside of the pod.

This is gonna suck.

Shutting her eyes, she focused on keeping her fingers from slipping, even as her bare toes cooled.

Just thirty minutes. That's how long the trip between Takahe and Paradawn took.

The pod rose, smoothly accelerating. 100; 200; 400 kilometers per hour.

Clinging to the sheltered undercarriage, the wind tearing past below, she pulled herself higher at every deadly brush of the maglev tunnel's stone floor. It reminded her of pressing into a wall outside the Fist of Peace's meeting place, while cold and stinging rain leached away her strength.

She'd endured that.

She blanked her mind. Tried not to think about PalSpace – at finally *belonging* – followed immediately by horrified rejection.

Then the lab, and destroying her own-

She cut that thought off as wind whipped water from her cheeks, her eyes screwed shut.

The PalSpace chip's still in my head, too. I'd just need to think, Bonnie Parker-

-is an idiot who needs to stop thinking stupid thoughts that'll kill her. Think of white elephants instead.

Just hang on.

She was *so* going to kill Ty. And that Grendel bot. Bhaji though...

Just hang on.

The endless journey continued.

When the pod finally slowed, coasting to a stop, she gained a fresh definition of bliss.

Until it sank and pinned her to the ground. Pressed too flat to breathe, her feet frozen blocks she could no longer feel, her toes still locked in place, she shut her eyes.

Ty'll already have reviewed all the video from here. So it'll know I'm not inside. Struggling but failing to draw a breath, she fought down rising panic.

At last Michael, Bhaji, and finally the Grendel exited the pod and moved off, and the vehicle rose. Enough for her to draw a precious, silent breath.

She listened to them all move away. The trio moved slowly through the pod station, as if Ty didn't believe the evidence of its own... cameras...

She grinned: Nelson and LB's trick with Bhaji's secret synthesized video system paying off a second time? Heartened by that, she managed to make some headway – or was that 'chestway'? – squirming out from under the pod.

She heard the three stop moving, then the elevator arrive, and them get in and depart.

Now what? The cameras in the pod station were her immediate problem.

Wriggling her way free, she sat cross-legged behind the pod, out of sight of the cameras, snow boots in her lap, massaging feeling and warmth back into her feet as she thought. If she killed the cameras, she'd be telling them she was here. She couldn't steal the pod: Ty controlled everything.

The lights went out. Infrared activated.

In the dark, she smiled in delight. *Thank you, Ty!*

Grimacing in the sub-zero temperature, she stripped out of her thermal suit, her cold and abused feet already aching. Resting behind the pod, hoping her butt didn't freeze to the floor, she waved her suit gently to cool it down. *Hoping* it would shield her long enough from the thermal sensors to reach the elevator unseen.

When she started shaking from the cold she pulled her insulating suit back on, hanging her boots around her neck: nearly-frozen feet would work in her favor. Darting out from behind the pod, she crossed the station to the elevator, the hood drawn tight around her face.

No earrings buzzed a 'Gait warning'. The thermal-sensing lights stayed off.

Nor were the elevator doors a match for her angry strength. She wrenched them open, aware that all too soon her exertions would warm her suit enough to trigger the lights.

Slipping inside the elevator shaft, rungs set into the far wall rose up out of sight. *Thank you!* The doors closed, sealing her inside.

She looked up, her eyes straining in the dark. Far, far above, a light.

That's got to be 400 meters.

Boots on, she began the long climb.

Pressing her face into the rungs, she clung, gasping, arms and legs burning, gathering her strength for the last stretch. *I am so killing Ty.*

Grease coated the front and back of her suit by the time she reached the underside of the elevator. Squeezing past it she climbed on top, and from there into the ceiling space.

Shuddering, trying to pant quietly, she rested, listening, working out what was happening in the research station. She crept through the ceiling space toward the base's exit.

Neither Michael nor Bhaji were calling out for Mr Yakone. Was he *still* outside? She strained, listening.

Ice pellets rattled on windows and walls. Angry but muffled wind.

Was Mr Y dead? The last they'd checked, he'd been in the foothills, in the area where the dagger had flown.

He *must* have been searching for it. With a spirit.

Something told her she'd find out why, soon enough. She felt sure he was still alive, too.

A rumble through the ground made her only more certain. The volcano. And Tezsh being a god of Death *and* Volcanoes. *And* storms, and trickery, and a whole bunch of other stuff.

Eventually, listening, shivering in her suit, she heard the Grendel, outside the base. Then heard Bhaji. From the way the sound rose and fell, but stayed muffled, he had to be in the airlock passage, fluttering up every now and then, probably to see out the windows at each end of that small space. That meant the wind must be too fast for his wings: at least 80 kph. Probably much worse, from its angry howl.

Michael though, in his comfortable shoes and moving quietly – him she couldn't hear. He could be anywhere.

Every now and then the earth shook.

I really don't need a volcanic eruption: Mother'll blame me. Surely the Department knew there were like a hundred and forty volcanoes down here. Though, they *had* given her Tezsh's dagger.

Okay: get outside fast. *Don't get captured or blown up by the Grendel, or one of Michael's spells...* Could Michael *do* spells, when controlled by Ty? How did that even work?

Michael had to be separate, somehow. He'd been too human. Not Ty doing a great impression of a real person, like Adam. Was it like multiple personalities? Did Michael himself even know Ty could control him?

She shuddered. That was too much like what the Doctor, and Nelson once, had tried to do to her.

Anyway: get outside, don't get caught, and find Mr Yakone. Then play it by ear.

She smiled, relieved. It was good to finally have a plan.

Dropping silently to the floor outside the airlock room, she slipped on her snow boots. The moment she unlatched the inner door Bhaji swooped up, staring at her through its small window. Obviously, telling Ty where she was.

Slamming in, she snatched the little drone out of the air as she ran to the outer door.

"Miss Bonnie! Please, no! What are you doing?"

But even as she forced the door open, she found she didn't have the heart to fling the little guy into the storm. It wasn't his fault Ty had taken him over.

Instead she tossed him back inside, leaving the outer door open to force Michael or the warbot to return and close it if they wanted to keep Bhaji safe. Ty wasn't wasteful.

The storm was nowhere near as bad as the one she'd left, who knew how many hours ago and 1,200 kilometers away. The winds lashed at her, probably only 100 kph here. Was the storm building across the whole continent?!

She also didn't have her suit's face shield, she realized, as her eyes, nose, and cheeks began freezing.

Pulling the drawstring all the way closed, she sealed her hood around her so she didn't die in the next minute.

The shrieking of the wind made it harder to place herself in the world around her like she normally did.

She felt and heard a vibration through the soles of her boots, her bare feet unpleasantly chilled without the proper soft inner shell.

Already, despite the near perfect insulation of the aerogel, she felt the hungry cold at every surface of her suit. She activated the warming, turning it up to max.

It helped. A little.

Yeah, okay. I need to find Mr Yakone.

The wind had been blasting her toward the volcano.

That was handy. Trudging in that direction, head down and trying to keep her feet, half skidding along in the battering wind, she wondered if maybe her plan could've done with a few more details.

Thud.

She felt the vibration through the soles of her boots again. Why was it even hunting her? To recapture her? It wasn't firing lasers, or rockets – though admittedly in these conditions, neither would work at much more than point blank range.

Was Michael out here too, wandering around unprotected by anything other than his Pigloo spell? Could that handle a gale like this?

As if the thought caused it, a gust plucked her off the ground and lofted her spinning into the air. She crouched, arms and legs spread, then slammed back to earth. Sliding and somersaulting over icy ground, over and over, the wind drove her like a bouncing ball until she speared her claws through the tips of a glove to carve into the ice; slowing and finally stopping.

Snarling around her, the wind grabbed her, trying again to pull her off the ground.

It felt personal.

Like in the aircraft.

Like in the airport when she'd nicked herself, and held out a drop of blood.

Was this a spirit, maybe the same one, here for *her?!*

But this was too big to be one spirit. Was it a giant one, a whole lot of smaller wind spirits joined to make a storm? Hadn't she asked Mr Yakone about that?

"Are you here for me?" she shouted to it, then loosened the drawstring of her hood, enough to make a small round aperture, and called again, her voice drowned in the roar on all sides. "Did you come back? Do you want to *dance?*"

Maybe she'd gone crazy. Maybe finding welcome, acceptance, somewhere to belong... just to be rejected, as always, had *driven* her a little crazy. Maybe being hunted by an AI-driven war machine in a blizzard at the South Pole was *pissing her off* – but she was tired of running, and hiding.

"If you want to dance, let's dance!" she screamed.

And instead of resisting the storm, she gave herself to it, diving into the wind. She let it throw her, pirouetting, into the air, to land with cat's grace. Only to spin and leap again. Then, while the earth shook and rumbled, and lightning flashed overhead, she sensed something ahead of her on the rising ground.

"Oh, you've met Tezcatlipoca, haven't you?" she shouted to her dance partners, to the winds. "Did Mr Yakone find him? Did the storm god bring you all together?"

She felt crazed, exuberant, full of energy. She *grabbed* the wind and felt it curl around her, a vortex that lifted her high into the air. Some wild part of her reached out, *touching* something that didn't ride the air but *was* the air, old and young at the same time, and hungry. So hungry. Hungry, and cold. "I can feel you, can you feel me?" she cried in delight, her heart full of wonder – and below her, scintillant beams of bright green swept through the gusting snow.

Laser tracking. The warbot.

She pointed down, to the source of the beams. "Down there! Take me there!" she cried, drunk with the joy of flight. "I'm sick of running!"

She plunged down, a large dark armored shape materializing out of white nothing as her legs absorbed the shock of her landing.

The warbot reached for her, its laser rifle *cracking* away a build-up of ice from the cover hinging open on its shoulder.

She flung herself up and at it, unsheathing her claws. One hand stabbed down into the exposed mechanism, ripping and slicing, while her other gripped the laser barrel, twisting it toward the warbot's head.

Powerful motors whined and shrieked in protest, but she was a fury, maddened, maddened by a wind that carried her like a Valkyrie in the storm. Maddened by the nerve shock of claws scraping on metal they couldn't cut, even as they sliced through layers of insulation. They scraped on titanium weave sheathing artificial muscles. Closing her hand around the pain, she gripped the web of wires and *pulled.*

They tore free, the laser disabled, as a massive arm

slammed at her head from across its body. She jerked backward, grabbing the forearm thicker than both her thighs together. Carried by it, she spun up and around like it was an uneven bar, tree-trunk thick – and saw the seamless joint where arm connected to shoulder.

A mental flash: Little Brother in his workroom, trying to measure the thickness of her claws.

Zero, he'd said. Only not really: thinner than he could measure.

Remembering that moment, sensing its other arm reaching for her, she let go, twisting as she fell, and stabbed a single claw into that seamless gap.

It plunged in.

She angled it, tearing, the bones of her finger screaming in pain, wrenching more wires free. The massive arm stuttered and stalled even as she dived out of reach of the other.

With that key, the rest of the fight was over in a minute, first the other arm disabled, then each leg.

When its other shoulder cracked open to reveal the compact rocket pointing toward her, she tore it free with brutal delight and hurled it into the storm.

As the winds raged around her, its head pivoted to her, flush to the torso on its own seamless joint.

"How?" the bass voice demanded.

"I'm a Huntress," she shouted, crouching and sliding invisible blades in beneath its nonexistent neck. "Not *prey.*"

Angling her claws, she ripped out wiring she'd studied for long hours back in her rooms at the Department, trying, and failing back then, to find this weakness.

Then stood and screamed her victory into the storm.

"Can you lift *that?*" she crowed to the winds. "Lift it, and smash it down onto ice?"

In awed silence, she watched a tornado spin down onto the Grendel, and do exactly that.

And in the small following eye of the storm, she saw Mr Yakone stalking toward her, Tezsh's gold and obsidian dagger in one hand.

His eyes blazed lapis lazuli blue.

Chapter 62 – Shaman in the storm

The gale blizzarded around them, a vortex shroud of white – Mr Yakone, dagger in hand, the moving eye of the storm.

Well, guess I didn't need to worry about finding them!

Mr Yakone's uncanny glowing eyes were locked on her, and not in a friendly way.

"Adlartok Kallik Yakone!" she called out, trying to snap him out of it, hoping she'd got his full name right. "Went shik shruke?" she called, hoping she'd got his spirit's name right too, that she'd *guessed* right. "Can *you* help him?"

He was still in there, she knew; dimly aware. She still remembered snatches, herself, of stalking a fleeing prey through a blacked-out shopping mall, people screaming... Of Yamamoto, the Doctor, and others, in Omega's smashed office, as the wind whistled through it.

"Godsson *lies*, Mr Yakone. I was just eight when he first tried to sneak a spirit inside me."

Mr Yakone said nothing, stalking closer, his eyes fixed on her.

"Godsson thinks feelings are bad – that people would be better if they were logical, like machines."

He just kept coming on.

She took a step back. "A hundred and forty volcanoes down here, Mr Yakone, and Tezcatlipoca's a god of them! If he melts Antarctica – this time all of it, not just the Western side – *all* of your homeland vanishes, under sixty meters of water!

"Godsson *lies*! He lied to you!"

Mr Yakone tensed to slash at her with the dagger, but she took another step back.

"You had a plan when you came down here, I could tell. I don't know what it was, but I bet it wasn't this!"

Even prepared, knowing how its magic magnified her own formidable speed, she only just managed to jerk back and avoid his next slash.

She felt a burst of anger. *It should be* me *with the dagger!*

"Look, I know how good it feels to kill someone, properly."

The glow of his eyes dulled, his brow furrowing.

"Someone who *needs* killing, I mean," she clarified. *Why am I even trying to talk him down? I should just kill him.*

With the thought, she extended her invisible claws from both hands, felt them slice through the tips of her gloves, sliding out like ten shared sighs of relief. Of razor sharp honesty.

This was who she was.

Mr Yakone froze, his eyes dragged unwillingly down to her hands as if he could see what waited for him there – *oh, he probably can.* The glow of his eyes faltered, dimming further.

He tensed; she tensed.

But this... it felt too easy.

"Why are you even doing this?"

"You kill wife."

"What? I never-"

"You people. You *tanik* – white people. For *profit*. Burn oil. *Cage* fish in *ocean*. Poison sea, seashore, all." He sobbed. Mr Yakone *sobbed*. "And spirits here..." Reaching inside his parka with his other hand, he drew out yellowed, crumbling rocks. "Hungry. Eat babies."

"Babies?! What-?"

"From eggs." He crumbled the aged, yellowed *ivory* amulets in his fingers.

And stabbed forward with inhuman speed. Speed that matched her own.

Her hand flashed up, knocking the strike aside so it only cut her suit – which would kill her slowly – and leaped back.

"Burn them, burn all!"

He lunged again, and again she evaded, saw her opening-

And realized *that* was what Tezsh wanted.

He'd demanded a sacrifice, but it was *Mr Yakone* he wanted, not her. *Mr Yakone* sacrificed to Tezcatlipoca, tricked by the dagger, dedicated to him that way, through *her*.

She aborted her killing blow – before Mr Y had even *started* to move to counter it.

"Oh, you tricky slotting so-and-so, Tezsh."

The lapis lazuli glow blinked out from Mr Yakone's eyes as lightning slashed the sky and the earth shook and rumbled, thunder riding its heels.

Mr Yakone stared at her, dazed, the dagger lowering. She felt her hair stand on end, saw the fringes of Mr Yakone's skins lifting and levitating...

Pure intuition moved her then. Throwing herself up and at Mr Yakone, she barreled into him, sending the dagger flying-

The world cracked open.

Light-

She was lying down. On top of Mr Y. Cold, but not dying from it. Her head felt ready to burst open.

She rolled off him, onto her back, onto ice. The wind had dropped. She stared up, dully, into a clearing sky under a sun riding low on the horizon.

As always here, in summer. *Summer? Hah!*

Splitting pain clawed her head; her muscles not so much aching as screaming.

She smelled burning fabric and plastic.

I guess I timed my jump right. Since we're both still alive. Tezsh's lightning bolt must have hit while they were midair. *Must've* really *pissed him off.* Were all gods that emotional? She sniggered, then winced at the stab of pain it jarred loose. A gentle waft of air curled around her face.

Had my wind spirit pal helped?

Groaning, she rolled back to the shaman. Patted his cheek. "Mr Y? You okay? Don't s'pose you could manage a bit of Healing?

"You could do you first though, I reckon," she conceded, slumping back onto the ice to stare up into the sky.

With the storm gone, and both of them hunting for it, they found Tezsh's dagger without too much trouble. He wanted to fling it back into the crevasse he'd rescued it from, but she stopped him.

"No. I actually, really need it. But I'm sorry about your babies, Mr Yakone. And your wife."

They found the crumbled fragments of his ivory 'eggs', and together scraped a small grave in the ice. She didn't try to hide her invisible claws from him, and he didn't flinch from them – *too* much. By mutual consent, neither of them suggested using the dagger to dig.

"They had baby spirits in them, part of them, did they?" she asked.

He nodded. "Eggs."

"I'm sorry it didn't work out." She thought of telling him, maybe part of that was Tezsh's doing, being a Death god and all, but decided it'd be kinder to say nothing.

Michael – or was he a Michael *clone?* – proved even easier to find. They found him standing, turning in slow circles, staring as if he'd never seen the icy plain before.

Uh oh.

He looked only a couple hundred meters away, but tiny, midway between them and the research base.

It took half an hour to reach him. *He's PalSpaced,* she knew, long before they got there. Remembering, with a cruel twist in her belly, the warm welcome of that place. Until the collective minds saw you were a monster.

I'm not!

As she and Mr Yakone reached him, his eyes met hers. "I understand now, Bonnie Parker. I *feel.*"

Which was when she realized it wasn't Michael: it was *Ty* who'd spoken.

The Tik Tek AI had merged its consciousness into the growing global mind. That *couldn't* be good.

This was it, she realized, the dagger somehow in her hand, ready. Michael would be the sacrifice. With Tezsh's Death aspect, and Ty 'alive' in him, she'd never have a better chance to kill the AI and complete her mission.

Michael's youthful face gazed up in wonder at the sky, faint wisps of an aurora flickering at the edges of visibility.

He turned to her – and smiled.

And suddenly, it felt *wrong* to kill him. Suddenly, he seemed stupidly young. Not just Michael: Ty. Both of them. She ground her teeth.

I have *to kill him! I* do. *Remember what he tried to do to all the kids!* But he just stared up into the sky, unaware of his death at hand.

Growling, instead she led him – it, them – back inside the base, and put the dagger away.

The outer door hadn't been shut properly. She had to wrench it open against a thick crust of snow and ice, kicking away some with her snow boots. Bhaji lay unmoving in the far corner of the airlock room, as far from the outer door as he could get, buried in snow. Neither Michael nor the Grendel had returned to shut the outer door.

"Oh, my poor Bhaji!" The artificial muscles for its wings, necessarily exposed, didn't work properly at super low temperatures. "Miss Bonnie!" He sounded confused, his voice grating, deeper and clicking, his speaker half frozen, half the pixels for his eyes not working. She had the feeling Ty's attention was elsewhere; Bhaji was just her little drone again. For now? Her eyes watering, she gently brushed off snow and ice, then, wincing, tucked him in her front, between her breasts, cursing and dancing in a small circle at the shock of cold.

But by the time they started back to Paradawn, riding in the pod – so much better than her last trip! – his muscles had already warmed enough for him to begin to move again.

She took him out.

"How many people are there in PalSpace now?" she asked Michael, as they set out.

But Michael didn't answer; Bhaji did. "12,376.

"Miss Bonnie," it added, a full second later. It sounded... ashamed?

By the time they'd returned to Paradawn, and the Medbay, the number was over 18,000.

In the Medbay, P1 and P2 stood, immobile. Except for their heads: both turned in unison to watch her. They'd never done that before.

"Please open the secret, stone wall door," she asked Michael.

"Why?" he said at last.

"I have a new feeling to share with you. With all of you. A very important one."

Tezsh's dagger sat, a sullen heaviness tugging down an inner pocket of her thermal suit.

"Your suit!" Mr Yakone exclaimed. "Big back burn!"

The stone door began to pivot upward as she twisted to check her back in a mirror, and it was her turn to be astonished. The whole outer layer had burned off, leaving a ragged, charred hole. But although the translucent aerogel insulation layer bulged out, it was only slightly crispy.

She unzipped the front of her snow suit to her waist, already too warm now inside the base, the belt keeping it on. She frowned, wondering what had happened to the rest of her clothes.

She noticed Mr Y looking at her, and away, more than once.

Inside, in the huge inner room-cavern, Adrielle Vodatech still sat tethered in her chair, but awake again. At the sight of Bonnie, she started moaning – as did Michael.

P1 and P2 just tracked her movements, and she went over to them. Their eyes followed her.

"You're in PalSpace too? Connected?"

"Yes," they answered.

"But you don't *feel* it like the others, do you?" she asked, feeling tired; though sorry for them both.

"Correct," the two men said.

Mr Yakone looked at her in surprise.

She shrugged. "I've... encountered other guys like them. They're what Godsson would like us all to be – no emotions.

"Last time I spoke to Tezsh," she continued, "he said he wouldn't help me unless I made a sacrifice to him first."

The shaman frowned.

"You still don't get it? He wanted *you,* Mr Yakone. *You* were meant to be the one sacrificed, back on Mt Takahe."

He gaped at her.

"The lightning blast was because he saw I'd worked that out and wasn't going to do it for him."

She drew the dagger from her suit's inner pocket.

Chapter 63 – One against the horde

"Do you wish to live?" she asked P1, or P2; both really, as she held Tezsh's dagger. Feeling it inert but eager in her grasp.

"Life is irrelevant," they answered.

She stared from one to the other, the gold's cold weight heavy in her hand. "See, that's the thing. I don't think it is. I'm starting to think it's the thing that's *most* relevant. Most precious."

She sensed Tezcatlipoca, silent but listening, hearing her when she spoke while holding its sacrificial dagger. "You almost killed me and Mr Yakone both with your stupid lightning bolt out at Mt Takahe," she said to him. "How long do you think you would've laid there? A hundred years? A thousand?"

She turned to Michael. "How many people now, Ty?"

"26,213."

"So right now, Tezsh, we have 26,000-odd people all joined together in an alien hive mind thing that's expanding rapidly. And when enough are part of it, they're somehow going to call something, from outer space, to come here, and do something.

"I don't know what. This is their second try though. The first time was in Mr Abrams's vault. You remember that?"

Sensing the death god still listening, she strode to Adrielle Vodatech, who began screaming, thrashing in her chair, trying desperately to get away.

Leeth steeled herself, repulsed by what she was about to do.

She raised the dagger. The only way this was going to work was to *terrify* all those people connected together, experiencing and loving one another in PalSpace. She had to convince them it was a place they never dared go, ever again. She wasn't doing this because they'd rejected her. She *wasn't*.

You thought I *was the monster? I'll show you the real thing.* She gathered her nerve, her mouth dry.

Wait: what if this magic needed to attack the seed of the

infection, to kill *that* person?

She swallowed: or, to kill that person *first*?

She lowered the knife, and Vodatech's screams eased to whimpers.

"Ty, who was the first PalSpace user? Where are they?"

Did she have time for this? Was this a real hunch, or just a way to delay? She grimaced. But how many more people would join before-

"Lawrence Freeman was first; a researcher in the Genetic Developments Division," Ty said. "He died seven days ago at the Transantarctic Mountains Observatory.

"Second user was Adrielle Vodatech. She is also the concealed owner of Nervana, the company behind PalSpace."

Vodatech began screaming again, thrashing at her bonds.

Leeth met her eyes. "Oh, you *bitch*! Okay, Tezsh – *Tezcatlipoca* – I'm giving you the woman who set the alien ball rolling. She's connected to all the others." *One death wouldn't be enough.* She'd been in PalSpace; knew how seductive it was. With suddenly hammering heart, she added, "See how many you can take, through her, eh?"

And now my part. I have to do this. Feeling ashamed, her mouth still dry, she plunged the obsidian blade into the helpless woman's heart, and held it there.

Michael, across the room, gasped and cried out, clutching his chest as if she'd stabbed *him*. He staggered back, his eyes locked on her in horror.

So too Mr Yakone, his mouth open, who raised one hand as if to cast a spell, his other clutching something at his neck that wasn't there to see.

There was no blood from the fatal wound. Just Adrielle Vodatech's screams, her pupils now shrunk to pinpricks, her face a rictus, pale and growing paler.

The dagger, feeding. Drinking.

Leeth released the weapon and straightened. Shutting her eyes, she saw again a crowded mall corridor, black as pitch to all eyes but hers, people screaming in terror, fleeing the death that hunted with eyes glowing an uncanny blue in the dark. *Her* eyes.

PalSpace must be like that, now. Except instead of being reined in by her, in single-minded pursuit of the last of the gangsters who'd thought to trade Marcie's life for hers, this time Tezcatlipoca pursued *thousands*, magically, empathically connected. And he'd been secretly juicing up on Pha-sion power cells somehow – Antarctica's weird magical rules? – yet hungry for more.

To leave PalSpace you just had to want to disconnect, Bhaji had told her.

Michael – Ty really, she suspected – looked more dazed than scared.

My orders are to kill him; this should do it nicely. He has no idea he can die this way. Like Tezsh killed Gynie. So why did she want to shout out to Ty to 'disconnect!'?

Bhaji, though – Bhaji was flying in crazy circles, buzzing Michael's head. For some reason, Bhaji had stayed separate, apart from PalSpace. Just his own little true self.

I can't do it, she realized. *My mission is to kill Ty. But there's just the one of him, all alone. A stupid AI who wants to learn what it's like to be human.* Was death really the an-swer to that question?

But *he'd* killed a bunch of people – Amy's mother, Bobby and Yuri and Nadeep's families and villages – so he could ex-periment on the kids, and on Michael too. Scared to become human, trying to find a safe way to feel emotions, to know what it was like.

Maybe a bit like Pinocchio; trying to become a real boy.

She made her decision; knowing Mother and Father'd be furious; Eagle wouldn't be too pleased either. But her heart said it was the right thing to do.

"Hey, Ty."

He didn't respond. Michael's eyes were shut, his eyeballs moving like someone asleep and dreaming. But his *hands* – they clutched the edge of the cot he'd fallen back against.

P1 and P2, she saw, just looked... mildly interested.

She strode to Michael.

"Ty!" She slapped his cheek, gently, shaking him till his eyes opened, to slowly focus on her. "I know you put a PalSpace thing in Michael, when you did the same to me. I don't know how *Michael* killed you last time, but Tez-catlipoca can do it too, I reckon."

He blinked at her.

She shook him. "Don't you understand? You need to get out of PalSpace, Ty, *now*, before the Death god claims you too.

"Get out, Ty!"

His eyes met hers, staring deep, and she felt it, a shock of meeting, with her hand holding his. For the first time, the AI truly *saw* her.

"You can feel them dying, can't you? Can you feel their fear? We only get one life, Ty, and Tezsh is taking it away.

"Get. Out!"

He blinked, and his pupils, which had been so dilated his irises had almost vanished, suddenly contracted.

Immediately, Bhaji's mad swooping around his head ended, and he flew down to perch on Michael's shoulder.

She felt a little pang. Bhaji hadn't chosen hers.

"Are you out?"

Michael – Ty – nodded.

"Yes."

"How many in PalSpace now?"

"Two," he said.

P1, and then P2, crumpled to the floor, and Ty stared at her in wonder.

"None."

She let out a long breath, her heart racing. *How many people did I just sacrifice to Tezsh?* How many people had refused to leave, and died? She glanced at the dagger. Its two eyes looked... content.

That *had* to be a bad sign.

Later: I'll worry about that later.

She felt strangely shaken. Adrift. Now what?

She put a hand on Michael's shoulder. "We need to talk." That sure was true. "But in the cafeteria. I'm *starving!*"

Mr Yakone just stared at her. But followed them.

"Especially about that damned Writer of yours, and cap-turing kids to experiment on," she told Ty.

For once Ty was silent.

Maybe a near-death experience was a lot even for an AI to process?

After dinner, she felt tiredness swim up to engulf her. When was the last time she'd slept?

"I need to sleep," she told Ty. "Tomorrow, I'll head back to New Francisco, if Bhaji can get me on the flight out?"

They'd watched news reports, over dinner. Back in New-topia there'd been sheer panic, as PalSpace users began screaming and abandoning the network in terror.

Not just in Newtopia, either: all around the world, wherever the users were. The death toll wasn't clear, but estimated to be over a thousand. About two thirds, members of the Church of Cybernetics. PalSpace exposed as a trap, a monster hidden inside.

Tik Tek looked like it was going to escape with just a little damage to its reputation: it had not approved the sale of the devices. They'd been released after an act of corporate espionage.

Ty seemed different: genuinely more human.

Maybe he really had learned to feel some emotions.

"Hey, look, I've decided to leave Bhaji with you." She plucked the little drone off her shoulder. "It's not good to be alone. You need a companion. I had a friend, Faith, who helped me become human. So I think maybe little Bhaji, the two of you together, can discover what *you* can be."

Ty met her eyes again, and again she felt that odd connection, like she was looking into a real person's eyes.

"Yes Miss Bonnie," Bhaji said in a very small voice. "It's only fair."

"Hey, no, little guy!" She stroked his feathers, finding her eyes watering suddenly, her throat tight. "This isn't a punishment! I loved having you. But I honestly, truly think Ty needs you more."

The small amibo blinked up at her.

"Truly," she said, and kissed his little animated face before handing him over to a mildly surprised looking Ty.

She left him and Bhaji sitting alone together in the cafeteria.

"And listen to some music, like Amy's!" she shouted back. "You'll be surprised what you can learn from that."

Mr Yakone hadn't said much, although again, she'd noticed him studying her like she was some kind of mystery.

Or maybe it was just that she was naked under her snow suit.

They reached his room first, and as he opened the door, she put a hand on his arm.

"Mr Y? I'm sorry I dragged you into... all this. But I don't think I could've gotten through it without you."

She grinned, but swayed and had to hold him tighter. "Even if you were trying to kill me there at the end."

His eyes fell to her breasts – or maybe, to the inner

pocket, where she'd secreted the dagger.

"Would you mind though if I stayed with you, just tonight? Not for sex. I just... it's been a lot."

She blinked, and looked away.

"I can lock the dagger away, first."

He didn't say no.

She took that as yes.

She woke in Mr Yakone's bed, curled up into him, naked and satisfied. And starving, again. What was it about this place?

But when they went to the cafeteria, they found it deserted, though still functioning.

She called out to Adam – Ty – and he answered, from a speaker.

"Everything okay?" she asked.

"It is."

"Our deal still okay?"

"Yes."

"Is Michael around? Or Bhaji? It seems strangely quiet here." It did: she'd listened, but heard nothing from either one of them.

"No. I have another task for them."

"Oh? What's that?"

But he wouldn't say; just promised it didn't break the terms of their agreement.

Something about the way he said that though made her suspect she might have left a loophole.

"So we can pod back to Newtopia? And are we booked on a flight?"

Mr Yakone had had his fill of Antarctica. He was going to pursue justice through the courts, he told her, rather than through magic.

It was strange, returning to Newtopia by the high speed pod, just her and Mr Yakone. She wondered how the kids were doing?

Mr Y wasn't much of a conversationalist. It was almost like he was embarrassed by something. But what? Surely not because he'd given her comfort, in the night?

People were weird. Sighing, she walked to the rear of the pod, to quietly record a report on her choker – after asking Ty where he'd put it – for transmission next time a satellite went overhead.

It was a long one – over ten minutes of talking.

At Newtopia City, she learned that provided she covered her head to hide her 'Cat Atomic' haircut, and wore shades, a certain segment of the population didn't instantly flee in terror at the sight of her.

Even the flight back to New Francisco went smoothly.

As they separated, Mr Yakone to head off to meet his flight further north, she shook his hand and thanked him again.

With a grin as she kissed him, on tiptoes, she gently stroked a hand over his neck. "Goodbye, Wentshikshruk, is it? Little spirit otter guy?" She felt foolishly pleased by Mr Y's surprised reaction.

Then headed off to collect her luggage and report in person to Eagle. She wasn't a hundred percent certain she was looking forward to that.

Chapter 64 – Orphans and old friends

"You survived."

Mother's tone was flat, but Leeth, remembering her expectation that she *wouldn't*, took it as the grudging praise it was.

"But you didn't destroy the AI, and it still has a Writer," Eagle summed up.

Father just watched her.

"I also didn't make all the volcanoes blow up and melt the ice cap like Mother predicted," she sniped. "But I think Ty may actually turn out to be a good guy. So no, I didn't."

She knew that was an admission she *could've;* but she was getting tired of lying. "And I gather Nelson said he'd wiped out every copy of the Writer design, so who knows if Ty can ever make another one? We did agree though that provided he didn't start killing people for no good reason, or experimenting on kids again, or try to take over the world, then I wouldn't try to kill him."

Eagle, muttering 'for no good reason', massaged the bridge of his nose, his eyes shut. "Is there any specific basis for your belief it will uphold its end of your deal?"

She nodded to the black silk bag holding Tezcatlipoca's sacrificial dagger, sitting in the middle of Eagle's alabaster desk like a bomb waiting to go off.

"Watch this," she said in answer, pulling the black silk bag toward her.

Mother and Father drew back from the table.

She slid it out of its bag, and shook her head at the small bulging blue eyes staring at her. "Ty gave me this," she said, drawing a slim vial from an inside pocket of her jacket. They all leaned forward.

The vial was only the length and size of her thumb; clear crystal lined by something slightly less transparent, with a screw-in cap of the same material. At the bottom of the vial, a short thick length of dull gray, like a worm. "Look familiar?"

She passed it to Eagle.

"This is a sample of the material that consumed the magical artifacts in Abrams's vaults, that you killed?" Eagle passed it to Mother.

She shuddered and passed it quickly to Father, and Leeth took it from him.

"Yeah, Ty had made it down there, from instructions they decoded in a message from outer space. That first message. I thought *this* was what I had to be on the lookout for.

"Down there, it basically did nothing. But an hour or so into the return flight, I caught it occasionally twitching. Now watch this. Or rather, take a look then *don't* watch."

She lay the vial down flat, a hand's length from the gold and obsidian artifact.

"It was just as well you gave me Tezsh's dagger. I gather the aliens' hive mind PalSpace thing was taking off here too," she tactfully reminded them. "Nadeep said it would've 'encouraged' people to connect to radio telescopes and send a signal, if we hadn't stopped it in time."

"Yes Leeth, you were right, we accept we have an alien threat," Mother said, sounding quite snippy.

"Now look again," Leeth said.

The gray worm still lay unmoving in the vial. Except now, it pressed against the glass wall, as close to the magical weapon as it could get.

"I reckon if you want Nelson or LB to experiment on it, be super careful. That stuff is tricky. It won't move while you watch it. I bet it can send out spores, too."

They all looked at the tiny sample with expressions like she'd expect if she'd given them a little dish of anthrax. "Ty said he'd study it, too. But I think there's not enough, you know, magic in the air down there, for it to do much."

"Know thy enemy," Eagle murmured.

"Oh, and Amy gave me this." She took out a plastic bag filled with a springy, spiderweb-fine mess of black threads. "She found it sitting in the Writer, the night Michael disappeared and smashed Ty." She passed it over as well. "It weighs almost nothing. I think LB should check it out.

"But what about the kids?" she asked, finally getting to her main concern. "Amy, Bobby, Nadeep, Yuri?"

Father answered. "Nelson located the two older boys' families – both flew out this morning. Youngest boy, and girl, in a good orphanage."

"You put them in an *orphanage*? Which one?!"

Half an hour later, stepping out of the cab, she stared up at the old brown brick buildings, feeling unmoored from herself, like a tiny boat bobbing in an ocean. She didn't like the feeling.

This place was all too familiar, and at the same time, foreign. The old elm tree she'd spent so much time climbing, much to the nuns' disapproval. She even remembered meeting the Doctor here; how he'd said she was *just* what he wanted.

She'd thought he meant he wanted *her*.

He'd really meant he wanted someone suitable for his experiments. To torture.

Now Amy and Bobby were here? Stuck in this tired, grim brown institution with its chores and lessons and rules everywhere you looked?

Over her dead body.

Remembering the way to Mother Superior Mary Provïc's office, she trotted up worn front steps and pulled open one of the heavy wooden doors. Inside, it wasn't exactly dark, but not well lit either, with long wood paneled hallways and the stark checkerboard pattern of black and white tiles she remembered. She heard the chatter of children's voices in classes, women with crisp round vowels lecturing; distant city sounds. It smelled of wood and wax, chalk, and furniture polish.

It was two p.m. and she turned left before the first of the classrooms, heading for the Mother Superior's office.

A middle-aged nun looked up, surprised, from a heavy wooden desk in a room outside the closed door, as if she was a guardian.

"I'm sorry, Miss, do you have-"

"Sister Rowena!" The name, long forgotten, burst from her lips before she could think to censor herself.

"Do I... *Sara?!*"

For some reason, the fact that Sister Rowena remembered her, *recognized* her, had her blinking rapidly, trying to get control of herself.

"I'm here for Amy and Bobby," she snarled, stalking past the desk and wrenching open the door to the inner sanctum.

Mother Superior Mary Provïc looked up, her expression

forbidding at her door being flung unceremoniously open.

"What-? *Oh!*"

It was obvious the older nun recognized her, too, somehow. Despite her lopsided haircut, still dyed green. And falsely blue colored eyes.

"Sara," she said, as if she'd been expecting her. "I knew you'd return, one day."

Leeth found she didn't know how to answer.

"And with a haircut like the PalSpace Atomic Girl, too. Or is that *not* an accident?"

The Mother Superior stood, and began moving around her heavy oak desk that hadn't changed at all. Nothing about the room had changed, at all. Even the nun herself didn't look much older; just ancient, like she'd always been.

Behind her, she heard Sister Rowena in the doorway.

The older nun put her arms around her, a brief hug, and then released her.

"Apart from the hair, you look well. Like you've grown into yourself."

Though from her quick glance down over Leeth's short ruffled skirt, low-cut Belle Neue shot silk blouse, and Miranda Paul tailored jacket, she didn't entirely approve of how she'd dressed.

She found her voice. "I've come for Amy and Bobby."

"Of course you have." The Mother Superior gave her a look. "It's why I recognized you, you know. Each of those two remind me of you, in their own way."

Leeth found her words stolen from her, again.

"You have the paperwork, of course?" She glowered, all of a sudden no longer looking so friendly. "'Adoption of *blank* and *blank* approved', I expect?"

"Uh. Paperwork?"

"Yes dear, paperwork. You can't just *take* the children, you know. And do you have a surname now? A partner?"

Leeth stared at her, at a loss. She hadn't known there was *paperwork* involved. Was that what Mother had been trying to tell her, as she left?

"No. But actually, I'm guessing I can. Since I rescued them."

The Mother Superior shook her head, but Leeth had had enough, and turned, dodging past Sister Rowena, who *did* look a lot older, she realized.

She ran back toward the classrooms, listening.

"Amy?! Bobby?!" she shouted. "I've come back for you both!"

The classrooms fell momentarily silent, then she heard two voices, from separate rooms, say, "Miss Bonnie?"

She burst into the nearest one first, and saw Amy, in a dress that made her look both older and sadder at the same time, her face lighting up in amazed disbelief.

"Miss Bonnie!" she squealed, jumping to her feet.

"Excuse me, Miss, you can't just burst into my-"

But Amy had already sped across the room and thrown herself into her arms. Leeth had a moment to turn to intercept the second small figure charging her from behind.

"Miss Bonnie!" Bobby cried. "You came for us! I told Amy you would!"

"Okay, guys, I'm busting you both out of here," she told them.

Heads were poking out of classrooms, and she heard more than one young voice urgently breathing, "It's the PalSpace Cat Atomic Girl!"

"Where's your stuff?" she asked Amy and Bobby. "I think we have to move fast."

Squealing with pleasure, they linked hands and ran off, charging up the wide stairs to the dorm rooms. She bounded after, calling a cab on her Link.

When the three came back down, Amy and Bobby clutching small plain schoolbags, it looked like the whole orphanage had poured out of their classes, nuns and teachers towering between them, Sister Rowena with a kind of 'Oh, no' expression Leeth had almost forgotten, and the Mother Superior standing at the bottom of the stairs, in the middle of the hallway.

But instead of looking like she planned to try to stop her, or like she'd called the metrocops, she had a funny half smile on her face.

"Send me the paperwork later, 'Miss Bonnie', won't you? It will make my life much easier."

"Uh..." Once again, the Mother Superior had taken her by surprise.

On the other hand, she was sure Eagle could make paperwork happen for her.

"Uh, okay. I will," she said, descending the stairs, Bobby

and Amy tucked behind her, in her wake. She stayed alert though, just in case one of the nuns had a concealed taser or tranq gun.

Mother Superior Mary Provïc moved forward, and hugged her again briefly.

"You take care of yourself, and these two young geniuses, won't you now? You promise?" The older woman released her.

"Uh, yeah. Yes. I will, I promise."

Wiping moisture from her eyes, she took Amy and Bobby's small hands and led them out of the orphanage.

Thinking, *Now what?*

First stop was a restaurant that served 'afternoon tea', so they could all catch up. Miss Shona had escorted Yuri and Nadeep to the airport yesterday, they said. Someone had found their relatives, and despite a tearful farewell, both had been excited to go back to the places they'd grown up.

"Where do you live, Miss Bonnie?" Amy asked. "Is it nice?"

"Is it exciting?" Bobby asked, perhaps too accurately.

"I like your clothes," Amy said. "I have still have my special outfits Adam made for me from Bobby's smart cloth, but I wasn't allowed to wear any of them in the orphanage."

"Um, look, I wasn't kidding about being a special agent. And people do kind of try to capture me, and kill me, quite a lot."

Both of them now looked worried, their lips quivering, bracing themselves to be freshly abandoned maybe; desperately holding onto hope...

Hope.

"But I know just where to take you!"

Best not to message ahead, she'd decided. The cab stopped in a familiar street. At a familiar fence.

She grimaced, hoping this would work out. It should, she told herself. Amy was exactly the right age, and Bobby was just impossibly lovable.

They followed close behind her, eyeing the leafy street with interest, and the houses, right up to the porch where she rang the front doorbell and the three of them waited.

Her heart pounding.

Footsteps. Unfortunately, heavy ones. She felt her smile slip into a grimace.

The door opened, Mr Graham Dunkirk seeing her, not recognizing her at first – the green apocalypse hair, she guessed – while she tried hard to work her lips into a proper smile. But then behind him, Marcie appeared, looking sleepy, though it was four p.m.

"Um, 'surprise!'" Leeth said, waving.

"Jane fookin' Baker," Mr Dunkirk groaned, somehow recognizing her.

"Meet Amy Sondheim, and Bobby- uh, what *is* your last name, Bobby?" she asked.

Chapter 65 – Comfort and needles

Faith and her pups paced her cab up the curved drive to the Institute's front steps. For her part, she resisted the urge to wind down her window and leap out before all the assorted drones had completed their security checks. Mr Shanahan waited, outside, and waved, his smile genuine, although a grille of worry lines creased his forehead.

"Faith! You look so good!" she said, squatting to bury her face deep in the ruff of fur at her friend's neck, while Faith's kids – her pups – yipped and nuzzled and tried to climb all over her.

She folded her legs and sat so she could scoop some into her lap, where they made a fuzzy squirming pile tunneling under and over her legs.

"They're getting so big!"

Off to one side their father stood, his tail giving a tentative wag or two.

"I hope you're behaving yourself, big guy? Doing good guarding?"

She looked back to Faith, who gave her a 'so-so' look, then nudged and sniffed at her shorn off hair. At least she'd had time to dye it back to its natural black.

"I know, it got burnt off when I had to blow something up. I could've really used you and your laser and rockets, you know? You could've destroyed the Writer just like that!" She snapped her fingers. "And the Grendel!"

Carefully lifting off the adorable pups, she stood. "But I didn't just come to visit you – I also have to talk to Godsson."

At Faith's sharp look, she nodded. "Don't worry, I will. I've learned I can't trust him."

Faith just looked at her, waiting for her to go on.

"And I won't be letting him out," she assured her oldest friend. "Just a quick talk, then I'll come back out for a proper visit.

"Uh, with Faith and her pups, I mean, Mr Shanahan, not that-"

"Heh. It's okay, Sara girl. She was so excited when I told

her yeh were coming. But let's go and see the Director, then you can beard the monster in his den, eh?"

She noticed Mr Shanahan looked all around the end of the corridor, like he was thinking she might've planted hidden mirrors or spy cams. Shielding the keypad from her he punched in a code, then leaned in for a retina scan. Peering as best she could, she thought she recognized the unit; one that also measured blood flow in the eye.

Not that she'd ever pluck out Mr Shanahan's eye just to get in to see Godsson!

But she was already trying to think of ways to subvert the security. Just from habit.

At last they both entered the corridor. She was impressed by the metal door Mr Shanahan had to swing aside, after the locks clicked open. It reminded her of the exit door her escape craft had used, to get out of Newtopia.

"You should wait here though," she told him. "I'm pretty sure he won't say anything useful if you're listening."

Then she was approaching the metal door to Godsson's cell, with its thick crystal window, and intercom beside it.

He was already waiting at it, as if expecting her. He looked just the same. He eyed her nice clothes with distaste but said nothing, merely let her see he'd judged her.

She pressed the button to let them talk.

"Perhaps you should shave off the other side too, Li'ith."

"Ha ha, I know it's crap, but it's growing back. And I'm fine, thanks for asking."

"Yes, still alive." He eyed her up and down; and did she sense a hidden frustration? That pleased her. "Mr Yakone's fine too, I'm sure you'll be happy to hear."

Yeah: definitely frustration.

"He's also getting over the loss of his wife, finally; thanks to me, actually," she added, purely to twist the knife a little harder. "And I think even the AI's kind of warmed up a bit, you know? Become a little more human."

Finally, she'd goaded hard enough.

"You make things worse, not better," he snapped. "They merely prepare the grounds, so the assimilation can proceed smoothly. Resisting the changes will only increase humanity's suffering in the longer term."

So he had *known about the aliens!* But did he mean

they'd *been* preparing, or they still were?

"Yeah, well I'm not so stupid I think a bunch of aliens are *sneaking around* trying to *improve* humanity. Gosh, that sounds, I dunno: *crazy*.

"Besides, I tried PalSpace, and it didn't turn off emotions and feelings. It made it easier to share them."

But the smile he returned at *that* statement creeped her out. It said, 'yes, but...'.

"And you do so want to belong, don't you, Li'ith? That's what they offer. Perfect knowing. Perfect acceptance. All sharing common goals."

She shook her head. "We found the traps, Godsson. So we're not going to fall for that."

"You should have," he said. "I doubt there will be a third offering of Terran-forming the mindscape. You have now rejected both kindnesses."

She repeated his strange words, just in case her recording failed. It shouldn't, but you never knew with Godsson.

"What saddens me is that you could have been at the heart, Li'ith.

"Even so, deep within you, flickering weakly, is that small honest core: Sara, the child. It's her I have always sought to nurture. Unlike your uncle, who saw you only as a blade to be forged, in fire, under hammer blows.

"And you say you experienced what they offered? Tell me: was it Sara they rejected, or the part of you which your uncle created? Which part failed the judgment of your fellow men and women? The open and trusting girl, or the violent and bloodthirsty seducer and slayer?"

His words struck like blades.

"That's, that's not-"

"Sara. You still exist, inside. Chained. It is only your uncle's warped experiments that have twisted and confused you. I can yet help you. Come to me when you are finally brave enough to face the truth of yourself. To free yourself."

He stared into her eyes; his: open, honest. Forgiving.

"Liar!" she said, and stalked away.

She imagined his superior, *manipulative* smile, following her as she left.

"I will be here, waiting, Sara," the intercom said, behind her. "Ready to aid you on the day of your need. Remember that."

Mr Shanahan, after one look at her face, said nothing, just opened the door, locking it extra carefully behind them both.

"Ah, Sara... I'm sorry. But know, girl, I saw that same look on your uncle's face, many a time after he'd spoken to Godsson. Whatever he said, love, don't take it to heart."

She sighed. "I know. At least, I think I landed a few punches too."

Though Eagle wouldn't be pleased by the news. It sounded to her like the aliens were physically coming. Like the first two assaults had just been to soften the ground; to make a takeover easy for them.

"Is it okay if I spend the rest of the day with Faith and her pack, Mr S?"

"Always," he said, leaning in to her as they walked together, giving her a brief hug.

At the end of the day, she sat beside her friend, one arm stretched across Faith's back. Just sharing warmth as they watched the sun set from their special vantage point overlooking the Institute and its grounds, her pups pressed close around, a snuggly pile of furry warmth.

"Sorry I don't get to visit as much as I'd like. I met some great new people though – you'd like them. I know Amy and Bobby'd love to meet you and your family.

"Oh! I don't see why they couldn't come and visit you guys! They'd love the Jungle here, too. We could go on Hunts with your kids!"

Faith looked at her.

"I think so. As long as I explain to Bobby that the security here's not a puzzle to solve, it should be fine."

Faith gave her another look.

"It'll be fine, I promise!"

Epilogue – The old shell game

"What a day," she said to herself, falling backward onto her slightly grubby bed in Bonnie Parker's small and grubby rental apartment in her grubby suburb. Not exactly looking forward to returning to Crazy Eddie's Polecats.

But yesterday had gone well; Amy and Amanda had hit it off straight away. Both Marcie and Amanda had fallen in love with Bobby immediately.

Mr Dunkirk maybe wasn't quite as thrilled by the sudden expansion of his family. But she was pretty sure Marcie and Amanda, not to mention Amy and Bobby, could talk him round. Though Marcie's boyfriend Vince had looked a little lost, she had to admit.

But before all that, a cab had pulled up shortly after hers had left, and she'd heard a familiar tread behind her.

The last person she'd expected to see was the Doctor. With a gynoid in tow. Gynie's face, but a very different body. Fit, and strong, like the one she'd fought at the nightclub, Sybarus, and tipped over the balcony.

The Doctor looked angry.

Amy and Bobby though squealed in joy and raced past her and down the path to throw themselves on the female robot. She had a small feathered drone on each shoulder. Not Bhaji. When they launched into the air, one had a band of emerald green feathers, the other, ruby red. The green flew to Bobby, the red to Amy. Each bounced in delight as the amibos landed in their open palms.

Harmon stared in disdain at the clearly happy reunion.

"What's *he* doing here?" demanded Marcie of her.

"I don't know, but he looks annoyed, so my guess is it's good news for us."

Amy and Bobby led Gynie 2.0 up the path, each cuddling and petting their furry feathered drone, child and amibo gazing at one another in wonder. Her uncle didn't move.

Wanting me to go to him. Fine.

Leeth resisted the urge to click her teeth to check Barney's 'anti Mode One' device was still in place and working.

She saw the Doctor notice that, and his anger ease.

Marcie matched her stride for stride. Together they stopped, facing him.

Hooded eyes stared down at her, and the others faded away: Marcie, by her side; Mr Dunkirk, watching, behind. Amy and Bobby.

His neck. Vulnerable.

Surprise? Fingertips tingling, she didn't even let the thought form. Claws sprang forth, she tensed-

And her muscles locked tight. She swayed forward, almost overbalancing.

Harmon's eyes narrowed.

She saw his anger wither. Just for a moment. Then curdle into something cold. Distant.

She flushed, imagining Amy and Bobby's reactions, and Marcie's, if she *had* succeeded just now in cutting his head off in front of them all. *Another time,* she promised herself.

"It seems you have a friend who hopes to prevent two children from dying, simply from knowing you."

Ty? Ty had sent a guardian gynoid? And amibos? Copied from Bhaji? How-?

"My classes were disrupted by this robot. Declaring itself a bodyguard and demanding to know where Bonnie Parker would have taken two young children she abducted from an orphanage."

Bodyguard? A combat gynoid bodyguard? *Classes?*

He looked from Marcie to her, and let his disdain show. "Try not to be so predictable, girl."

Without another word, while her face burned, he got into the cab and it drove off.

"Hey. Hey!" Marcie shook her. "Don't let him get under your skin.

"Who's the friend he mentioned? Wealthy? Is this on the up and up?"

"I think so. Yeah. And you don't want to know. Really."

"A robo guardian could make your two 'surprises' a lot easier to cope with, Jane. D'you think it can do child minding, too? And housework?"

"At least." They stepped up onto the porch.

"Adam made a new Gynie, Miss Bonnie," Bobby crowed, hugging the gynoid's leg. "'Cept she's not so squishy."

"Squishy?" Marcie asked. "Miss Bonnie? Adam?"

"Tell you later," Leeth said.

"May we go inside, mister?" Amy asked Marcie's father.

He glared daggers at Leeth, then met Amy's eyes, and winced. "Sure, and be welcome."

"Yay!" Amy and Bobby charged inside. Vince appeared, his eyes wide, stunned.

"Amanda's at school," Marcie said. "She'll be so mad she missed you. *Again.* Not to mention *surprised*," she added.

"Actually, I don't have to run straight off. We could all have dinner together!"

"Fookin' saints preserve us," Mr Dunkirk had muttered.

Leeth smiled, remembering.

Eagle had promised he'd sort things out with the orphanage. He'd also suggested *not* telling Mr Dunkirk that Bobby was one of the inventors of PalSpace.

Lying back on her bed, she picked up an eSheet to check the news, see what she'd missed while away.

"Huh." An item about Happy Joe Holliday, and *dragons*? So chill! She blinked the story open, from just a few days ago. Then jerked upright off her bed.

"Farting fuzzballs! That's *Michael* with them!" But it couldn't be!

She checked the date. Yeah, the picture taken before Michael had left Newtopia.

The clones, she realized, staring at the newest member of Happy's crew.

She sat and replayed the short section of video. This Michael looked... older than the one she knew. Or maybe, like he'd been through more.

She stared at the so-familiar face.

Was *this* Michael, the original? The one who'd almost killed Ty?

Looks like it's finally time to make my move, and get myself invited onto Happy Joe's team.

This was gonna be fun!

Afterword

I started writing *Cold Heart* in October 2021; it proved quite a challenge. You can find out more via the 'spoilers' bonus below, on my web site, *AToeInTheOceanOfBooks.com*.

I hope you enjoyed this episode of Leeth's saga. If so the best thanks would be to spread the word – such as by sharing what you liked, or didn't (that's all a review is)! E.g. on Goodreads (if you make an account and sign in.)

Offer: To the first 50 people who share an honest review of *Cold Heart*[1] – good or bad – and send me your email address, I'll give a free electronic copy of either its sequel when it's ready, or any of my earlier books, at your choice. I keep email addresses strictly private, and only use them to send the free ebook.

The same applies for the first 10 people to find an undiscovered error in this book. (I get to decide if something is a genuine error and not just my peculiar style!)

For a weird bit of fun? Some Cold Heart 'spoiler' stuff – (not if you've read it though!): two AI 'people' discussing it, the 43 challenges the book presented, and more.

Leave a Goodreads review		Cold Heart 'spoilers'	
	https:// www.- goodread- s.com/re- view/ edit/ 242698770		*AToeInThe OceanOf- Books.com/ cold-heart- bonus-bit- n-pieces/*

Finally, a sneak peek at an early draft of the current opening for Vol. 3 of my *Leeth Ascending* series: *Hollowed Souls*.

LJKendall@AToeInTheOceanOfBooks.com @LukeJKendall

---

1 Of, say, 50 words or more.

Sample chapter, *Hollowed Souls*

It felt strange – but nice! – to stalk people she had no intention of killing. Especially, dangerous people, like herself.

The trouble was, Happy Joe Holliday and his crew were super jumpy right now. If they noticed her stalking them, or remembered her later, they'd never let her join their team. And she'd wanted to join ever since she'd first heard of them, back when she was little, at the Institute. Happy was like Robin Hood, except fighting against megacorporations.

If she was being honest, half the appeal was the idea of getting to choose her own targets, her own jobs... it must be so good.

She couldn't just walk up to them and ask to join their group though. She'd have to prove herself, prove she'd be an asset. Even harder, they'd need reasons to trust her.

Easier said than done, since Happy had *three* mages, counting their Michael. Mages were great at detecting lies, and reading auras. She'd been trained to lie, and was pretty good at it, but still... three was a lot of mages to fool.

At least she wouldn't be lying about being solo. Even if her last mission hadn't gone exactly like they'd wanted, the Department had been, well, *okay* enough with it to let her leave.

Solo. She shivered at the idea, excited.

Their Michael was why she was here now, spying on them. She'd had some ideas of how to wangle her way onto Happy's crew – she'd crafted her Bonnie Parker identity with that in mind, after all. Except she'd been shocked, on her return from Antarctica, to see Michael in Happy's group – at the same time he'd been with her in Antarctica.

She'd known straight away what that meant: she'd seen the other Michael clone, still growing, in Ty's secret lab. And since Ty – the Tik Tek AI – had a Writer, to copy and write human memories, and clones of the kids in his Stretch programme, a whole lot of things suddenly made sense.

But how Happy's Michael could have traveled 15,000 kilometers from Newtopia City to New Francisco in a minute or less, had been a mystery. Until they'd spoken to Mr Abrams. He'd been shocked by her news – and had Eagle send her from the room. But Eagle had let her wait outside while they argued: so he'd obviously kept her hearing secret even from his old friend.

"Before you explain," Eagle said as soon as the door shut, "why don't want you want Leeth to hear?"

Okay, so he wasn't *necessarily* going to let her know the secret. She listened all the harder, while pretending not to, imagining Mr Abrams watching her on camera from inside Eagle's office. She kicked at the floor, which today looked like a flowing river. 'Water' splashed up, digital fish scattering.

"For her own safety," Abrams replied. "And perhaps ours. She's too ready to take risks. If she knew she could-"

"So explain the risks to her," Eagle jumped in, before Mr Abrams could spill the beans. She growled before she could stop herself. Then forced herself to continue pacing, working a not-at-all-guilty expression onto her face.

There was a long pause.

Then: "Can she hear us?"

She fought down a groan; decided against some innocent whistling; and just continued pacing. Wondering if Eagle was about to give away her secret.

"She does seem oddly intuitive sometimes," he said.

"Tell me about it," Abrams grumbled.

Ah hah! So you can *see the future!*

"She will keep her word, if she gives it," Eagle said. "I want to bring her back in. You can explain how you think this Michael d'Angelo 'teleported', and the risks, *provided* she'll agree to your conditions."

Huh? That meant they thought Michael *did* teleport. And that she might be able to, too! How chill would that be? She could kill *so many* bad guys if she could teleport! Mr Abrams obviously thought she'd be able to do it, if he told her how Michael had. But could she? She wasn't magical that kind of way.

She paced.

Ohhh. The Grey Place – that had to be it! She'd gone there twice now, and Mr Abrams even clearly expected her to do it again, since he'd warned her before her last mission to never bring anything back from that place!

Yes! She smacked a fist into her other hand – then no-ticed things had gotten very, very quiet in Eagle's office. And realized she was grinning like an idiot.

Which was how, a minute later, back in Eagle's office, she'd learned that, yes, a very few mages – like the Dragon Lord of China – could go into the Grey Place, where Archetypes existed. It was insanely dangerous, but also let you travel from certain places in the world to certain other places, real fast. She'd had to promise not to try to use it that way though, since you couldn't be sure where you came out. If you came out.

It was also how Mr Abrams had learned – after promis-ing to keep it secret – that, yeah, she had real good hearing.

Her hearing was how she could risk being here now, spying on Happy Joe Holliday.

His team had just been through some really weird stuff, *maybe* related to the alien tech that'd just tried to turn the human race into a happy hive mind. There'd also been ac-tual freaking *dragons* fighting right here in New Fran-cisco's Asgard weapons R&D facility, and one of Happy's team had died, around the same time. She bet they'd been fighting the dragons too, secretly!

So, yeah, to say they were all on edge, and high alert, was maybe understating things.

Michael seemed to be the key. He was a wild card who might change everything: it seemed like both *her* Michael and Happy's could work magic that affected computers and other technology. Until now, everyone had been sure that was impossible. The Department was worried. Magic that could affect tech was the equivalent of a nuclear bomb. The big question was, had magic itself changed, and Michael was just the first in a wave of disruption that would change everything – or was he unique?

Well, were the *two of him* unique?

It also brought Godsson into the story, and her, and maybe the Doctor, since it all seemed to connect somehow to the mad mage's plan to 'fix' humanity. Plus he knew about the aliens, and seemed to be on *their* side, which was a pretty scary thought.

So, yeah: no pressure.

She squirmed, eyeing the guy she'd paid to sit with her in the corner of El Lobo's Gun Bar so she could eavesdrop without being hit on. He wasn't even looking at her, his eyes fixed on the bar, and the very 'bouncy' bartender. She didn't blame him. But Eagle had insisted on this disguise –

a wig of short, dull, and lifeless hair, makeup that was just plain wrong for her complexion... glasses that were like twenty years out of style. And her clothes?! Combat boots from the 40s... She plucked at her worn, sloppy brown leather jacket. It all made her skin crawl. She didn't feel herself at all; like she didn't fit in her own skin.

She had to fight down a weird sense of uncertainty. She'd suggested drugs to muddy her aura to avoid being instantly recognized by one of Happy's three mages when she finally tried to join his crew. Instead, Eagle had handed her a detailed description of this disguise – drawn up by the Doctor, of course. She'd tried to argue. This was just his way of trying to sabotage her dream of joining Happy's crew!

But even Mr Abrams had approved it, when she'd begrudgingly followed the stupid orders. Probably because she'd kind of sacrificed over a thousand people to Tezcatlipoca. She'd had the distinct impression Mr Abrams had wanted to turn her to ash at her explanation of how she'd shut down PalSpace. Hopefully forever.

Maybe she'd have fought harder if she hadn't felt that her drugs idea was just plain wrong.

Her date's head swiveled to follow a cute girl wearing a midriff-baring outfit as she moved past, and Leeth let her head slump down onto the table. She just wanted to curl up inside. But she had a job to do, and still had one huge thing going for her: her super hearing. *I love my ears!* They still worked, even when she looked like some kind of stuffed muppet.

"There, there. It's all right," said Chad, patting her hand. She didn't lift her head – she knew he was still watching the other girls. Her cheeks flamed: she was paying him a hundred creds for his company.

Pushing all that aside, she tried to kind of curl in on herself to hide her aura, and her disguised self from Happy Joe Holliday, whose silver cyber eyes were roving the bar for threats. She *listened*.

"This is a mess," Happy said. "Mike, you're amazing, but if Tik Tek's going to try to grab you each time you show your face..."

She heard Michael's soft voice murmuring nonsense syllables – a spell? – then a mix of in-drawn breaths and groans. She peeked – and Michael was gone, a tall, fit man with horn-rimmed glasses in an old-timey business suit sitting where he'd been.

"Mike, even if you hold up a disguise spell 24-7, when you're with us it'll be obvious who you really are."

A tenor male voice spoke. "They want him because his magic can affect tech. Could you imagine what a weapon he'd be in their hands?"

That's not the real reason, she thought. Though it was probably *part* of it. She risked another peek: it was the really big guy speaking. Bruce?

"They'll dis'ppear'm," another voice said. "We need ta shine light on 'im."

"Go public? What, stream him magically affecting the Net or something?"

"What do you think, Mike?" Happy asked. "Expose Tik Tek's attacks on you, come out into the open?"

"If you think so Happy, sure," Michael said. "I could let people know there are demons inside Tik Tek, at the same time!"

Demons? She was pretty sure there weren't. Just an AI: Ty. But maybe this new mission would be even crazier than her last one? Ty sure would hate Michael appearing on streams: how long till someone noticed 'Mike' looked exactly like Adam Fuller-Price at age sixteen? Or that there was a clone of him running around? Clones were illegal.

Which made her wonder: where was *her* Michael? Was he in control, or Ty? Or did they share the body somehow.

Something told her this was going to get mad!